Chances

A Novel

By

Bud Shuster

BURD STREET PRESS
SHIPPENSBURG, PENNSYLVANIA

This Burd Street Press publication
was printed by
Beidel Printing House, Inc.
63 West Burd Street
Shippensburg, PA 17257-0708 USA

The acid-free paper used in this book meets the guidelines for permanence and dura-bility of the Committee on Production Guidelines for Book Longevity of the Council on Library Resources.

For a complete list of available publications
please write
Burd Street Press
Division of White Mane Publishing Company, Inc.
P.O. Box 708
Shippensburg, PA 17257-0708 USA

Library of Congress Cataloging-in-Publication Data

Shuster, Bud.
    Chances : a novel / by Bud Shuster.
        p. cm.
    ISBN 1-57249-314-3 (alk. paper)
    1. Computer industry--Fiction. 2. West Virginia--Fiction. 3. Mountain life--Fiction. I. Title.

PS3569.H8644 C47 2002
813'.54--dc21

                                                                2002071234

PRINTED IN THE UNITED STATES OF AMERICA

To My Teams
in Public and Private Life

We seize our chances or they pass us by, and through that solitary act we soar into the sunlight or sink into despair.

Chapter One

Clifford Cross had everything—and now he might end up with nothing—or so he thought, as he settled into his first-class seat, sipping a Perrier aboard United Flight 101 from Washington, D.C., to Chicago. Leaning his forehead against the port-side window, he stared down at the western slopes of the Allegheny Mountains, cast in the shadow of the morning sun, coming alive with the leaves of early spring. Somewhere down there, a little off to the south, were the roots he had left behind, but never could quite forget. Grimly smiling, somehow he sensed that he was on his way to his destiny—or, could it be, to his destruction?

"Excuse me, Mr....Mr. Cross, is it?" the willowy blonde flight attendant smiled down at him as she checked the passenger list.

"Yes, ma'am. All day today," he smiled back.

"Excuse me?" her eyes twinkled as she cocked her head with a quizzical look on her sun-bronzed face.

"That's my name all day today," he laughed.

"Oh, I get it." She smiled again, this time so radiantly that she reminded him of a young Farrah Fawcett, the actress.

"My name is Krissy...Krissy with a K, Mr. Cross, and please let me know if I can get you another drink, or perhaps something from the snack tray."

"Thanks, but no thanks," Clifford replied, as his eyes followed her down the aisle toward the cockpit. He noticed a thin ankle bracelet on her right ankle and chuckled to himself, why would anybody want to be bothered with a useless ornament on their body. He had resisted even wearing his college class ring or his wedding ring, but to no avail.

Mindlessly outstretching his left leg, he inserted his hand deep into his pants' pocket, fumbling with his change. Eventually, he located and extracted a worn, discolored, slightly oversized die which once had been part of a pair of dice, crudely fashioned by his great-grandfather, Alonzo Collins, from two black bear teeth. Staring down at the strange die, in his mind's eye, Clifford could clearly see the coal-pocked, craggy face of his great-grandfather, seemingly sculpted right out of a bituminous vein, as if descended from the earth's geology, hard and weathered, sad and yet serene. Clifford could almost feel the old man's presence, although he had died when the boy was only seven.

Alonzo had carved the unique dice from two molars he had extracted from the mouth of a giant black bear he had shot on one of his many bear hunts atop the rugged Allegheny Mountains, a half-day's hike north of Beckley, West Virginia.

Instead of drilling the usual dots in them so they might be used for Saturday night gambling in the coal camps of southern West Virginia, Alonzo had turned them into his personal good luck amulets.

On one face of each die, he meticulously had etched the symbol of a bear paw—five toes extending from a tiny pad—the ancient Indian symbol of power and direction. On the opposite face of each die, he had drilled a single dot—the snake-eye of an evil omen. He packed pure black coal dust deep into each marking and sealed them shut with a thick, translucent lacquer. The other four sides of each cube were left untouched. He had carved the strange totems by lantern light during his free moments, far beneath the earth inside the coal mine where he began working as a fourteen year old. A half-century and a dozen deep mines later, he hung his lantern hat on the pantry wall for the last time and rolled his bear-toothed dice across the wooden kitchen table.

"See!" he exclaimed, as little Clifford gazed, wide-eyed as the dice stopped a few inches from his nose at the table's edge. "Double bear paws! No snake eyes for me and you, Cliffy. Not today. Kept me safe...nary a scratch down in them goddamned holes for a black-assed lifetime. Here...you take one of the dice...rub your thumb, gentle-like, over that bear paw. Feel the power? Feel the direction? Feel it guiding you? Feel it...**feel** it, boy!"

Although little Clifford wasn't certain he could feel anything, he shook his head enthusiastically, as he gingerly rubbed the talisman, "Reckon maybe I can, Pap, Pap. Yep...yes, sir...I surely can!"

"You take that one, boy...stick it in your pocket. I don't need them both no more. I'll have this here one buried with me. But you...you, Cliffy, you hang onto that there one. Always...**always** keep it with you. Don't pay no mind to old snake eye. You just rub your thumb real easy over old bear paw and everything will turn out right."

When Alonzo Collins lay dying a few years later, coughing up black blood and phlegm, his last words were, "Old snake eye's finally got me. Mind you now, make sure old bear paw's facing up atop me in my casket."

Clifford was given the honor of affixing the bear-pawed die, face up, securely inside the top buttonhole of his great-grandfather's black vest. His mother, Ruth Ann, had widened and restitched the buttonhole so the venerable talisman would fit.

* * *

As United 101 leveled off to cruising speed, Clifford smiled to himself as he jiggled the totem in his hand, gently rubbing the bear paw with his thumb, and then carefully inserting it back into his pocket.

Digging into his briefcase, he pulled out the three-ring notebook he had begun to organize, stretched the long legs of a six-foot-four-inch frame under the seat in front, and quickly lost himself in the new world he was about to enter. What a chance! What a chance, he thought.

* * *

Back in a Washington suburb, Dr. Sidney Martin, a middle-aged, cadaverous, chain-smoking chiropractor turned entrepreneur, bellowed into his phone to an investment banker who stood at his office window, holding his phone at arm's length, staring down at Number One, Wall Street. "Dammit, Oscar, why did you offer the job to that young Cross fellow and give him forty percent of the company without asking me? Hell, I've got over five million tied up in that dog, and it's going to take another four or five million to get us out of this mess...if we ever can."

"Sidney, he's the third person we offered the job to...when the others saw our financials, they just laughed...said we'd be throwing good money after bad...wouldn't touch us with a ten-foot pole. The only way I got Cross interested was to offer him a big piece of the company. But that's forty percent of nothing, unless he can turn it around. He'll use some of that stock to attract his management team. You're the one who insisted on looking for someone to bail us out. You knew it was going to take several million more. And then, it's a long shot."

Oscar McMillan was the antithesis of Sidney Martin: tall and trim for a man in the twilight of his life, who spoke in deep, soft, self-assured tones, his thick, white-maned, perfectly sculpted hair lapped the white-on-white collar of his French-cuffed shirt from the Custom Shop. His regimental tie, tucked neatly in his pin-striped suit jacket, meant he surely was a Yale man, probably Skull and Bones. The two of them were the oddest of couples, but Sidney had the money and Oscar had the connections. Ample green mixed with the bluest of bloods produced a most seductive combination.

"At least you should have talked to me about it first. It's my money, too," Sidney grumped.

"With all due respect, Sid, bringing him up here to Wall Street, letting him sink his shoes into the thick carpeting of a prestigious investment banking firm, made more sense than sending him over to that dump of yours. And, frankly, with the problems you're having with the SEC, letting him know how deeply involved you are didn't seem like the best idea in the world. He still doesn't know you hold most of the company's notes."

Sidney's eyes darted nervously across his paper-strewn desk in a cramped basement office of a dilapidated apartment building which he owned in Capitol Heights, across the river from Washington. The sallow-faced, rumpled little man easily could have passed for one of his seedy tenants, rather than a multimillionaire, whose portfolio ran from AT&T to Xerox, and whose stock manipulations made him feared by all who knew him. "Well, when do I get to meet this golden boy of yours?" he asked, disgustedly. "How old is he, anyway?"

"He just turned thirty-one. But, hell, Tektron made him a vice president three years ago. Our headhunter couldn't find anyone to say anything bad about him. Turned their software division around in eighteen months. Talk about a dog...it was hemorrhaging losses."

"Ya, but what does he know about hardware? And when do I get to meet him? Hell, he lives right here in the Washington area...Tektron's offices are out by Dulles. By God, I should have been able to at least meet him before you gave nearly half the company away."

"Nearly half of nothing, Sidney. And he started out as a systems analyst, so he's got to know something about hardware."

"Did we actually put anything in writing to him? Could we still get out of it?"

"Of course I put it in writing. Do you think he'd leave a top job at a Fortune 500 company without a firm commitment? He knows the odds. Fact that he's so young is probably why he's willing to roll the dice. He's on his way to Chicago now to introduce himself to the employees...and lower the boom. Part of the deal is that he can move the headquarters to Washington, so you'll meet him next week when he gets back. But Sidney, it's got to be gentle. He's the boss. You can't roll over him like you did the others. He might still have peach fuzz on his face, but he's got the cojones. He didn't get a scholarship to play college basketball by being a wuss."

"Ya, ya. Gentle. Put a meeting together. If he can dig us out of this hole, I'll be as gentle as a pussycat."

* * *

Sitting on a bench in front of the pool hall in Beckley, West Virginia, Jumper Ramsey was reading the article about Clifford Cross for the second time. His hand shook as he dug his can of Copenhagen out of a deep pocket of his faded combat fatigues. Extracting a pinch, he inserted the moist snuff between his lower lip and rotting teeth. Turning to an older man leaning against the doorframe of the hall, he called, "You read what Clifford up and got himself into now? Says he's gonna head up some computer company in Chicago. Sure don't let no grass grow under his feet."

"See, Jumper. Not all of us got stuck in this coal hole for the rest of our lives. That could'a been you too," the older man wheezed. "You was just as good as Cliff. If you got control of that temper of yours, and paid attention to your grades, you could'a been playing ball up there in Morgantown with Cliff. You had the chance."

"Ya...sure. Tell that to Uncle Sam when he come and got me in '73."

"You could'a got one of them deferments like Cliff if you had half the grades."

"Least I done my duty...and look where it got me." Clifford Cross's old high-school teammate let a glob of brown spittle drool from his lower lip down onto the sidewalk.

Jumper Ramsey and Clifford Cross had led the Beckley Miners to the West Virginia state basketball championship...and they both were legends in the valley, for it was the only time little Beckley even got past the semifinals. Jumper was only five-feet-ten, but he could dunk a basketball as easily as Cliff. He was the point guard whose ambidextrous ball handling and defensive steals helped Cliff become a star. His lean frame seemed to be one sinewy bundle of erratic energy, quick as a cat, with a temper even quicker.

Cliff, who graduated magna cum laude, was offered half a dozen scholarships, but once the recruiters saw Jumper's grades and heard about his reputation, they lost all interest in him. In fact, he never even graduated from high school, although they let him walk across the stage on graduation day, handing him a certificate of achievement, so very few people really knew the story. He and Cliff were the two town celebrities that year, and no one really cared. When it looked like his number was coming up at the Draft Board, he enlisted in the Marines, and within a year, while Cliff was running up and down the basketball court at the University of West Virginia, Jumper was slogging through the rice paddies in South Viet Nam, killing gooks and learning to like it.

He was one of the lucky ones to complete his tour and come home unscathed. At least, physically. He had vowed that he would never work in the mines, but the pay was too good to pass up. His pap and his uncles broke out the moonshine to celebrate on the day he got his union card, but he lasted less than a month.

When the foreman yelled, "Ramsey, what the hell's wrong with you? Get your foot off that loader! You want your leg taken off? You dumb rednecks are all alike!" Jumper slammed him against a shuttle car, told him what he could do with his loader, and quit before they could fire him.

"Damned if I want to spend my life like a mole grubbing beneath the earth," he fulminated at his embarrassed parents, as he threw his miner's hat against the kitchen wall, shattering its light and gashing the thin plasterboard. So he lived at home, putting his talent as a backyard mechanic to work repairing old junkers, and got a job, evenings, tending bar, where he indulged his taste for whiskey. Eventually, he found himself working to pay his bar bills, and, but for his local celebrity, probably could not have held those jobs as he moved from bar to bar in Beckley.

As thirty-one-year-old Jumper sat on the pool hall bench thinking of his former teammate's success, he was filled with loathing for himself and anger at the world. He was nothing but a no-good drunk, and thank goodness that Cliff had never seen him that way. They had been like brothers once. But only Cliff had gotten the chance.

* * *

As Flight 101 began its descent into Chicago, Krissy paused at Cliff's seat, lightly touching his arm. "Pardon me, Mr. Cross. Is your belt fastened?"

"Which one," he grinned.

"Very funny. Come on, put that tray up and let me have a look."

"Yes, ma'am. Are you this concerned about the safety of all your passengers?"

"Sometimes big men have to be treated like little boys."

"Wow! You're a little testy for so early in the morning."

"This is just the beginning of a very long day. From Chicago, we go on to Dallas, and then back to Chicago. But of course, I get time off," she gave him her Farrah Fawcett smile.

"Is Chicago your home?"

"No, I'm based in Washington. When we overnight here the crew stays at the O'Hare Marriott. It's real convenient. Better put that briefcase under the seat."

"Yes, ma'am," he saluted, stuffing his precious notebook and loose papers into the battered case and shoving it beneath his outstretched legs.

"Have a nice day, Mr. Cross," Krissy purred as he brushed past her out of the plane. "Hope you fly with us again."

"Afraid you'll be seeing a lot of me on this flight over the next several weeks," he called back over his shoulder. "Take care, Krissy with a K."

* * *

As Clifford entered the baggage claim area, a dapper, graying at the temples gentleman approached, extending his hand. "Cliff? Good to see you, boy. We've been looking forward to your arrival. I'm Jamison Tackaberry."

"Well, thank you for meeting me, Mr. Tackaberry."

"Certainly glad you're here, Cliff. Would have recognized you anywhere from the press release picture Oscar sent out. Should have come from my office, but I guess you know Oscar. Understand you're a marketing wiz...just what we need to get the product moving. Let's get your bags...the limousine's right outside. I'll get a skycap over here."

"Never mind. I've just got one. I can manage it myself. Here it comes now."

"Didn't bring your golf clubs?" Jamison smiled as he settled into the back seat of a Lincoln Towne car. "With that suntan of yours, and only early spring...and your athletic background according to the press release, I wouldn't be surprised if you were a scratch golfer."

"Afraid not," Cliff unconsciously began tapping his right foot on the carpeted floor of the limousine. "Don't get much time to play golf. And it's not a suntan. I'm one-eighth Indian. My great-grandfather was Cherokee." Actually, his complexion was like an unvarnished slab of red oak, and his body just as solid. Beneath his thick, black, curly hair, his incandescent blue eyes sometimes playfully danced, and sometimes narrowed into piercing slits.

"My, you don't say. Well, ah, I've always liked the Indians. Always thought they were a lot different from...well...you know...the other minorities. We had an Indian aboard ship during the war. Kept to himself. He didn't cause any trouble."

"Well, I'm seven-eighths white, so I guess you don't need to worry about me scalping you." Cliff's broad smile revealed a lustrously white, perfectly proportioned set of upper incisors, eclipsing his smaller lower teeth which, incongruously slanted forward like microscopic shovels. Obviously, he had never had the benefit of braces.

As the car glided out of the airport, Jamison asked, "Would you like to go directly to the plant, or check into your hotel first? We put you up here at the O'Hare Marriott since you said you wanted to be near the airport, but you might want to stay somewhere closer to the office. Wilfred, here, can pick you up and get you back and forth."

"Marriott's fine for now. Let's get to the office. Tell me about yourself, Mr. Tackaberry."

"Well, Cliff, after the war I got my degree at Cornell in business, and then directly went to work for IBM. Spent thirty-four years there, until a headhunter approached me two years ago about heading a new start-up. That's how I got here at Speedcom."

"I see," Cliff nodded, noting that Jamison was still wearing the IBM "uniform" of navy blue suit, starched white shirt, blue and white rep tie, and spit-shined black wing tips. "What did you do there?"

"Spend most of my time in finance. Started here in Chicago in accounting. Ended up in Poughkeepsie as director of finance in the OEM Division. Getting back home here to Chicago was one of the attractions of the job. Plus a three-year contract. You know I have a three-year contract?" his eyes narrowed as he stared into icy, unblinking eyes. "With my financial background and your marketing background, we'll make a great team. The way I see it, you can really put some spark into the sales force. That's been one of the problems."

As the limousine pulled onto Interstate 90, heading toward the Southside, Cliff looked puzzled. "I thought the problem was interfacing the new printer with the software and the PC you buy from IBM. I was told the first production run of several hundred systems is sitting in the warehouse, except for the demos you put out...and they've got bugs in them. Please correct me if I'm wrong."

"Cliff, you've been in the business. You know new products always have bugs. We're working them out."

"When we arrive, first I'd like to meet the management team...just say hello...then tour the plant...then meet privately with you to go over financials, including your business plan for the rest of the year, and your evaluation of each of the managers...and then meet privately with each of them."

"Fine. I'll call them in, one at a time, and we can brief you on their responsibilities. Obviously, they're a little nervous about you showing up here. They know they've been slow in getting the business off the ground, but they've been working their tails off."

"No, I'd prefer to meet with them alone, one on one. I'll just take the vacant conference room I saw in the blueprints. Let's make that my office for the time being."

"Are you sure that's wise? After all, they report to me. And I thought we'd build you a corner office down at the end of the hall."

"I don't believe we should be spending any more money, Mr. Tackaberry, until we start making some. And I'd prefer to meet with each manager alone."

As the limousine pulled off the interstate and under the Chicago skyway into the Southside, Cliff saw the run-down row houses, vacant store fronts, and off in the distance, the brownfields of what once had been the booming Southside Works of US Steel. So this is where they got such a good deal to build the company's plant and headquarters, he thought. No wonder the politicians came up with grants and low-interest loans to entice them here.

Driving through the plant gate and stopping in front of the headquarters building, Wilfred bounded out of the vehicle and opened the door for the two executives. "Have a good day, gentlemen," he smiled.

Tackaberry grunted at him, heaving his well-fed body out of the limousine.

Pausing on the sidewalk, Cliff turned to the driver, "Wilfred, thanks for the ride. What's your last name?"

"Koppshinski, Mr. Cross. But everyone calls me Kopp."

"You drive for the limousine service?"

"Oh, no. This here's a company car. Been working for Speedcom for the past two years...since Mr. Tackaberry got here."

"What did you do before?"

"Worked over on the open hearth at South Works for over twenty years."

"Got a family?"

"Yes, sir. Wife and three teenage kids. Sure glad I got this job. Times have been hard around here."

"Driving keeps you busy?"

"Well, I pick up Mr. Tackaberry in the morning and drive him home at night. In between, I might take him or the other executives somewhere. In my spare time, I look after their cars in the lot over there."

"Their personal cars?"

"Yes, sir."

"I see," Cliff nodded soberly.

Listening to the conversation from atop the steps, Jamison wondered if Cliff was going to be a problem. Why had he been reading the blueprints? The press release said he was the new president of the company, but what did that mean? He, Tackaberry, was CEO. Why had Oscar, as chairman of the board, issued the release? It should have come from the CEO. Why hadn't he been brought into the decision-making process? Why hadn't Oscar told him more? What was going on? He was a seasoned computer executive, and this...this part Indian was still a boy. Didn't look much like an Indian either, except for the high cheekbones and complexion. And where'd he get that curly hair? Indians had straight, black hair. Looked more like a French Canadian...like that giant hockey player, Mario Lemieux.

"Come on, Cliff," he barked, perplexed by the appearance of this seemingly friendly, yet intense, young man who couldn't keep his foot still. What were his intentions? Exactly what authority had

Oscar and the Board given him? What did it mean to a sixty-two-year-old computer executive who was slowly beginning to realize that holding an important management position at IBM was a world away from trying to build a fledgling little computer company from scratch?

Chapter Two

"This big fellow is our new President, Clifford Cross, and I'm sure we're all going to get along just fine. You've all seen the press release about him on the bulletin board," Tackaberry explained to his people sitting around the mahogany table in the oak-paneled conference room. "Cliff, it's all yours."

"Well, thanks, Mr. Tackaberry. I'm looking forward to meeting with each of you today or tomorrow. I'd like you to be prepared to discuss your areas of responsibility and your business plans for the balance of the year...your objectives and how you plan to achieve them...your budgets...your people. Not personnel...**people**. I hate the word **personnel**. I expect to be here through Wednesday, back to Washington, then in New York early next week, and back here the following Wednesday. I've got a lot to learn, and let's start by going around the table and introducing yourselves. I've seen your employment files, but I need to begin putting your names with your faces," he smiled, encouragingly.

"I'm Smokey Lee, Vice President of Systems Integration and Software," a disheveled young man in a mismatched green sport shirt, blue pants, and loafers without socks nodded sardonically.

"Red Cermak...Engineering."

"So, you're the inventor of our ink-jet printer. Heard a lot about you, Red," Cliff nodded his approval. "Where'd you pick up all your knowledge about ink-jet technology?"

14

"Actually, I was involved in developing some of the technology for the serial impact dot matrix printers at Cybersystems around 1975. That got me interested in looking for a less expensive and more reliable printing mechanism. So, in my spare time, I started fooling around with ink-jet technology. I'm a chemical engineer by training, and early on developing the ink was the most critical element in an ink-jet printing system. Once I thought I had it down, I left Cybersystems and filed my patents. Shopped the idea on Wall Street...met Mr. McMillan, who brought Mr. Martin in as an investor. They bought my patents and formed Speedcom."

"I'm told the quality of our ink is one of the pluses."

"Yes, sir. And it's proprietary...and we want to keep it that way. The repeat business we can get on our ink cartridges can be **extremely** profitable. Once we sell a printer, we've got a captive customer."

"Excellent. And you are..."

"Glenn Johnson, VP of Sales. Came from IBM."

"They're number one. Not sure, though, why we're limiting our printer to their PCs. But that's a question for another day. And..."

"Sam Finn, VP of Manufacturing," answered a middle-aged, slightly rotund but obviously energetic man in neatly pressed coveralls.

"Jane Hammon, Vice President, Finance and..."

Turning away from her before she finished her sentence, and slightly tapping his foot under the table, Cliff looked over his shoulder to a diminutive, yet compact, young woman sitting with one leg folded under the other along the wall. A pencil stuck out of her jet black hair, twisted in a bun behind her head. The symmetrical features of her small face and soft, full lips reminded him of a china doll. "And who are **you**?"

"My name's Annette Yablonski, but people call me Nettie. Secretary, office manager, and chief cook and bottle washer," she smiled, her whole body exuding energy as her face lit up. Cliff knew from her file that she was thirty-four and widowed. Her husband had been killed in Viet Nam.

"Well, thank you, Annette," he returned her smile, thinking she should put on a little makeup. "Thank all of you. Now, Sam, why don't you show me through the plant?"

Sam Finn explained as they walked through the new government-financed facility, "We're set up to do a hundred Speedcom systems a month, plus the cartridges, which are fully automated. We're only doing twenty-five systems, until we get the bugs out and the work force trained. Even so, you can see we're building an inventory...have nearly a thousand units over there. We've restarted shipping demo units to the sales offices, but frankly, until we get our problems fixed, I worry about getting too many in the field."

"I count only about fifty people at the workstations. Where are the rest?" Cliff asked.

"Well, we laid off forty-five, and have another twenty-five in training. With all the money the government put into the building and equipment, we're under pressure from the politicians to keep people working."

"Only part of the system that we actually manufacture ourselves, aside from the cartridges, is the printer. How's it performing?"

"I'll tell you, Mr. Cross, that's the one bright spot. Extremely reliable...requires minimum maintenance...the new ink-jet technology Red designed puts out perfect copy."

"We hold all the patents on that, right? And please call me Cliff."

"Yes, sir...Cliff. Red sold them to the company for cash. I think he wanted some stock...guess we all would have liked some...at least the options, for the risk we're taking joining a start-up company. But Mr. McMillan promised us they'd come in due time, once we started making money."

"Well, that's the name of the game. If we don't get the product fixed and out in the field soon, there won't be any company."

Closing the door behind him as he sat down in Red Cermak's laboratory with Red and his engineers, Cliff nodded approvingly, "Well, boys, I hear you're the stars of the show. Tell me about this new ink-jet printer...although I won't pretend to understand much of the engineering lingo."

Well dressed, in a necktie, buttoned-down blue shirt, blue blazer, gray slacks, and tasseled loafers, Red was not the stereotype of an inventor who held several patents. Articulate and pleasant, he introduced his engineering team and explained the theory behind his ink-jet printing mechanism. "As you probably know, the problem with ink-jet printing has been the intermittent clogging of the diaphragm—the nozzle—when the ink drops through it. By reducing the tolerances around the pinhead of the diaphragm, we've been able to eliminate the clogging. Bottom line is we can get to three hundred dpi resolution without any degradation of quality...reliability at least as good as your standard impact dot matrix printer."

"What about speed?"

"We're still getting four pages a minute, but I think in a few years the whole industry will be moving toward faster printers. That should be no problem. The rest of the industry is still stumped by the clogging, so that's where we have a real advantage."

"I know this isn't your bailiwick, Red, but tell me how we could get real quantity production with our small sales force? After all, we're only a peanut in the industry."

"Mr. Tackaberry's got big plans. Thinks we can go head to head with the big boys, once we get our problems fixed. I'll tell you one thing, Cliff...hope it's okay calling you that...I'll stack my printer up against anything on the street, or anything we know about coming down the pike."

"You've got a gem, Red. You and the boys just keep trying to squeeze another ten percent out of the cost. Let me know what kind of volumes you'd need to do that." Cliff shook a determined clenched fist high in the air as he rose to leave. "Your printer's going to save all our jobs, and make us some money, too!"

He found Smokey Lee leaning against the coffee machine talking with his programmers. After introducing himself around, Cliff said, "Sounds like you guys are having some problems with the bugs in the software driver for the IBM PC. Are you sure it's the software, and not the cable interface between the printer and the PC?"

"Shouldn't be the cable. They're pretty standard. We're using a serial hookup," Smokey replied.

"I assume you're hooking our software driver onto Microsoft's DOS Operating System for the IBM PC."

"Right. Problems might be in our install program hooking the driver into the operating system. That's what we're trying to sort out right now. Have all six programmers on it."

"How long before you get the bugs out?"

"Got to be within a month."

"Good. Once we get that solved, let's suppose we write some software drivers for other operating systems...Macintosh...Digital...Wang. How long would that take?"

"Whew...I don't know. Let's see...we're getting our learning curve behind us...probably take three people about three months for the driver...another month for the install program. What do you say, fellas?"

Jeremy Thorpe, the senior programmer, spoke up, "Probably about right for Wang and the Mac, but Digital uses three different operating systems for their mid-frame computers. That would be more complicated."

"Interesting," Cliff nodded. "Well, keep plugging away. First things first. Let's get the bugs out of our driver in the next few weeks, and then maybe we can talk turkey about some other projects. Look forward to seeing you next week."

Jamison had been tagging along behind Cliff, scowling at most of the answers Cliff was receiving. "Why don't we just get Glenn and go over to the South Shore Country Club for lunch?" he suggested. "He can fill you in on sales over there. His people are spread out, so there's no one else here in his department for you to talk to."

"Why don't we just get some sandwiches and soft drinks out of the machines, and ask him to come into the conference room." It really wasn't a question. Tackaberry shrugged and motioned for Glenn Johnson to join them.

After spending a long hour, restlessly tapping his foot under the table throughout, listening to the sales manager's complaints about the unreliability of the product, the inadequate sales force, the lack of experienced systems maintenance men, and the superiority of the competition, Cliff thanked him for his briefing, and said he would look into the various shortcomings.

He then spent another hour having Jane Hammon explain the accounting system, and a half-hour having Nettie Yablonski walk him through the paper flow procedures. She seemed to be the only one who had a handle on everything that was happening in the plant and office.

Dropping his earlier plan to meet separately with each department head, for he had already talked with them, he suggested that Tackaberry pull together his financial reports, forecasts, and business plan, take them into the conference room, where Cliff would join him in a few minutes.

Asking Nettie how she took her coffee, he got her and himself each a cup of black from the coffee machine, and pulled up a chair next to her desk. "Tell me about this place, Nettie," he smiled.

"What's to tell...sure beats working over at the steel mill."

"Ah...come on, you know...how's the morale, and all that stuff?"

"Well...since we don't have a product that works...and since we've just about spent the whole ten million that Mr. McMillan and Mr. Martin put into the company...and since IBM is going to shut us off if we don't pay our bill for all those PCs you saw sitting in inventory...and since Congressman Romanowski is threatening to stop our federal job-training grants even if we don't have enough work for those who are here...and since we've got a sales force sitting in six cities across the country with nothing to do but pass out brochures of the nifty system that they might be able to sell someday...except for all these little problems, everything is just hunky-dory."

"Whew! You don't miss a trick. What about the oak-paneled conference room, these executive offices, the limousine...how does all this sit with the employees?"

"No you don't. Not going there, Mr. Cross. Mr. Tackaberry's my boss. If there's a problem, it's your problem, not mine."

"Fair enough, Nettie. But in the long run, it's all our problem, if we can't get this business off the ground."

"Yes, sir. But as long as Mr. Tackaberry's my boss, I'll give you the facts as I see them, but I don't get paid to express my opinion about my boss."

"You've got the smarts...and spunk, Nettie...and I respect that," he nodded as he put his chair back in its place. She can't be more than five-feet-two, and weigh more than a hundred pounds soaking wet...but she sure is built like the proverbial you-know-what...he smiled to himself. Wonder why she never remarried. She's the whole package. It was only Monday afternoon and already he was missing his wife.

Tackaberry had elaborate four-colored charts and graphs laid out on the mahogany table and on easels around the room. With pointer in hand, he explained that they could produce and market approximately one hundred Speedcom systems a month at an average price of $10,000, which would generate about $1 million in revenue monthly, or $12 million annually. His Cost of Goods Sold was running about $4,303 per unit, giving him a Gross Margin of $5,697, or $569,700 a month. His Overhead was running a little over $200,000 a month, giving him a projected PBT, allowing for contingencies, of around $350,000 a month, or over $4 million annually. Before bonuses, that is.

"Dammit, Tackaberry," Cliff exploded. "You haven't sold any product yet, the system doesn't work, and you're running out of money! You can put all of these fancy charts back in that fancy bathroom and use them for fancy toilet paper!"

"Cliff...boy...what are you getting so riled up about? This is normal for a start-up operation. Why, when we'd bring a new product out at IBM, it could take months to get the bugs out...cost one hundred million dollars after we introduced it before we could see daylight. That's the way this business works. Surely you saw that at Tektron. Those birds in Wall Street, and that shyster, Sidney Martin, have plenty of cash. They just want us to do this on the cheap. Don't be naive."

Staring down at the floor for a moment and rubbing his eyes, Cliff replied softly, "Please do me a favor...rather than look at these projections...put out your monthly Payroll records, monthly Accounts Payable, and Cash Disbursement records. Set them on the table here for me tomorrow morning. I'm going back to my hotel room."

"If you insist...wait, I'll call the car for you."

Spinning around, seething, Clifford looked down at Jamison and muttered through clenched teeth, "No!" and then regaining control of himself, said, "I'll have Nettie call me a cab. I don't ever want to ride in that limousine again. In fact, I recommend it be gone before I get here next week."

When he came out of the conference room to Nettie's desk, she rolled her eyeballs, "Temper...temper, Mr. C. People don't miss much around here."

"Thanks, Nettie. You're right. Would you please just call me a cab?"

"I'm taking a night class at DePaul. If it's all right with Mr. Tackaberry, I could drop you off and double back to school."

"It'll be just fine. Grab your purse, and let's get out of here."

Chapter Three

Laughing as he squeezed his body into the front seat of Nettie's yellow VW Beetle, Cliff said, "You sure have a fancy car. Glad it's got a floor in it. What year is this, anyway?"

"It's a '76...and it gets me where I want to go. Push back that sun roof. Don't roll down your window, though, until we get out of this part of town."

Although it was only late afternoon, young, toughs—blacks, whites, Puerto Ricans, Poles, Slavs, Hungarians, Italians—seemingly all nationalities were loitering on the street corners in their Malcolm X or Chicago Bears tee shirts, baggy pants, and unlaced sneakers, smoking what one hoped were only cigarettes. Some were nonchalantly swigging from bottles of beer, while a few passed around a brown paper bag out of which protruded the neck of a bottle. At a stoplight, one of them, leering at Nettie, called out, "Yo, babe," grinding his hips and motioning with an obscene gesture for her to join him.

Cliff started to open the door, cursing under his breath, "Why you..."

"No, Mr. C! **Please** don't say anything. Just ignore them."

When the light changed, she sped away, forcing him to hurriedly slam the door shut. Gusts of wind blew old newspapers along the sidewalk and into the doorways of boarded-up old buildings. Wire garbage baskets overflowed with trash. The stench of life gone sour was in the air.

"Is this where you live, Nettie?"

"All my life."

"Ever thought of moving someplace else?"

As she pulled onto the interstate and rolled down her window, she sighed, "Not really. Got married right out of high school. Then Nick got drafted, and I moved in with my family. Pop passed away a few years ago, so I still live with my mother. My brother wants her to go live with his family. Help take care of the kids so the wife can go back to work...that's if she can find work. Don't know what I'll do if Mom leaves. Maybe look for a roommate."

"Attractive, bright young woman like you must have plenty of beaus knocking on your door."

"Oh, I get around. Hang out with Nick's old friends at the corner pub. Nick and I went to high school together. His buddies look after me. I don't mean to put them down, but unemployed steelworkers don't exactly turn me on. I guess that's why I started taking night classes. I enjoy the young people, even though most of them are a lot younger than I am. But there's one or two professors...now that's a different story," she smiled.

"You know, I really like Red. Soft-spoken...well organized...obviously brilliant, but not like some of the off-the-wall geniuses I've known in the computer industry."

"Red's solid as a rock. If he wasn't hitched, I'd set my cap for him in a millisecond. But to tell you the truth, Mr. C., there aren't too many eligible men in my little world that I'd be comfortable with. Not that I'm anything special."

"Don't underestimate yourself, Nettie. After you briefed me this afternoon, and watching you handle yourself, I confess, the thought that went through my mind was, 'This young lady is not only like the Energizer bunny...she's the whole package!'"

"That's nice of you to say, Mr. C., but when you get to know me a little better, you'll see my faults. Sometimes, I can be a little pushy."

"You...pushy? No," he teased.

As she turned into the off-ramp onto the airport road, neither spoke until they came to a stop in front of the Marriott.

"Thanks a million, Nettie. I enjoyed our little talk. Would you have time to come in for a drink?"

Looking at her watch, she winced, "Afraid not, Mr. C. Got to get to school. Say, you're not hitting on me, are you?"

"Why, Nettie, how could you think such a thing? I'd just like to get to know you better since we're going to be working together, and I have a feeling, you're someone I can count on," he said, twisting his body around to get out of the little car, and then sticking his head through the window. "And, call me Cliff."

"Maybe...once it feels right...if you give me a rain check," she called back as she drove away.

Once inside his hotel room, he flopped down on the bed and opened his three-ring notebook. Staring at it for a moment, he threw it aside, thinking, I need a break. He had specified that he wanted to stay in a hotel with a health club, so thumbing through the hotel's booklet of services he located the club, saw that it had treadmills and a sauna, and was into his running clothes and on his way.

After signing into the club on the third floor of the hotel, he climbed onto an empty treadmill and began his thirty-minute run. Halfway through it, he heard a lilting voice on the treadmill next to him as it started up, "Why, Mr. Cross, hello there. Remember me? I'm Krissy, your flight attendant."

"Krissy with a K! Don't tell me you're a fitness buff." Her hair was tied back in a ponytail with a very...**very** feminine pink ribbon. Her long-sleeved, black, tight-fitting turtleneck jersey and skintight pink pants left little to the imagination. Her loose-fitting flight attendant's jacket had been quite deceiving. Obviously, she had just put on fresh makeup. The eyebrow pencil and eye shadow had been applied perfectly, and one of those delicate lipstick brushes had traced the outlines of her thin, curved lips.

"No more than you appear to be," she replied. "Stay here often?"

"First time, but probably not the last. Involved with a business on the Southside. Probably should move closer."

"Oooo...don't do that," she whimpered. "Too dangerous in that part of town. Can't beat this club or the lounge upstairs."

As he slowed his treadmill to a stop, he observed, "Krissy with a K...you must be doing a seven-minute mile. Where do you get all that energy after a day's work?"

"Don't you think you could keep up with me?"

"Heavens, no. These old knees couldn't stand the pounding. Ten-minute mile at a five percent elevation is about my speed. Well, I'm off to the sauna. Have a nice evening."

"Why don't you join my two girlfriends and me for a drink in the lounge after you shower?"

"Oh, so you think I need a shower after sweating in the sauna?"

"Only if you want to be within ten feet of another human being," she bantered.

"I've got a pile of work to do in my room. Think I'll just order room service for dinner. But I might drop by for a beer."

"Please do."

"We'll see. Take care, Krissy with a K."

After washing his running clothes and draping them over the lamps in his room to dry, he showered and slipped into khakis and a Mountaineer shirt. He picked up the phone to order room service, held it for a long moment, and then put it down, muttering, "What the hell."

Entering the lounge, he spotted Krissy and her two girlfriends at a table in the corner. Sizing them up, he thought: Whew, if Krissy's a nine, they're both at least eight plus!

"Evening, ladies."

"Hi, Mr. Cross. Please sit down. This is Jeannie and Mary Catherine. They're both flight attendants."

Shaking hands with them, Jeannie said, "So, you're the tall, dark, handsome hunk Krissy was telling us about."

"Come on. If you promise to knock off that stuff, you can call me Cliff." Turning to the waitress, he said, "I'll have a Coors Light. How about another round for you ladies?"

After ordering three more daiquiris, Krissy said to her friends, "Cliff, here, is a workaholic. He had his nose buried in a notebook all the way from Washington this morning."

"What do you do, Cliff?" Mary Catherine asked.

"I'm heading up a small computer company over on the Southside. It's a new start-up. Speedcom's its name...at least for now."

"Oh, how exciting," Jeannie gushed. "You're so young to be the president of a high tech company. Why don't you join us for dinner so you can tell us about it? Is your stock publicly traded, or are you going to be making an Initial Public Offering? Maybe we could get in on the ground floor?"

Finishing his beer, Cliff chuckled, "Now why would sweet young girls be worrying your pretty heads about an IPO? You know, they're extremely risky. And no, our stock is not publicly traded, and an IPO is, at best, a long way off. Anyway, I've got to get up to my room to get some work done, or there won't ever be an IPO."

"Oh, come on, Cliff, have dinner with us," Krissy pleaded.

"Maybe next time we bump into each other," he replied, rising, "but I have to get up to my room."

"I'll be overnighting here next Monday and Wednesday," Krissy purred, giving him her Farrah Fawcett smile.

"I might be here next Wednesday. Maybe I'll see you then...Krissy with a K. Nice meeting you ladies."

As he walked away from the table, he overheard Mary Catherine say, "Krissy, he wasn't wearing a wedding ring."

"I know...I know," Krissy giggled.

* * *

In his room, Cliff called room service, ordering a green salad, T-bone steak, mashed potatoes, and another Coors Light. Opening his three-ring notebook, he started writing his impressions of the day, studied the financial data that McMillan had given him, and then reflected on the fancy forecasts of Tackaberry. "No way...no damn way," he shook his head, and then, for the first time in his life, the palms of his hands became sweaty, his whole body turned clammy, and his stomach began to churn.

He stood up, looked in the bathroom mirror, doused his face with cold water, and spoke to the figure in the mirror. "Mr. tough guy, you're having a panic attack...a damn panic attack! There's no way you can save this company. You've got a wife and two kids, and you've just jeopardized your family's future."

Suddenly remembering that he hadn't called home, he went for the phone as he heard a knock on the door. Opening it, the waiter entered, laid out his dinner on the serving cart, thanked Cliff for the tip, and departed.

Cutting into his steak, he took two bites and pushed it aside. He couldn't stop his stomach from churning. He should call home...talk to Sarah and the kids...that might calm him.

"Cross residence," Greta answered the phone.

"Greta, this is Cliff. Could I please speak to Sarah?"

"Sorry, Mr. Cross. She isn't here...went to the country club for dinner with some friends."

"What about Tyke and Sally? Put them on."

"They're both in bed. Shall I get them up?"

"No...no, just tell Sarah I called. I'll call tomorrow."

"Yes, sir. Have a nice evening."

"Thanks, Greta. You, too."

Some nice evening, he thought, closing his notebook, undressing for bed, and crawling between the sheets. Tossing, unable to sleep, he got up, took a Sominex, downed it with a cognac from the minibar, and scooped his lucky die off the nightstand as he crawled back into bed.

Lying on his back in his boxer shorts, feeling sorry for himself, studying the strange cube as he slowly turned it between his thumb and his forefinger, suddenly his jaw tightened as the snake-eye side stared up at him. A jumble of thoughts raced through his mind: Why wasn't Sarah at home when he needed her? At least, she couldn't be complaining about his sleeping in his shorts instead of the silk pajamas she had given him. Can take the boy out of the hills, but you can't take the hillbilly out of the boy, she constantly complained. And how was he going to turn the little company around...and make his fortune...show her and her parents that he is just as good as they are?

Eventually, the Sominex kicked in, and he fell into a deep and troubled sleep, his tight grip on the odd amulet gradually relaxing.

Chapter Four

Jumper Ramsey finally got the wrecked four-door Ford he had bought for nearly nothing at the junkyard back in running order. Now, if he could talk his old buddy Jep Bittle down at the Exxon station into putting an inspection sticker on it, he could make himself three or four hundred dollars.

"Come on, Jep. The bumper's back on secure. Welded it myself. Grinded off the rust spots around the gas tank. New paint job. Got ninety-seven thousand miles on it, which proves I didn't tinker with the odometer. Listen to that engine. Hardly rattles."

"Dammit, Jumper, why do you always put me in this spot? I could lose my inspection license. Promise me this is the last time. Put it over on Joe Joe's lot with all those old clunkers he's got. Won't stick out like a sore thumb. Get over there and ask him if he'll take it. I don't want it setting out on the street with a For Sale sign. Troopers will spot it in a minute."

"Sure, Jep. You got my word. I'll talk with Joe Joe right away."

Crossing the potholed, winding main street of little Beckley to Joe Joe Karns's corner used-car lot, Jumper found his drinking buddy watching "As the World Turns" on his fuzzy black-and-white TV inside his office trailer. Joe Joe was a few years older than Jumper, but they knew each other well, having played sandlot baseball together in the summertime. He was a beet-faced, beefy lout, with straggly strands of hair combed across his prematurely balding head. Jumper considered him the town's fashion plate, for he owned nearly every color of sport coat, shirt, and pants, which he mixed and matched with artistry. His favorite seemed to be his fire engine red jacket, canary yellow pants, and black, buttoned-down shirt with creamy tie. His zippered, patent leather boots, out of a mail-order catalog, came all the way from Italy. Although no one dared call him "slick" to his face, he could have passed for the barker at the county fair, or even a pimp in a Kansas City brothel. A wide gold ring, with diamond chips forming the letter J, appeared to have squeezed all the blood out of his stubby pinky finger.

"Got a dandy for you, Joe Joe. Inspected...painted...sets yonder over there. You could move it in a week. Give you twenty percent of what you can sell it for. Right off the top. Won't cost you nothing. 'Course, you probably don't even need the money. But, if truth be told, I sure could use it. I'm a little short."

Stretching his neck to look across the street, Joe Joe shrugged, "Thirty percent. Put it in the back row. Don't want it near the street."

"Aw, come on, Joe Joe, I've got a whole week's work plus the parts and paint in it. It's a cream puff. Split the difference...make it twenty-five percent."

"Well...hell...for you, Jumper...I'll do it. But I don't know why you keep piddling around with this penny-ante stuff. Didn't your grandpap leave that old dilapidated farm of his up in Possum Hollow to you?"

"Ya, but it ain't worth nothing. Been setting idle since I was a boy. All growed over. Why? Want to buy it?"

"Hell, no. But if you was interested, we just might be able to form ourselves a little partnership. Ain't there an old worked-out coal mine halfway up the hill behind the pastures?"

"Sure. But what good is it?"

"You smoke pot, don't you?"

"Not no more. Used to over in Nam. Why?"

"Got anything against it?"

"Hell, no. Guess I just got stuck on booze. Easier to get. My old lady'd have a fit if she smelled pot on me. Whiskey's bad enough."

"Pull the door shut...let me turn up the TV...you sit down and listen."

Pulling his chair closer to Jumper, Joe Joe half-whispered, "I got real good connections up at the auto auction in Charleston. I could sell as much marijuana up there as I could lay my hands on. Problem is, I'd be the middle man, and I can only get it from a middle man, so there ain't no margin in it for me. Now, if we was to set out some plants back in on your grandpap's farm, we could process the leaves up in that old, abandoned mine. I could sell it at the auction, and we could make a ton of money."

"Ya, but what if we got caught?"

"Who's going to catch us? State police and DEA are on the lookout for the pot smokers to track them back to their suppliers. That ain't us. We'd never be selling to the end users. We'd be the wholesalers...and the producers. Anyway, that new drug task force is making a big stink about cocaine and heroin. Pot ain't no big deal to them."

"But I read how they use planes and helicopters to spot the growing fields—go in and arrest the farmers and burn the fields."

"Sure. But the beauty of our operation would be that there ain't no plane or even helicopter that's going to chance coming up that winding hollow or get down below those narrow ridges."

"How much could we make?"

"Well, you got to work backwards. Figure I could move whatever we could produce. Say we set out a thousand plants...maybe up along the old, abandoned road leading to the mine. Probably some old logging roads up there, too, that we could use. Good to have the open spaces with tree cover nearby."

"We got logging trails running all through the woods."

"Good. Gotta get seeds first. I got a safe connection for that down in Kermit. Hell, the city fathers run the rackets. We get 'em started indoors in pots. This time of year is just right. Could use your grandpap's old farmhouse for that. Right?"

"Sure. Nobody goes up there."

"Then we plant them in May, after the last frost. Set about three feet apart...we could get...let's see...a thousand plants on both sides of an old trail...in less than half a mile."

"We got at least a couple of miles of mine and logging roads."

"Don't be getting too greedy, Jumper. Let's just see how it goes. One plant produces about a pound of MJ. We could wholesale it by the pound for about two hundred dollars, but we wouldn't want to do that."

"Why not? At two hundred dollars a pound, we'd be making two hundred thousand dollars on a thousand pounds. Holy hell!"

"Not so fast. There's a lot of work in harvesting the leaves and buds...trimming it...drying it...packing it. I'm not even sure we could handle it. Might take some more help."

"But why wouldn't we want to sell it by the pound?"

"Can make a lot more selling it by the ounce...or even in nickel bags...one-fifth of an ounce. Can get about ten joints out of an ounce. Probably retails for sixty dollars an ounce. We could wholesale nickels for half that. But now we're talking real work making up the packets."

"What's it going to cost us to get started? How soon?"

"Seeds'll cost peanuts. Pots...gas mileage...practically nothing. But it's going to take a lot of work. Crop'll come in around late July or early August. We'd do the processing and storing up in the old mine...cool and damp'll keep it fresh. Then I'll start moving it at the auction this fall."

"What's our split?"

"Right down the middle. You provide the land. We both do the work...I do the selling...only wholesale."

"What about all those drug kingpins? Don't they control everything from the production right up through the distribution to the users? Don't they have their territories divvied up, and if they catch you poaching, you end up wearing cement shoes at the bottom of some lake?"

"Hey, those guys are the big time operators. They're mostly into cocaine or heroin, anyway. We're just small potatoes. They ain't going to bother us."

"I hope you're right. I don't need no bullet in the back of my brain."

"Nothing to worry about. They won't even know we exist. Best you post the land with No Trespassing signs, so hunters or hikers don't come stumbling onto our operation."

"But what if we get caught? They gonna lock us up? For how long? I don't know if I could take that."

"Hell, no. It'd be our first offense, so we'd probably get off with a fine and put on probation."

"Then we'd fold our tent. Right? Second offense would mean the slammer for sure."

"Right. That'd be our deal. Grow it out on your grandpap's farm. Process it in the farmhouse. I do the selling...wholesale only. We'd split the profits even, and the first time we get caught, we hang it up. Deal?"

"Well, I sure could use the money. Okay. Let's give it a try."

"Good. I'll make the arrangements to get the seeds and start feeling out some of the guys at the auction. You get out to the old place and figure out where we should do the planting. We're gonna make a killing!"

Taking a deep breath and slowly letting it out, Jumper shrugged, "Or maybe we get ourselves killed."

Chapter Five

Six-year-old Sally answered the phone with a mouth full of cereal, "Crosh reshidence."

"Sally, how are you, honey?"

"Hi, Dad. Where are you?"

"I'm still in Chicago. Put Mommy on the phone, please."

"She's still in bed. Greta's here."

"Put her on!"

"Wait...Tyke wants to say hello."

Four-year-old Tyke grabbed the phone from his older sister. "Daddy, when you coming home?"

"In a day or two, buddy. I'll bring you and Sally a present. Okay? I love you."

"Okay. I love you, too. Here's Greta."

"Morning, Greta. Where's Sarah?"

"She's still in bed, Mr. Cross. Didn't get in till late last night."

"Is everything all right?"

"Far as I know."

"Good. Please tell Sarah I'll call tonight. Bye."

Irritated, Clifford smacked the elevator button, got out in the lobby to get some breakfast in the restaurant, and ran into Tackaberry.

"Morning, Cliff. Hope you don't mind my getting here early. Drove my own car. Thought maybe we could talk on our way to the office. Could I join you for breakfast? Cup of coffee. Already ate."

"And a good morning to you," his spirits rising slightly. "I'll just get a roll and some coffee at the carryout, and we can beat the traffic."

Settling in to Tackaberry's midnight blue Chrysler for their drive to the Southside, Cliff asked, "Where's the limo?"

"Oh, I thought maybe we should get rid of it...could use the cash...so I told Kopp to shop it around to see what we could get for it."

Cliff nodded, "Good move. What's on your mind?"

"Well, I guess I'm not quite sure what's going on. Oscar didn't tell me much more than they hired you, and you'd be out. Didn't even know you'd been named president until I got the press release. That was one of my titles, along with CEO and COO. Nobody told me exactly what your duties are...where you fit in...and frankly, where I fit in."

After a long silence, Cliff responded, "I don't know what to tell you at this point. Right now, I need to learn as much as I can. Then, in a few weeks, I think things will sort themselves out."

Now it was Jamison whose palms became sweaty, whose body turned clammy, and whose stomach began to churn. "Cliff, you wouldn't have taken the job without knowing what your responsibilities would be...what your **authority** would be. I have a right to know where I stand."

"Well, as you said yesterday, you have a three-year contract. I guess that means you have another year to go on it. Beyond that, I'm in no position to say anything further right now. Like I said, I expect things will sort themselves out in a few weeks. Tell me about Sam Finn. It must be frustrating for him to try producing a product with the software problems not solved. Inventory keeps stacking up. Means all those units are going to have to be retrofitted if we have a hardware problem. Are we sure our problem's only software?"

"Well...er...ah...I think so, Cliff."

"I'd say, we better be sure. We know the IBM PC works. Have we double-checked our cable interface?"

"Hell, Cliff, I can't do everything. That's Sam's problem. He's our hardware guy."

"Mr. Tackaberry...sir...it's all our problem, if we don't soon get this product up and running. And what if we want to market the printer to other PCs? Then we'll need both serial and parallel interface cables. Have you thought about that?"

"Well, not exactly. I guess that's something we should look into."

"I'll say it is! And it doesn't make any sense to keep producing a product that doesn't work. Shouldn't we shut down the line until we've solved our problems?"

"You don't understand, boy. We're under tremendous pressure from the politicians to keep people working. Oscar, and especially that snake, Sidney Martin, want us to look like we're busy."

As they turned into the Southside, Cliff prodded, "What about Sam? Does he know what he's doing?"

"Sure. Sam's a pro. Ran a production line at IBM. Came highly recommended."

"I see," Cliff clamped his jaw shut and stared blankly, both his feet rapidly tapping the floor. As the car pulled in the lot, his stomach began to churn again.

Attempting a smile, nodding to the employees as he hurried through the office to the conference room, he closed the door behind him, removed his coat, and began pouring over the accounting documents he had requested.

"Can I help?" Tackaberry stuck his head in through the door.

"No thanks. I'd just as soon be alone. I'll get you if I need you."

Around midmorning, Nettie tapped lightly on the door and asked, "Coffee, Mr. C?"

"You're a lifesaver...come in, Nettie," Cliff pushed his calculator away and stretched his arms.

"What's all your penciled spreadsheets?" she asked, setting down his coffee. "All our accounting data is printed on the computer. You've got the stacks right there."

"Yep. But I've got to play with the numbers to get them in my head. Need to make sure I understand them...and need to make sure different reports jibe with each other."

"So what have you learned, Einstein?"

"Not much yet. Here's some money. Please get me a sandwich and a Diet Coke around noon. Ask me then."

Promptly at 12:00 noon, Nettie opened the door, a lunch tray in her hands, and Tackaberry peered in behind her. "Here you are, Mr. C."

"Can I help?" Tackaberry called in.

"Thanks, Nettie. No thanks...wait a minute, Nettie. Eat your lunch yet?"

"Got it at my desk."

"Good. Bring it in and let's have an executive lunch together."

"Fine," she smiled, looking askance at her boss as he shrugged and turned away.

Setting her tray on the table and pulling up her chair, Nettie asked, "So, do you have it all figured out?"

"No, but I'm getting there," he replied, biting into his ham and cheese. "Going to spend the afternoon taking another run through the plant...talk some more with Sam, Red, and Smokey. How good is Sam?"

"Solid as a rock. Has the production line well organized. Now all he needs is a product that works."

"What about Smokey?"

"Wild as a March hare. But smart. His software team is all a bunch of eggheads, but they don't seem to be able to get the different software packages to work. Maybe they are trying to do too much. I don't know enough about it to say."

As they finished their lunch and emptied their trays into the wastebasket, Cliff said, "By this afternoon, I think I'll have everything I need here...for now. Get me on an evening flight to Washington, and please cancel my room at the Marriott and get me a late checkout. I'll pick up my things on the way to the airport."

"Want me to drive you?"

"Sure, I'd like that...and please, get me Mr. McMillan on the phone."

"Yes, sir. I'm pretty sure I can get you on a six-thirty to National...gets in around nine, your time."

* * *

"McMillan here."

"Hello, Oscar. This is Cliff."

"Hey, how's it going? Got our problems solved? Give Tackaberry his walking papers yet?"

"Things are a little more complicated than that. I'd like to meet with you and Mr. Martin early next week. I hope to have a plan laid out by then. I'll come up to New York, or we could do it at Mr. Martin's office down here."

"I'll come down there, but let's make it at the University Club for lunch on Monday...say, noon. I'll reserve us a private room. No need to go over to Sidney's office. He can join us there."

"Fine. Noon, Monday, at the University Club. See you then. Bye."

After spending the afternoon confirming his initial impressions with Sam, Red, and Smokey, and sticking his head into Tackaberry's office to inform the puzzled-looking CEO that he was leaving, Nettie drove him, by way of the Marriott, to the airport. He was strangely silent, even though Nettie tried to cajole him into talking. "Come on, Mr. C, don't look so glum. Don't you think we have some real talent?"

"Maybe."

"Brighten up. I was too negative yesterday. That's not my nature. I know you can fix what ails us..., can't you?" she asked hesitantly.

"Maybe. There are a few bright spots, Nettie, and you're one of them," he patted her arm as she pulled alongside the curb at the United entrance. "Look forward to seeing you next week...when I think we can begin straightening things out. Thanks for the ride."

"Look forward to seeing you, too, Mr. C. **Yes, I do!**" she repeated emphatically, smiling and smacking her steering wheel as she drove away.

* * *

Pulling into the circular driveway, bordering the manicured lawn in McLean, Virginia, Cliff beheld a five white-columned red brick colonial, shaking his head in awe for the hundredth time. Setting back off Old Dominion Drive in an elegant suburb bordering the Potomac River, it was shielded from the road by the leaves of giant red oaks from spring to fall. Even in winter, after the leaves had fallen, the stately oaks, which obviously had been there for over half a century before the land was developed, served as a shadowed trellis, hiding from view all but patches of red brick, and green roof shingles, sandwiched between two chimney tops.

Cliff had been flabbergasted, bemused, and a bit uncomfortable when Sarah's parents had presented the deed to them at their engagement party. Cliff had never even seen the property. Sarah's mother, Odessa, had chosen it.

The marble-floored foyer opened into a wide hallway that led back into the kitchen, which was divided by a black walnut bar and stools, separating the kitchen proper from the rustic table and chairs. To the right of the hall, was a spacious stone-fireplaced living room, and behind it, a formal dining room, both done in soft blue and white, early American wallpaper, and rich burgundy wall-to-wall carpeting.

To the left of the hall was Cliff's oak-paneled den, the built-in bookcases supplied with books Odessa thought he should be reading. Behind it was the family room, opening into the kitchen! Jutting off the family room, was a wing containing the master bedroom and the children's rooms.

Upstairs were three guest rooms and Greta's quarters. The pantry and laundry behind the kitchen led into a three-car garage and stairway down into the basement, which housed empty metal shelves and a complete home fitness center. Cliff never completely adjusted to the sheer spaciousness of the place. He often mused that his boyhood home in Beckley could have easily fit inside two rooms.

* * *

"Hey, where is everybody?" Cliff called as he burst through the front door.

"Shush, sweetie...it's past ten...the kids are in bed. Give me a hug...I missed you," Sarah threw her arms around Cliff and pressed her body tight against him.

"I missed you, too, honey," he dropped his suit bag and briefcase, wrapped his arms around her waist, lifted her four inches off the floor as he kissed her while backing her toward their bedroom.

"Greta's still in the family room," she whispered, without trying to extricate herself.

"Hi, Greta," he called, as he kicked their bedroom door shut with the heel of his shoe. "To hell with her," he smiled.

"You're terrible," Sarah snickered.

"I know...and you love it!"

* * *

Sarah Wilson Cross was the only child of Walter Wallace Wilson, III, a prominent Charleston attorney, and his socialite wife, Odessa McFadden Wilson. She and Cliff had met at the university in her junior year at the pep rally on the day she was named the head majorette of the marching band. Cliff, as the senior captain of the Mountaineer basketball team, sat next to her on the stage at the rally and couldn't take his eyes off her. She was WVU's new Golden Girl, nearly six feet tall, with extraordinarily long, curvaceous legs, a compact body, deliciously rounded above and below her slender waist. She smelled of lilacs in springtime. But cleaner, purer, more fragrant than the purple lilacs beneath his mother's kitchen window, forever flawed by the slightest taint of coal dust. Her pageboy golden hair, obviously lightened to match the school's colors, was exquisitely coiffed, each strand in place, sprayed stiff to withstand the swirling winds of a football field, or her own acrobatic twists and turns. But what captivated Cliff most was her round, perfectly proportioned face...the dimples on her sweetheart smile.

But, a boy with his background could only look at her, perhaps smile and say a word or two. And so that was what he did on the day when he first met her, sitting next to each other at the pep rally—two stars from different galaxies. What he couldn't know was that she was smitten from the first moment he touched her, taking her arm to help her off the stage.

Who was this blue-eyed, seemingly tongue-tied giant, who would look at her and smile each time they passed, and as she turned to look back at him, would catch him watching her as she walked away? She knew he was the captain of the basketball team...the yearbook said he was from Beckley and was majoring in business. But who was he **really**? What was his background? Who were his parents and grand-parents? What did his parents **do**?

There wasn't much going on down in little Beckley. Unless his family was in coal. Not that she cared. Well, not too much. But Mother and Father would certainly want to know everything about him if she ever brought him home. And that eventually was going to happen. Clifford Cross **would** be hers!

And Clifford Cross's family was, indeed, in coal. Deep in coal. His father, Clint, had quit school at sixteen to go into the mines, and was still digging coal thirty-five years later for the Beckley Lick Run Company. Both his grandfathers as well as several of his uncles and great-uncles were coal miners. Only his grandfather, Josey Cross, was still alive, but barely. The black lung had finally got him, and only an inhalator kept him breathing.

But even though he could only wheeze out three or four words at a time between deep gasps of air, propped up by huge white pil-lows, his gaunt body stretched corpselike atop a fetid, discolored mattress, each time his grandson visited him, his lecture was the same,

"Boy, don't you...never...never set foot inside a goddamned coal...coal mine." Raising his voice, his bloodshot, watery eyes seemed to nearly burst out of their sunken sockets as he painfully raised his blue-veined hand, pointing his bony finger at Cliff. "Promise...promise...never in no...coal mine!"

"No need to worry, Grandpap," Cliff had tried to assure him, "I'm going to college. Wouldn't go in the mines. Not even for the summer. I'm getting a real education, and coach got me a summer job up in Morgantown."

But the old man was obsessed with the notion that his grandson had to be kept out of the mines, even physically restrained, if necessary. He would mumble to himself, or greet members of his family as they entered his room, or admonish them as they were leaving, with the same halting words, "Keep Clifford...out of...the goddamned mines."

Retired on a pittance for nearly a decade, Josey still could taste the coal dust in his mouth each time he took a breath. He had entered the mines as an overgrown twelve year old, witnessing the West Virginia coal wars of the 1920s, the Matewan massacre of striking coal miners in nearby Mingo County still fresh in people's minds. Before he was old enough to vote, he was marching with the strikers in Raleigh County, fighting for their right to unionize in the anti-union strongholds of southern West Virginia.

When the Great Depression engulfed the coal fields, wiping out thousands of jobs, he and his brothers opened a bootleg drift mine, nothing more than a hole in the side of a hill on Spruce Mountain, eight miles northwest of Beckley. Digging bituminous by hand, they hauled it out to their mule-drawn wagon in bushel baskets. Returning to town after dusk to avoid detection, they used it to heat their homes or barter for food and secondhand clothing.

Josey had purposely tried to frighten Cliff when he was little, by telling him gruesome tales of the "Black Maria", which was a mule-drawn black-boxed wagon used as both ambulance and hearse. Dead or injured miners were delivered in it to their homes and dumped on the front porches. In gory detail, he told Cliff of the men suffocating behind collapsed mine entrances, or having their arms blown off while lighting sticks of dynamite inserted into coal seams, or being crushed to death by cave-ins.

"Be good, or the Black Maria will come and get you," was a thoughtless threat to little children in the coal country long after it had been replaced with modern ambulances and miners' hospitals. But Josey's hatred of the coal mines had sunk deep within his grandson's consciousness.

And Cliff's mother, Ruth Ann, reinforced his fear of coal mines from the time he was a toddler. As a child, and even occasionally as a grown man, he experienced a recurring nightmare of being stuffed inside a Black Maria, of being carted home and dumped, lifeless, on his parents' porch. He would awaken in a sweat, his hand fumbling in the dark over the nightstand beside his bed to find and clutch his bear tooth charm.

Ruth Ann Collins Cross was a force of nature to be reckoned with. Telling no one, not even her strong-willed husband, Clint, who she loved dearly, even though he drank too much, Ruth Ann vowed to herself and to her God that her son would not be permitted to enter the mines. She was a robust, healthy woman, always in command, yet the thought of her son eking out his life, trudging with a metal lunch bucket and lighted hard hat deep into the earth each day, made her physically ill. By God, he would make something of himself, be somebody someday, get an education, although she had not the slightest idea how. She cooked and baked and took in sewing, saving her nickels and quarters in a shoe box in her dresser. She cleaned and scrubbed and prayed out loud at every meal. She made Clifford do his homework at the kitchen table every evening, and wouldn't let him up until she had gone over it herself. Sometimes when she was alone, she sensed that she was different from her neighbors, from other coal miners' wives, even from her family. She was stronger, more alert, more energetic. She decided it was her grandfather's Cherokee blood coursing through her veins. And she was determined that her son, Clifford, would grow strong and driven to excel. Like her, he would be a force to reckon with. And although it would break her heart, she wanted him out of the damn dreary valley, far away, so there would be no temptation to return, hemmed in, trapped by mountains that hovered forebodingly, bare and cold in wintertime, and mockingly beautiful in the summer, verdant, blossoming reminders that their dull gray days, their plodding, painful lives would seldom see the sky, but through a haze of coal dust in the air.

So, when Cliff went to the university on an athletic scholarship, he carried deep in his subconscious the smoldering drive instilled in him since childhood, and in his pocket, his great-grandfather's bear-pawed die to infuse in him the power and direction needed to succeed.

But he also carried the unconscious inferiority of growing up dirt poor amid the soot and squalor of the West Virginia mountains. He knew, deep down, that Sarah Wilson, the daughter of Walter Wilson, III, and Odessa McFadden Wilson, was far beyond his reach.

When she finally invited him to her Kappa sorority dance he hesitated, even though the very thought of her made him ache. "Thanks, Sarah. Well...I don't know...ah...never been to a sorority dance. Hang out with the jocks at the field house when I'm not studying. Got rushed by a couple of fraternities in my freshman year, but didn't have any time for that," nor the money, either, he thought.

"Surely you've been to dances before."

"Sure, but nothing very fancy."

"I promise it won't be fancy. I'll dance in my bare feet before the night is over."

His face flushed as he thought of his own barefooted childhood, wondering if she was making fun of his rural roots. But she had struck a nerve that got his competitive, aggressive juices flowing. "Well, good," he smirked, "then it may not be too tame for me. Tell me when and where."

On that first date, their chemistry clicked —and it was Cliff and Sarah from that moment on. They met in the cafeteria for breakfast and lunch nearly every day. During football season, he would work-out in the weight room while she practiced with the marching band, and then stroll together along the campus walks, hand in hand, the emblazoned October leaves crunching beneath their feet. He would gulp down his dinner at the training table while Sarah ate at the Kappa house, and then they both would rush to the library to sit across from each other at a long oak table, in the dim lighting of ancient table lamps, casting their pale green glow through tinted glass shades, form-ing overlapping concentric circles upon their open books. Silently, she would rub his ankle with the tip of her shoe, and he would glance up from his book, smile, and wink.

Cliff always felt secure, surrounded by the musty rows of books running from floor to ceiling, as if, somehow, beyond the pages and chapters he was reading, a few particles from a thousand years of knowledge might seep into his bones. And when the chapel chimes told them it was ten o'clock and time to leave, a tiny part of him was sad, even as his body tingled at the thought of walking Sarah home. He refused to ride in her Thunderbird around campus, but they ended nearly every evening in it, parked behind the Kappa house.

On clear, crisp Sunday mornings they would take five-mile runs over the mountain trails above the campus, she keeping up with him, step for step, both in baggy gray sweats, lettered on front and back, Property of Athletic Department West Virginia University. About half-way through their run, at a particularly secluded spot where a thicket of vines and scrub brush obscured a nearby pine grove beyond the trail, Cliff suddenly would grasp her hand and, without a word, pull her off the trail, through the brambles to a grassy knoll beneath the pines. Twenty minutes later, she would rise, tug at his hand as he lay stretched out on his back, squinting up through the pines at the noon-bright sun.

"Huh uh, big fellow. Time to go."

"Can't blame a red-blooded American boy for trying," he would shrug and smile.

When basketball season began, Cliff practiced after class each afternoon while Sarah worked out in the gym, and then waited for him high up in the bleachers of the field house where the healthy smell of steamy sweat seemed to rise and hover in the air.

Their first crisis occurred over the Thanksgiving holiday when she invited him to have dinner with her family in Charleston. Initially, he declined, but a mixture of her pleading and pouting finally brought him around. He agreed to have a noon Thanksgiving dinner at home with his family, and drive to Charleston in time for an evening dinner with the Wilsons. But he was worried for a week about pulling up in front of their ritzy home in the snobbish South Hills section of Charleston in his father's pickup truck.

Theirs was a different world. Sarah had spent a summer traveling through Europe and a Christmas vacation skiing in Switzerland. Cliff had not been beyond the hills of West Virginia, except with the basketball team, and then they would be in and out of a city, seeing not much more than a city's skyline from a distance, smell the pungent odors of a locker room, and hear the anticipated boos and catcalls of hysteric hometown fans.

Fortunately, one of his old high-school teammates, Jumper Ramsey, solved the problem. Jumper was tight with Joe Joe Karns, a used-car salesman, who loaned Cliff a spiffy Jeep Cherokee for the day.

What Cliff didn't know as he knocked on the Wilsons' door at precisely five o'clock on Thanksgiving evening, was that Sarah had already been put through the third degree by her parents, over, "Just who is this Clifford Cross?" In fact, her father had called the president of the Beckley Bank to learn about the family.

Walter Wallace Wilson, III, was not a man to be trifled with. A senior partner in Charleston's most prestigious law firm, he was a block of granite wrapped in velvet. Although only of medium height, he seemed to tower over everyone in any room. His flat stomach, barreled chest, broad shoulders, and bull neck were crowned by a steel gray, bristled crewcut atop his large round head and piercing eyes, together conveying a highly charged magnetic field. As a younger man, he had won the handball championship at the Charleston Athletic Club several years in a row, and continued his fitness regimen, running and weight training at least three days each week. When his friends and colleagues commented that Sarah got her athleticism from him—and they did so often for they knew that was what he wanted to hear—he would reply, "You got that right, sport!" Although he played golf only to cultivate his clients to promote his varied business interests, he relished the poker games that followed, where he usually walked away a winner. Walter Wallace Wilson, III, was, indeed, a man in full. And although he had been married to Odessa McFadden Wilson for a quarter of a century, she easily could have passed for a new trophy wife, or Sarah's older sister. Odessa had made her formal entrance into society as a debutante in both Charleston and New York, and no one was permitted to forget it. Although approaching fifty, she moved in a leggy, slender, elegance, right out of Vogue. Occasionally, she would have her platinum blonde hair bobbed like Sarah's and appear at cocktail parties in a black-fringed, white chemise, adorned with spangles and beads, a flapper throwback to the 1920s.

But on the night their servant opened the door to let Cliff in, she was dressed demurely in solid black, a single-strand pearl necklace disappearing inside her cleavage, as she and Walter stood like frozen statues to receive the unwanted guest.

At dinner, a very nervous Sarah tried to make conversation, but her parents could be described, at best, as coolly courteous.

They seemed to listen attentively as, at Sarah's urging, he outlined the courses he was taking, his dedication to basketball, and his desire to find a job in computers upon graduation. But they responded with not much more than an occasional nod or "that's nice."

Finally, as Walter finished his mincemeat pie and pulled his napkin out of his collar and onto the table, he studied Cliff for a moment and then pronounced: "Damn shame about the election. **Peanut** farmer for president. What's the country coming to! Did you vote, young man? It's a civic duty, you know."

"Yes, sir. Absentee. My Grandpap Cross would put a strap to me if I didn't...that's if he could...although he's laid up pretty bad these days."

"Oh? Sorry to hear that. What's his problem?"

"He's got black lung...pneumoconiosis."

"You don't say. How'd he contract that?" Walter raised his eyebrows in mock surprise, already knowing the answer to his question, by wanting to extract from the young man a detailed description of his family background in front of Sarah. Surely, she would see for herself the unsuitability of any serious relationship with this unpolished hillbilly.

The corners of Cliff's mouth turned up into a slight smile, "As I'm sure you know, Mr. Wilson, black lung comes from a lifetime in the coal mines."

"Well, that's what the United Mineworkers Union claims, but I understand you could just as easily get it working in the steel mills or stone quarries."

"I believe that's called white lung...silicosis...sir."

Squirming, unused to being contradicted, even so politely, Walter grabbed his napkin and swiped it across his mouth, "Hell, those kind just want something for nothing! Probably catch it smoking three packs of cigarettes a day!"

Hesitating, Cliff half-whispered, "I believe that'd be lung cancer...bronchial carcinoma, sir."

"What the hell are you...a pre-med student?"

"No, sir. Where I come from, Mr. Wilson, we're all too familiar with these diseases."

"Oh, Daddy," Sarah interjected, "why don't we talk about more pleasant things? It's Thanksgiving."

"Sweetie, I'm glad to hear Cliff's family takes its civic duty seriously. I take it, Cliff, that your grandfather was active in politics?"

"Yes, sir. At least with the UMW." Cliff suddenly realized where Walter's subtle interrogation was heading. Stiffening, he could feel the blood rushing to his face. Smile and change the subject, he told himself, but Walter was on a roll.

"Involved in some of those coal wars down in the southern part of the state, was he?"

"I expect he was, Mr. Wilson. Standing up for his rights."

"Ever get arrested? Put in jail?"

"Don't know, sir. But a lot of good people were. Standing up for their rights. It's easy for you to...aw, I don't know what I'm talking about. Everything I heard was second or third hand." Cliff shrugged, smiled, and then twisted in his chair away from Walter towards Odessa, "Mrs. Wilson, this certainly was a scrumptious dinner. You must be a gourmet cook."

"Thank you, Clifford. I have a gourmet cook prepare it."

After a long, chilly silence, Cliff said, "Well, you surely have good taste. But now I'm about as stuffed as that turkey was, I better be heading home. It's a long drive, and traffic's bound to be bad. Thank you so much for your hospitality," he rose, shaking hands with Odessa who simply nodded her head, smiling, and Walter, who smacked him on the back, saying, "Wait 'til you get in management, young man. Your world is going to look a lot different."

As the disastrous evening dragged to a close, Sarah walked Cliff to his car, squeezed his hand, and stifled a sob, "Oh, Cliff, I'm so sorry about tonight. My parents are, well...they do live in a different world. They expected me to fall in love with some lawyer's son."

It was the first time the word "love" had passed either of their lips. "And...," he smiled down at her as she leaned back against his borrowed Cherokee. "So, you've fallen in love with someone else?"

She stared down at the ground for a long moment, and then looked up at him, her eyes glistening, "Yes...yes, I have. With all my heart. And I only hope he feels the same about me."

Taking hold of her hands and jiggling them, he replied, "I think he just might."

"Just might?"

"Sarah, I love you so much it aches!" He pulled her to him and clutched her in a long embrace.

* * *

From that day forward their lives were intertwined in planning for their future. They would become engaged by Christmas, and assuming he could find a decent job, would be married after his graduation in June. She would handle her parents and if they could not be brought around, she insisted that they should elope.

"Sarah, if they don't want me, then perhaps, you shouldn't either. We do come from different worlds. They haven't even met my parents yet, and you only saw them briefly at the Pitt game. They don't exactly fit in your social circles."

"Shush up and listen. My daddy hasn't ever denied me anything I've really wanted. And I want you, Clifford Cross, more than anything else in the whole wide world! So...they **will** accept you. Guaranteed! And once I get Daddy on my side, Mother will follow. They may not be thrilled, but eventually will get used to the idea. Once Daddy gets to know you...I mean, really **know** you...a few years from now he'll think he pushed me into your arms."

It worked out exactly as Sarah had predicted. They were engaged at Christmas, married in June, and after a honeymoon at Niagara Falls, were on their way to Washington, where Cliff had accepted a job with Tektron in their systems division.

By the time Cliff had risen through the ranks to become the youngest Vice President in the company, Walter Wallace Wilson, III, couldn't stop talking about his successful son-in-law to his cronies at the country club, or anyone else who would listen. Odessa McFadden Wilson never could feel quite comfortable around the dark-complected giant, resented her daughter leaving school without graduating because of him, and winced each time she thought of her daughter being married to a coal miner's son, and part Indian at that. He just had to become more sophisticated—more like **them**—and she would see to it that she and her daughter, working together, would turn him into a gentleman. Sarah's taste for the finer things in life would be Odessa's chosen weapon.

Chapter Six

Cliff awoke before sunrise, plotting the next few crucial days behind his closed den door. It would be a test of his persuasiveness. If he could lock up Harold Greenburg and Mike Gattuso to head his marketing and field maintenance, respectively, his team would fall in place. He had already decided to keep, or at least try to keep, Red Cermak, Sam Finn, and Smokey Lee. They were the key to his engineering, manufacturing, and software operations. He would worry about accounting later, after he had moved the headquarters to the Washington area. But he had to strengthen marketing and product maintenance—assuming they ever got the product working right. He had three days, plus the weekend to put his plan together before meeting Oscar and Sidney.

By ten o'clock, he was standing at the Delta gate waiting for Harold Greenburg who was flying in from Atlanta. Harold had been Cliff's top regional manager at Tektron. He was twenty-nine, recently married, smart, and energetic. His dark, chiseled face, his entire short, slender body could light up with enthusiasm around customers or prospects, yet he could be cool and calculating when developing his marketing strategies. Cliff needed him on the team. But was he willing to take the chance? He had a good future at Tektron, even though he felt passed over when Cliff's position was given to an older man. Seniority had counted more than performance, and Cliff was pretty sure that Harold was still smarting over the perceived slight. He would have to be straight with Harold. He could match his salary and give him five percent of the company's stock. But if they couldn't turn the company around, they would all be on the street looking for other jobs, probably within a year. The stock would be worthless. However, if they could make this little company click, Harold could be a very wealthy man.

And so could I, Cliff thought, as he spotted Harold making his way through the crowd of passengers to meet him.

"Hey...I could have used you as a blocking back to get me through this mess. I thought Dulles was supposed to be a white elephant...it's a zoo!" Harold grabbed Cliff's hand and poked him in the chest. "Good to see you, Tonto."

"What am I going to do with you, Hal? I invite you up here to make your fortune...and I still get no respect. How are you? And your new bride? Has she kicked you out yet?"

"I'm fine...and Bev's never had it so good. Why, the first thing she says every morning is how lucky she is to have married a wonderful guy like me."

"Ya, sure. Come on, let's get in my car and head over to Burning Tree Country Club. I've got us a private room there where I can lay out the deal I told you about on the phone. Get a bite to eat, and then let you have at me with any questions, if you're still interested."

"Sounds fine with me. Burning Tree Country Club, you say?" Hal raised his eyebrows. "Hey, old buddy, where in the hell did you get the money to join a posh club like that?"

"Well, that's sort of a touchy subject, but Sarah's parents paid for it. They were here over the holidays, and her mother had a hissy fit over our not belonging to a country club. She badgered Sarah over the phone for several weeks until Sarah got on my case. I finally agreed to look at some of the clubs in the area...Chevy Chase...Belle Haven...ones we could afford. But when her mother heard that, she dragged Sarah's Dad into it. He insisted on giving Sarah the money

for it. Ended up with Sarah accusing me of being selfish by not wanting her to have the very best. So rather than the hassle, I finally gave
in and said okay."

"But I thought it took years to get into a place like Burning
Tree?"

"Her dad pulled some strings, and presto, here were are," Cliff
smiled as he pulled into the driveway.

After settling into two plush, deep-cushioned easy chairs in front
of a marble mantled fireplace, Cliff opened his notebook and laid his
spreadsheets across the coffee table in front of them. For the next
two hours, he explained the company's product, the problems, the
strengths and weaknesses of the current management team, the financial structure, and the backgrounds of the two financiers, although
he admitted not knowing much about Sidney Martin. Oscar McMillan
had offered Cliff the job and had negotiated the deal with him.

Hal listened carefully without interruption until Cliff began out-
lining the current market strategy of hooking Speedcom's ink jet to
IBM's PC, which they purchased from IBM, interfaced together, and
marketed as a system. Or, planned to market as a system once the
bugs were out.

"Wait a minute, Cliff. Even if you get the systems running
smoothly, how do you expect to compete with the big boys? Word on
the street is IBM's about to announce the megabit memory
chip...storing a million bits of data in one computer. Another first.
Anybody can buy the PC. Anybody can write the software. Hewlett-
Packard's got a standard driver for printers. Sounds to me like all you
bring to the table is the ink-jet printer. And a darn good one...I'll give
you that."

"You've seen our printers?"

"You bet. Went over to your sales office in Atlanta, off Peachtree
Avenue. Your manager there ran a standard demo for me, but he
couldn't input any variables...couldn't change the format."

"Well, what did you think?"

"What I think is, you've got the best ink-jet printer in the industry...but it's not worth a damn hooked into an off-the-shelf PC, running on software that doesn't work. I don't know why you even have a sales office in Atlanta. I don't know why you have one anywhere, until you redefine your marketing strategy and get a product that works."

"Exactly! You've just confirmed what I've been stewing over ever since I started talking to Oscar McMillan. Their whole approach is wrong."

For the next hour and a half, over chicken and Caesar salads, they roughed out what the company's new strategic plan should be. It wasn't until midafternoon that they got around to discussing Hal's deal.

"My deal, Hal, is I've got forty percent of the company to keep or use as I see fit. My plan is to keep at least fifteen percent for myself, and use the rest to build our management team. No one will get more than five percent. That's what I'd like to offer you, along with matching your current salary and the standard Blue Cross medical package. You'd headquarter here in the Washington area, along with me, our field maintenance operation, once we get it put together, and our accounting and administrative operations. The only contract I have is a letter committing forty thousand shares out of the hundred thousand issued, at a dollar a share. Oscar McMillan...he's the Wall Street financier...will loan us the money to buy the stock at no interest, with his loan being secured only by the stock. So if it's worthless a year or two from now, he takes it back and we're out of here. Of course, that means we're all looking for a job. You'd get the same deal I have...for five thousand shares at a dollar a share. What do you say?"

"Damn! It's a crapshoot, isn't it?"

"If we succeed, take the company public...with splits...our stock could be worth from a hundred to a thousand dollars a share. You could make a million bucks or more in the next few years. Or we all could be out on the street. What do you say?"

"Sure sounds exciting. Running my own marketing operation. Have a chance to make some real money. What would my title be?"

"You'd be vice president of marketing...and, you'd have a seat on the Board. It's a five-man Board, and I'm entitled to two seats, so you and I would represent management."

"Damn! Tell you what, Cliff...I'm interested. I'm really interested. But I'd like to sleep on it...talk it over with Bev. What about moving expenses?"

"We could cover the actual moving of your household goods, plus, say, up to a month's living expenses up here until you and Bev get settled."

"Sounds reasonable. Shouldn't have any trouble selling our house...Atlanta market's hot. Probably smart to rent here until we see how things are going. Promise I'll be back to you with an answer by Saturday morning. How's that?"

"Fair enough."

After driving Hal back to Dulles, he scurried home and back into his den, with the door shut. He rejected Sarah's proposal that they go out for dinner, asking that she bring him something to eat in his den. When Sally and Tyke knocked on the door to say goodnight, he realized he had lost all track of time.

Emerging from his den to tuck the kids in bed, he found Sarah standing in the middle of the family room, her hands on her hips, glaring at him. "So nice to have you home with the family, Cliff. We've had just a wonderful evening with you. The children certainly enjoyed their quality time with their father."

"Come on, Sarah. Knock it off. You know these are critical days to get this company put together. You agreed that it was our big chance to make some real money...to achieve financial independence. You understood. You agreed. You knew what it was going to take for me to do this."

"Well, it seems to me, that since you're supposed to be such a great manager, you might **manage** to spend a little time with your family," she slammed the front door, got into her car, and drove away.

"Nice...real nice," he muttered. "Greta," he yelled, "would you please put these kids to bed?" Slamming his den door behind him, he went back to his spreadsheets until midnight.

He was up again at dawn, in his den studying the literature on his competitors' printers. Today would be another crucial day. Pouring himself a cup of coffee at midmorning, he called into Sarah, who was still in bed, "Don't you think it's time to get up? Where'd you go last night?"

"What do you care?" she sneered, coming out of her bedroom, bleary-eyed.

"Come on, Sarah," he moved toward her to put his arms around her, but she pushed him away. "Don't be like that. We're in this together. It's for us and the kids that I'm doing this."

"I know...but I feel so alone all the time. It was bridge night at the club last night, so I thought I might get in on the tail end of some games, but there weren't any openings."

"So what did you do?"

"Pamela Parker and her husband were in the lounge, so I had a few drinks with them."

"Do you think that was smart?"

"Now don't you start on me, Cliff."

"Fine. Come here and give me a hug." As she submitted to him in her flimsy negligee, he whispered, "Where's Greta?"

"Gone to the store...then she's picking up Tyke at kindergarten."

"Good!" he smiled as he led her back into the bedroom.

By eleven-thirty, he had showered again and was on his way into Washington to meet Mike Gattuso at the Black Angus for lunch. Mike was a field maintenance troubleshooter for Tektron.

As Mike squeezed his hulk into a corner booth facing Cliff, he glanced around, "If any of the big shots at Tektron see me with you, they'll know something's up."

"Hey, it's a free country."

"You got that right. Anyhow, tell me more about Speedcom. Your telephone call made it sound interesting."

Over beer and cheeseburgers, Cliff outlined the structure, the product, the problems, the risks and opportunities, as he had to Hal Greenburg.

"So, where do you think I fit in? Cut to the chase. I know you too well, Cliff. You wouldn't have left Tektron if this didn't have real possibilities."

Cliff offered Mike a deal similar to Hal's, including three thousand shares of stock. Mike could be vice president of field maintenance, and Cliff said he expected a very good mutual friend to take over marketing.

"That's damn important. Goofy salesmen promise the moon and make my job impossible. Who's the guy?"

"I hope to be able to tell you by this weekend. Interested?"

"Interested...sure. Wouldn't be here if it wasn't for you. But I'd like to know who's going to peddle the product...and I'd like to get my hands on that printer before making up my mind. Already told Glenda we'd be talking, and she'll go along with whatever I decide."

"Fine. Tell you what. You free Saturday?"

"Sure. Figured on getting the lawn mower out to go over it before the grass starts popping, but that can wait. Why?"

"Why don't you and I fly out to Chicago, Saturday morning, so you can get a good look at the operation...get some ink on your fingers. Should be able to tell you more about the marketing operation by then."

"Suits me. Let me know what flight we're on."

* * *

Cliff spent Friday locked in his den typing a rough draft of his business plan. Late that afternoon, he called Hal in Atlanta. "Hal, this is Cliff. Just wondering if you might have made your decision already. I'm not pushing, but I've got a mutual friend of ours who is flying out to Chicago with me tomorrow to look at the operation. He'd be a perfect fit to run field maintenance. Struck me, if you are going to come on board, you might want to come out also. See the operation, and maybe help me close the deal on a maintenance VP. Goodness knows, marketing's dependent on maintenance."

"Bev and I talked it over, Cliff, and she's more excited about moving to Washington than she is about the job. You got a deal, Tonto. The Lone Ranger is going to ride to your rescue."

"Hey, I thought it was the other way around, kemo sabe. But that's great news. I've got a feeling that we're going to be riding to each other's rescue in the months ahead. What about tomorrow?"

"Absolutely. Let me know what time to arrive in O'Hare and we can hook up there. Now tell me who our maintenance wizard is going to be?"

"Mike Gattuso's going out with me. Hopefully, we can clinch the deal with him tomorrow."

"Mikey! He saved my ass a dozen times. If you can get him to trim up that beard, lose forty pounds, and put on a clean shirt every other day, you might be able to turn him into an executive. The guy's an animal."

"Who cares. As good as he is, he can come to work in his undershirt."

Friday night, Cliff and Sarah took the kids to McDonald's and then to Tyson's Corner Mall to buy them new swimming suits, and a baseball glove for Tyke. On the way home, Cliff sighed, "Got to go to Chicago tomorrow, honey. Don't know what time I'll be back tomorrow night."

"Cliff...how could you! Tomorrow night's the spring dinner dance at the club. You promised. We put it on the calendar two months ago. I bought a new dress."

"Damn. I forgot all about it. We surely didn't know what I'd be into two months ago. I'm sorry. But I've got to go. You go ahead and go to the dinner, and I'll try to get back in time for the dance. I'll meet you there. But this is a chance to build my team. To show Hal Greenburg and Mike Gattuso the plant. Lock them up to run marketing and field maintenance. I'm sorry, but I've got to go."

"Well, I'm sorry, too, Cliff. And someday we're both going to be sorry you put your business ahead of me and your family."

Chapter Seven

While Cliff was laying the plans for his new venture, Jumper Ramsey and Joe Joe Karns were doing likewise for their little scheme. Jumper had posted No Trespassing signs around the perimeter of the old farm, ran his weed trimmer along the edges of an old logging road, brushed the cobwebs out of the dilapidated farmhouse, swept its floor, and cleared the kitchen counters. Joe Joe met his connection from Kermit at the Twin Falls State Park to buy his cannabis seeds, and was careful to purchase his pots and Miracle-Gro Potting Mix at several farm and garden stores off Interstates 77 and 64 on the way to the auction in Charleston. Buying a thousand pots, or even a few hundred, at one location surely could have aroused suspicion.

Jumper had the rural electric company turn on the electricity to the farmhouse. He and Joe Joe ran a string of heat lamps above the seed pots laid out across the kitchen counters, tables, and on wooden crates stacked end to end throughout the house. They quickly discovered that the wiring couldn't handle the electrical load, so they plugged the lamps into timers, so only half of their tender crop would be heated at any given time. Stapling black plastic over the windows so no one could see the lights in the house, they then began the task of planting the seeds in their pots and cramming them along the counters and the crates set in rows in the two first- and second-floor rooms.

It was a tight fit, and the chore of carrying water from the well every day to water them would be Jumper's job. It took them three days from sun-up to dusk to get the seeds and Miracle-Gro in the pots, with Jumper's knees rubbed raw from crawling between the aisles planting, as Joe Joe shuffled along behind, pouring fertilizer in the pots. But they were as giddy as two schoolboys, calculating and recalculating the hundred thousand dollars apiece which they expected to net from their venture within the year.

"Where we gonna hide all that cash, Joe Joe? I seen that money box you carry home from the car lot each night. Damn dangerous. How come you don't use the night deposit at the bank?"

"Oh, I put the checks in the bank every day. But the cash...now, you think on that, Jump. Uncle Sam can't tax what he don't know about."

"Ain't safe...carrying all that cash home at night."

"Hey, I ain't packing this .38 for nothing. Anyone come rooting around my bedroom closet at night, they'll go a'flying out the door faster than they come in and with air conditioning through their gut."

"I got a big metal suitcase that I'm gonna bury with my share way back in the old coal mine. You're welcome to stash yours there too."

"Just might do that...at least until I invest it proper-wise."

"Invest it? In what?"

"I'm thinking that maybe I can buy me a new-car dealership. At least I'll have enough money for a down payment. Hear old-man Siefert up in Oak Hill has his Ford dealership for sale."

"Might you be wanting a partner? Bet I could run a Service Department, I know cars."

Studying his old friend and now new partner in their illegal scheme, Joe Joe hesitated, "Well...let's just see how things work out...sure could use the money, but you know, Jumper, you been hitting the bottle pretty hard, and that temper of yours sure gets you in trouble. Think you could really hold down a full-time job...ten-hour days...managing some prima donna mechanics?"

"Hell, I know I'd have to sober up, and not get so riled up about little things. But, it would be a chance of a lifetime...to make something of myself. If we can pull off our deal without getting caught, by next spring, before we set out another crop, maybe we should think about calling it quits...get out before we get snagged...buy out old-man Siefert...you run the front and I run the back. Get respectable. Maybe even find a steady girl and get hitched."

"It'd take more than our two hundred thousand...and wouldn't be smart to tie it all up. Maybe hold back twenty-five thousand each. Pay old-man Siefert a hundred fifty thousand down, get him to take a note for the blue sky part of the deal. Maybe lease the property from him. I could move my used-car lot up there...probably keep that line of credit with the bank."

"Where would we get the money for the new cars? Would Ford finance that?"

"Maybe. But we'd have to have someone respectable to guarantee our loan. Fact is, we'd have to have someone respectable and with the financial wherewithal to be part of the deal to get Ford to give up the dealership. It ain't automatic. My being in the business is a plus. But you ain't never worked for a real garage, have you?"

"Hell, no. But I know how to fix cars."

"Running a Service Department takes a lot more than that. You got to get along with people, too. Best we pay attention to what we're doing here. Best you not get your hopes up too high, Jumper. I ain't so sure it'd be a good fit for you."

"Damn you, Joe Joe!" Jumper threw a pot across the front parlor room, missing Joe Joe and smashing against the wall, the Miracle-Gro leaving a black smudge on the faded wallpaper. "I got connections too, you know!"

"Ya, sure, Jumper. Nice shot. You study that black mark on the wall every time you come into this room...see if it might tell you something about yourself."

"Don't play games with me, Joe Joe. You don't want me involved in your new-car dealership...fine. I'll just take my money and invest it elsewhere. Maybe open up a brand new repair and body shop right in Beckley. And I got just the friend who will back me up. He's got respectability, and money, too."

"And who might that be...one of your drinking buddies over at the pool hall?"

Jumper cocked his head sideways, closed one eye, and squinted at some broken plaster in the corner of the ceiling.

"Come on...tell me...who's your big financier? President of the bank?"

"Wouldn't you like to know! Better than that. Clifford Cross—that's who!"

"Cliff? Hell, he don't even know who we are any more."

"Me and him was teammates. You played sandlot ball with him, too."

"So what? I loaned him a Cherokee, so's he didn't have to use his old man's rattletrap when he was courting that society babe up in Charleston. Married her, he did. Probably knocked her up in the back seat of my Cherokee."

"You don't know nothing about Cliff. He married that girl, all properlike. Didn't have their first young'un until a couple of years later. Ruth Ann told me they got another kid now. Living in some fancy part of Washington. I'm still tight with Cliff's family. Me and Cliff was like brothers once."

"You really think we could get Cliff to come in with us on the dealership?"

"Class reunion's coming up in July. Let's just get reacquainted with our old buddy...plant a few seeds, so by next spring when we got the money, we'll be in a position to talk turkey with him. You come as my guest. Cliff won't forget you."

"Jumper, maybe you just might fit in this deal—that's if you can clean up your act. But I'd say the seeds we better be worrying about right now are them what needs watering in these here pots."

Stacks of crisp one hundred dollar bills danced through Jumper's head as he went about his daily chores. Driving out to the old farm, squishing through the mud in his old combat boots to haul water from the well to coax along the seedlings, stopping to watch a robin perch atop the rotting fence post of his grandmother's overgrown, long-abandoned garden, and then dart into the underbrush, emerging with a worm securely in his beak. He was fascinated by the moles burrowing for grubs in among the weeds, reminding him of the life in the coal mines that could have been his lot. With each passing day, the bare, brown, bleakness of the rugged mountain slowly turned a speckled green, then finally full and lush, verdant and alive. As Jumper trudged up the abandoned logging road with his weed trimmer to keep the edges trimmed for the days ahead when they would be planting their future fortunes in the ground, he often thought of Cliff, his teammate, his best friend, and how they had hiked the mountain trails in springtime. He recalled how they had unknowingly crawled through a patch of poison ivy to drink with cupped hands from a cold, clear mountain spring. How the welts rose up on his fair skin from his elbows to his wrists, nearly driving him insane. Yet, Cliff, with his tough, dark hide, could lie in it unscathed. But he, Jumper, was just as tough as Cliff, even tougher, for Cliff couldn't gut a rabbit or a deer without shuddering. No...Cliff had a soft spot at his core that even his giant frame or masculine agility couldn't hide. But Jumper never let on he noticed Cliff's squeamishness. Their friendship was too close for that.

* * *

Cliff and Mike Gattuso met Harold Greenburg in front of the Delta ticket counter at O'Hare a few minutes before eleven. His plane had been late.

"Got plenty of time before Mike and I catch the six-thirty back to D.C. Got you on the seven o'clock to Atlanta, Hal. Hope that's okay."

"Sure, let's just get to this new plant of yours."

Nettie was waiting at the curb in a rental car. Cliff had sworn her to secrecy. He had told her to have Kopp take the plant guard's place that Saturday, and explain to him the confidential nature of the visit. No one else was to know, except Red, Sam, and Smokey, whom he was counting on to help sell his two prospects, while counting on Hal and Mike to show the boys that Cliff could bring real firepower to their team. Let them take the measure of each other, see if their chemistry clicked, as he was sure it would.

It took Nettie about two minutes to figure out what was happening. By the time they reached the plant gate, she knew their names, where they were from, what they did at Tektron, and how long they had known Cliff. The absence of any makeup on her face accentuated her freckles, which seemed to dance about as she spoke and smiled. Her coal-black hair, which she usually wore in a bun, was loose and flowing, the tips nearly touching her shoulder blades above her white-muslin peasant blouse. Her blue jeans fitted snugly, tapering down tightly around her ankles, atop her small bare feet. Her manicured toenails were painted apple-red.

There was no doubt in her mind that by the time she slipped into her black, toeless, spiked heels to run ahead of them up the steps to ring the bell for Kopp, that Cliff had taken new notice of her. But then, so had Hal and Mike, and she knew right then that these two young Turks could be real trouble.

Red, Sam, and Smokey were waiting in the lobby. After introducing everyone, Cliff asked Nettie to take Hal and Mike into the conference room. He then explained to his managers who the two were, and why they were there. He was building a new team, and he wanted the three of them on it. They would each get stock in the company, and he would discuss it with them in detail next week. Now he needed their help to bring Hal and Mike on board.

"Damn, Cliff! We just might be able to save this sinking ship," Red grinned. "Count me in."

"Me, too," Sam nodded.

"What about you, Smokey?"

"Hell, yes. What have we got to lose, that we haven't already just about lost?"

Calling the others out of the conference room, Cliff turned over the responsibility of explaining the operation to his three managers. After going through the plant, Nettie brought them sandwiches and Cokes into the Engineering Lab. Red explained the printer as Mike held up the tiny diaphragm and ink-drop generator to the light to study them.

"So it's this drive rod that creates the ultrasonic pressure waves in the ink, creating the jet?" Mike turned to Red.

"Yep. Each ink drop is given an electrostatic charge. Size of the drop determines the resolution of the print."

"Neat," Mike nodded.

They spent the next thirty minutes running several test routines, and then went back into the conference room to talk.

"Hal confirmed my doubts. Our whole marketing strategy's wrong," Cliff announced. "We should be marketing the printer to the whole industry. Eventually making it available to virtually all the PCs. Forget about selling a whole system."

"That means different software," Smokey spoke up.

"Right, but you're committed to getting the bugs out of our driver and install packages by next month. Right?"

"Yeah, we're almost home. Might take some more programmers to get compatible with the other operating systems. Depends on how fast you want to move."

"What about all the IBM PCs we've got in inventory?" Sam inquired.

"They're new product. If IBM won't take them back, we can get rid of them at a discount," Cliff shrugged. "Nettie, make sure the Accounting Department doesn't pay our IBM bill. If they begin to think we're not good for the money, they'll be happy to take back their product. The few we have out on the field we can probably use for demos once we get our software working."

By late afternoon, they had defined their respective responsibilities, Mike had agreed to join the team, and they swore each other to secrecy. Cliff avoided any discussion of the headquarters location. That would come later.

On the way back to the airport, Nettie asked, "Where do I fit in to this grand conspiracy, Mr. C?"

"We want you on the team, Nettie, but let's wait until next week to talk about it." She sighed, nodded, and shrugged her shoulders.

After discussing the details for their starting dates, Hal punched Cliff on the arm, saying, "See you in Sodom on the Potomac, Tonto. You, too, Tarzan," he waved at Mike as they headed toward their respective gates. Suddenly, Cliff realized that the perpetual knot in his stomach was gone.

Filing into the jetway, Mike squinted at Cliff, "Where'd you get that little spitfire, Nettie? She bounces around like Dolly Parton without the hillbilly accent."

"Don't be knocking hillbillies. I **are** one, you know," Cliff wrinkled up his face and looked cross-eyed at his new vice president.

"Ya, boss, and I'm Louie off the pickle boat," he laughed.

"Don't be fooled by her bubbly act. She's the only one who knows everything that's going on back there. Got to admit though, I saw a different side of her today. Actually, she looks good without any makeup. Can't say that about many girls. 'Course, that outfit she was wearing didn't hurt...But don't you be getting any ideas...we don't need any more complications than we already have."

Cliff shaved with his electric razor and changed into a clean shirt on board the airplane, but didn't make it to the country club until after ten o'clock. He found Sarah sitting alone at the bar drinking a Manhattan.

"Hey, honey, sorry I'm so late, but I had a great day. Both Hal and Mike are signed up. And the key guys out in Chicago are pumped up, too."

"Well, I'm glad you had a nice day. I've certainly enjoyed myself, sitting here alone."

"Pam and Jim Parker are sitting over there. Why didn't you join them?"

"Because I didn't feel like it! That's why! This isn't some stag affair. Maybe it would be better if it were...then I could find myself a partner."

"Come on, Sarah. The band's playing a slow song. Let's dance."

"You think you can just waltz in here, after letting me get treated like an orphan by all these couples, hold me in your arms, and everything will be just fine. Well, I'm not your squaw!"

"No, you're not, because no good squaw would treat her man this way," he hissed into her ear. "Come on, we're going home right now." As he grabbed her arm to pull her off the barstool, she stumbled, her ankle twisting over her high-heeled shoe.

Catching her, he frowned disgustedly, as she stared daggers at him. Aware that people were watching, he smiled sweetly, "Come, my dear, you've had too much to drink." Digging his long fingers into the soft flesh of her arm, he escorted her hurriedly through the room and out into the fresh night air.

Chapter Eight

Oscar met Sidney at his office in the basement of a run-down apartment building on Capital Heights an hour before their scheduled lunch with Cliff. "Sid, we better get our story straight before you meet Cross," Oscar seemed exasperated with his partner even before they began plotting their strategy.

"What's to get straight? Speedcom owes me seven million plus interest on my notes...owes you a million plus interest...and we each put up a million for our stock. We got ten million sunk, and you just gave away forty percent of our company."

"Sidney, this is Oscar you're talking to. You know damn well that our stock isn't worth the paper it's written on. Company's Accounts Payable alone exceed the few real assets it still has. The way things are, we'll never see a penny on our notes, either."

"And you expect me to plunk another two or three million in to keep it afloat."

"No, Sidney, I don't **expect** you to do anything. We can pull the plug right now and kiss your eight million and my two million goodbye. Or, we can pony up enough more to give Cross the chance to bail us out."

"I read the copy of that letter you two signed. By the way, thanks for letting me see it **after** it was signed. You gave him forty percent of our stock at a dollar a share...said you'd loan him the money personally to buy it. That was mighty big of you. But you didn't put any restrictions on issuing additional common stock. Think about this...if he pulls a rabbit out of a hat and turns this around for us, nothing would stop us from converting part of our loans into more stock for us, at the same price...watering down his shares."

"Sidney, that's not our deal, so don't even think about it."

"Well, what kind of cash commitments does he expect from us today?"

"He'll give us a new Pro Forma, and I told him we'd advance the necessary funds monthly until he can generate a positive cash flow. You and I know we could pull the plug any month simply by not advancing the cash. But let's think positively...he's got to feel that we have confidence in him. He's our last chance, Sidney. He makes it, or our ten million goes down the rat hole."

"You mean my eight million and your two million...plus the additional cash we advance him."

* * *

Cliff already was at the table in the private dining room when Oscar and Sidney arrived.

"So this is our new champion," Sidney gushed, sticking out his hand.

After Maryland crab cakes, beer, and some small talk about their families, Oscar pushed his plate away and said, "What say we get down to business. What have you got for us, Cliff?"

Reaching into his briefcase, Cliff pulled out two thin three-ring binders which he handed to them, and a thick one for himself. Thumbing through each section, he explained his new Business Plan to change the name of the company to Jet Speed Printers, Inc., focus solely on producing their ink-jet printer for virtually the entire PC market, return or resell the IBM PCs in inventory, move the headquarters to the D.C. area as previously agreed, bring on board his new management team, replace the dead wood, double the size of the programming staff to write software drivers and install packages for IBM, Wang, and Mac PCs initially, and eventually for Digital's mid-frame computers. Oh, yes, and shut down the plant and the six sales offices until he had the software to support their printer. Cash infusion needed for the first six months: $500,000 monthly. Then $300,000 monthly for the next six months, with Break-even projected for May of '87.

"Hold your horses, young fellow!" Sidney exclaimed. You're proposing to scrap our whole approach when we're just about ready to start marketing our complete system."

"Mr. Martin, we're never going to make any margin on the IBM PC...that's a pass-through cost. And by tying ourselves to one system we're limiting the market potential for the best ink-jet printer in the industry. That's really what we have to sell. That's our advantage. And that's where we have a healthy gross margin. We can make it available to all the major PC manufacturers...promote our specs...and their sales forces can offer our printer with their systems. I think we can get our printer approved on the GSA list for the federal government. Then the agencies can spec our printer on their system RFPs."

"How much more did you say we'd have to kick in?" Sidney grimaced, as Oscar fumbled with his napkin, smiling faintly.

"Three million for the next six months, and $1.8 million for the second six months. But if things go well, we'll need another four million in our second year."

"Huh?"

"The industry-wide market potential for printers like ours is over three hundred thousand annually, and darn near doubling every year. I figure it will take us the next three months to begin selling our printer as an optional spec with other PCs. We'll have our first software package ready next month, and then follow-on every three or four months with packages for other systems. I'm projecting a hundred units in the fourth month, two hundred the fifth, and three hundred in the sixth. We'll be working our various inventories down, so we won't have to restart production until the third month. In the second twelve months, I'm projecting six hundred units a month, with a buildup in the last quarter so we're at a thousand units a month going into the third year, building up monthly to a rate of twenty-four thousand units annually by the end of the third year. The market will continue to explode, but there will be enormous downward price pressure. That's okay. With quantity production we can get our unit cost down so by the third year, we can gradually drop our price from $3,000 to $1,500 per printer. At twenty-four thousand printers annually we're only talking about us capturing eight percent of the market...and that's with the best inkjet printer in the industry. These are conservative numbers. Take them and study the projections. We can hit a Break-even in twenty-four months, and twelve million in thirty-six months. That's PBT, but the start-up losses will shelter most of the profits into the third year. But, if I'm right, we're going to need another four to five million in the second year to cover the cost of increasing production, plus a sixty-day lag in our mushrooming Accounts Receivable."

"Boy, you're telling us you want $4.8 million in the next twelve months, and another $4 or $5 million thereafter?" Sidney winced again. We've already got $10 million sunk in this operation. That's $20 million your are talking about!"

"The real risk, Mr. Martin, is in the first six to twelve months. If we can't come close to our projections, then I'm all wet...we don't have a viable business."

"And we're all broke!" Sidney exclaimed.

"Respectfully, Mr. Martin, that's not what Dun and Bradstreet says about your net worth," Cliff's icy eyes narrowed, staring, unblinking into Sidney's eyes. "This is a small part of your net worth...sir." Cliff's foot commenced a staccato tapping.

"You don't need to be telling me my business, young man!" Sidney glared back at Cliff.

"Calm down, Sidney," Oscar patted him on the arm. "Why don't we just take your projections here...study them for a few days...and get back to you."

"That's what I would expect you to do," Cliff replied. "But I do need next month's cash...so we can proceed...at least in the short term."

"You'll have the first five hundred thousand wired out to Chicago by week's end," Oscar nodded. "Right, Sidney?"

After a long pause, Sidney replied, "If you say so, Oscar...but we've got to sit down and talk."

"Of course. Of course. Cliff, we'll study these projections, and get back to you within the week. You just go ahead and put your plan in motion. Whom do you want on the Board with you?"

"Harold Greenburg. He'll be our VP of marketing."

"Good. Good," Oscar smiled. "I'll have our attorney, Winslow Rooke take care of that this week. Put you both on at the same time. Why, we'll make you the vice chairman. How'd you like that?"

"Whatever. But I have no illusions about who controls the Board or the company, Oscar. I'm well aware of the fact that my value simply lies in making this company profitable, for which I get forty percent of the stock to use as I see fit. If we don't succeed, our stock's worth nothing and we're out. That's the chance we take."

"We have total confidence in you, Cliff. Don't we, Sidney?"

Squirming in his chair, Sidney took a gulp of water, "Yes...yes...of course we do."

"Well, thank you, gentlemen, and the first phase of this Business Plan will be rolled out before the week is over. And I look forward to hearing from you on the longer range plan by then, too."

"Wait a minute," Sidney interrupted. "Shutting down the plant is going to bring the politicians down on us like locusts. How the hell are you going to handle that?"

"That's Cliff's problem. He's our new CEO. It's his plan...it's his problem. Right, Cliff?"

Suddenly the churning returned to Cliff's stomach, but he jutted out his chin, hoping he sounded confident, "Absolutely. It's my problem. I'll handle the politicians."

Chapter Nine

Cliff rushed home after his meeting with his financiers, threw some clothes in his suit bag, left a note for Sarah who was playing tennis at the club, and headed for National Airport to catch the first plane to Chicago. On boarding the United flight, he caught himself searching the aisle for Krissy, but then realizing she probably was on the early morning flight, was glad she wasn't on board because he didn't need her distraction. Working furiously on his business plan, he didn't realize they were about to land, until the flight attendant stopped to check his seat belt. She wasn't nearly attractive as Krissy, but he quickly put that thought out of his mind.

Red, Sam, and Smokey were standing in the baggage claim area waiting for him as he had requested. "Over here, boss," Red called out.

"Thanks for being here, boys. Why don't we head over to the Marriott where we can talk, get a bite to eat, and I'll check in."

After they were settled in the restaurant and had ordered, Cliff said, "Here's the deal." He then summarized his meeting with Oscar and Sidney, told them they each would get four percent of the stock at a dollar a share, the four thousand dollars to be loaned to them by Oscar McMillan, secured only by the stock. He outlined his plan to change the name of the company to Jet Speed Printers, Inc., drop their efforts to assemble a complete system, and concentrate instead on producing and marketing their ink-jet printer to virtually

76

the entire industry. He intended to make all his changes—shutting down the plant, closing the sales offices, except for Washington, which could be located in the plant, and Los Angeles, which would remain open. Tackaberry, Johnson in sales, and Hammon in accounting, along with most of their staffs, would be terminated. He hoped to persuade Nettie to take over the accounting and administrative functions, which would be greatly simplified if they were not marketing directly in the PC systems market, but largely to system suppliers in the OEM market. A small headquarters operation would be set up in the Washington area, where he hoped to move accounting and administration...that's if he could entice Nettie to make the move. Greenburg and Gattuso would be on board next week.

"Well, what do you think, boys?" He locked eyes with each of them individually for several seconds.

Finally, Red spoke, "It's one hell of a chance. But if we can't make it with the printer...we can't make it...period."

"I agree," Smokey shrugged. "You give me the programmers and I'll give you the software. In fact, while we'll need different packages for the different systems, I think we can hook on to some of the standard stuff that's already out there or coming online. We'll have to write our install packages, but we can hook onto some standard drivers. Hewlett-Packard's developing a standard driver for printers, and Microsoft and Apple are including the HP driver in their software. So, at least there, we only will need to tie into their software with our install package. It's a risk. But what are our chances going down our present path? Close to zilch!"

"Makes my life easier...focusing our production on our printers," Sam Finn nodded. "I can get another ten or fifteen percent productivity out of the line by eliminating the interface steps onto the PC. Maybe even twenty-five percent increase. That will really reduce our manufacturing labor costs."

"Now you're talking, Sam," Cliff motioned with his clinched fist in the air.

"What the hell are you going to tell Congressman Romanowski when you shut down the plant? He's the one who got us the money to build the plant and the related infrastructure. He'll go ballistic when we lay off the workers. He's no one to be trifled with."

"Who's dealt with him in the past?"

"I think Oscar and Sidney put the deal together with him in Washington, but Tackaberry is the contact, although I don't think he and the Congressman hit it off too well. A big, gruff, no-nonsense guy like Romanowski didn't cotton too well to a smooth-talking, corporate blue suit like Tackaberry," Sam replied.

"Well, I'm sure all he cares about are the jobs for his people, so we've just got to show him, that in the long run, this will mean more jobs," Cliff shrugged. "I guess that's my job."

When they were leaving the restaurant, Cliff saw Krissy sitting in the lounge with some of her girlfriends, he hesitated, and then started to go into the lounge, but upon seeing the girls surrounded by several United pilots, he thought better of it, turned, and took the elevator to his room.

The following morning, Nettie picked him up at the hotel so they could have the talk he promised her.

"Happy to see you, Mr. C, and sure anxious to hear what you have to say. Traffic's bad so you do the talking and I'll do the listening."

After extracting her promise of confidentiality, he outlined his plans for the company, the new risks involved, the management changes he would be making that week, and after letting it all sink in, he said, "So...I've got a proposition for you, Nettie."

"Won't be the first time I've been propositioned, Mr. C."

"Oh, I believe it'll be the first time you've had the kind of proposition I'm going to make," he smiled.

"Shucks...and here I thought things might get exciting. Not that my answer would have been yes."

"Let's get serious, young lady."

"Oooo...now it is getting interesting. Why, Mr. C, I didn't know you felt that way."

"Come on. I want to get this all covered before we get to the plant."

"Okay, spoilsport. Have it your way. Shoot."

"As part of the headquarters move, I want to consolidate accounting and administration in the Washington area. It will be streamlined and simplified. I'd like you to move to Washington to head it up. You'll get a thirty percent pay increase, moving expenses, and two thousand shares of stock in the company at a dollar a share, and you won't have to put up any of the money to get the shares. You'll own two percent of the company. If we succeed, you can make several hundred thousand dollars, or more. If we fail, it won't be worth anything. But it will be one heck of a ride...living in the nation's capital...being a part of an exciting chance to build a company...and maybe make a pile of money. What do you say?"

"Boy...this is a switch. I thought I might be helping you find an apartment in Chicago. I don't know what to say. I'm dumbfounded. Two thousand shares, you say...living in the nation's capital...pay raise...promotion...Mom wants to live with my brother, Mr. C...I'm weak-kneed."

"You sleep on it, Nettie. Talk it over with your family. But I want you to know that I really want you...really need you to be a full partner on this team."

Arriving at the plant, Cliff scheduled a series of fifteen-minute meetings. First he gave Tackaberry the bad news. Handed him a check covering the year's balance of his contract, asked for his keys, company badge, credit cards, and suggested that he gather up his personal effects and leave at his convenience, but by five o'clock that evening. A stunned Tackaberry blinked uncontrollably as his eyes suddenly became bloodshot and teary. "Cliff, where am I supposed to go?" he pleaded. "I'm sixty-two years old. Who will have me?"

"I know," Cliff sighed. "This isn't easy, Tack." It was the first time Cliff called him by his nickname. "It's a bitch. But I've got to make the decisions that I believe will give this company a fighting chance to survive. Otherwise, we'd all be out on the street in another few months...you included. And then there might not be any money to pay you that twelve-month salary check you're holding in your hand. I'm sorry," Cliff rose, shook hands with the dazed executive, and walked out of the room.

Similar scenes were repeated with Glenn Johnson and Jane Hammon, although they were given a month's pay since they had no contract. Sam Finn announced the temporary closure of the plant, while Cliff dispatched Smokey to give the good news to his programmers that they would be taking on expanded responsibilities with a doubling of their staff, and the bad news to the people in the Atlanta, New York, and Dallas offices that they were being terminated and the offices closed. Cliff spoke by phone to the Los Angeles and Washington branch managers and in person to the Chicago manager to brief them of the changes and assure them that they still were on the team. Nettie took over the headquarters accounting and administration functions, at least until she made her decision about moving to Washington.

As the evening shadows cast a doleful gray pallor through the windows into the unlit conference room, a weary Clifford Cross sank into the captain's chair at the head of the mahogany table and kicked off his shoes.

"Want a drink, Mr. C?" Nettie whispered from the doorway.

"I'd love one, Nettie...but where are you going to get me one around here?"

"Oh, Mr. Tackaberry has a good supply in his credenza. What'll it be?"

"Got the makings for a vodka martini? And invite the boys in, please."

"Sure, but Smokey's already left for Dallas to shut down that office...then he's on to Atlanta and New York."

Red and Sam joined them in the conference room, mixed their own drinks from the tray Nettie brought in, and reported on their progress.

"I think people saw this coming," Red said. "Everyone realized things couldn't continue this way much longer. It's bitter medicine, but necessary if we have any hope of keeping the patient alive."

"I feel sorry for my folks," Sam nodded. "They'll sign up for unemployment, but that won't stretch far. You better get to Congressman Romanowski fast, Cliff, before he hears about the layoffs from someone else."

"I've already called his Chicago office and have a meeting with his staff director there, tomorrow. Things are going to be chaotic around here for the next few weeks."

"For the people still here, Cliff, morale's shot up a thousand percent. Everyone's enthusiastic. At least now we've got a chance," Red waved his fist in the air, unconsciously picking up Cliff's habit.

"We're pulling an all-nighter," Jeremy Thorpe reported in Smokey's absence. "We're so close to getting the software driver and install packages running smoothly, we can smell it. This weekend, we're taking home the specs of the Wang and Mac PCs."

"Good. What about you, Nettie? How's your operation?"

"Really not that much to do. Our two accountants have everything on the computer, so that's easily transferable when you decide to make that move. Already called IBM and told them they could pound salt for their money. Threatened to sue us, but what else's new? Said they'd take our proposal to return all our IBM PCs upstairs to their management. Far as I'm concerned, it's a done deal. That'll be a hefty credit to bring down our Accounts Payable. But I agree with Sam. Explaining what you're doing to Congressman Romanowski before he hears it from someone else is really crucial. He could pull the plug on us, and we'd be in bankruptcy tomorrow. There'd be a padlock on the doors."

"Right. You pick me up tomorrow morning to take me over to his office, since you know your way around town. And for plant security, now that we're shut down, let's keep Kopp on the job. Lay off that young plant guard. He doesn't have a family, does he?"

"Mr. C, you do have a heart, after all," Nettie glanced at him affectionately. "If you like, I'll drop you off tonight. I've already missed my class at DePaul."

"Sure...and maybe you can take me to one of your Chicago fancy restaurants. I'll spring. I'm starving. Any of you guys want to join us?"

"You two go ahead," Red motioned. "We've all got our work cut out for us tonight."

Nettie took Cliff to a candlelit, checkered-cloth, little bistro over-looking Jackson Park and Lake Michigan, where they settled into a corner booth for spaghetti and a bottle of Chianti. A Russian-clad old gentleman strummed on a balalaika in the background. He was playing "Laura's Theme" from *Dr. Zhivago*.

"Have you given any more thought to my offer?" leaning forward, Cliff raised his wine glass to Nettie. "To a new chance?"

"It's all I've been able to think about," she stared down at her glass, turning it slowly. "Inevitable, beautiful chance. Will it guide my blind feet to destruction? It's a stone that starts an avalanche...the pebble that widens the sea."

"What?"

"Oh, that's Thomas Wolfe...*Look Homeward Angel*...my favorite author."

"Damn, Nettie, you're downright cultured. Maybe some of that can rub off on me."

"Don't make fun of me, Mr. C. I'm just a Polish girl from the Southside, trying to make some sense out of my life."

"Aren't we all? I really want you on the team, Nettie."

"I want to talk to my mom, but I need to talk to you more, too."

"Fire away."

"Well, I don't really know anybody in Washington. I'd be all alone. I'd love the job...the challenge. I'd love working for you, Mr. C. But what would I do in the evenings and on the weekends? Sure, I could fly home, maybe, once a month...on the holidays. But I'd miss my old gang and my family."

"That's a decision only you can make, Nettie. But there are a million things to do in Washington...and an opportunity to meet lots of interesting people. And we wouldn't abandon you. You'll get along fine with my wife, Sarah," he hoped he was being forthright, as those words escaped his lips. "You can hire your own little office team...and Hal and Mike will be on board. They're good guys."

"Maybe too good, Mr. C. I can spot red-blooded American boys when I see them...and those two have the making for trouble with a capital T."

"I admit, both those boys are gunners...but they are winners. They'll do damn near anything to get the job done. Those two are going to help us succeed. Anyway, you're a big girl...you know how to take care of yourself. I'm sure those steelworker buddies of yours aren't choirboys. Fact is, you'll be on the team...you'll just be one of the boys."

"If you say so...but let me ask you this, Mr. C. How much time am I going to be able to spend with you? Are you going to be flitting all over the country, or are we going to be working together on a daily basis?"

"More than that, Nettie. I'm going to be counting on you not only to run the office, but when I'm traveling, to be my eyes and ears. I **need** you, Nettie."

"If I say yes, will you promise to look after me?"

"Nettie, you're going to be a full partner on the team. We're going to have to look after each other. We're going to war. I'll cover your back if you cover mine."

"Promise?"

"Promise."

"Then I'll tell Mom tomorrow. It's a deal."

Reaching across the table, Cliff shook her hand...and then he kissed her on the cheek.

Chapter Ten

The following month was both chaotic and exhilarating. Hal and Nettie relocated to Washington, and Mike joined the team, bringing with him four of his crack maintenance engineers. Cliff leased a modest office suite for his headquarters and the Washington sales office, including basement space for the maintenance engineers and inventory off Route 7, adjacent to Tyson's Corners. Smokey's software team solved the bugs in the driver and install packages, hooking them onto Microsoft's DOS Operating System for the IBM PC, and began work on a software package for both Wang and Mac. Oscar McMillan forwarded the $500,000 operating capital as promised, and Winslow Rooke's law firm had the company's name changed to Jet Speed Printers, Inc.

Hal refocused his sales team in Washington, Chicago, and Los Angeles to promote the printer as a unit to be specified by buyers in their RFP—Requests for System Proposals. Hal and Cliff decided to handle their marketing efforts with the federal government themselves. But that would have to wait. Dealing with an irate Congressman Romanowski over the plant shutdown had to be Cliff's top priority. If the government pulled the plug on its economic development support, the company would be in bankruptcy within thirty days. Cliff's stomach churned each time he thought about it. If he couldn't persuade the powerful Congressman, all their dreams would evaporate, he would have let down, even mislead, the very people who depended on him, who had agreed to take a big chance largely because of their faith in him.

* * *

Standing in the Congressman's outer office, waiting to be escorted in, Cliff extracted his lucky charm from his pocket, rubbed his thumb across the bear paw etching, and muttered, "Come on, old bear paw...stick with me now."

"You talking to yourself, Tonto?" Hal nudged Cliff, as a door opened and an aide motioned for the two of them to enter.

"Nothing! Look alive...we're on," Cliff motioned his head toward the door.

The burly Congressman was standing in his stocking feet, looking out his plate-glass window at the Capitol dome as Cliff and Hal were ushered in. His profile reminded Cliff of Dick Butkus, the great Chicago Bears' linebacker—and just as menacing. He turned his head slightly, not looking at them, but rather staring at a picture on the wall of himself shaking hands with Lyndon Johnson, "Why'd you shut down my plant...put over a hundred of my people out of work?"

"Mr. Chairman, I'm Clifford Cross, the new CEO, and this is..."

"Why'd you shut down my plant and put over a hundred of my people out of work. That slick-talking dude from Wall Street promised me that we'd build up to over two hundred jobs if I got you a low-interest economic development loan and got the state to put in the money to build the infrastructure...the water and sewer system...the road...and all that crap. Where the hell is he?...What's his name? McPherson, or something like that?"

"Oscar McMillan, sir. We're here to explain how we are going to build up to two hundred jobs, probably more. But if we don't shut down the plant temporarily, we'll be in bankruptcy...and then there won't be any jobs for anyone."

The young man who had escorted them into the room spoke up, "What's this about you moving your headquarters out of Chicago and in here to Washington?"

"That's a strategic decision to enable us to..."

"What? You shut down my plant and move the high-paying jobs to Washington? Nobody votes in Washington. Too damn many jobs here already."

"If I could explain, sir..."

"Well, make it fast...I've a mind to call down to the Economic Development Administration and tell them you've welshed on our deal."

Cliff laid a color photograph of their ink-jet printer on the Congressman's desk in front of him, and handed another to the staff assistant. He explained that the previous management had made a fundamentally bad decision to try to market their proprietary printer—on which they held the patents—with other personal computers which they did not manufacture...that they should not try to market an entire system, but rather only their own printer, which could be specified by potential customers to be tied into whatever system they chose. That way, they could be the printer of choice for many different systems. But they needed time to make the transition. If EDA called their loan, they would be out of business. There would be no jobs for his people, and, of course, no opportunity for expansion to three or four hundred jobs in the future."

"Hmmpf...," the Congressman grunted. "What about pulling your headquarters out of Chicago?"

"Only a few people are involved in that move, and it positions us better to deal directly with different PC suppliers in the industry...as well as with the federal government."

"That sounds like a bunch of crap to me. How long before you could call my people back to work?"

"We'll start next month...build up to the full workforce by September. Then if things go as expected, we can start adding on by the end of the year."

"That a commitment?"

"Mr. Chairman, if I'm wrong...there won't be any company...I won't have a job...and none of your people will be back to work."

"That doesn't sound like a commitment to me."

"Mr. Chairman, I can only promise you that is what I intend to do. If I fail, then I'll be gone."

"Well, let's hope that doesn't happen, young man," the Congressman smiled broadly, stuck out his bear paw of a hand, smacked Cliff on the shoulder, and leaned his face to within an inch of Cliff's nose. "You get my people back to work and I'll come over to that plant of yours and sing your praise...but if you screw me...I'll nail your ass against the wall. Now get out of here and let me get back to work," he turned, still in his stocking feet, and resumed staring out the window at the Capitol dome.

* * *

Cliff's routine included traveling to Chicago each week to review the progress of his engineering, software, and manufacturing teams. Usually, he would fly out early in the morning, spend the day, and return home late that evening, but always packing his shaving kit and a clean shirt should he have to stay over.

Boarding a United flight in mid-June, he hesitated without consciously thinking about it, before sliding into his seat in the front of the plane, and peered back into the tourist section to see if Krissy was working the flight. A surge of adrenalin shot through him when she emerged from the rear pantry and started making her way through the aisle of passengers toward him.

"Why, Mr. Cross, I do believe...Cliff...where have you been? I haven't seen you in weeks. You're not flying American, are you?"

"Well, hello. Krissy with a K. You look particularly fetching this morning."

"Where have you been?"

"Hey, you're the one who's been missing in action. I've been one of your airline's best customers on the Washington-Chicago run."

"Well, I did take a week's vacation...and then I got temporarily bumped onto a puddle-jumper. But I've been back for several days. When you had that drink with us at the Marriott, I thought you promised to take me to dinner," she pouted.

"As I recall it, I said, 'Maybe,' if we bump into each other again."

"Does this qualify as a bump?" she gave him her Farrah Fawcett smile. "We're overnighting at the Marriott. What about you?"

"Gee, I don't know. Been up to my ears. If I can't wrap up all my meetings at the plant today, I just might stay over."

"That'd be great."

"I really don't know. I've got to get back to Washington."

"Come on...you promised."

"Now, that's not true," he felt his neck flushing.

"We'll be back from our Dallas leg around five. I'll be in the health club with some of the crew. Why don't you join us? You look like you could stand a little exercise."

"Thanks a lot. Fact is, I've been losing weight since I've been on this job."

"I just meant...I don't know what I meant. Forget it. Better buckle up...we're set for takeoff."

After the seat belt sign was turned off, she pushed the food tray through the aisle, stopping at his seat and giving him an icy glare, "May I serve you, Mr. Cross...sir?"

"No, thank you, Miss Conlon, I've already had my breakfast. Or, is it Ms.?" he winked at her.

"You better be careful, sometimes it gets a little bumpy up here and I could spill some coffee on an unsuspecting passenger...especially one who was getting me upset," she leaned down and whispered, unable to repress a slight smile.

"Then you might have to pay to have my shirt laundered."

"They have one-day laundry service at the Marriott."

"Get back to work, or I'll report you to management," he grinned, his soft eyes locking for a moment on hers.

As he was debarking past her in the Jetway, he hated himself the moment the words passed his lips, "See you at seven in the lounge," and then, as an afterthought, "...with your friends."

* * *

All three of his key managers were waiting for him in their car at curbside, like little boys who couldn't wait to tell the news. Before the car door was closed, Smokey began, "Got a call last night from a buddy of mine who's a systems big shot at Prudential...said they've been looking at our ink-jet printer...saw it demoed at the spring trade show. Said they're going to standardize on IBM PCs, but want to spec our printer—if it holds up on a thirty-day test—which should be no problem—and if...get this...we could commit to delivering a hundred a month starting in sixty days, for the next year...did you hear that, Cliff? For the year! Hell, that's twelve hundred units!"

"Good news, boys. Did he ask about a quantity discount?"

"Holy hell, Cliff," Red threw up his hands, beaming. "We give you the best news yet, and you want to talk about the numbers right away."

"Hey, guys, this is absolutely the best news I've had since coming on board in April. But I don't care how big an order we get if we can't keep up our margins. Has anybody talked to Hal? He should be on top of this."

"I just got the call last night," Smokey answered, "...and no, he didn't even mention discounts. All he talked about was our quality, and if we could deliver on time. I plan to call Hal first thing this morning and put the two of them together."

"Good. If we can reel in a few more orders like this...build up the production line...you ought to be able to get some economies of scale...squeeze some direct labor costs out of production...reduce unit manufacturing overhead. Probably get some direct labor efficiencies, too. I guess this means I can start calling back our workers."

"Just wait till we have the order in hand. But let me tell you, that will be a happy phone call for me to make to Romanowski. I don't know if I could take another one of his tirades without telling him where he could stick it."

As they pulled into the parking lot, Cliff said, "You guys come on into the conference room with your latest progress reports, but, first, I want to talk to Red about the modifications to the printer head, and how much that's going to save us."

By late afternoon, Cliff had satisfied himself that everyone was on target. In fact, the software team was a little ahead of schedule in developing their driver and install packages for the Wang systems. He was having second thoughts about staying over, even though he had asked the new office secretary to get him a reservation at the Marriott, when he received an urgent call from Nettie.

"Cliff, there's a man on the phone who says he's got to talk to you right away. Says it can't wait. Said it's personal, and just to tell you it's Jumper. Said you'd know. Sounded sort of weird to me. What should I do?"

"Patch him through, Nettie," Cliff sighed, "patch him through."

Chapter Eleven

"Cliff, Cliff...that you, boy?" Jumper Ramsey shouted into the phone.

"Jumper! You still alive?"

"Hey, man...how the hell are you...mister chief executive?"

"I'm fine, Jumper. What about you? What brings on this phone call?"

"Cliff, we got our lucky thirteenth high-school class reunion coming up next month, and May Belle says you haven't replied. You coming, ain't you?"

"Boy, Jumper, I don't even remember getting any notice. Maybe they sent it to my old address at Tektron."

"No...May Belle says she talked to your ma and got your home address."

"Well, maybe Sarah mislaid it. When is it?"

"Saturday, July 12th. Me and Joe Joe Karns was hoping to see you. You remember Joe Joe, don't you?"

"Ya, sure. He was selling used cars. Loaned me one once."

"Well, can you make it?"

"Boy, I sure would like to see you guys, but I don't know. I've got a tiger by the tail in this new job of mine."

"Hell, it's only a Saturday night. You could visit with your ma and pa, too. May Belle says they miss you and those two little grandkids something awful. 'Course, I guess they don't cotton to your wife too well...maybe she don't cotton to them...but that ain't none of my business. When's the last time you saw your folks?"

"Had them up to Washington during the Christmas holidays...spent a whole day with them," Cliff replied defensively, ashamed that he had not seen them more often, even though he called them every Sunday night, and regularly sent his mother little gifts from airport shops as he passed through, always enclosing a crisp one hundred dollar bill with the admonition that she should spend it only on herself.

"Why don't I tell May Belle to sign you up for two reservations? Dinner's at the VFW and we're blocking off rooms at Motel 6...unless you want to stay with your folks."

"You go ahead and mark me down, Jumper. Send me the details and I'll send May Belle a check. I'll do my best to be there. Don't know if Sarah will make it. She may want to visit with her family in Charleston. July 12th, you say? I'll put it in the book. Sure would like to see the old gang."

"Hell, Cliff, you'll be the star of the show. You're 'bout the only one who's made it big. We're all proud of you...and me and Joe Joe, in particular, want to renew old acquaintances."

"Now, Jumper, what's that supposed to mean? You and Joe Joe got something up your sleeve?"

"Hey, can't old buddies—old teammates—just want to get together?"

"Jumper, I know you and Joe Joe too well...but sure, I want to see you guys—everyone—so I'll be there if at all possible." After hanging up the phone, Cliff smiled to himself, remembering Jumper and Joe Joe—his teammates—the old gang. Yes, he missed them. It was a different world—a simpler world. Sarah was right. He would never get those boyhood days in the mountains of West—by God—Virginia out of his blood. If she wanted to call him hillbilly—fine—he was damn proud of it. And his family, too—if she—or especially her mother, felt uncomfortable around Ruth Ann and Clint, too bad. Yes, come hell or high water, he was going to his class reunion, and so would Sarah. He would insist. It wouldn't kill the kids to spend a few days with their grandparents in Beckley. They needed to know how the other half lived. And a little old Sunday-go-to-meeting religion wouldn't hurt them either.

* * *

Loping up the old logging trail at sundown, Jumper was out of breath by the time he reached Joe Joe to give him the news. "Cliff's coming," he shouted, "he'll be at the reunion. We can ease him in, real gentlelike."

"Not so loud. You don't know who's over on the next ridge hunting groundhog this time a'day. But things is working for us," Joe Joe grinned. "Got another two hundred seedlings set in. Come on, help me with this last fifty and we'll be done. You work the planting bar, and I'll stick them in."

As they completed their planting of the marijuana seedlings, the first lightning bugs of summer flickered in among the trees, and the sweat-flies feasted on Joe Joe and Jumper's bare necks and arms. They nonchalantly swatted them away, too pleased with the progress of their little scheme to be bothered by such minor annoyances. Reaching the old farmhouse, they rewarded themselves with two icy beers out of Joe Joe's cooler. Plopping down on the rotting porch steps, they sat silently, studying the harvest moon as it rose, full, above the Allegheny Mountains, savoring their dreams of becoming wealthy men...of owning their own car dealership...of driving fancy cars...of wearing expensive suits...of buying drinks for pretty girls in the town's best bars...of being looked up to...being respected...maybe even being invited to join the Rotary. Yes, their marijuana crop was going to be their ticket to prosperity. So what, if it was a little shady? Didn't old John D. Rockefeller get his start by tramping on a few toes? More than a few. He was a mean SOB. And they weren't hurting nobody.

And his kin ended up being governor of their state. Yes, they were on their way. And their old teammate, Cliff, was going to help them get there. He just didn't know it yet.

* * *

The same full moon shone brightly over Lake Michigan as Cliff's cab pulled into the Marriott, but it made no impression on him for his mind was on other things. Should he meet Krissy in the lounge? He told her he would. "Damn, I wish I hadn't said that," he muttered to himself. But then, he told her he would meet her with her friends. Nothing wrong with that.

Entering the lobby, he couldn't avoid her if he wanted to, for she was sitting, alone, on a couch facing the revolving door. Her long blond hair fell across her shoulders, barely touching the top of her low-cut black cocktail dress, the hem of which was at least seven inches above her knees. She looked like she had been poured into it. As she slowly rose upon seeing him, she broke into her Farrah Fawcett smile. "Cliff...Cliff, I knew you wouldn't disappoint me!"

"Hey, Krissy...where's your uniform...and all your friends?"

"This is my uniform after the sun goes down...and I guess they all had better things to do. Where are you going to take me for dinner?"

Pursing his lips and frowning, he held up his hands, "Now wait a minute...I said I'd meet you and your friends in the lounge...for a drink."

"Come on...don't be a party pooper. You have to eat. You said yourself you're losing weight. Let's just get a bite in the restaurant here. They have good food...and it's no fun eating alone." She slid her arm through his, tugging him in the direction of the restaurant. "I'll even buy."

"Well...why not? It isn't every day that a fellow gets to have dinner with a beautiful girl. And you're not buying...Krissy with a K."

"So, tell me about yourself, Cliff," she bubbled with enthusiasm as they slid into a booth.

"Why don't we order first," he replied, rattled by her question.

"You order for both of us...and maybe some Merlot."

After ordering two filet mignons, medium rare, with garden salads, baked potatoes, and a California Merlot, Cliff cautiously began describing bits of his life. "Not much to tell...grew up in a little town in West Virginia...went to the university in Morgantown...got a job in the computer industry...and this spring, got a chance to take over a little company that was heading for bankruptcy." I should tell her I'm married, he thought, but she hasn't asked...maybe she doesn't care. Steering the conversation away from himself, he asked, "What about you?"

"Oh, I grew up in Cleveland, went to Ohio State for two years, and then had a chance to get this job with United. But what did you do in college? Tell me all about it." She plied him with questions about his boyhood, about his life at the university, about his work, but never once asked about his marital status. And when he told her he was the captain of the basketball team at West Virginia, she squealed, "I knew it! I just knew it!"

"Knew what?"

"That you were a jock. I could tell it...the way you walked...your size and build...your quiet confidence...I just knew it."

Cliff shook his head, smiling, perplexed, yet pleased by her effervescence. After coffee, and paying the bill, as he held her chair for her to get up, she again gave him her best Farrah Fawcett smile, and said coyly, "You know, mister captain of the basketball team, I have an apartment with a girlfriend over in Virginia, just off Shirley Highway. She has the Washington–LA run. We have different schedules...we're almost never home at the same time. Why don't you let me cook you dinner...to reciprocate for this evening?" Before Cliff could answer, she slipped her arm through his and said, "But first, why don't you be a gentleman and walk me to my room."

Now's the time to tell her I'm married, he thought. But the second bottle of Merlot was working its mellowing magic. Why spoil a perfect evening...and it was nice to be called a gentleman. Sarah always chastised him for not being sufficiently considerate and polite, especially after she had spent a few days with her mother in Charleston, or on one of their shopping trips to New York. "I'd be delighted," he responded, patting her hand.

As she unlocked the door to her room, she said, "Coming in for a nightcap? The minibar's stocked. Anyhow, I need to write down my address and phone number if you're going to let me cook you that dinner."

Suddenly sobering up, Cliff thought, now I am in the soup, yet he couldn't bring himself to tell her he was married, even though he sensed that it probably made no difference. Thinking quickly, he said, "Oh, your phone number's in the book," even though he hadn't checked.

"I'm impressed...you've already looked it up. Coming in? We can't stand out here in the hall talking."

"I've just got to get to my room. I've got some reports to get through before tomorrow morning. I'll take a rain check."

"Killjoy," she pouted. "Call me soon." She stood up on her tiptoes and kissed him before he knew what was happening. He took hold of her elbows, but then, didn't push her away.

* * *

He actually completed his business at the plant, so early the next morning, he called Red to see if there were any messages, and then, Nettie, to let her know he was catching an early plane back to Washington and would be in the office around noon. "How come you stayed over in Chicago last night, Mr. C? The boys told me you wrapped things up yesterday afternoon."

"You checking up on me, Nettie?" he asked, a bit miffed.

"Yes," came her dry, one-word, matter-of-fact answer.

After an awkward silence, he gently replied, "Well...thank you for caring. See you soon. And please call Sarah and tell her I'll be home for dinner. In fact, why don't you come on over and join us? Tell Sarah I invited you."

"Oh, I don't know, Mr. C. It's not my place to be telling her that."

"Dammit...I'm in a hurry, Nettie. All right...patch me through to my home."

"You're always in a hurry," she replied softly. "Hang on while I put you on hold."

Greta answered the phone, "Cross residence."

"Hi, Greta, this is Cliff. Let me talk to Sarah."

"She's not here, Mr. Cross. I think she's over at the club."

"Well, when she comes home, tell her I'll be home for dinner around six-thirty, and I've invited Nettie to join us. Kids okay?"

"Yes, sir. They're fine. I'll give Mrs. Cross the message."

* * *

Arriving in the office at little after noon, Nettie had a tuna fish sandwich and Diet Coke waiting for him on his desk. After checking his mail, touching base with Hal on his sales progress, and Mike on the latest printer maintenance statistics, Cliff turned his attention to the staffing of his newly created Accounting Department. He had assigned Nettie the task of working with a headhunter to find an accountant, two computer-literate bookkeepers, and a secretary with some accounting background. Transferring the accounting system from Chicago to Washington should be no big deal. Marketing the printer to the OEM market rather than part of a whole system to end users should greatly simplify the record keeping. If the accountant performed well, after thirty days he would be promoted to controller. Nettie and Hal had interviewed several candidates and narrowed it down to three. Cliff spent most of the afternoon interviewing the three final candidates, and then, after conferring again with Nettie and Hal, offered the job to Arnold Shearer, a CPA from Price Waterhouse, who had been on the team that audited Tektron's books. Arnie was a no-nonsense, bispectacled, marathon runner in his late twenties, with already thinning curly blond hair. He was excited about the opportunity, but would only take the job if he was hired as the controller and received an equity position in the company. Cliff decided on the spot that Arnie was the right fit, not only because of his professional credentials, but because he represented a serious, stabilizing counterbalance to the hot-blooded team that he had assembled. Rather than immediately agreeing to Arnie's terms, but not wanting to lose him, and knowing he was single, Cliff suggested, "Tell you what, Arnie, why don't you join Nettie and me for dinner out at my house with my wife this evening? We can nail things down then."

"Sure. Sounds good, Mr. Cross."

"Call me Cliff...and Nettie, why don't you give Arnie the directions...say around six-thirty, and please call Sarah and tell her one more will be joining us."

"Why don't you call, Mr. C?"

"Nettie..."

"Yes, sir."

A few minutes later, Nettie stuck her head in Cliff's office to report, "Mrs. Cross wasn't at home but I left the message with Greta."

"Fine. I'm going home to get a run in before dinner. See you two around six-thirty."

* * *

Sarah still was not home when Cliff arrived. Agitated, he called the club, locating her at the bar. "Sarah, didn't you get my message? I'm bringing people home for dinner. It's nearly five. What the hell are you doing there?"

"Why, Cliff...what a surprise. I thought you might have died...or gone off on one of your hunting trips to Montana or Wyoming."

"Come on, Sarah. I'm sorry, honey. I know I should have called from Chicago...called sooner...but I've really been tied up," he felt a pang of guilt, remembering his dinner with Krissy the night before. "I'm trying to hire this new fella for accounting, so I invited him...and Nettie out to the house for dinner tonight."

"Well, I'm sorry, Cliff, but tonight's bridge night at the club...not that you'd remember that. I've made plans to have dinner with the girls. It might be nice if you consulted me, just once before you made arrangements that included me."

"I'm sorry, honey. You're right. I'll call Greta and have her put something together...maybe feed the kids early. Why don't you try to join us after dinner?"

"Cliff, as usual, you're not paying any attention to what I said. It's bridge night. I won't be home until late."

* * *

Before going on his run, Cliff spent a few minutes in the back-yard with Tyke and Sally tossing a Frisbee around, and then located Greta in the laundry room. "Got two people coming for dinner around six-thirty, Greta. Sarah's tied up at the club. Think you could whip up a salad, throw some steaks on the grill, some baked potatoes in the oven?"

"No problem, Mr. Cross. Maybe some mixed vegetables, too?"

"You're a lifesaver, Greta."

Greta Larson had emigrated from Sweden to the United States after World War II with the expectation that her GI boyfriend would marry her. For whatever reason, it didn't work out, so she began her career as a nanny. Now in her early sixties, she had held a series of jobs, moving on after children in her care had become teenagers, always highly recommended, always dedicated to the little charges in her care. Although the years had added a few pounds to her five foot-four-inch frame, there wasn't a wrinkle on her fair, cherubic face, and her ice-blue eyes blended nicely with her Nordic ash-blond hair, wrapped back in an efficient bun. She loved Sally and Tyke, spending hours with them each day, hoping that she might be able to remain with the Crosses until retirement time, and then she planned to return to Sweden to live out her life among her extended family.

Odessa had insisted upon providing a nanny for the children, had personally conducted the search, interviewing several and finally deciding on Greta. Cliff hadn't liked the idea of having a stranger in the house, of Odessa, once again, taking charge and imposing her will upon them. But he could hardly refuse, since it would be a big help to Sarah, and he was away so often. Eventually he acknowledged that Greta was a wonderful find, a calming influence in the home. He actually came to like her.

* * *

Nettie and Arnie arrived a few minutes apart and were ushered by Greta into the family room where Sally and Tyke were sitting on the floor at a coffee table, finishing their dinners. Nettie immediately plopped down on the floor with them, wanting to know all about them, while Arnie stood silently at attention, smiling quizzically. Six-year-old Sally, who had her father's curly, coal-black hair and ice-blue eyes, explained that she was entering the first grade, that her hobbies were reading, playing the piano, swimming on the eight and under swim team at the country club—where she fully expected to win several ribbons next summer—and was lobbying her parents to buy a golden retriever puppy. She was little Miss Efficiency. Four-year-old Tyke, who also had his father's dark complexion, was taller than the six year old, and had little to say. He wanted to get back outside where he could ride his new two-wheeler in the driveway.

On entering the room, Cliff clapped his hands together, saying, "Okay, what'll you have to drink?"

"Got any beer?" Nettie asked.

"Is the Pope Catholic?" Cliff asked, bending down to the refrigerator under the bar. "Arnie?"

"Just some soda water will be fine."

"Boy, are we in trouble," Nettie exclaimed. "You a teetotaler?"

"Nettie...," Cliff frowned.

"Oops. Sorry, Arnie. I'm supposed to be on my good behavior. I forgot. We're trying to seduce you."

"Nettie...you're incorrigible," Cliff shook his head.

"Sounds to me like this might be a fun place to work," Arnie smiled. "You might as well know now, I'm a Mormon, so I don't drink. But that doesn't mean I don't like having a good time. Guess I'm just a little quiet."

"No wonder you're quiet. I understand you Mormons spend all your time with a bunch of wives making babies."

"Nettie...," Cliff looked exasperated at her.

"Don't worry, Mr. Cross...Cliff...I think Nettie and I are going to get along just fine. I'll bet she makes the office sparkle."

"Keeps the office jumping, is a better way to put it, Arnie. When she cracks that whip of hers, none of us escape. But, come on, let's move into the dining room," Cliff motioned, handing Arnie a club soda. "Here's a glass, Nettie."

"Bottle'll do just fine. Thank you."

Nettie chattered on pleasantly through dinner, with Arnie staring at her in a perpetual grin, chuckling between bites, while Cliff injected a word or two, slowly realizing that Nettie had completely captivated his prospective employee.

Over coffee and strawberry shortcake that Greta had whipped up, Cliff got down to business. "Been thinking about your terms for coming on board, Arnie. I'm not going to haggle with you. We've looked at over a dozen candidates. Narrowed it down to three. You're the man. We want you on the team. The controller's job is yours if you want it. We'll match your Price Waterhouse salary and get you two thousand shares of stock representing a two percent equity position in the company at a dollar a share financed at no risk to you. Plus the standard Blue Cross package. What do you say?"

"I'd say we've got a deal. I'll turn in my two weeks' notice tomorrow...if you can get me a letter confirming your offer tomorrow morning."

"Great. Nettie?"

"Consider it done, Mr. C."

After shaking hands all around and saying their goodbyes, Cliff stuck his head into the kitchen to thank Greta for a wonderful meal, and then into the kids' bedrooms to tuck them in. He was in his den going over some reports when he heard the car pull into the driveway. A few minutes later, Sarah was standing at the den door, gorgeously tanned, her Golden Girl hair perfectly coiffed, her long, deliciously curved legs planted firmly apart.

Looking up from his papers, Cliff exclaimed, "Damn, Sarah...you look ravishing!"

"You don't look so bad yourself, tall, dark, and handsome!" she purred, strolling toward him slowly, like a model down a runway. Spinning his chair around to face her, she straddled his leg, wrapped her arms around him, and inserted her tongue deep into his throat.

Although he detected the strong smell of alcohol on her breath, he wasn't about to complain. Easing her off his leg and down onto the floor, he was completely oblivious to the rug burns that would bring a smile to his face each time he rubbed his sore knees in the days that followed.

Chapter Twelve

The next few weeks seemed to bring nothing but good news. The big Prudential order was solidified. Every aspect of the Chicago operation was running smoothly. So much so that, other than getting daily reports over the phone or by fax, Cliff decided that he could best spend his time focusing on sales with Hal. He made a happy phone call to Congressman Romanowski's office to tell his chief of staff that the employees had been called back to work, flew up to New York for a Board meeting and to inquire about the status of his stock certificates, and made several high-level sales calls with Hal, promoting the printer with corporate systems executives, as well as the New York Stock Exchange.

PC manufacturers began listing the Jet Speed printer as an option with their systems, several businesses started specifying the printer on their Requests for Proposal, and after several meetings with the General Services Administration, GSA agreed to run their own thirty-day test on the printer, with an eye toward approving it in their catalog for federal government procurement.

The knots in Cliff's stomach, the panic attacks, all but disappeared. He was spending more time at home, playing with the kids on weekends, taking Sarah out to dinner. As more printers were shipped to customers, minor maintenance problems cropped up, but Mike Gattuso and his growing band of maintenance engineers pounced on them quickly. Mike started flying to the plant weekly, conferring with Red and Sam, faxing change order fixes to the field within days, sometimes within hours, of discovering a problem. Cliff had complete confidence in Mike, so much so that he began relying on him to be his eyes and ears at the plant, taking some of the pressure off Cliff, permitting him to travel less frequently to Chicago.

* * *

With each new weekly report, Oscar McMillan and Sidney Martin grew more excited. "I think the kid might pull it off," Sidney shouted through the phone to Oscar.

"Can't you lower your voice," Oscar shouted back. "When my time comes, I should have you deliver the eulogy...it could make me sit right up out of my casket."

Oblivious to Oscar's complaint, he shouted back, "Hey, we may not need to dig our graves, after all. You didn't transfer that stock to them yet, did you?"

"No, but Win tells me you called him and told him to hold it. What are you up to, Sidney?"

"Think about it. If we delay the transfer until the value of the company increases, those boys will have to pay a higher price for their shares, or take an income tax hit on the spread between their lower price and the true value."

"Why do that? What's in it for us?"

"Come on, Oscar. Use your head. Say an independent appraisal values it at ten dollars a share. We go on notes for them to the company for their cost. Don't put up any cash...just notes. When we go public and that stock hits, say, twenty, to be conservative, they sell...pay us our ten dollars a share in cash...and they make their ten dollars."

"Sidney, no accounting firm is going to stand for that. No wonder you're in trouble with the SEC. Did you even take first-year accounting? Even if the firm took our notes in payment for their stock—which might be illegal—eventually we'd have to pay the company cash to cancel the notes."

"Who would ever know?"

"Our accounting firm...the auditors...would know. Cross and his boys would know. They're not dummies. All you need is another lawsuit. Then the Securities and Exchange Commission would know. Forget your crazy scheme."

"Well, there's got to be a way to maximize the return on our investment. We're the ones who took the chance. Those young Turks are making decent wages, and ought to come out of this with something, but they don't deserve to make a killing on our risks."

"Sidney, get out of the car. We don't have anything worth selling, yet. And a deal's a deal. Let's keep our fingers crossed, and I don't mean a double-Cross. Get the pun?"

"Ya, sure, if you say so. But there's got to be a way."

* * *

One day toward the end of June, as Cliff and Hal returned to the office, all smiles, with a RFP in hand for COMSAT, specifying the Jet Speed printer for a minimum of two hundred fifty PC systems, Nettie stood scowling at her desk. "What's up?" Cliff asked.

"I certainly don't have a problem, Mr. Cross. But you received a strange phone call."

"Oh?"

"A female called, wanting to confirm the time and date of your dinner reservation. I asked her for the name of the restaurant...told her I didn't have any dinners on your schedule. She said, 'Well, just give Cliff the message. He'll know what it's about.' Here," she threw the yellow telephone memo at him.

"Phew...," Cliff stooped to pick it up off the floor. "Sure sounds like a mystery to me. Must've been a wrong number."

"Sure...Cliff...she just happened to dial the wrong number and get your name right!"

"Knock it off, Nettie. I get some weird phone message, and you throw it at me. I don't have time for this!"

"You never have time for anything!" Tears welled up in her eyes, as she turned abruptly, leaving the room.

"Damn," Cliff muttered to himself. "Damn...damn...damn." I better call Krissy, he thought, because if I don't, she'll just keep calling here. But I better not use the office phone. Nettie watches me like a hawk.

On his way home, he stopped to get gas and use the pay phone. Thumbing through the directory, he found Krissy's phone number and called. There was no answer. Good, he thought. When the answering machine clicked on, he tried to lighten up, "Hi, Krissy. Got your message forwarded to me. Doing a lot of moving around. I'll give you a call." Then, as an afterthought, "Uh...best you don't call the office...uh, I'm hardly ever there. Bye."

Feeling guilty about Krissy's phone call, he stopped at a florist's to get a dozen yellow roses for Sarah. Quietly entering the house, he tiptoed up behind her as she stood at the kitchen sink rinsing out a glass. Grabbing her around the waist with one hand, he thrust the flowers in front of her with the other.

"Oh...," she dropped the glass in the sink, which, fortunately, did not break, "Cliff! You nearly scared me to death."

"Hey, can a husband surprise his wife with a little present every now and then?"

"Absolutely, sweetheart," she replied, throwing her arms around him and squeezing.

"What say we go over to the club for dinner?" he whispered in her ear. "Just you and me. Greta can feed the kids."

"Only if you promise to let me have the dessert after we get back home."

"You got a deal. But keep talking like that, and I'll be willing to skip dinner and get right to dessert."

"Shush...let me put these flowers in a vase, throw on a dress and some makeup, and I'll be with you in a jiffy."

* * *

It never failed. Every time Cliff and Sarah strolled into the dining room at the country club, the eyes at every table turned toward them. What an imposing, perfect couple! He was back down to his two hundred twenty-pound college-playing weight, which he carried confidently on his six-foot-four-inch frame. His broad shoulders and narrow waist made him seem even taller than he was. His dark complexion created the illusion of a well-tanned giant in command of all around him. His tailor-made, English, Austin-Reed of Regent Street, double-breasted, pin-striped suit accentuated his muscular build, his broad shoulders. The suit, though, had been a sore spot with him from the day he got it. Sarah's mother, Odessa, had obtained his measurements from Sarah without his knowledge, and then had the suit made for him in London, as a birthday present. He couldn't very well object, because it was, indeed, a very special gift, even though he sensed that the unspoken message behind it was an admonition, rather than a compliment: Dress properly, you dumb hillbilly. Look like you deserve to be the husband of Sarah Wilson, the daughter of Odessa McFadden Wilson. He bought perfectly good suits off the rack at Raleigh's, and vowed never to wear his English-tailored suit to work. Surely, the boys would think he was putting on the dog. But Sarah loved it, so when he wanted to make her happy, when he felt guilty about something he had done, he dressed up in what he called his "English costume."

His dominance in any room was both heightened and softened by having Sarah on his arm. At thirty, she was even more beautiful than she had been as WVU's Golden Girl, twirling her baton high in the air, doing a somersault, and catching the baton before it touched the ground. She had filled out in all the right places, and the clothes that her mother had insisted upon buying for her on their shopping trips to New York City were right out of Vogue. The eight, one-carat diamonds set in her gold necklace, along with her diamond earrings, and the diamond-studded gold bracelet—all given to her by her parents—made her presence stunning in any room. Together, she and Cliff created a larger-than-life sensation wherever they went.

Halfway through their poached salmon, as Cliff emptied the bottle of Montebelluna Prosecco—Sarah's favorite Italian wine—into her glass, he gingerly raised the subject of his class reunion. "Sarah, my high-school class reunion's coming up. One of my old teammates called...said they sent me an invitation to the house. I never saw it. Did you?"

"Oh...seems to me some kind of notice came a long time ago when you were out of town. I probably mislaid it or threw it away. It didn't look important."

"Well, it was important to me. It was about our class reunion."

"Surely you've outgrown that kind of stuff. We don't even go back to our college reunions. Why in the world would you want to associate yourself with those losers in that little coal-mining town?"

"They're not losers, Sarah. They're my friends. Anyway, honey, it's weekend after next. I was thinking why don't we take Friday afternoon off, drive down with the kids to my parents, leave the kids with them, take everyone out for dinner...," he reached across the table taking hold of her hand and winking, "...you and I could shack up in some motel...play golf Saturday, go to the reunion...pick up the kids Sunday morning and drive up to Charleston to see your folks. What say?"

"Why do I have to go, Cliff? I don't know any of those people. The kids aren't even comfortable staying at your parents. They're afraid of the hunting dogs and the cat. Why don't you just drive down Saturday afternoon, visit with your folks before the reunion...come back Sunday morning. We can do something special here Friday night, if you want, and then you'll have most of Sunday with the kids. Maybe take them swimming and for a picnic at the club."

"Dammit, Sarah, I **expect** you to go with me to my class reunion...to spend some time with my parents...to let them get to know our kids better. Our kids **need** to understand our roots...my side of the family too. I never object when you're running back and forth to

Charleston with them...or when your parents...your mother, especially, pops in here, unannounced...all the time," he threw his napkin on the table.

"Fine. If you want to equate the things **my** parents do for us with the things you parents **don't** do for us, go right ahead. I'm ashamed for our children to see how your parents live...back there in the sticks...among a bunch of grimy, ignorant coal miners."

Staring down at his plate, slowing folding his napkin and placing it neatly under his fork as his foot began to tap beneath the table, Cliff replied softly, almost plaintively, "Sarah, I never asked for any of the things your folks give us...fact is, their largess makes me uncomfortable. As for my family...you knew where I came from...you knew my background...and my parents are good people...the miners and their families that I grew up with are good people...salt-of-the-earth people. Sure, they're not sophisticated, but they're hard-working, God-fearing people. I love them...and not just my family...the neighbors...the kids I grew up with...my classmates...my old teammates. I'm asking you, please come with me. It means a lot to me. And Sarah, don't ever...ever put down my family to our kids."

"I'm sorry, sweetheart," she placed her other hand on top of his. "It's the Prosecco talking. It's just that you're so different...so out of place with the rest of them...even in the way you talk, the way you walk. It scares me. I'll go, but let's just drive up Saturday morning. That means the kids will only be away from us for one night. I'll call Mother and tell her we'll be up that Sunday."

"Sure. That'll be fine. Thanks for understanding, honey. And one more thing...let's not use the Mercedes. The minivan will do just fine. Truth is, I don't want the guys seeing me driving a big Mercedes."

"Cliff...it's my car! Oh, I understand...one more of those awful presents from my parents that you were happy enough to accept...but resent their giving to me."

"That's not so, Sarah. Well...maybe it is. But it's important that the old gang doesn't think I'm putting on the dog. Probably only Joe

Joe drives a fancy car...because he's in the business. Jumper and the rest of the guys probably still drive pickups."

"What kind of names are those...Joe Joe...Jumper?"

"Knock it off, Sarah. They're my friends! Come on, let's get out of here."

* * *

While Cliff got back to work, helping Hal with important sales calls, keeping in touch with the Chicago operations, pressing Oscar to get the cash advances on time, and the status of their stock certificates, his old gang in Beckley was immersed in nailing down every detail of their big event. May Belle Hanik reported daily on the confirmations she received, followed up with phone calls to those who hadn't replied, checked and rechecked the menu with the VFW— roasted turkey with all the trimmings—went over the room reservations with Motel 6, assigned table decorations and door prizes to her girlfriends, told the boys how to set up the tables and chairs, and how to block off the parking lot so everyone would have a parking spot.

Jumper borrowed two hundred dollars from Joe Joe so he could buy a new suit, shirt, tie and shoes. Doc Ketterman agreed to fix his cavities, pull his rotten tooth, and put a spacer in between, all for twenty percent down and five dollars a week over the next twelve months.

Jumper and Joe Joe carried five-gallon cans of water from the old well to Jumper's pickup, drove as far as they could go up the old logging trail, and then lugged them the rest of the way to water their precious marijuana plants which soon would be budding.

"How do I look when I smile?" Jumper asked Joe Joe one evening when they stretched out on the old porch for their nightly bottle of beer after completing their watering chore.

"Open up wider...smile. Hell, can't hardly tell it ain't a real tooth in there, Jumper."

"Good. You think Cliff will notice? Bet he'll be surprised at how spiffy I come off. What'a ya think? You always look good with all them duds you got."

"You and me'll look better'n everyone else in the room...except for Cliff and his woman, that is. Boy, was she a looker. Wonder what she looks like now after a couple'a little brats."

"Oh, I figure she probably hasn't aged a day. Them society dames go off to spas...sweat off the fat...get face-lifts...Some of them even get the fat sucked out of their body."

"Get out'a here...how the hell they do that? Damn...that's a job I'd sign up for."

"I don't know...read it somewheres. Anyway, we better try to get Cliff off in a corner away from her. She'll think we're just a couple of dumb yokels. One-on-one with Cliff, we can ease him into gettin' interested. After all, he'd be helping some hometown boys get started. That's the tack we take...him puttin' a little bit back into the community. Helping his old teammates."

"You know, Cliff always had a soft spot. Tough as he was on the basketball court..."

"And a mean sucker on the mound. Remember the time he beaned the kid at Fayetteville? He must'a decked three or four of them coming out of their dugout before we could get to them. But you're right...Cliff's got a soft spot...long as he don't get riled up. That's what we got to appeal to. He wouldn't let his old buddies down."

"No sir. Not Cliff. He's one of us."

* * *

When Sarah called to tell her mother that she, Cliff, and the children would be up to visit them on Sunday after the class reunion in Beckley, her mother asked if the children couldn't stay in Charleston for a few days. "We'd love to have them," she pleaded. "Your dad and I will drive them over to Washington the following weekend."

After checking with Cliff, when Sarah called back to tell her mother that the children could stay, Odessa informed her, "Your father and I have talked it over, and we'll just drive down to Beckley

Sunday to pick up the children. Your dad would enjoy taking some of the old back roads...down through Whitesville and Dry Creek. You know, that's where the firm sent him to handle some cases just out of law school. Hasn't been back there for thirty years. Said it'll make a lovely Sunday drive, and bring back some old memories. Said it's really where he got his start. Send us the directions to the Cross house, and we'll pick up the children Sunday afternoon."

"Why don't we meet you somewhere, Mother? Perhaps somewhere for lunch. Once I get there, I'll pick out a nice restaurant and phone you."

"No, dear. I think your father would like to mosey down. We'll get there around midafternoon. Just send us the directions. Talk to you soon. Ta-ta."

* * *

When Sarah told Cliff that her parents would be picking up the children at his parents' home, he arched an eyebrow, "You sure that's good idea?"

"Why, Cliff," she smiled coyly, "you said you were **proud** of your parents. You said our children should see how the other half lives...your half. So what's wrong with my parents stopping at your parents' home? Getting to know each other better."

"Very cute, Sarah...this is my payback for making you go to the reunion. And another thing...I didn't say I was **proud** of my parents. I said I **loved** them. Nothing good can come from this little stunt of yours."

She didn't bother to tell him it wasn't her idea. After all, it served him right, she thought.

Chapter Thirteen

As Cliff pulled the minivan into the dirt driveway beside his parents' house, his mother rushed down off the porch, beaming, her arms extended to greet her grandchildren, while his father stood in the yard grinning, his thumbs hitched on his two-inch-wide, mustard-colored suspenders.

"Come here and give your grandma a hug," Ruth Ann exclaimed, tugging on the door handle. She reached in, unbuckling their seat belts, while they sat still, warily studying her.

"Say hello to your grandma," Sarah instructed, as Cliff unpacked their bags.

Sally and Tyke both gave their grandma a cautious hug, and then shook hands awkwardly with their grandpa, Clint. Sarah gave Ruth Ann and Clint a peck on the cheek, and Cliff hugged both his mother and his dad. Tyke ran around the side of the house to see the hunting dogs in the pens, while Sally climbed up the porch steps to pet the cat.

"Let's get out of this hot sun...come on up on the porch and sit a spell," Clint smacked Cliff on the back. "Good to see you, boy."

"You, too, Pap," Cliff nodded, easing himself down into a bent, hickory rocker. Clint Cross was only fifty-one years old, but his weathered face and long, gaunt body were mute testimony to a lifetime in the mines. His most distinguishing physical characteristic was huge, purple-veined, bulging, bony hands, which usually were folded gently across his lap as he sat rocking in the porch. Their cinder block home once had belonged to the Beckley Mining Company, along with the other houses that sat in a row halfway up a steep hillside above a recently oiled dirt road. The pungent smell of tar still wafted through the screen door into the house when the western wind swept through the valley below. Their home, like every other house on the row, originally had only four rooms, but Clint and Ruth Ann, working together, had built on two more behind. Indoor plumbing had been added in the '50s, but the hand pump in the backyard was still in working order. And the privy with its half-moon cut in the door still stood on the rise above Ruth Ann's garden. The potbelly stove in the parlor still gave off a rosy glow on bitter-cold winter nights, when the snow swept down from the hovering mountains, locking them in with ten-foot snowdrifts until the snowplows did their work. But the coal stove in the kitchen had been removed on the day the electric lines were strung along the row. The entire kitchen, including the faded linoleum on the floor, was so crisp and clean, it would have put the chef at Burning Tree to shame.

Even Sarah had to comment, "You certainly keep a neat house, Mrs. Cross. I'm always picking up at our place. Sure hope the children don't give you any trouble."

"Sarah, how many times must I ask you to call me Ruth Ann? And don't you be fretting about those little darlings." She bustled about her kitchen, filling glasses on a tray from a pitcher of lemonade, unwrapping the cellophane from a plate of brownies, removing the glass cover from the creamy chocolate cake. "Cliff's favorite," she smiled, setting a knife, fork, and plate beside it. "He'll help himself when he sees it. Yellow cake with chocolate icing...made from scratch. He can't resist it."

Ruth Ann exuded energy. She was a large woman, but certainly not fat; muscular yet she seemed to glide through her domain effortlessly, totally organized. Behind her deep, dark eyes, her olive skin, and her curly once jet-black, graying hair lay a will of iron, a determination to make the most of every precious minute in her modest life. Although her prayers for more children had not been answered—even though, goodness knows, she and Clint kept trying—her most earnest supplication had been granted; her son had made it out of the mountains and was an educated, successful man. And in her heart she was sure that it was both her prayers and her constant prodding that had made it possible.

By the time Cliff and Sarah finished their lemonade, and Cliff had wolfed down two large pieces of his mother's cake, running his finger around the edge of the cake plate to lick the icing, the children had persuaded their grandpa to bring one of the beagle pups out of the pen, and were rolling around on the ground with her. When their parents attempted to get their attention as they were leaving, the children waved nonchalantly and then turned back to their new-found friend, certain that she would be theirs before the weekend ended, if only...if only, their parents would agree.

* * *

Checking into their motel room, Cliff and Sarah found a welcome basket filled with trinkets produced in the state, including a picture of the class of '73, along with Cliff's graduation photo pasted on a card listing the addresses of the seventy-eight students in his graduating class. Beside Charlie Houston's name only a single word appeared: Deceased. Charlie had been killed in Viet Nam.

After showering and changing clothes, they departed for the VFW, Cliff filled with anticipation to see his boyhood friends, while Sarah nervously fingered her pearl necklace.

On entering the hall, May Belle squealed, "Hey, everybody, Cliff's here...Cliff's here!" Hugging him, she pinned a red rose on his lapel and practically curtsied to Sarah, as Cliff was surrounded by his old friends. Turning from one to the other, shaking hands, slapping them on the back, kissing the girls, he was ecstatic.

"Jep...Bucko...Skeeter...Nell...Jake...Agnes Fay...Will...Walter...Patsy Lou...Erma...Donnie...Ike..." He was home...**home**...where you didn't have to worry about balance sheets, or ulterior motives, or making a payroll, or putting on airs. He was home again, where everyone knew everybody's whole life story—warts and all—and didn't care. Home among his kind, the people who once had been his entire world. And leaning on the bar with Joe Joe was Jumper, his closest friend, grinning from ear to ear, waiting to be seen.

Sarah, who all her life had been the center of attraction—her daddy's girl, the **Golden** Girl—stood back, glumly watching everyone cluster around her Cliff. To her, it was nothing but a smoke-filled run-down room, reeking with the stench of stale beer. Even worse, her husband, her Cliff, was totally oblivious to having exposed her to this human pigsty. He actually **liked** this place!

Cliff threw his arms around his old teammate, exclaiming, "Jump...Jump!" then stepped back at arm's length. "Look at you...just look at you!"

Jumper grinned, hoping Cliff would notice his teeth, "Well, Clifford, I guess you and me was the brothers we never had."

Cliff nodded approvingly, then turned to Joe Joe, "What bandbox did you step out of, you old rascal?" punching Joe Joe lightly on the arm.

"Cliff, good to see you, too, buddy," they hugged and then Cliff smacked the bar, calling out, "Three boilermakers for the three musketeers, bartender. Say, ain't you Willard that lived up yonder by the coal tipple? Used to come sniffin' 'round Dora, next door to us."

"Sure am, Cliff. Me and Dora got hitched. Got seven kids."

"Well, I'll be damned. You ain't got no problem getting it up!"

Turning back to Joe Joe, Cliff frowned, "Sorry to hear about your brother Spike. Guess he's still in?"

"Ya...got another three to do. Damn dumb thing...holding up a liquor store in broad daylight," he laughed nervously.

Remembering Sarah, Cliff looked around for her, but she wasn't in the room. "Shit...," he muttered. "May Belle, you see my wife anywhere?"

"She turned and went out the door. Hear tires screeching in the parking lot."

"Jump! Run me over to the motel."

"What's the problem?"

"Never mind...just do it! Get a move on!"

"Yes, **sir**. But you can kiss my ass for ordering me around. I ain't one of your high-priced flunkies," he shouted back over his shoulder as he and Cliff ran toward his pickup truck.

As they sped down the highway, Cliff reached over, putting his hand on Jumper's shoulder, "Sorry, back there, Jump. Looks like my wife is pissed off at me...don't know what she'll do. And by the way, old friend, looks like you still got that short fuse of yours."

"Hell, Cliff, you know I ain't no good at taking orders. It ain't in me." And then, remembering the real objective of the evening, he added, "But I'm getting better at it. I really am, Cliff. I really growed up a lot these last few years. What'a you think of my clothes? Look a lot better that I used to. Right? I got my head screwed on right, I do. Honest, Cliff, I can hold my temper when it counts."

"Well, for your own sake, Jump, I hope that's true."

Pulling into the parking lot, Cliff saw the lights on in their room and noticed that the car was still running. Bursting through the door, he found Sarah stuffing her clothes into her suitcase, sobbing.

"Sarah! What are you doing, honey?"

"You know damn well what I'm doing! I'm not staying in this godforsaken hole for another minute. You and your buddies! I saw you standing there...putting down shots of whiskey...murdering the English language, like you were one of them. You can put on your white shirt and necktie, but underneath you'll never be able to scrub away the coal dust. My mother was right about you. You can take the boy out of the hills, but you can't take the hills out of the boy. You disgust me! I'm sorry I ever married you...you...you bastard!"

"Sarah, you don't mean that..."

"Yes, I do. You left me standing over there all by myself, like a fool, while all those hicks kept fawning over you."

Turning toward the open doorway, where Jumper stood wide-eyed, Cliff hissed, "Shut the damned door, Jumper, and wait outside!"

"You stay away from me!" she held her arms out, palms out.

"Sarah, I'm so sorry, honey. I got carried away, seeing all my old classmates...my old teammates. I apologize. I'm the most inconsiderate SOB in the world. And I'm just an asshole. Please forgive me." He took a few steps toward her as she lowered her arms a little.

"Don't you touch me," she said softly, unconvincingly.

"I'll try to be more considerate. Give me another chance?" He took a few more steps toward her, taking hold of her hands and shaking them gently.

"Oh, Cliff, why are you like this?"

"I know...I know...," he whispered soothingly, cradling her in his arms.

"Why can't we be like other people?" she pouted, playing with a button on his shirt. "You're always gone. I end up having to do everything."

"I know...I know. But I'm doing it for us. It won't always be like this."

"Promise?"

"I promise," he squeezed her tightly. "Why don't you wipe your tears, put on a little makeup, and let's go back to the party?"

"You won't leave me alone again, will you?"

"You'll be by my side all evening."

After apologizing to Jumper for being so curt, Cliff drove Sarah back to the VFW. Taking her by the arm, he introduced her to every person in the room. Being seated across from May Belle and her husband, Gary, they drifted easily into a conversation about their children and the superb quality of a home-cooked turkey dinner. To Sarah's surprise, she discovered that she actually liked May Belle.

After dinner, Cliff was careful to have only one beer, and Sarah, uncharacteristically, drank only water. As the evening wore down,

Jumper and Joe Joe approached Cliff, asking if they could have a private word with him.

"Sure, boys. But Sarah can hear whatever you have to say. I don't do anything without her, do I, honey?"

"You go ahead. I'll stay and have a chat with May Belle," she smiled. "Get the real scoop on your wild and wooly childhood."

Huddling in a corner of the room, Jumper leaned into Cliff's face, explaining in hushed tones, "Cliff, we got a big chance. Old-man Siefert's Ford dealership is gonna be up for sale. Me and Joe Joe got some money put aside...well, will have it put aside by next spring. With my mechanical know-how and Joe Joe's car lot experience, we're pretty sure he'll sell it to us. It's a damn gold mine! But it ain't automatic that Ford would approve. We need somebody with respectability in the deal, and we was thinkin', what with us being lifelong friends and all, maybe you'd be interested."

"You'd be investing in the community...sort of renewing your ties back here at home...helping to create jobs," Joe Joe added.

"Whoa...now hold your horses, boys. What's he asking for it? Have you seen his financials...say for the past five years?"

"Well, not yet, Cliff. Figured we ought to get our ducks in order before we got too serious with him. Knowing you was involved would carry a lot of weight with him. Think about it. Be just like old times...you, me, and Jumper back together again."

"I don't know. I'm up to my ears right now. Wouldn't want to get involved unless I could be on top of it. You need more facts. Tell you what, I'd be happy to take a look at it...give you my analysis of the deal...but I doubt that I'd want to get too deeply involved. Why don't you get his financials...work on your Pro Formas...then I'll take a look at it."

"Pro Forma?" Jumper looked quizzically at Cliff.

"Our projections," Joe Joe glared at Jumper. "Sure we can work up our projections. Good idea, Cliff. We'll get right on it."

"Drive out with us tomorrow to see the place. No one will be there. **Please**, Cliff," Jumper begged.

"Well, I guess I could. We've got to get over to my parents' place by early afternoon. Pick me up at the motel around eleven."

"Great...old buddy. You won't regret this. It'll be just like old times. Us against the world!" Jumper shouted.

"Well, we'll see," Cliff replied, hesitantly.

As Cliff and Sarah moved through the room saying their goodbyes, Jumper was ecstatic. "See, Joe Joe...Cliff practically signed on with us. We work him over again tomorrow...about it being like old times and helping the community...show him around the outside of the place...the car lot...the location, and we got ourselves the partner we need to put this deal together. Next year, this time, we'll be respectable businessmen at the class reunion."

But as Cliff and Sarah drove down the road to their motel, Cliff had quite a different description of their meeting. "You know, Sarah, I love those guys. But they don't have the foggiest notion of what it takes to run a business. I told them I'd help them analyze a deal they're looking at...to buy a Ford dealership...I'm going over with them tomorrow around eleven to look at the place. But I wouldn't put two cents of our money into any venture with those good old boys. They may be my buddies, but they ain't never gonna be my business partners."

"Well, thank goodness for that, honey." Walking into their room, Sarah said, "Why don't we just snuggle up in bed and have a drink?"

"Where are we going to get a drink this time of night?"

"I've got a bottle of vodka in my suitcase."

"Sarah...," Cliff raised his eyebrow.

"Come on, honey, just one drink. I was a good girl."

"Okay. I'll get some ice from the machine down the hall. You get the glasses out of the bathroom."

Propping themselves up on pillows, they slipped under the covers, sipping their watered-down vodka on the rocks, watching an old movie classic, *How Green Was My Valley*, on their TV. Eventually, Cliff dozed off. When he awoke around nine the next morning, Sarah was still asleep; three-quarters of the bottle of vodka was gone. Frowning, he shook her gently, but decided to say nothing about the vodka for it would only cause another argument, and he didn't need that after their little set-to the night before, and their pending visit to his parents' home that afternoon.

She woke up groggily, threw her arms around him, and pulled him down on top of her. Maybe a little vodka wasn't a bad idea, after all.

After showering and dressing, he brought back some complimentary coffee and sweet rolls from the front desk, and then left with Jumper and Joe Joe to survey their proposed Ford dealership.

It was about what he expected. A little rundown, but the only Ford dealership in the area. A real captive market for someone who knew how to run a business. He told that to his old friends, but again emphasized, "Got to see the financials...and your Pro Formas. I'll help with the analysis, but don't think I can get involved."

After they separated, with Jumper and Joe Joe promising to send Cliff the documents, Jumper was ecstatic, "See, Joe Joe, he said he'd help. I think we got ourselves a partner. Old Cliff wouldn't let us down."

"You sure called that right, Jump. Old Cliff is gonna help us put this deal together. You and me are gonna be somebodies in this town!"

* * *

Cliff took Sarah to lunch at the Kozy Korner, a clean little home-cooking restaurant in town where, once again, everybody knew him, slapped him on the back, and wanted to reminisce. In fact, his picture was on the back wall, with Jumper beside him, and the rest of their teammates from the '73 championship basketball team. But while they were enjoying a leisurely lunch among the townsfolk, an unforeseen development was occurring at his parents' home.

Odessa and Walter Wilson had picked up their gourmet picnic basket at the deli on their way out of town. Taking the back roads to

Beckley, it quickly became apparent to Walter that the rural communities of West Virginia where he had begun his law practice had changed beyond recognition. Traveling down Route 94, they picked up Route 3, south through Whitesville and Dry Creek. Disappointed, he suggested that they pull off the road alongside the Coal River, outside of Arnett, to have their picnic lunch, and then push on to pick up their grandchildren.

"Good idea. I can't wait to see the little darlings," Odessa agreed. "I'm sure they won't mind if we get there a little early."

Following Sarah's directions, as they drove up the recently oiled dirt road along the row of miners' houses, Odessa exclaimed, "My God, Walter, do people really still live like this?"

"Some, a lot worse that this, my dear."

As he slowed the new sleek Cadillac, looking for the address on the mailboxes, Clint came out into the yard, motioning for them to pull into the driveway. It had to be them, Clint reasoned, for no one else would be driving such a car up miners' row.

Sally and Tyke were frolicking with the pup in the front yard, but upon seeing their other grandparents, rushed to hug them, breathlessly explaining that Grandpa Cross said they could have the pup if their parents agreed. "Please...please tell Mommy and Daddy it's okay," Sally pleaded to Odessa. "Mommy always listens to you."

"I want Ginger...I want Ginger!" Tyke jumped up and down, having already named the pup.

Ruth Ann came down the steps, wiping her hands on her apron, "My, oh my, you're early, but it's good to see you. Cliff and Sarah aren't here yet, but they should be along shortly. Come along up on the porch and rest your bones, while I go in and get us a pitcher of lemonade. You children fetch a bowl of water for the pup from the pump out back."

Settling into the rockers on the porch, Walter motioned to the Appalachian Mountains rising all around them, "My, but you have a spectacular view. I'll bet it's especially gorgeous in the fall when the leaves are changing."

"Nothing quite like the fall in the mountains, Walter," Clint nodded. "Flaming red maples, yellow oaks, and crunchy underfoot. Once the hardwoods are bare, smell of the pines fills the forest like perfume."

As Walter and Clint made friendly conversation, Odessa looked up and down, turning from side to side, attempting to note the smallest defect in their home, their yard, their surroundings.

"You know, I started out as a young lawyer, handling cases down in these parts. We took the back road down Route 3, thinking it might conjure up some pleasant memories, but everything's changed so much, I didn't recognize anything. Maybe it's just my senior moment," he laughed.

"Do tell. Folks in these parts didn't have much need for lawyers in those days, except for drawing up deeds or defending moonshiners. Certainly not for big city fellas like you."

"Well, there was one case that involved over a thousand acres, west of Dry Creek...got quite complicated...a dispute over legal ownership. Must have been right after the war."

"Dry Creek, you say? That's where Ruth Ann's from. Still has kin up there. Who were the folks you represented?"

"Oh, I'm sure there's no connection. It was a family dispute. My firm represented the Robertsons against a family named Collins."

"Collins, ya say? Why Ruth Ann's a Collins. What was the man's first name?"

"Oh...well...ah...I don't think I remember. It was such a long time ago. Anyway, enough of my talking about my legal practice. Tell me about the coal mines. I understand enormous improvements have been made in both automation and safety since I was last down in these parts."

"Well, things have improved a lot, but it's still a hard life. Hey, Ruth Ann...get out here. Walter, here, had a case against your kin up by Dry Creek onto forty years ago."

"You don't say," Ruth Ann backed out against the screen door, carrying a pitcher of lemonade, glasses, and cookies. "Well, I hope you didn't hurt us too bad."

"Her pap was Abner," Clint continued. "Her grandpap was Alonzo Collins, a full-blooded Cherokee. That's where we figure Cliff got some of his athletic ability. 'Course, I wasn't too bad a first baseman on our American Legion team in my early years."

"Alonzo Collins, you say?" Walter looked from Clint to Ruth Ann, staring at her, studying her intently.

Just as Ruth Ann was about to say something, Cliff and Sarah pulled into the driveway. The children shouted to their parents. Tyke pulled the puppy toward them on a cord tied around his neck. "Grandpa gave us Ginger," Sally ran up to her dad, hugging his knee. "Can we keep him...please, can we keep him?"

"Has he had his shots?" Odessa asked, the first words she had spoken since her arrival.

"He's a she," Ruth Ann laughed. "No, but I'm sure they've got plenty of vets up there in Washington who can do it."

"Well, Sarah, **if** you're going to take the dog, you've got to get all the proper shots right away," Odessa announced firmly.

"Of course, Mother. What do you think, Cliff? Are they old enough to care for a dog?"

"Sure they are. I had a dog before I could talk."

"It's easy enough for you to say. You're gone all the time. It'll be up to me to make sure she's taken care of. But...," she reached down and tickled the pup behind the ears, "maybe she can help keep me company when you're gone."

Tyke and Sally were nearly delirious with joy, watching over Grandpa Cross as he made a makeshift cage out of a wooden corn crate, fondling the little brown beagle as Ruth Ann filled a bag of dog food for them, and found a tiny red collar to put around Ginger's neck. After the excitement of getting the pup settled on an old blanket in her cage in the rear of the minivan, the children tugged on their parents to get them home so their friends could see their new possession. Upon learning that the pup would be going back to Washington, but they would be going with their other grandparents to

Charleston, they both started crying, Tyke throwing his body on the ground, kicking.

Unable to calm the children, Cliff finally said, "I think we better take them with us. Sarah can run over with them early next week. Best we get them settled with the pup, first."

"Hmmpf, this certainly means we made a trip for nothing," Odessa stared daggers at Ruth Ann and Clint.

"Gee, I'm sorry. I didn't mean to cause a problem," Clint winced. "Kids fell in love with the pup...I just thought..."

"No problem, Clint. I think it's just as well we...ah...head back alone," Walter nodded, soberly.

Odessa stared at her husband, bewildered, and then shook her head, snapping, "Fine. Let's go." Without another word, she walked over to the children, hugged them, got in the Cadillac, and slammed shut the door.

As Cliff kissed his mother goodbye and slapped his father on the back, Clint said, "She sure has a burr under her saddle."

"Don't pay any attention to her, Pap. She's that way half the time."

As they pulled out of the driveway, after Sarah had said her goodbyes and got the children settled, she looked over at Cliff with a smirk on her face, "What a way to end your wonderful weekend. I hope you're satisfied."

Chapter Fourteen

Stone-faced, gripping his steering wheel, Walter Wallace Wilson, III, drove north on Interstate 77 toward Charleston, staring straight ahead, silently trying to reconstruct the details of the case he had handled so many years ago deep in the mountains of rural West Virginia. Odessa babbled on about the poverty, the utter embarrassment of their dear daughter having married into such a family. "Walter, you're not listening to a word I'm saying. What's wrong with you? Aren't you feeling well?"

Sliding his hand across the seat to take hold of hers, he half-whispered, "Dess...I don't think you want to know. I feel like someone unloaded a ton of coal on top of me."

"What? What are you talking about? Tell me this instant...I have a right to know. Was it something about Ruth Ann's family? You clammed up when Clint told you about her kin. What was their name?"

"Collins."

"Well...go ahead."

"Dess, some stones are better left unturned...but if you insist," Walter took a deep breath and slowly exhaled. "The firm sent me down there to handle a land dispute over rights of ownership. The Robertsons brought a claim against one Alonzo Collins, arguing that he had no rights of ownership to land which had been handed down to him because he had Melungeon blood in him."

"Melungeon? Wasn't that some kind of half-breed Indian tribe that settled back in the mountains?"

"Not exactly. The Robertsons wanted to bring their cause of action based on an old Virginia statute called the Racial Integrity Act. It required everyone with mixed heritage to be registered with the state...everyone with Negro or Melungeon blood as nonwhite, regardless of how far back it might be. Caucasians were defined as those with one hundred percent European ancestry, or with one-sixteenth or less Indian blood. The law made it illegal to marry outside one's own race, to vote, or to own land. The Robertsons argued that since West Virginia had been a part of Virginia until Lincoln created the new state during the Civil War, the Virginia law should apply. They really didn't have a leg to stand on. The Virginia law clearly did not apply to West Virginia. But that really wasn't the point. The Collins had no money. Alonzo tried to defend himself, but the judge wouldn't even let him appear on his own behalf. Even if the Robertsons didn't have the law on their side, they certainly had the judge...in fact, most of the population...racial feelings still ran pretty hot back in the '40s. Seeing the handwriting on the wall, Alonzo reluctantly agreed to an out-of-court settlement...to selling the land to the Robertsons for a mere pittance. As I recall, he got ten dollars an acre."

"But, I don't understand. Why are you upset now? We learned about Cliff's Cherokee blood long ago."

Letting out a deep sigh, Walter patted Odessa's hand, "The problem, Dess, was that Melungeons aren't just a mixture of white and Indian. There's a debate over whether they're descended from Portuguese sailors, but there's no debate over the fact that they are descended from Indians, the Scotch-Irish, and...slaves."

"Slaves? You mean blacks?"

"I'm afraid so. Alonzo was not a full-blooded Cherokee. He was a Melungeon...a mixture of Cherokee, Scotch-Irish, Negro, and God knows what else. He admitted it in a sworn deposition."

"Oh, my God, Walter," she clutched his arm, wincing, "that means are grandchildren are **colored**! Sarah's married to a colored man!" She began sobbing, moaning, rocking her body, twisting her head, not knowing where to look, as if, somehow, she could make the dreadful revelation go away.

Pulling off onto the shoulder of the road, Walter reached over and took hold of both her hands, "Calm down, Dess. Don't overreact. Our grandchildren are as white as we are. Old Alonzo probably only had a speck of Negroid in him...probably less than one-eighth...or one-quarter at most. That would make Cliff...worst case...one-thirty-second...our grandchildren, worst case, one-sixty-fourth. They're white, Dess...they're **white**!"

"Oh, Walter...how could Clifford have done this to us? To Sarah? I knew from the first time she brought him home, nothing good could come of it. Even if he had been an **Italian**, or a **Catholic**, we could have learned to live with it...but this..."

"Dess, you're talking like Archie Bunker. This is the second half of the twentieth century. The world's changing. There's no room for that kind of bigotry anymore. I admit, the **black** part of it comes as a shock, but put it in perspective: The problem, if you want to call it that, probably goes all the way back to Cliff's great-great-great-grandparent. Alonzo was his great-grandfather, and he was mostly white and Cherokee. Cliff's a fine man...a good husband to Sarah...a good father to the kids...an educated man...and a damn successful one at that. There's no reason for us to dredge this up. Nothing to gain, and everything to lose. Best we forget about this ancient bit of family history. Who knows how many horse thieves or scalawags we'd find on our own family tree if we dug back far enough. Best we let it go...never mention it again."

* * *

But Odessa McFadden Wilson couldn't let it go. It was an affront to her very being, to the core of who and what she was. The next day, she went to the West Virginia Historical Society, then to the library, then to the state archives at the capitol. Pouring over documents, she learned that the Melungeons were, indeed, a combination of white, Indian, and African blood who, themselves, claimed to be descended from the "Portyghee"—the Portuguese. In 1834, Tennessee declared them officially to be "free persons of color," which deprived them of their right to own land, vote, or sue in court. The Melungeons faded back into the mountains, migrating deep into the Appalachians of Virginia, part of which later became southern West Virginia. Odessa uncovered an 1891 report in the magazine *Arena* which stated, "The Melungeons are filthy; their home is filthy. They are rogues, natural born rogues, close, suspicious, inhospitable, untruthful, cowardly, and to use their word, sneaky. In many things they resembled the Negro. They are unforgiving people, although they are slow to detect an insult, and they expect to be spit upon." Another report described them as sometimes being born with six fingers or toes, and having strange, small, outward-protruding "shovel" teeth.

"Oh, my God...his lower teeth!" Odessa caught her breath, glancing around the dimly lit reference room to be certain no one knew her.

That evening, after dinner, when Walter went out on the back porch with his nightly glass of Chivas Regal on the rocks to watch the sun go down, Odessa went upstairs to her bedroom where she telephoned her daughter. When Greta answered the phone, Odessa demanded, "Greta, put Sarah on the phone, right away."

"Mrs. Wilson, is that you?"

"Of course it is. Who'd you think it was? Get Sarah, and be quick about it."

"Mother?" Sarah asked, picking up the phone.

"Yes," Odessa answered in a hushed voice. "Now listen, carefully. I need to see you, alone. Is there some place we can meet tomorrow afternoon? Perhaps for lunch, in Staunton. That's about halfway."

"Why, I suppose so. What's this all about? You sound frantic. Is there a problem? Are you and Dad okay?"

"Yes, we're all right. I can't talk about it on the phone. Just meet me at noon...say, at the entrance to the Military Academy. You know where that is? We'll find a place to eat."

"Yes, Mother, but I wish you'd tell me what this is all about. I won't be able to sleep tonight."

"Just be there, Sarah. I've got to go." Hanging up the phone, she thought, nor will I be able to sleep tonight, my darling daughter. It will be sleepless nights for both of us when you hear what I have to say.

* * *

Coming out of his den, Cliff saw Sarah standing at the telephone, staring at it, her hand on the receiver. "What's up, honey?" he asked.

"Oh, nothing. That was Mother. She wants to meet me for lunch tomorrow."

"Good. You can take the kids so they can spend a few days in Charleston. That's if they're willing to part with Ginger for a little while."

"I don't think she's up to it. She sounded worried. I better just go alone."

"Whatever you say. I hope your parents are okay. She certainly left Beckley in a huff yesterday. Anyway, I'll be going up to New York tomorrow. Won't be home until late, so take your time. Come on, I'll help you tuck the kids in, and then maybe you'll let me tuck you in."

"Clifford...," Sarah cocked her head at him and smiled, as he took her hand, leading her toward the children, who were playing with Ginger in the laundry room where they had placed her wicker basket.

* * *

When Cliff arrived at Oscar McMillan's office on Wall Street for a hurriedly called Board meeting, he carried Hal's proxy in his pocket, not knowing what to expect. Oscar, Sidney, and Winslow Rooke already were seated in the conference room. Obviously, they had been conferring.

"Hey, Cliff...come on in and grab a cup of coffee," Sidney shouted, pleasantly.

Cliff nodded, smiling, and shook hands all around. He had spoken with Winslow on the telephone, but had never met the man. The attorney was middle-aged, middle-girthed, with a bald spot in the middle of his graying head. He sported a pencil-thin mustache, probably blackened with Grecian Formula to match his floppy black bow tie. When Cliff shook his hand, he simply muttered, "Cross," staring blankly into Cliff's eyes. This is one cold fish, Cliff thought.

"Meeting will come to order," Oscar pronounced. "Big item on the agenda is formalizing the sale of your stock to you and your boys. Win's made out all the paperwork...in the folders in front of you. I've included certified checks for each of you, Cliff, which are in the folders. You can have the boys sign their promissory notes and mail them back to me. Any questions, anyone?"

"Looks fine to me, Oscar," Cliff replied after scanning the documents, including the stock certificates. Stuffing them in his briefcase, he said, "The fellas will be pleased. They were beginning to worry about where their certificates were. This will be a real shot in the arm."

"I'll say it should be," Sidney bellowed. "You boys have a good chance to make a pile of money."

"Which brings us to our next item on the agenda," Oscar flipped through his papers. "Let's have your financial report, Cliff."

Cliff passed out updated Balance sheets, P&L, and Cash Flow statements, including projections. They were ahead of target, and the large volume of multiple printer orders caused the Directors to nod approvingly.

"Excellent progress," Oscar stated.

"Looks like we're going to need more cash up front, sooner than we expected. That could be a problem," Sidney frowned.

"Surely, with the way we're cleaning up the Balance Sheet, we could go to a bank for an operating loan against our Inventory and Accounts Receivable," Cliff interjected.

"That might pose some problems," the attorney commented, glancing at Sidney, but not wanting to reveal the extent of Sidney's problems with the SEC or the pending lawsuits against him relating to his other ventures.

"Let's just keep a steady course, for now," Oscar smiled. "We'll have next month's five hundred thousand wired to the bank this week, and then we can reevaluate at the Board meeting next month. Anybody have anything else? No? Okay, let's plan to get together around the middle of next month. Give me a call, Cliff, when you've got your financials ready."

As Cliff packed up his briefcase and started to leave, Winslow casually turned to Oscar, "Why don't you sign the papers extending Sidney's loan...might as well get that done today."

"Fine. Routine extension, right?"

"What's this all about?" Cliff asked.

"Legally, Sidney could call his loans anytime," Rooke answered matter-of-factly. "We know he won't, but if he died tomorrow, his estate could. That's the last thing we'd need, with the progress you're making now. So, this is just boilerplate, nailing his loans down for another twelve months, giving him an extra interest point for the commitment, et cetera. I'll just include it in the minutes of the meeting so everything's legal."

"Give it here," Oscar reached for the documents and signed them.

Cliff shrugged, "Last thing we need right now is a cash crunch. If it takes another interest point to buy us stability in our cash position, I guess that's fair."

Sidney sat, unusually silent, an angelic glow of satisfaction on his face.

"Come on, Cliff, I'll walk you to the elevator," Oscar took his arm. "I want to hear more about Smokey's progress with the other software packages."

When Oscar walked back into the room from depositing Cliff on the elevator, Sidney shouted, "Hot damn!" giving a thumbs-up to Oscar and Win.

"Sidney, I don't like it. I don't like it one bit," Oscar pushed his chair under the table.

"What do you mean? It's legal. Tell him, Win...totally legal."

"Well, he was present at the Board meeting," Winslow nodded. "The subject of the new terms of your loan was referred to...he did seem to agree...but he didn't actually read the document...and we didn't actually outline the new conditions."

"Hey, whose fault is it if he didn't read the document? He's a big boy."

"I think it probably would stand up in court," the lawyer opined, "but when he finds out we tripled the shares of stock that could be issued, and gave you two an option on another two hundred thousand shares at a dollar a share, in exchange for you changing the terms of your loans, he isn't going to be a happy camper. You, potentially, have taken away two-thirds of the value of their stock."

"So...if this thing turns around, they'll still walk away with a nice piece of change," Sidney grunted.

* * *

Sarah pulled up behind her mother's car at the entrance to the Staunton Military Academy a few minutes before noon. "Follow me," her mother commanded, motioning through the window.

After parking on a side street and walking around the corner to the Beverely restaurant, a quaint little establishment in the heart of Staunton's historic district, they slid into a corner table.

"What's this all about, Mother?" Sarah asked, perplexed.

"Let's order first...and I need a drink to get my stomach settled." They both ordered vodka martinis and Cobb salads. Halfway through their lunch, Odessa ordered another martini, pushed her plate back, and began her story. "I'm afraid I've got some very disquieting news for you, Sarah. I don't know quite how to say it...so I'll just spit it right out: Clifford's got colored blood in him."

"What?"

"You heard me right, dear. Your father stumbled onto it Sunday at the Cross's. We're just sick about it. We debated whether we should even tell you...but you have a right to know...particularly because of the hereditary implications."

"What are you talking about, Mother?" Sarah pushed her plate away, and as she picked up her napkin to wipe her lips, her hand began to shake.

"We arrived a little early, and your dad sat out on the front porch making small talk with Clifford's father. Your dad was telling him that he handled some cases in the southern part of the state when he was a young attorney with the firm. Well, it turns out that he was involved in a land dispute case with an Alonzo Collins up in the mountains behind Dry Creek. When Clint heard that, not knowing any better, he volunteered the information that Alonzo Collins was Ruth Ann's grandfather."

"So..."

"Well, you see, dear," Odessa leaned across the table, looking from side to side to be sure no one was listening, "the whole case was about Melungeons owning land. Alonzo Collins was a **Melungeon**!"

"What in the world is a **Melungeon**? I never heard of them."

"They're a mongrel breed of mountain folk...a mixture of white, Indian...and **colored**! Alonzo Collins, Cliff's great-grandfather...has **colored** blood in him! You're married to a man who has **colored** blood in him. Your children...my grandchildren...have **colored** blood in them!"

Sarah's lips began to tremble. She turned her head away from her mother, staring into space, her face contorted, trying to hold back the tears. "Mother...how could you say such a thing?" she jerked her head back, glaring at her mother. "It's bad enough, the way some people try to make a big deal about Cliff being part Indian...a tiny part, at that. Some of his friends call him Tonto...think it's funny. But this...you take some old backwoods tale and try to denigrate my husband. You never liked him...you **never** liked him...," tears streamed down her cheeks, her voice rising.

"Shush up, Sarah! People are looking at you! Do you think I'd make up something like this? Do you think I **want** this to be true? Goodness knows, we can't let it get out. But there are hereditary implications. You don't plan to have any more children, do you?"

"Mother! For God's sake. What's that got to do with it?"

"Well, dear, you never know when certain hereditary traits that have been buried for generations will show up. And I don't just mean color. The Melungeons have birth defects." Leaning closer to her daughter, Odessa whispered, "They've been known to be born with six fingers, six toes, and tiny shovel-shaped teeth. Look at Cliff's lower teeth. He's got the mark of a Melungeon. It's in his blood!"

"Oh, Mother...you make them sound like freaks."

"Believe me, Sarah, I wish with all my heart that these things weren't true. But your dad said Alonzo Collins admitted to being a Melungeon in a sworn deposition. And I spent all day Monday at the West Virginia Historical Society, the library, and the archives at the capitol researching it. These people have a terrible reputation...of being shiftless, dirty, ignorant, dishonest. Thank goodness, none of those traits seem to have been carried over into the little ones. But you never know, Sarah, you never know. Just look at his lower teeth...and his curly black hair. He's got the features. He's one of them!"

"My God, Mother, stop it. Let me pay the bill, and let's take a walk. I can't stand this, Mother." Sarah's eyes turned watery and a tear ran down her cheek, streaking her makeup.

"I'll pay the bill, dear. You go to the powder room and fix up that beautiful face of yours."

Emerging from the ladies' room, Sarah met her mother in front of the restaurant. "Let's just walk." She took her mother's arm. "Assuming everything you said is true...and I guess it is...what hurts...what really hurts the most is that Cliff would do this to me. I don't know what I would have said, or done, if he had told me when we started dating." A bitter sneer crossed her face as she suddenly stopped, facing her mother, "He was always so...so **obsequious** about being sure that his being part Indian didn't bother me. Frankly, I thought it was something to be proud of. But this...it's such a tiny fraction. I...I don't know what to think. I'm still in shock. Not **telling** me...that's the thing, Mother. Cliff and I have a chance for a wonderful life together. Now this. What am I supposed to do? Ignore it? Ignore the fact that he lied to me about something so fundamental. His heredity. Something that could affect our children? I don't think I could ever forgive him for that."

Rounding the corner to their cars, Odessa took her daughter's hand, "Think of the children, dear. Just don't do anything rash. Just think of the children. Words can't adequately express how terrible I feel, telling you this. But you have a right to know. You're my daughter...and I love you."

"I know, Mother. I'm going home right now and confront him this evening."

Hugging each other, they both went to their cars, when Sarah realized that she had left her purse in the restaurant. "Oops, left my purse and my keys to the car in the restaurant," she called over to her mother as she turned to retrieve them. "I'll phone you tonight."

"Be careful, dear," her mother waved. "I love you."

Sarah turned to the restaurant, locating her purse under the table. As she sat down in her chair, fumbling in her purse to find the car keys, she noticed that the table had not been cleared and that her mother hadn't finished her second martini. Slumping in her chair, she sighed, mumbling to herself, "How could this be?" Staring for a long minute at that half-full martini glass, she sighed a second time, reached across the table, slowly raised it to her lips, and drained it in a swallow.

Looking out the window, disgustedly, she motioned to the waiter, pointing to her empty glass. She sipped her refill slowly, drumming her fingers on the table, becoming more and more agitated as she rehashed her mother's revelation.

"The dirty bastard never even told me!" she muttered. She ordered another martini, gulped it down, threw some bills on the table, and weaved her way out of the restaurant.

Chapter Fifteen

While waiting for the shuttle back to Washington, Cliff couldn't wait to tell the troops that he finally had their stock certificates. Together, they were the proud owners of forty percent of Jet Speed Printers, Inc. Or so he thought.

"Nettie, put Hal on the phone...you stay on, too," he instructed her from a pay phone at LaGuardia. "Guess what, guys? We finally got our stock. All the certificates...right here in my briefcase. Nettie...see if you can conference in the boys in Chicago...Red, Smokey, and Sam. Oh, and you better get Mike and Arnold on an extension, too."

"Mike's out, but hang on and I'll see if I can get Chicago on their squawk box," Nettie answered, while Hal went looking for Arnold. A few seconds later, Nettie pushed off the hold button, "We're all here, but Mike," she announced.

"Hey, guys. Got good news. Finally have our stock certificates along with our loan agreements to purchase them. We're in business!"

"About time you came through, Tonto," Hal teased, winking at the others in the room. "No wonder the pale faces won the West."

"Up yours...," Cliff responded playfully. "Now we really have something worth working for!"

"You ought to stay out of the office more often, old buddy," Hal retorted, laughingly. "We got good news for you, too. The Air Force just sole-sourced three thousand printers for their bases around the world. Don't know how they can do that without going through GSA...or at least a competitive procurement. But I got the order right here in my hand."

"Damn, I'd say today's our lucky day," as Cliff instinctively raised his fist, the man standing next to him at the phones jumped back, looked at Cliff like he was demented. "Oops, sorry, buddy," Cliff apologized.

"What'd you say?" Hal asked.

"Nothing. Just getting a little too demonstrative here in a crowded airport. Sam...can you meet the delivery schedule?"

"Yep. Already went over it with Hal," Sam yelled into the squawk box in Chicago.

"Good. Gotta go...but I'll be back in the office in a couple of hours...let's go out and celebrate. And you guys in Chicago...go have a few on me."

* * *

It was nearly quitting time when Cliff bounded through the door, swinging his briefcase, grinning, but he was stopped short by Hal, Mike, Arnie, and Nettie, all clustered in the outer office, grimly awaiting his arrival.

"Hey, what's up?" he raised his eyebrows, standing transfixed.

Nettie's face quivered as her teary eyes met his. She started to speak, "Cliff, there's...," but she broke down and cried.

Hal reached out and gently took hold of Cliff's arm, "Cliff, there's been an accident..."

"What? Who? Are my kids all right?"

"It's Sarah. She was in an automobile accident. You're supposed to call the Fairfax County Police. Here's their number. Ask for Sergeant Webster," Hal handed Cliff a slip.

"Is she okay? How serious was it?" he asked over his shoulder as he rushed into his office, with everyone following.

"You better talk to the police," Hal answered.

Getting the Sergeant on the line, Cliff demanded, "This is Clifford Cross...what happened to my wife? Is she all right? Where is she?"

"Mr. Cross, are you the gentleman who lives on Old Dominion Drive in McLean?"

"Yes, I am."

"I take it you're the husband of Sarah Wilson Cross?"

"Yes, dammit. Get to the point. How's my wife?"

"I'm sorry, Mr. Cross. Your wife was involved in a one-car accident on Route 123 just outside Vienna. She apparently lost control of the car...went off the road...hit a tree...she...ah...she didn't make it, Mr. Cross."

"What? What are you telling me?" Clifford roared into the phone, frantically.

"I'm sorry, sir. Apparently, she died instantly. She was pronounced dead on arrival at the Fairfax County Hospital. We'd appreciate it if you could come over to identify the body. That way we can avoid sending it to the morgue."

"The morgue," Cliff murmured plaintively, slumping down into his chair. Shaking his head, he spoke, looking up beseechingly to his friends, "No...no, we don't want that. I'll be there right away. I know where it is." Choking, he started to say, "That's where our children were born," but garbled the last words as he broke down crying.

Nettie took the receiver from him and said soothingly, "He'll be right there, officer. Thank you for your help."

Hal again took Cliff by the arm, gently, "Come on, Cliff, we'll drive you there."

"Fine...fine," Cliff shook his head, wiping the tears from his eyes, dazed. "But what about the children? What about my kids? What about **our** kids?" he broke down again.

"I'll go to the house." Nettie sighed, walking over to Cliff and hugging him. "We all love you," she whispered.

Halfway through the door, he turned, "What about her parents? Someone's got to tell them."

"Why don't you call them from the hospital, after you...after you...do what must be done," Nettie suggested. "Arnie, why don't you stay here to take any calls? These things get picked up on scanners. The press may get hold of this. If you get any inquiries, just say the family hasn't been notified, so you'd appreciate them not putting out anything publicly. Mike, you go with Hal and Cliff. I'll get out to the house right away."

* * *

Hal and Mike walked on either side of Cliff, holding his arms as he walked, still dazed, unsure of his steps, down the long corridor to the room of death.

A physician, two attendants in white coats, and two police officers met him at the door.

"How could this have happened...in broad daylight...on a four-lane road?" Cliff implored the officers. "Was she speeding?"

"Mr. Cross, we don't know for sure, but the head-on impact on the car indicates that she was traveling quite fast. And there are no skid marks, so she didn't have time to brake. Or chose not to brake," he lowered his voice, looking down at the floor.

"What? What do you mean? She did it **on purpose**?"

"No, we're certainly not saying that, sir. Under the circumstances, we just can't exclude any alternatives at this time. You understand, there will have to be an autopsy. I'm afraid...ah...it **appears** that she had been drinking. They've already drawn blood for a blood-alcohol test. I'm sorry, sir. Best you step in here and we'll get this over with."

Cliff looked dejectedly at Hal and Mike, "Do I have to do this?"

"It's a formality, sir," the physician nodded. "It will just take a few seconds."

As he entered the room, one of the attendants lifted the white sheet from Sarah's face. "My God!" Cliff exclaimed. "She's hardly recognizable! She was a beautiful woman...honest...I wouldn't exaggerate...she was beautiful," he looked imploringly from the physician to the attendants to the police officers. "She was the Golden Girl at the University of West Virginia."

"I'm sorry, sir," the physician replied softly. "I'm sure she was."

"She wasn't wearing her seat belt, sir," one of the officers interjected. "Force of the impact threw her up over the airbag into the window."

"You say she was drinking. How could you tell?" Cliff asked, almost afraid of the answer.

"Smell was pretty strong, sir. She...ah...she must have had quite a bit."

"No one else was involved in the accident?" Cliff asked. "Maybe she had to swerve to avoid hitting another car."

"Not that we know of, sir."

"Thank you...thank you...," Cliff mumbled, turning to leave.

"Excuse me, sir...just for the record, that is your wife, Sarah Wilson Cross?" one of the attendants with a clipboard in his hand asked.

Scowling, Cliff let out a guttural sound, "Yes...that **was** my wife."

Walking back down the corridor, Hal suggested, "Don't you think you better call her parents?"

Still dazed, Cliff mindlessly reached in his pocket for a coin and then realized he could dial the number, simply using his credit card. His fingers touched his bear-toothed totem. He stopped, took it out of his pocket, and turned it over in his hand until the snake-eye side seemed to pierce his very being.

"What are you doing, Cliff?" Hal frowned.

Without saying a word, Cliff sneered, and then thrust the die back into his pocket. He walked over to the pay phone, put his hand on the receiver, leaning his head against it before lifting it, shook his head again, and sighed. "Telling them is going to be even more difficult than telling the kids. What am I supposed to say? Your daughter got drunk in the middle of the day and killed herself in a car accident?"

"You don't know that, Cliff," Mike squeezed his shoulder. "Just give them the sad news, before they hear it from someone else."

Walter was on the porch having his Chivas Regal as Odessa sipped an iced tea in the lounge chair facing him. Having already told Walter of her lunch with Sarah, and received his blistering excoriation for her poor judgment, they sat silently, brooding, when the phone rang.

Odessa answered it on the portable phone beside her.

"Odessa, this is Cliff. Could I speak to Walter?"

Without answering him, she hesitated for a moment, and then thrust the phone at her husband, "Hmpf...it's your son-in-law," she said in a singsong voice. "Guess I'm not good enough to talk to."

"Yes, Cliff? What's wrong?" The lawyer in him sensed that Cliff would not have asked for him unless there was a problem.

"Walter, I've got terrible news. Felt I should let you handle it as you best see fit with Odessa. Are you sitting down?"

"Spit it out, boy!"

"Sarah was in an automobile accident driving back from Staunton...," he swallowed hard.

"Yes?"

"Walter...Walter, she didn't make it," he broke down again, sobbing.

"Cliff...what the hell are you telling me?"

"I'm so sorry, Walter. I'm so sorry. She's...her body's in the Fairfax County Hospital. It happened late this afternoon."

Stunned, the urbane, erudite attorney was at a loss for words.

"What's he saying. Walter? What's he saying," Odessa insisted.

Lowering the phone to his lap, he gasped out the words as the last whisper of a dying man. "He says...he says...Sarah's been killed in an automobile accident. It happened this afternoon, on her way back from Staunton."

"No! No!" Odessa shrieked, bolting out of her chair, falling down at Walter's knees. "No, Walter! Say it isn't so!"

Cradling her with one arm, as she let out intermittent shrieks between sobs, Walter regained his composure, returned the phone to his ear, and matter-of-factly said, "We're on our way, Cliff. We'll be there as quickly as possible."

Walter's composure seemed to have a calming effect on Cliff. Hanging up the phone, he turned to his friends, "Mike, would you please stay back here to see if anything else needs to be done. Give me a call at the house. Take a cab home. Hal, will you please drive me home? We'll leave my car at the office. I don't know anything about funeral arrangements. I suppose the Wilsons would want things done a lot different from the way funerals are handled in Beckley. I need to see the kids. Maybe you could talk to somebody who knows about these kinds of things."

Both Mike and Hal nodded their assent.

* * *

As they entered the house, Nettie met them in the hallway, taking Cliff's arm and walking back outside with him. "They're in the family room playing with Ginger. I said their mother was in an automobile accident. I told them she was in the hospital. I said you were with her, and you'd be home soon to tell them all about it. I felt it wasn't my place to break the news to them. After all, they're only little children. That's all I told Greta, too. Although she seemed to understand. She's with the children now."

"Thanks, Nettie." Walking back into the house, Cliff suggested, "Why don't you all go on into the living room. I'd like to talk to the children, here, by myself for a few minutes."

Taking both Sally and Tyke up on his lap, Cliff smoothed Tyke's hair, and began. "Hey, guys, I've got some real bad news for all of us. Your mommy's been in an automobile accident. She was hurt real bad...and...," choking up, he lowered his voice, "...and she didn't make it. Your mommy's in heaven. She...she won't be coming home again. But...but she loves you very much...and...and she's up in heaven watching down on you...watching over all of us."

Teary-eyed, little Sally looked up at her father, "Why, Daddy? Why isn't she coming home? We want her to come home."

"I know, honey. This is something that happened, and we can't change it. Now, it's going to be very hard for us to adjust to this...to learn how to get along without your mommy. But, we'll make it. She would want us to. Think of it this way, you have your own angel in heaven looking after you now. Mommy will be with you now, not just when she was here with you at the house, or when she was taking you somewhere. Mommy will be with you now, always. Wherever you are...in school...on the playground...no matter where...Mommy will be there. She's going to be your guardian angel."

"Is she here now?" Tyke asked.

"Yes...yes, she's watching over you right this minute."

"Then why can't I see her?" the little boy asked.

"Because she won't be with us physically anymore. Her body won't be here. But her spirit will always be with you. Close your eyes. Good. Now, can't you see a picture of Mommy? All you have to do is close your eyes, and you can see Mommy. Right? Always. Always...Mommy is with you, watching over you."

"I can see her, Daddy." Tyke had his eyes squeezed tight shut.

"Good. You try, Sally."

Squeezing her eyes shut, Sally nodded, "Yes, Daddy, I can see Mommy, too."

"Good. Real good. Now, let's go find Greta and get you some ice cream. Then, it's off to bed. It's way past your bedtime."

After tucking the kids in bed, and again trying to explain that their mother would be with them always, Cliff collapsed into a cushioned chair in the living room with Hal and Nettie.

"Can I fix you a drink?" Nettie asked.

"I don't care if I never see another drink," he scoffed.

"Mike called while you were in with the kids. He suggested having the body taken to the Everly Funeral Home in Fairfax. Then you can decide on the details...whether you'd like to have her buried here...back in West Virginia, or whatever," Hal reported.

"Hal, I don't know. I'm brain-dead. I suppose we should wait until her parents get here. They'll probably be pulling in after midnight. Greta...where's Greta?"

"Here, Mr. Cross."

"Please have the guest room ready for Sarah's parents. Leave the light on and the front door unlocked."

"Yes, sir. Could I get you some hot chocolate?"

"No, thanks. Kids asleep?"

"I think so."

"Fine. I can't thank all of you enough for hanging in here with me. Why don't we all call it a night? I'm going to pop a couple of Sominex and try to get some sleep. Tomorrow's going to be very difficult."

As they were leaving, Hal said, "What about the funeral home?"

"Everly will be fine for now. Please ask Mike to take care of the temporary arrangements. Then we'll make a decision tomorrow, after Sarah's parents arrive."

"Done. I'll have Mike call you in the morning. Don't worry about the office. I'm available. Just let me know what you want me to do," Hal hugged Cliff, patting him on the back.

"I'll come out tomorrow morning, if you want me to," Nettie offered.

"Might be a good idea, Nettie. Probably have a million things to decide, and I've got no experience at this."

Hugging him again, she whispered again, "We all love you, Cliff. Just tell us what to do."

After locking the door behind them, Cliff went into his bedroom, slowly undressing, letting his shirt and pants fall where he stood, pulled his blue silk pajamas from beneath his pillow where Sarah always put them, but which he seldom wore, and mindlessly put them on. Tears welled up in his eyes and streamed down his cheeks. His broad shoulders convulsed as intermittent sobs erupted from deep within his lungs. "Damn you, Sarah!" he cursed, snatching the bear-toothed die from the top of his dresser and hurling it at the mirror. The hard cube cracked the center of the mirror and bounced back onto the dresser.

Cliff stared at the cracked glass and muttered, "Seven more years of bad luck, huh?" He picked up the die, grunted at it, then jerked open his bottom dresser drawer and flicked it into a pile of old Mountaineer sweats that he hadn't worn in years. Slamming the drawer shut, he muttered, "Stupid superstition!"

He took two more Sominex, swallowed them with a gulp of water, turned off the light switch, crawled in bed, and sobbed himself to sleep.

* * *

Cliff woke a little after seven, splashed some water on his face, brushed back his hair, and groggily padded toward the kitchen for some coffee. Walter and Odessa were sitting at the counter. Walter looked up at Cliff, nodded wearily, and said but a single word, "Clifford."

"Walter...Odessa...I'm so sorry...how could this have happened... it's unbelievable."

"How could this have happened?" Odessa's shrill voice rose, her eyes went wild with anger. "As if you don't know...you...you rotten scum!"

"What? What did you say?"

"You...you caused her to kill herself! We learned your dirty secret. Our dear daughter was so distraught when she learned of your deceit that she obviously lost control of her car...probably blinded from crying all the way home to confront you. How could you? How could you?"

"Dess, now's not the time," Walter interjected.

"The time for what?" Cliff demanded. "My wife...your daughter is lying over there on a coroner's slab, and you walk in here accusing me of being responsible. What in the hell are you talking about, Odessa?"

"As if you don't know," she sneered. "Your colored blood...
your...Melungeon ancestry."

Mystified and furious, Cliff threw his coffee cup into the
sink, spilling it, "Colored blood? Melungeon? What the hell is
Melungeon?"

"Humpft...so I suppose you didn't know your mother's grandfather, Alonzo Collins, was a Melungeon...had colored blood?"

"Odessa, I don't know what you're talking about. My great-
grandfather, Alonzo Collins, was a Cherokee Indian. Sarah knew that.
Everybody knew my mother was part Cherokee. So what? The woman
we all loved is lying over there dead, and you're bringing up some
irrelevant bizarre fact."

"Dess...that's enough!" Walter glared at her. "I want to speak
with you privately back in the bedroom. Cliff, I'll apologize for Dess's
outburst. She's very upset. We all are. Let's plan to sit down in the
family room in about half an hour to talk about the funeral arrangements." Scowling at his wife, he pulled her off the stool and led her
into the guest room.

Mike and Nettie were standing in the hallway as Cliff passed
through. "Cliff, I'm sorry if we're intruding," Nettie grimaced. "We
didn't mean to barge in on a family...well, you know, a family...
discussion."

"You should have knocked!" Cliff snapped. "Exactly what did
you hear?"

"Nothing...nothing, really, Cliff. Just voices. Raised voices. I'm
so sorry. We'll leave right now," Nettie replied.

"No, I'm the one who's sorry, Nettie. Forgive me. I'm distraught."

"You got a right, buddy," Mike nodded. "Thought I ought to tell
you the temporary arrangements I worked out with the Everly folks."

Mike explained that following the autopsy, Sarah's body would
be prepared by the funeral director, and then they would await in-
structions from the family on how to proceed. They understood that
the body might be shipped to West Virginia for the funeral.

Nettie then asked, "Have you called your parents, Cliff?"

"How the hell could I have forgotten to do that? In the confusion, it slipped my mind completely. Gotta do it right now."

"We'll go over to the office, if you don't need us for anything else," Nettie said.

"Fine. Thanks so much for everything. I'll let you know what's happening."

When Ruth Ann took the phone call, she was surprisingly calm. In her lifetime, in the mountains and coal mines of West Virginia, death had been all around her far too often.

"I'm so sorry, Clifford," she spoke soothingly. "What about the little ones? How are they taking it? Who is taking care of them? Can I help? Do you want your father and me to come on? What are the funeral arrangements?"

"Everything seems to be under control, Ma. The Wilsons are here. Once we work out the funeral arrangements, I'll let you and Pap know." He almost asked her if she knew anything about Melungeons, but decided now was not the time.

"Fine, son. Our prayers will be with you and the little ones."

After showering, shaving, and dressing, Cliff went into the family room for what he expected to be a very tense confrontation. But instead, Odessa sat silently, slumped in the corner of the couch, staring at the coffee cup in her hands.

Walter spoke with a gentleness Cliff had never before seen in Charleston's most prominent attorney. "Son, we're all in a state of shock. Sarah's **your** wife. The funeral arrangements are your call. We'd **like** to suggest that she be buried in the family plot in Charleston...have her laid out and have the services at our home...where she grew up...the home she loved so much. Our Episcopalian priest could perform the service, or you could have your Baptist minister from down home, if you wanted. Or, for that matter, we could have them both. It's totally up to you."

"Walter, you're being very gracious. I know how hard this is on you and Odessa. That flare-up we had earlier this morning is

something that we can certainly set aside for now. Although...
eventually...eventually I'm going to have to understand it. I think
Sarah would want to be back home in Charleston. Your suggestions are thoughtful and appropriate. Sure. Mike Gattuso's handling
things for me on this end. Just give me the names and phone numbers for the proper people in Charleston to be contacted, and I'll
give them to Mike. He tells me that with the autopsy and the other
preparations we probably wouldn't be ready for the viewing until
Monday. Should we have two days or one before the burial?"

"There's no sense in putting everyone through this ordeal any
longer than necessary. I think an afternoon and evening viewing on
Monday will be sufficient. We'd like to have the Barlow Bonsell
Funeral Home handle it. Let's have the service and burial Tuesday
morning. Then we can have a little gathering of family and friends at
the house afterwards, if that's okay with you."

"That's fine, Walter."

"We might as well start back to Charleston, if there's nothing
else you want us to do here. Would you like us to take the children
with us?"

"Thanks, Walter, but I'd like to have them here with me. I guess
I **need** to have them here with me."

"We understand." Walter walked over to Cliff, shook his hand,
and patted him on the back. But without saying a word, Odessa
stood up, stared at Cliff forlornly, and followed her husband out of
the room.

* * *

The next few days seemed to drag on forever. There wasn't much
Cliff could do. Before he could get the words out, Greta assured him
that she would do whatever...**whatever** he wanted her to do to look
after Sally and Tyke. She loved them like her own children that she
never had. Thank goodness for Ginger, who kept the children en-
grossed, taking her on her walks, feeding her, brushing her, cuddling

her. Cliff went into the office a few times, but Nettie and the boys had everything under control. They saw to it that there was nothing for him to do. He tried working out with weights and on the treadmill in the basement, but couldn't muster the energy. He thought about packing Sarah's clothes, sending them to Goodwill, but decided Odessa should make that kind of decision. Each time he opened her closet, he started to cry again. And he couldn't let the children see him that way. He was embarrassed by his own weakness. He **had** to get control of himself. He **would** get control of himself.

When Mike called to say that the body would be picked up and transported to Charleston by the Barlow Bonsell Funeral Director, Cliff insisted that he and the children, along with Greta, would follow behind in the minivan. And so, with Ginger curled asleep in Sally's lap, they began the long, mournful journey to Sarah's home and her final resting place.

* * *

Flowers spilled over the great room at the Wilson estate. The flag of the University of West Virginia was draped over the casket— closed because of the crash had so horribly disfigured the once beautiful face of the university's Golden Girl. In the upper left-hand corner of the flag lay three yellow roses, not quite in bloom, with a little note: "With our love forever. Cliff, Sally, & Tyke."

Cliff read the card on every floral arrangement, but recognized only a few of the names. Most were from prominent Charleston citizens whom he had never met. There were flowers from Nettie, Hal, Mike, and Arnie; from Red, Smokey, and Sam; from his Tektron friends; from Oscar and Sidney; from Sarah's sorority sisters; from their neighbors in McLean and friends at the country club; from his parents and grandfather, Josey. And there was a little plant of mountain laurel with a bent three-by-five card stuck down in it bearing the simple pencil-scrawled signature, Jumper. When Cliff saw it, tears welled up in his eyes.

On Monday afternoon, people filled the great room, and the line extended out of the house, down the driveway, and onto the street. Two policemen appeared to help direct traffic. Monday evening was more of the same. Cliff knew few of the people. His family and friends were coming for the service on Tuesday. Walter made most of the introductions, taking charge, handling the solemn occasion with great dignity. Odessa sat in a corner-stuffed chair, dabbing her eyes with her embroidered hankie, accepting the condolences of their many friends. In spite of the long-standing tension between them, in spite of the bizarre, inexplicable recent attack on him, Cliff found himself feeling sorry for her. She was a wilted, pitiful woman who suddenly looked her age.

* * *

Cliff, the children, and Greta were staying in the guest wing of the Wilson home. After taking milk and cookies to the children, who insisted on sleeping together in a king-size bed, and reading them the story, *Sleeping Beauty*, Cliff kissed them, turned off the light, and went to his room.

Throwing his coat and tie on his bed, he walked over to the window and stood, mindlessly mesmerized by the water in the garden fountain below, splashing over a clump of rocks, trickling down into a narrow spillway, then pouring into a lily pond. He remembered how he and Sarah had sat on the edge of the pond, their bare feet dangling in among the lilies, talking about their future. Suddenly, he shuddered, bringing himself back to the present. He yanked the window curtain closed, abruptly turned, and went out of his room to find his father-in-law.

Walter was sitting alone, in the dark, on his back porch staring at the garden fountain, with a short glass in one hand and a bottle of Chivas Regal in the other.

"Excuse me, Walter, can we talk?"

"Get a glass and some ice over on that tray, and I'll pour you a drink. Chivas okay?"

"Sounds good. I guess we both could use one."

"What's on your mind, Cliff?"

"I was really stunned by Odessa's outburst the other day. I know how shaken she is...we all are...but I don't understand what she was talking about. My family...**Melungeons**...I don't even know what Melungeons are. I never heard the word before. I meant to look it up, but with all the excitement, I haven't got around to it."

Walter told him the story of the case he handled so many years ago in Dry Creek involving Alonzo Collins, Cliff's great-grandfather, and explained who the Melungeons are.

"I'm sorry, Cliff. Those are the facts. So, if Alonzo had, say, a quarter Negro blood in him, that would mean you would have one thirty-second. I don't think it's a big deal. Certainly not in this day and age. And I believe you when you say you've no knowledge of this. It was quite common back then for the Melungeons to hide their backgrounds. I wouldn't be surprised if your mother wasn't aware of it. I apologize for Dess. She had no right acting the way she did. You're a fine young man, and I'm proud to have you as a son-in-law. I don't know what Dess said to Sarah, but it must have been upsetting. It just makes our loss doubly tragic. I don't know if Dess can ever face up to the consequences of her actions."

* * *

On Tuesday morning, a few minutes before ten, when the service was about to begin, people began pouring into the row upon row of folding chairs set up in the great room. Additional chairs had to be hurriedly set up in the adjoining rooms. Cliff's parents entered the hall, not sure where to sit. Ruth Ann's dark complexion, without a hint of makeup, was highlighted by the wide white collar of her flower-printed dress. Her black-tied Cuban-heeled shoes seemed a throwback to the '30s. Clint stood, ramrod straight, his gaunt body surely sweltering in his brown wool suit. His unstarched white shirt was fastened at his neck by a half-broken button, without the benefit of a necktie. He could have been the model for a Norman Rockwell painting.

When Walter saw them, he motioned for them to sit in the second row behind Cliff, who held on tightly to Sally and Tyke's hands, sitting on either side of him.

Odessa, who sat one chair over, leaving room for Walter, was crying softly, fidgeting with her handkerchief in her lap. Ruth Ann leaned forward, patting Cliff on the shoulder, who responded by reaching back and squeezing her hand.

When everyone was seated, the Episcopal priest made the sign of the cross and began the service. It didn't last long. His opening prayer was followed by the Twenty-third Psalm; then one of Sarah's sorority sisters gave a moving eulogy, describing Sarah as, not only their Golden Girl, but as a golden person, both inside and out; their dream girl, who set a standard of excellence to which they all aspired. The priest then read the One Hundred Twenty-first Psalm, delivered his own eulogy about how Sarah, as a little girl growing up in Charleston, created a sparkle simply by her presence in any room; how her involvement in activities at church or in school lifted the spirits of all around her. They **knew** she was a very special, gifted, talented child, the likes of which one might see only once in a lifetime; how she was loved not only by her parents, husband, and children, but by virtually everyone who was privileged to have known her. He then closed by commending her soul to God and asking everyone to join in the Lord's Prayer.

Cliff did not hear a word of what was said. He sat staring grimly at the closed casket, his jaws clamped tightly shut, thinking of what might have been, remembering the first time he saw her, sitting next to him at the pep rally, her exquisite body, her perfect smile, the golden hair with not a single strand out of place, and most of all, the warmth of her lilting voice, as he sat tongue-tied and entranced.

He was inundated with guilt. If only he had spent more time with her, she would not have felt so much alone. If only he had more thoroughly understood his own family background, he could have—he certainly would have—told her the truth, so she could have decided whether she wanted to get involved with him, so she, at least, never would suddenly be confronted by the shocking revelation that she was married to a man with colored blood in him. That her children had colored blood in them. He felt so guilty, so ashamed. And yet, why should he? Tightly gripping the hands of his little children, he looked down at his hands and theirs. We haven't changed...I haven't changed, he thought. I'm the same person I was yesterday, and last year, and on the day Sarah and I fell in love. I'm still **me**, by God, and I've nothing to be ashamed of. I **made** something of myself! I'm **proud** of who I am and what I've done. And Sarah...Sarah was so very proud of me, too. Nothing's changed. Except now she's gone. Forever. And I've got to live with this forever. But who I am is not...**cannot** be the reason why she's dead."

As the pallbearers walked forward and began pushing the casket down the aisle, he snapped out of his reverie, rose with the children, still gripping their hands tightly, and, with head held high, slowly followed them out of the church. The funeral procession wound its way through Charleston and up a steep grade to the cemetery.

The service at the cemetery was even shorter, high atop a hill, overlooking the city. Surrounded by the lush greenery of the mountains and the manicured lawns encompassing a thousand well-kept grave sites, the sun shown down upon the Wilson family headstone, a giant obelisk dwarfing those around it. The priest read another passage from the *Book of Common Prayer* commended Sarah's body to the grave, and it was over. Once again, Cliff heard not a single word, his eyes locked on the casket, his heart burning with contrition: Forgive me, Sarah, for not being a better husband, for not just being with you when I should have, for not telling you how much I loved you, every hour of every day. As they led him away from the grave, he felt crushed and crippled, a solitary burnt-out ember, useless, disconsolate, and cold.

* * *

The great room, as well as the adjoining rooms, had been cleared and a catered buffet spread on long white-clothed tables. Cliff stood alone in the corner, absent-mindedly accepting the condolences of those around him. Greta had taken the children outside to play.

When the crowd has thinned out, Mike walked over to Cliff and leaned close to his ear, "Cliff, I thought you should know, the coroner issued the death certificate. Cause of death: Traumatic trauma to the cranium in a single vehicle crash...with...with...ah...presence of alcohol."

"Will it be made public?"

"I spoke to the coroner. The death certificate is a matter of public record. Her alcohol level was .18. Pretty bad. That will be in the toxology report which won't be out for another two weeks. I'm sure there won't be any surprises in it. The good news...if you can call it that...is that in an accident like this, as part of the autopsy, they dust the sole of the shoe for latent ridge marks from the brake pedal to see if the driver attempted to brake. She did, Cliff. This wasn't a suicide. She was off the road before she could hit the brakes. That's why there weren't any skid marks. It was an accident, Cliff. Pure and simple."

"Thanks, Mike. It was an accident, all right. An accident caused by alcohol. An accident caused by her mother? No...it was an accident...an accident...caused by me. I'm the one who killed my Sarah. I'm the one who killed my Golden Girl."

* * *

Our golden chances turn to dust,
Crushed by life's harsh blows,
Or slowly harden into gems,
To be seized anew, or tossed aside.

Chapter Sixteen

For Cliff personally, the next six months were absolutely the worst of times. Yet, the business flourished beyond his wildest dreams.

He couldn't shake his sense of impending doom, even though he reminded himself repeatedly that the worst tragedy of his life was behind him. He *had* to overcome his grief. He *had* to focus on the future. He owed it to his children, to the people at Jet Speed who depended upon him, to himself, and perhaps most of all, to the memory of his dear wife. But even before the alarm would buzz before dawn each day, he lay awake, his stomach knotted, tortured helplessly by his overwhelming sense of guilt.

Each time he thought of Sarah, each time he saw her perfect dimples, her golden hair-crested face, each time he saw her battered bloody skull, her lifeless eyes staring into space upon the gurney, his chest would tighten and his heart felt as though it were being constricted by barbs of a jagged, rusty wire.

Reaching over to the empty side of the bed, he would cradle Sarah's pillow in his arms, somehow irrationally, half-expecting, hoping, she would be there. Gazing through the snowflaked window panes, at the leafless giant oaks and the snow-covered lawn beneath, they too, like his Sarah, had gone to sleep, yet in the spring would come to life again.

Their past problems receded deep into his consciousness, oblit-erated by the vision of the Golden Girl he loved. He was consumed by the emptiness all about him. He saw her stepping from the shower, her marvelous body glistening as she vigorously toweled her golden hair. He heard her lilting laughter as she lay on the rec-room floor, throwing Tyke high in the air, with Sally perched atop her bended knees. He smelled the fragrance of her French perfume each time he opened the closet that once had held her clothes.

Odessa, who had not set foot in the McLean house since the day after Sarah's death—the day of her terrible accusations—had directed Greta to pack and ship all of Sarah's clothes, including her jewelry, to Charleston. Cliff couldn't muster the energy to object, although he rescued Sarah's engagement and wedding rings, saving them securely in the wall safe behind the children's picture.

Cliff often thought, thank the good Lord for kindly, competent Greta, who relished her increased responsibilities, becoming the de facto head of the household.

Tyke asked about his mother, talked about her more than Sally, who seemed to sense her father's pain at the mere mention of her mother's name. At Greta's suggestion, Tyke's bed was moved into Sally's room so neither would be alone at night.

Cliff did his best to be home each evening by dinner or at least in time to read the children a bedtime story and tuck them in. Their favorite was Hans Christian Anderson's *Ugly Duckling* which they begged him to read time and again. "Will I grow up to be a swan?" Sally wanted to know each time he read the story. And Cliff's answer always was the same, "You already are a little swan, and when you grow up, you'll be a big beautiful swan."

"Like Mommy?" Tyke would ask.

"Yes, like Mommy," Cliff would swallow hard as he replied. Each night after their bedtime story, the children would slide out of their beds and stand holding hands with their dad in a little circle.

"Now, everyone close your eyes tight, and let's see Mommy," he would say. "Do you see her, Tyke?"

"I think so, Daddy. Yes...yes, I see Mommy."

"Good. Sally?"

"Yes, Daddy. I see Mommy. Do you?"

Squeezing his children's hands, he answered softly, "Yes, Sally...I see Mommy...always. Now let's kneel down, say our prayers, and go to sleep."

* * *

Walter usually called Cliff at least once a week to see how the children were, and every few weeks he and Odessa drove over to Washington to take the children out for an afternoon. But Odessa never got out of their car and never so much as acknowledged Cliff if he were standing in the doorway or on the porch.

As the weeks went by, Cliff eventually became reimmersed in the business. Hal had hired several more salesmen and opened three more sales offices to keep up with their explosive growth. Likewise, Mike had brought a dozen more field maintenance engineers on board and had opened a small training center for his new hires, as well as for maintenance engineers from other companies using their Jet Speed printer, charging them a fee and turning the school into a profit center. Arnie had the Accounting Department well in hand, although he constantly was worried about cash flow and kept pressing Cliff to get the Board's approval to secure a substantial line of credit.

Sam was pumping out several thousand printers a month from the plant, but the order backlog kept growing. "We've got to expand the production lines...we need more inventory...we need more people. Cliff, we need more capital, or we're going to piss away our chance to become a market leader. Please...Cliff," he implored.

Smokey's success in churning out additional driver and install software packages for other systems, including packages to move Jet Speed up from the PC market to the mid-range computer market, was creating additional pressure for increased investment.

Red claimed his shop was on the verge of being able to demonstrate a twenty-five percent increase in dpi resolution, along with an increase in printing speed. It sounded almost too good to be true, but then, Red was unusually cautious for an inventor and had always come through in the past. But that would mean scrapping some equipment and investing in new.

Finally, one late afternoon, when Cliff was alone in his office, Nettie stuck her head in the door, "Mr. C, can I talk to you for a minute?"

"Sure. Come on in. What's up?"

"I think you've got a morale problem on your hands."

"Oh?"

"There's a lot of grumbling over our inability to meet deliveries...to take advantage of our growth. The guys don't understand why you aren't out pursuing a line of credit with a major bank. We know you've been distracted, more than that, broken up over Sarah...but it's been several months now, and we **need** you here on top of things. You hardly ever go out to Chicago anymore. They're feeling like orphans. As great as sales are, Hal says he's losing orders every day because we can't deliver. I know you rely on Mike to spend a part of every week at the plant. But that's not the same as your being there. The guys worry that we're passing up the chance of a lifetime to really hit it big. That if we don't institute a major...and I mean a **major** expansion soon we're going to miss the boat. I'm sorry about bringing this to you, but somebody's got to say it."

"Nettie, you're absolutely right. Honest, I'm not blind to what's happening. But...and I want this to stay in this room...I've got problems with the Board. They've already come up with some additional capital, and, for some reasons, are very reluctant to turn to a major lender."

"Boss...you've got to find a way. We can't pass up this chance."

"I know, Nettie. I know."

"Oops...gotta go."

"What's your hurry?"

"Meeting Arnie for dinner over at Seven Corners. I'm already late. See you tomorrow."

"Sounds like you two are hitting it off. Have a good time," he called after her.

Dashing through the office, she unfastened the barrettes out of her hair, shaking it down around her shoulders, as she called back, "We will...we will!"

"Damn, she's wearing makeup," Cliff spoke aloud to himself. "Now she's **really** got it all together!" he shook his head, smiling wistfully.

* * *

The following morning, Cliff called Oscar McMillan, insisting on a prompt meeting with the Board of Directors. "This can't wait, Oscar. Just because the business has taken off, doesn't mean we don't have serious problems. I've run the numbers and we've got to expand...and quickly...or we're going to miss a golden chance to become a dominant player in the printer market. I'll lay it all out, but I need decisions."

"I hear you, Cliff. But you've got to understand, Jet Speed is only one of the companies in our portfolio. We've got other capital needs.. other problems...we've got to look at the big picture."

"Dammit, Oscar, don't patronize me. I don't need to understand your other problems. What I do understand is that there are vast capital markets out there wanting to invest in growth companies. Maybe going public is the answer, although we really should have a longer track record to command top dollar. You're sitting up there on Wall Street, in a prestigious firm, in the middle of the investment capital of the world. I don't understand your reluctance to deal with this. It's a **happy** problem, for God's sake. I want a Board meeting **now!**"

"Fine. Just calm down, Cliff. How's next Tuesday, say, one o'clock in my office. I'll confirm it with Sidney and Win. Unless you hear differently from me, it's on."

"Thank you, Oscar. I'll come prepared."

"I'm sure you will, Cliff. You always do."

* * *

Upon hanging up the phone, Oscar immediately placed a conference call to Sidney and Winslow. "We've got a problem, fellas.
Cross is no dummy. He wants to know why, with the track record
they're building, we can't approach a major bank for a substantial
line of credit for expansion. Or for that matter, go into the equity
markets, although he recognizes that would be premature. And, you
know what, he's absolutely right, we're going to miss the boat if we
don't get the money to finance a major expansion. Hell, this, potentially, is the best investment we've got going for us."

"We know that, Oscar, but the minute we approach a major bank,
or file a 10K with the SEC, Sidney's problems are going to come to
light. As it is, we've been dragging out our negotiations with the
SEC to avoid their filing an enforcement action against Sidney. When
that happens, the cat's out of the bag," the attorney responded.

"Sid, have you given any more thought to settling?" Oscar asked.

"Ha. Fat chance. You tell him, Win."

"They've got him cold on insider trading, Oscar. You're lucky
they haven't got on your trail, too. This new Congress has already
announced hearings into SEC practices. Now would be the worst
time in the world to try to settle. We could become the poster child
for the SEC being too cozy with Wall Street. If we can drag this out
for another year, things will calm down, and we'll have a much better shot at a reasonable settlement...just a fine and a slap on the wrist."

"So, you're saying our hands are tied...we can't approach a bank
or the equity market," Oscar grumbled.

"If those Congressional investigators got a whiff of Sidney's
shenanigans, we all could be in the soup."

"I know it would cost us an arm and a leg, but what about finding another private investor," Oscar asked. "That way, we don't have
to disclose anything publicly."

"Ya...and give away another big chunk of the company," Sidney
bellowed into the phone.

"All right, Sidney. Can you come up with another five to ten million?" Oscar asked.

"You know I'm stretched like a rubber band. And I don't know what it's going to cost me to settle this SEC thing. And the damn lawyers' fees are bleeding me to death...**Winslow!**"

"Under the circumstances, we probably would have to give away most of the company to get another private investor in at this point. Any sophisticated investor is going to do an awful lot of due diligence before plunking down the cash we need. Cross and his boys really didn't do their homework. They're damn good managers, but they're not financiers. From day one, they haven't understood our machinations," Winslow opined.

"Don't use a word like that, Win...**machinations**...you make us sound Machiavellian," Oscar winced.

"Oscar, this is your attorney you're talking to. Don't bullshit me...I do it for a living."

"So, what are we going to do?" Sidney asked.

"I don't have the foggiest...," Oscar replied. "But put your thinking caps on, because we've got to have some kind of an answer for Cross next Tuesday."

* * *

Cliff, Arnie, and Nettie spent the rest of the week updating the company Business Plan, projecting Revenue, Accounts Receivable, Accounts Payable, Operating Expenses, Cash Flow, and Capital Investment required, under three scenarios: No further growth, modest growth, and expected growth with adequate capital investment. Working past midnight every day and through the weekend, they were bleary-eyed by Monday morning when Nettie fed the last piece of data into the computer to produce the final product.

Sarah's parents had arranged to drive over to Washington on Sunday afternoon to take the children to the zoo. When Odessa learned from the children that they hadn't seen their father for the entire week, it simply confirmed the fear that had been gnawing at her for several months: Cliff was unfit to be a proper Father.

Returning from the zoo, she entered the McLean home for the first time since Sarah's death.

"Too bad Clifford can't be here with the children, isn't it?" she soothingly observed to Greta, as she strolled from room to room, running her fingers across the table tops, opening closets in the kitchen and in the children's room.

"Oh, he spends every minute he can with them, Mrs. Wilson," Greta assured her.

"I'm sure he tries. But a man with his responsibilities...I guess he's got to put them first. The children tell me they haven't seen their father all week," turning toward Greta, she raised her eyebrows.

"This has been an unusual week. Apparently, they're planning some big expansion. Nettie says the next few weeks are really going to be critical."

"Nettie? Who's Nettie?"

"Oh, she's the girl who works with Mr. Cross. She sometimes stops by to look in on the children, or brings Mr. Cross papers from the office so he can work at home. She's awful nice. The children love her. She's always bringing them things."

"Candy...ice cream...sweets?"

"Well...yes...sometimes."

"You know that's bad for their teeth, Greta. You really shouldn't let them get hooked on sweets at their age. It isn't good for them."

"Yes, ma'am."

"What's this girl's name?"

"Nettie."

"I *know* that. I heard you the first time. I mean her last name?"

"Nettie...ah, Yablonski, I think."

"Yablonski? Is she Polish? Where's she from?"

"I think that might be her married name. She came from Chicago. Mr. Cross had her transferred here when he took over the company."

"She moved here without her husband? Is she a divorced woman?"

"I think her husband was killed in the Viet Nam war."

"How old is she?"

"I don't really know, Mrs. Wilson. I guess in her thirties."

"Hmm. Has Clifford ever talked about sending the children to private schools?"

"Not that I know of, Mrs. Wilson."

"Hmm. Well, it was nice talking to you Greta. Let me give these two little darlings a hug, and we'll be on our way. For now."

* * *

Once in the car, Walter looked askance at his wife, "What was the third degree all about, Dess?"

"It's obvious, isn't it? The children aren't being raised properly. He's never home. Greta's just a housekeeper...a foreigner raising our precious grandchildren! And that pushy Pollock, trying to muscle her way in..."

"Dess, you don't even know the woman...and you're the one who picked Greta...who insisted that they hire her."

"Well, it's clear to me that the children need to be sent to a private school, where they can be taught a proper upbringing. Sarah did just fine at Porter-Gaud, and it's only a few miles from home. They could stay with us, expose them to the finer things, of **our** way of life, instead of letting them grow up around that...that **Melungeon** hillbilly."

"Dess...get off it. There's no way you're going to get your hands on those children. Cliff's their father...and he's a good Father, a good provider. He's a young man. He may well get married again. It's quite possible that Sally and Tyke could be raised by a Stepmother. It breaks my heart to think of it. But our Sarah's gone. That's the sad reality we've got to face. And we had better be careful that we don't alienate Cliff, any more than you already have. We should be supportive. That's our proper role as grandparents."

"That's easy for you to say. You're a man. But every time I think of what he did to our Sarah, it makes my blood boil. I'm willing to bide our time, for now, but after the children are home from school all summer, I'll wager by September he'll tire of the responsibility. He'll be happy to have us take them off his hands."

"Dess, you're still in shock over Sarah. This had been a blow that I don't think we're ever going to get over. But, sweetheart, stop deceiving yourself. We're never going to get those children."

"We'll see, Walter. We'll see. If Greta finds another job...or another job finds her, he won't have anywhere else to turn."

"Dess, don't do it."

"Oh, be quiet, Walter. Keep your eyes on the road."

Chapter Seventeen

When Cliff walked into Oscar's conference room on Tuesday with Harold Greenburg at his side, everyone was surprised. Introducing Hal, Cliff casually commented, "Since you put Hal on the Board with me, I thought it was high time he attended a Board meeting. After all, he's my number two, and the man largely responsible for our sales success."

Sidney and Win glanced at each other uneasily, but Oscar extended his hand to Hal, smiling, "Of course. Good to have you here, Hal. Cliff has been voting your proxy...looking out for your interests...while you've been out beating the bushes for us, but there's nothing wrong with you getting exposed to this end of the business. It's a different world, right, boys?"

Both Sidney and Win shook hands with Hal, somewhat reluctantly nodding their assent.

"Well, let's get down to business," Oscar opened his folder. "First item...minutes of the last Board meeting approved...all in favor say, aye. The ayes have it, minutes approved."

"Excuse me, Mr. McMillan," Hal interrupted. "Since I wasn't here at the last meeting, maybe you should put me down as abstaining."

Taken aback, Oscar stuttered, looking over to Cliff, "Well...ah...if you say so...Mr. Greenburg abstains. Now, let's move on to Cliff's monthly report."

Cliff handed out copies of the updated P&L Statement, Balance Sheet, and Cash Flow Report, along with a separate document showing the growing backlog of unfilled orders, and employee overtime hours and costs.

"Damn! You got us in tall clover, boy," Sidney pounded the table. "You sure lowballed your projections last year."

"But the way we're taking off, Sidney, you can see it creates its own set of problems. Backlog's growing...can't meet delivery dates...even with sales booming, we're losing a lot of business because we can't commit to quick delivery. Overtime costs are eating us alive."

"That ought to make old Romanowski happy," Oscar smiled.

"Oh, he is. Sam had him over to the plant for a tour...he gave a little speech to the employees. We gave him all the credit."

"You were there, weren't you?" Oscar asked.

"No, Sam handled it."

"Cliff, you've got to pay more attention to handling the politicians. You should have been there with the Congressman. It's important. The day may come when we'll need him again," Oscar said, nodding at Sidney. "We don't want some low-level factory manager squiring him around."

"I've had a few other things on my mind, Oscar."

"I know, son. We all sympathize with your personal grief. But Romanowski can be very important to us in the future. Why don't you call on him in his Washington office. Make sure he remembers who we are. Find out when he's going to hold his next fundraiser. We'd like to participate...heavily. That'll get his attention."

"Yes, sir. Can we talk about our expansion problems now?"

"Of course. We're just as concerned as you are, son. It's our future..."

"And our money, too!" Sidney emphasized.

Cliff then handed out his forecasts, showing his three scenarios, explaining them in detail, but, hopefully, guiding them to see that only the potential growth scenario made any sense, created the opportunity for them to become the market leader in printers, to maximize their Return on Investment, to make all the stockholders multimillionaires. Although he assumed that the three men he and Hal were dealing with, already were millionaires, many times over.

When he finished, Oscar spoke up, "Excellent! Excellent presentation, my boy. Win, Sidney, and I got together this morning in anticipation of you presenting to us a very persuasive set of facts. You didn't disappoint us. Right, gentlemen?"

"Outstanding...outstanding!" Sidney slapped the table.

"It's all there in black and white," Win nodded his approval.

"We'd like to propose that we pursue three different avenues to raising, say, another ten to fifteen million. That should do the trick, shouldn't it?" Oscar asked.

"Oh, I think ten to twelve is what we need, but, sure, if we could raise another fifteen, without it costing us too much in either interest or equity, that would be great."

"Let's proceed this way: Win and I will talk with our banking connections about a substantial line of credit; I'll explore a possible public stock offering with some of my friends on Wall Street; Sidney will pitch a few of his buddies to see if they might be interested in taking an equity position in the company...maybe a combination debt-equity investment; and you get together with your contacts in the industry to see if we might get one of the big boys interested in buying us. You're well known in the industry. Hell, **Datamation** wrote you up as a **wunderkind**. You could do that, couldn't you?"

"I guess I could. But isn't it premature to be selling out? Don't we need another year's track records under our belts to maximize our potential?"

"Cliff...boy...you're the one who's pushing to get additional capital into the business. We're simply saying let's pursue every option...divide up the effort...each one of us handle the part that we're most familiar with. We do want a substantial cash infusion, right, Hal? Do you agree?" Oscar shook his head affirmatively, turning to Hal.

"We certainly need the cash to expand, Mr. McMillan. How we get it...that's out of my league."

"Well, you just keep on selling those printers. And you start talking to your friends in the industry, Cliff. Quietly, of course. Leave the line of credit and potential stock sale to us. We'll handle that end of it."

"If you say so. I want to think about who might be the best candidates to acquire us...Hal and I can kick it around for a few days...and then I'll start making contacts."

"Good. Let's all get to work," Oscar clapped his hands together as he rose and escorted Cliff and Hal out to the elevators.

* * *

Returning to the conference room, he shrugged, "Well, maybe we've got him off our backs for awhile. Between running the business and looking for a buyer...that ought to keep him busy."

"You know, it's a damn shame that we really can't follow through and get the capital he needs. With that product and that organization he's put together, Jet Speed could become the market leader," Winslow sighed. "Then it **really** would be worth something. Any chance you could find us a private investor, Sid?"

"Not without giving away too much of the company. I say, let 'em make do with what they've got. They've turned the corner. They're making money. Pretty soon we'll be able to start repaying our loans to ourselves. The key is to not let them invest in any expansion. Then we can milk the cash out of the company. Who knows, maybe a year or so from now we'll be in a position to raise more capital. But not ours. Somebody else's."

"I agree with Sid," Win nodded. "Keep stringing them along. Maybe the kid will find a buyer. He's got moxie, I'll give him that."

"Well, leading him on like this doesn't pleasure me, fellas, but I guess we've got no choice. You're right, Win, maybe he just might find a buyer."

* * *

On their flight home, Cliff and Hal rehashed the meeting and began compiling a list of potential buyers with the names of the key executives they knew personally. They decided that their old company Tektron might be a good fit. Tektron wasn't in the printer business. Nor were they in the PC business. Jet Speed could give them a toehold in both. Cliff, Hal, and the rest of the fellows had all left the company on good terms. Everybody knew one another's strengths and weaknesses. Tektron wouldn't be buying a pig in a poke. And it certainly had the financial wherewithal to fund a major expansion at Jet Speed. Yes, they decided, their old company was a prime candidate.

As they parted at Washington National, Hal to catch a cab, and Cliff to get his car, Cliff said, "How we approach them is very important. They can't think we're desperate...and we're not. Let's sleep on it and put our heads together tomorrow. But not a word to anyone else."

"Wouldn't it be nice if we could get them to approach us?"

"Hey, Hal," Cliff called out to his departing friend, "you figure out how to do that and I'll owe you a big one."

* * *

As Cliff was dodging vehicles to get across the street to the parking lot, a voice from the curb on the other side squealed at him, "Look out! You're going to get run over!"

Hopping up onto the curb, he nearly stumbled into a flight attendant. Looking up, his eyes widened in surprise, "Krissy!"

"Hello, stranger," she replied, coolly.

"Gee, it's good to see you. It's been a long time."

"Too long." After posing for a moment in her practiced pout, she bathed him in her best Farrah Fawcett smile.

"Need a lift?"

Even though her car was in the parking lot, she didn't hesitate, "Sure, I'd like that...if it's not out of your way."

"Of course, it's out of my way. That's what makes my offer special."

"Haven't lost your charm, big guy."

"Hope not. Here's my van. Hop in," he held the door for her as she tossed her clothes bag in the back seat. Following her directions, he drove south on Shirley Highway, turning off on Seminary Road and into the parking lot in front of her high-rise.

"Want to come in for a drink? My roommate's on her LA run."

"Sure."

"Well, that's progress. You never did take me up on my invitation to cook you a gourmet dinner."

Cliff simply shrugged and said nothing until they both were settled on the couch with two frozen daiquiris on the coffee table in front of them. "Krissy, there's something I'd like to tell you."

"I'm a good listener, Cliff."

"Well...when we first met, I was married. I admit I was..."

"I know."

"You knew?"

"Well, not at first. But I saw the story in the *Washington Post*...computer executive's wife killed in car crash. Mrs. Clifford Cross...then I read the obituary the next day. I'm sorry, Cliff."

"Well...I don't know what to say."

"Don't say anything," she leaned over and put her finger on his lips.

He took her hand, patted it, half-whispered, "Thank you," and then raised his glass to her. She responded by raising her glass to him and taking a sip while not taking her eyes off him.

"You free for dinner Saturday night?" he asked.

"I'm not free...but I'm cheap," she giggled. "What time?"

"Pick you up around seven?"

"You got a deal."

"I better get going. If you read the story in the paper, you know I've got two little ones to worry about."

"I'd love to meet them," she said as they walked to the door, holding hands.

"I don't think it would be appropriate, yet, Krissy. In fact, I'm not sure our going out together this soon is proper. I guess that's something I'll have to think about. Maybe get some advice. I'm really not up on these kinds of things."

"But we are having dinner Saturday? You're not backing out...again?"

"No, I'm not backing out," he smiled, "but I never did actually commit to dinner before. I said maybe."

"No matter. I forgive you, anyway," she put her arms around him, and he pulled her to him, embracing.

* * *

The next morning, Hal walked into Cliff's office, closing the door behind him. "Been thinking about our conversation yesterday. Got an idea for you, Tonto."

"Shoot, kemo sabe."

"Why don't you contact some of the people you know over at Wang. They might be interested in us. Sometimes they buy OEM printers and put their brand name on them. While you're doing that, I'll talk to some of our buddies at Tektron...let it slip that Wang's talking about acquiring us. Tell them it worries me about being gobbled up by a company that's already so big in the PC and mid-range markets. Gently suggest that it's a new market Tektron might want to get into. We'd certainly give them a ready-made toehold. If they bite, I'll tell them I'll feel you out and see if you'd be willing to meet with them. We'll wait a couple of days, then I'll call them and say, sure, you'd be willing to listen. Doesn't cost anything to listen. Then let them call you and set up a meeting. What do you think?"

"Sounds good to me. I worry about word getting out that we're looking for a buyer. But if Wang has any interest, and I think they probably would at least want to talk to us, they'd want to keep our talks quiet. The last thing they'd want would be for one of their competitors to get wind of our discussions and enter into a bidding war. Let's do it. *Caveat emptor.*"

"Hey, I didn't know you Indians could talk Latin."

"Get the hell out of here before I scalp you."

Cliff then went out to Nettie's desk, picked up her Rolodex, and took it into his office to get the phone number at Wang. He returned it, went into his office and closed the door. His contact at Wang wasn't in, and Cliff didn't want to leave a message, so he said he'd call back later.

At noon, when Nettie delivered a tuna sandwich and Diet Coke, she scowled at him, "Okay, Mr. C. What's going on?"

"What are you talking about?"

"Come on. If you and Hal are going to have a hush-hush meeting, and then going to place your own secret phone call with the door shut, when you return my Rolodex, you at least shouldn't leave it open to Wang's phone number."

"Uh-oh. Caught in the act. Nettie, for once, will you tend to your own knitting? Trust me. There is nothing you need to know right now. Nothing that anybody needs to know. If and when there is something real to discuss, you'll be among the first to know. I promise you. Now, get out of here and let me eat my lunch in peace."

"I just thought, maybe, I could help. You usually ask my opinion on things."

"Nettie..."

"I'm going. I'm going."

Cliff wrapped up his work at the office, stuffed his briefcase full of papers, and left in time to be at the bus stop when Sally arrived home from school. Greta had picked up Tyke from kindergarten in the new Jeep Cherokee he had bought to replace the wrecked Mercedes.

Waiting at the bus stop, he worried about inviting Krissy out to dinner Saturday night. Was it too soon? Who could he ask? How serious should he let it get? Assuming she was interested. She certainly came on strong. And she certainly turned him on. Truthfully, he admitted to himself, from the first time he saw her. Then he felt a pang of guilt. As much as he loved Sarah, how could he let himself even have these thoughts? Maybe Odessa was right. Maybe I am no damn good. He shook the thought out of his mind as Sally jumped down off the last step of the school bus, ran toward him, and threw her arms around him. "I love you, Daddy."

"I love you, too, sweetheart," he squeezed her tightly.

* * *

Friday afternoon, Hal walked into Cliff's office, closing the door behind him. "Having lunch with Charlie Lambert and Gus Sarius next Friday. They wanted to know what it was all about, so I gave them a teaser...said there might be one of the big boys interested in acquiring us, and I'd appreciate their thoughts on how to go about it. Told them we didn't have any experience with something like this. Right off, Gus said, 'Don't be moving too fast. Let's sit down and talk about it.' I think his wheels started turning right away."

"Good. You know, the more I think about it, Tektron would be one hell of a good fit. And we all know each other. Less chance of a clash of personalities turning the deal sour down the road, like you read about happening so often in mergers. Too bad though that we couldn't put this off for another year...develop a longer track record first."

"Based on our New York meeting, I guess we've got no choice. Maybe Mr. McMillan and his cohorts will come up with a line of credit so we don't have to sell out."

"Tell you what bothers me, Hal. The way we turned things around...and with your bulging order book, I don't understand why it wouldn't be relatively easy for us to get a line of credit. I was tempted to start pursuing one on my own, but Oscar was adamant about their handling it in New York. There's more to this than meets the eye. I just hope they know what they're doing. Best we run the business, do our part looking for a potential buyer, and keep our fingers crossed."

"You're the boss, Tonto. You've brought us this far. My money's on you."

The old knot returned to Cliff's stomach, as he stared at his compatriot for a long moment. "Can I ask you something personal, Hal?"

"Sure. What is it?"

"Well, this is probably a dumb question...but, after a man's wife dies, how long should he be in mourning? I mean...well, you know...ah, in one sense, I suppose you're in mourning...grieving...for years...especially if you really loved her. I mean, really, *really* loved her. But is it all right to look at another woman? Now, that's a stupid question. Of course it's all right. But how soon? When, for example, would it be proper to invite someone out for dinner. Nothing serious, mind you. Just dinner."

"Cliff, it's been how long since Sarah's death...nearly eight months?"

"Eight months last Monday."

"Old friend, you've been handling yourself in an exemplary fashion. We've all been bleeding for you. Sarah wouldn't want you to shrivel up and die. You're honoring her memory by the way you're so devoted to those two kids. Hell, we've talked about you not spending enough time on the business. But we understand. You got your priorities straight. You're also human...a young man. There's nothing wrong with you starting to see someone else. Hey, go to it, man. You're entitled. Nobody's going to find any fault in it."

"Thanks, Hal. I appreciate your words. But I feel so damn guilty when I even think of seeing another woman. And yet, I guess it isn't going to stop me."

"Is there someone special?"

"No. Well, at least not yet. But there might be."

"Do I know her?"

"No."

"Hmm...I guess I was thinking maybe...never mind. Let me know if I can do anything to help. Maybe Bev and I could have you and what's-her-name over for dinner."

"I'm not there, yet, Hal. But maybe later."

* * *

Saturday night, Cliff knocked on Krissy's door at exactly seven. It seemed to open itself, ever so slowly, and standing there, in the dark, in front of her picture window, in the early moon glow of a late March evening, she appeared ravishing. Her snug black-knit mini-dress was belted by a narrow gold chain accentuating her ample curves. Her long blond hair hung loosely at her shoulders, half-hiding a gold choke collar around her neck, which matched the gold tips and spiked heels of her black suede pumps. Her best Farrah Fawcett smile glistened in the shadows.

"Hi, Cliff," she murmured.

"Evening, Krissy. You look...you look...**pulchritudinous**," he stammered.

"What?" she laughed.

"That means four thousand percent better than okay. Okay?"

"If you say so," she held out her hand until he walked over to her, and then she kissed him on the cheek. "Throw my wrap, there, over my shoulders and tell me where I'm going to be wooed tonight."

"I made dinner reservations at the Four Seasons. Suit you?"

"Wonderful. Come to think of it, the Basin Street Blues isn't too far from there. It's really a hot jazz place. Could we go there after dinner?"

"Sure, if you like."

After valet parking the Cherokee, as they strolled the long length of the Four Seasons entrance hall and down the stairs to the five-star restaurant, people glanced admiringly at the dazzling couple. For an instant, Cliff thought he was with Sarah again.

As they were handed menus, Cliff asked, "Would you like a cocktail before dinner?"

"Why don't we just have wine with dinner, if we're going to have a few drinks later at the Blues."

"Fine. You go ahead and order. Ladies first."

"No. You order for the both of us. I like everything. Surprise me."

"Okay. Let's see...how about a bottle of Mouton Cadet Red Bordeaux, two Caesar salads, and two steak Diane flambés, medium rare, with stuffed baked potatoes."

Midway through their dinner, Cliff felt the tip of Krissy's shoe rubbing his ankle. "Keep that up," he smiled, "and we may never to make it to the jazz joint." Then he remembered Sarah doing that in the school library and was awash in shame.

"The evening's young," she blew a kiss at him.

Although the Basin Street Blues was packed, a twenty dollar bill got Cliff a table near the stage. He decided that was a mistake because they couldn't hear each other talk, but Krissy seemed to enjoy the jazz and the ambience, rocking her body and drumming on the table to the beat of the music. He was surprised when a gentleman with a French accent, who appeared to be the owner or at least the manager, made his way through the crowd to their table, held out his arms, and droned, "Krissy, *mon cher*, where have you been?"

"Jean Paul...it's lovely to see you," she replied, accepting his kisses on both her cheeks. "Please meet my friend, Clifford Cross."

After exchanging pleasantries, as he retreated, Jean Paul shook his finger at Krissy, "You must come back soon. I missed you. Call me. *Bon soir*," he bowed to Cliff.

"Well, you get around," Cliff seemed disconcerted.

"Oh, Jean Paul's just an old friend." Finishing her second daiquiri, she said, "Come on, pay the bill and let's get out if here. I know a great after-hours club. We can dance."

"Gee, Krissy, I'm not much of a dancer. Actually, I think we better be calling it an evening. It's past midnight."

"Cliff, you're not a party pooper, are you? The night's still young."

"Not for me, it isn't. I really do have to get home. Remember, I've got two little ones to think about."

"Surely, they're asleep by now. Do you have a babysitter problem?"

"Not exactly. But I really do have to go. Okay? We've had a great time tonight. Haven't we?"

"So far...perfect."

After paying the bill and retrieving the car, on their way to Krissy's apartment, Cliff reached across the seat and took hold of her hand. "I really enjoyed this evening, Krissy. Thanks."

"Me, too, Cliff. You can come up, can't you? Mary Catherine might be there, but she'll be asleep, or otherwise busy in her bedroom."

He didn't answer her until they were in the elevator on their way up to her apartment, because he couldn't decide what his reply should be. He knew what he wanted it to be, but then another wave of guilt washed through him. At the door, he said, "How about next Saturday night? Maybe dinner and a show?"

"Aren't you coming in?"

"Not tonight. Maybe next Saturday night. You free?"

"Why don't you give me a call when I get back in town Thursday evening."

"Fine. It's a deal." He reached to pull her toward him, but she gave him a peck on the cheek and disappeared behind her door.

The following Monday morning, Cliff closed his office door, phoned the florist, and sent Krissy a dozen long-stemmed red roses, with the card, "You make Saturday night come alive—Cliff."

Chapter Eighteen

Jumper Ramsey and Joe Joe Karns were practically delirious over the success of their marijuana venture. It had exceeded their fondest expectations. They had begun their harvest about a month after the high-school class reunion. Of the one thousand plants they set in along the abandoned logging road, about eight hundred survived. By Labor Day they had completed the harvest, trimmed the leaves and buds, and hung them throughout the old farmhouse to dry.

As the early morning frosts glistened atop the valley meadows, and the leaves of fall turned the Appalachians into a cacophony of blazing colors, Jumper and Joe Joe worked long hours into the night, packaging their precious product in one-pound plastic bags. By mid-November, Joe Joe made his first sales at the Charleston Auto Auction, delivering five one-pound bags to his used-car buddies for $450 a bag. That Friday night, flush with over thousand dollars each in their pockets, Jumper and Joe Joe hit every bar in Beckley. Rousted out of bed at noon the next morning by his mother, Jumper swallowed four aspirins, a quart of water, shaved while soaking in the bathtub, and gobbled down six powdered donuts with a mug of black coffee. By late afternoon, he had purchased a new gray and white checkered suit, a cashmere sport coat, two pairs of pants, three pairs of shoes, several shirts, and paid off Doc Ketterman for his dental work. At suppertime, he met Joe Joe at their favorite hangout, the

Moonshiner, where they dined on beer nuts and boilermakers, again setting up several drinks for his buddies. By the time he staggered up the steps to his bedroom and emptied his pockets onto his dresser, he had eleven dollars left.

* * *

The following week, Jumper and Joe Joe decided they had had their celebration and resolved to save every penny from their new business. Joe Joe could easily survive on his income from the used-car lot, and Jumper persuaded May Belle Hanik's husband, Skeeter, who ran the Moonshiner, to put him back behind the bar four nights a week.

Within a few weeks, Joe Joe had connected with all the right boys at the auction. He was delivering twenty-five one-pound bags of MJ weekly at $450 a pound. Each Friday night, he and Jumper met at the farmhouse, counted out the cash in two stacks, $5,625 each. Relenting on their resolve, but only slightly, each peeled off $125, stuffed it in their pockets, and carefully wrapped the rest in two plastic bags. With their flashlights in one hand and their booty in the other, they picked their way deep into the abandoned coal mine. At the very end, they unearthed a boulder, reached down into a hole, and together lifted out a metal suitcase. Unlocking it, they tucked their plastic bags in alongside the others already there. Relocking and replacing the suitcase in the hole, they rolled the boulder back over it, high-fived each other, and stumbled out through the coal mine, whooping and laughing hysterically, into the cold night air.

Their operation could not have gone more smoothly. After all the leaves and buds had been cured, weighed, and packaged in one-pound plastic bags, they were stored on makeshift shelves deep inside the abandoned mine, where the humidity and 60-degree temperature would keep their product fresh. Every Thursday evening they stuffed twenty-five bags inside the deflated spare tire of Joe Joe's Cadillac, and on Fridays, before dawn, Joe Joe departed for Charleston. At the auction, he dealt only with used-car dealers he had known for at least a few years, even refusing to deal with their friends to whom he was introduced. Nor would he ever make an exchange with a customer within sight of anyone else, not even another customer. He usually conducted his transactions sitting in his car, in his customer's car, or underneath two adjacent stalls in the men's room. Late that evening, he and Jumper would go through their ritual of dividing and hiding their cash.

During the New Year's Eve celebration at the Moonshiner, after several drinks, Joe Joe couldn't resist sauntering into the back room where the usual illegal card game was under way, pull a wooden chair out from the wall, turn it around backwards, and slide up to watch the play.

Skeeter, who was running the five-stud poker game, said, "Want in, Joe Joe? Twenty dollar limit."

"Not now. Maybe later," he took in a deep breath and glanced up at the blanket of cigarette and cigar smoke curling around the shaded lightbulb hanging from the ceiling. The room was redolent with the sweet smell of marijuana. "Who's got the MJ?"

"I got a couple'a joints left," Skeeter replied. "Want one?"

"Naa. Smokin' blunts, myself." Joe Joe reached into his inside coat pocket and pulled out what appeared to be a normal cigar. Lighting it, he tilted his head back and blew a smoke ring into the air.

The four poker players took a whiff in unison, and Jep Bittle exclaimed, "That's potent stuff, Joe Joe. Where the hell did you get it?"

Smirking, Joe Joe winked, "Oh, I got my sources."

"Come on, Joe Joe, don't hold out on us," Skeeter laid his cards facedown on the table, and sat back, staring at Joe Joe in silence. The others followed.

Looking around the room and out through the swinging doors leading to the bar, he then shrugged, "Guess I know you bums a lot longer than the people I been dealing with. I got a connection. This here blunt's nothing more than a hollowed-out cigar filled with a couple'a grams of Mary Jane. Packs a wallop of about four joints. Here, try them." He handed out cigars to his four friends. They all lit up, leaned back, and looked up into the ceiling.

"This mean you got access to nickel bags?" Jep asked.

"Sure...I could supply ya...nickel bags, by the ounce, or by the pound."

"You gotta be shitting us," Skeeter lowered his head, looking askance. "For how much?"

"Oh, I guess...about sixty dollars an ounce...maybe a little less for you guys. You can get about sixty joints out of an ounce...so you figure."

"Hey, at that price, I could go for couple'a joints a night. So could some of the young guys that come into the gas station," Jep nodded. "If you're sure you can deliver, put me in for an ounce each week."

"Me and Walter could split an ounce, right?" Jake looked across the table.

"Sure. Count me in."

"I bet I could move at least half a pound right here in the bar," Skeeter rapped the table with his knuckles. "When can you deliver?"

"Saturday nights," Joe Joe replied. "But you guys gotta swear you ain't tellin' nobody. I mean *nobody!*"

"You got our word, Joe Joe," they all nodded soberly.

Although the Moonshiner was closed at two o'clock, several of the regulars stayed until sunup. Jumper hung up his apron on a wall peg and joined his buddies. Joe Joe took him by the arm and led him over to a quiet corner of the bar. "Jump...got us a real sweet deal."

"Like what?"

"Boys in the back was lighting up joints, so I give 'em a whiff of one of my blunts. One thing led to another, and before you know, they were all over me to supply them with several ounces a week...retail! Skeeter says he can easy move half a pound a week right in the bar. Be good for business. Didn't even ask for a cut. Hell, we can probably move a pound a week right here in town... retail...without no trouble."

"Joe Joe, I thought we agreed we was only going to be selling wholesale...only up to Charleston, to the guys you know."

"Ya, but listen to me. We only sell it to guys we know. Retail, Jump...retail! At sixty dollars an ounce, we can clear nearly a thousand a week extra. Think about it! Without no trouble."

"That wasn't our deal. How do you know somebody isn't going to blab it around town?"

"Only to our friends, Jump. The guys in the back gave me their word...their solemn promise...nobody would know where it came from."

"Well, you're the salesman. If you want to do it, go ahead...but I'm not touching it."

"Hell, Jump, with you being here in the bar four nights a week...knowing everybody...you at least could make some of the deliveries. We'd still split fifty-fifty. All right, I'll do all the selling. But if somebody we know real well comes asking, you at least could pass it on to me. Right?"

"Well, I suppose I could do that. But, I'm not lifting a finger to sell any here in the bar. You got that straight?"

"Ya, sure, Jump. I'll sell it. Me and you can make it up in ounce bags out at the farmhouse, and I'll deliver it...unless it's one of our real close buddies you see in here all the time. You could slip him a couple'a ounces. Wouldn't even be out of your way. Wouldn't even have to do it direct. There're real slick ways of makin' an exchange without even talking or touching each other."

"Like how?"

"Well, first, I agree with you, Jump, we don't deal with nobody we don't know real well. Then, let's just say, one of our buddies comes in and buys a beer...gives you a wink, and taps the bottle with two fingers. You let me know it's two ounces for whoever, we make it up on Thursday night when we're packing up my run for Charleston, and then, Saturday, when he shows up in the bar, you tape his packet inside a paper bag behind the commode in the men's room. He goes in...gets it...puts the money in the paper bag...sticks it behind the commode...and you retrieve it. Slick as a cat's ass. What'a you say?"

"Well...I suppose we could try it. But, by God, Joe Joe, you better know what you're doing!"

"Trust me, Jumper...trust me."

Although Jumper had misgivings and was extremely nervous when he made his first delivery, taping it behind the toilet in the men's room, as weeks went by, he had no problems and grew accustomed to the routine. It was simple and seemed quite safe.

As the snows blanketed the mountains and piled up drifts in the valleys, Joe Joe had to open the lane leading back to the farm with his snowplow from the car lot. But they worried that the plowed road might attract attention, so they veered off away from the farmhouse down to a frozen little creek, where they stopped plowing. Each Thursday night they trudged up along the creek in a wide circle, coming down through the upper woods to the back of the farmhouse to prepare their packages. Then, with their carefully doled-out twenty-six pounds of marijuana, they retraced their steps.

By the time their boots were squishing through the first thaw in the valley, they had nearly two hundred thousand dollars between them stashed securely in the coal mine.

"I'd say we're about ready to make our play for old-man Siefert's Ford dealership." Joe Joe grinned at his partner.

"Best I be giving Cliff a call. We need him to make it work."

That night Jumper went home and dug out the program from the class reunion which listed everyone's home address and phone number. He dialed up Cliff's number, but a pleasant lady on the other end informed him that Cliff wasn't expected until late that evening, but would give him the message.

"Thank you, ma'am, but just tell Cliff, Jumper called. I got his office number. I'll try there tomorrow."

The next morning, Nettie stuck her head in Cliff's office, "That fella, Jumper, is on the phone for you. Want me to handle it?"

"Nobody can handle Jumper," he rolled his eyeballs. "Put it through."

"Hey, Jump, what's up?"

"Cliff...how you doing? Boy, that was a great reunion we had, wasn't it? Sure sorry about your wife. Must'a been quite a shock."

"Certainly was, Jumper. But thanks for the mountain laurel. It sure was different from all the other flowers. Sure brought back some memories of you and me hiking and hunting through the mountains. Really was thoughtful."

"Hey, what are old friends for. Really felt for you, Cliff. Ah...reason I'm calling...remember we talked about buying that Ford dealership up in Oak Hill?"

"Ya. How you coming on that?"

"Me and Joe Joe got a good bit of money saved up...we really been socking it away from a little side venture we got...you'd be proud of us. Like we talked before, if you was to come in with us, that'd go a long way with old-man Siefert, and with the Ford people, who'd have to approve the deal. Me and Joe Joe would like to come on over to Washington to talk to you about it. I think you'd be surprised at how...how...*ma-chured*...we both are. We got our heads screwed on right, Cliff. We could come whenever you say, to suit you...only Fridays ain't no good."

"Jump...you know, I've already bitten off about more that I can chew."

"You said you'd help. Be like old times...us together...getting all juiced up for a different kind of competition. Be like homecoming for you...back to your roots...helping the community...creating jobs."

"Jump, I said I'd be happy to help, analyzing the deal..."

"Let us come over to at least talk. I think it's important that we sit down before we approach Siefert."

"I don't know, Jump. Tell you what...I'm bringing the kids over to my parents for Easter weekend. Maybe we could sit down then."

"Sounds great, Cliff. I knew you wouldn't let us down. How about Saturday night? I'm bartending at the Moonshiner...just for pin money...but I could switch with Skeeter. Maybe have a few pops and get down to business in the back room. Maybe dinner first. I'll buy."

"I'd like to spend the evening with my folks. Make sure the kids get settled in bed. Why don't we figure, I'll slip down around ten o'clock?"

"Sounds terrific. Just like old times. See you then."

* * *

Hal's lunch with his former Tektron colleagues went extremely well. Before he could say very much, Gus Sarius expressed their interest. "You tell Cliff not to move too fast. He should be leery of selling out to one of the big PC makers. They'll take your printer...which is damn good...integrate it into their system, and dump you guys. We've already talked it over with Gil, and he's given us the green light to explore you getting together with us."

"How is the old rascal?"

"Since he's been made CEO, he's calmed down a bit," Charlie Lambert replied. "But he's a goer. Suggested we get together with you and Cliff...sign some nondisclosure agreements...you give us your financials to look at. After we digest them, let us have a look at your facility in Chicago...probably on a weekend so as not to arouse suspicion. If we're still interested at that point, you give us your asking price, and Gil will sit down with you and your investors to see if we can negotiate a deal."

"Makes sense," Hal nodded. "We're in no hurry, but I'm concerned about these other negotiations that Cliff apparently is engaged in. I really don't know the status. Why don't you guys give Cliff a call. I'll suggest that he try to slow down any other discussions."

After they agreed on their approach, Hal returned to the office to report to Cliff. "I think they're really serious. I suggested that you were already talking to other players in the industry. Implied that we were being courted. Have you talked to Wang yet?"

"No. Let's keep that one in our hip pocket until we see where this one leads."

"We should begin putting together a nice-looking package for them...more that just our financials...but not make any further move toward them until they contact you."

Grinning, Cliff replied, "They already have."

"What? I only left them forty-five minutes ago. Stopped off at the cleaners on my way back here."

"Yep. Gus called me. Didn't beat around the bush. You know Gus. Asked if we could get our financials to him early next week. Give them a few days to look at them, and then, possibly take him, Charlie, and Lester Berry from Engineering out to Chicago next weekend."

"I assume you agreed."

"Sure. But we're going to have to bring Arnie and Nettie into this, if we hope to get a packet put together that includes more than just financials. Looks like another weekender."

"No problem. But don't you think we should bring Mike and the boys in Chicago into it too? They could be helpful, putting together part of the package...emphasizing the capabilities of their departments...And if they found out we were doing this behind their backs, they could get ticked off."

"Right. Good point. Nettie...hey Nettie...get Red, Smokey, and Sam on a conference call, and you, Arnie, and Mike come on in here."

It was nearly six...five o'clock Chicago time...before Nettie had everyone assembled, either in Cliff's office or on the phone. Cliff outlined the possibility of selling the company to Tektron, emphasizing that it would provide them with the cash they needed to expand, and that it would be opening up a new market for Tektron, so they should not be absorbed into any existing operation. In fact, if the negotiations got serious, he would insist that they continue to function as their own operating unit. Possibly, down the road, they could even become the nucleus for a larger integrated systems division. To his great relief, everyone was enthusiastic.

After dividing up their assignments to prepare a first-class packet emphasizing Jet Speed's capabilities, including updated projections of their growth potential with the necessary cash infusion, Cliff shook his fist in the air, beaming, "What a team we've got! What a chance! Let's get some pizza in here and get to it right away. You guys in Chicago know what to do, right?" he called into his squawk box. Back came a simultaneous jumble of replies—all boisterously positive.

"Ah...would you mind if Nettie and I got started tomorrow morning?" Arnie looked at Cliff, wincing. "We're meeting some of her friends from Chicago for dinner tonight. They're in for the weekend. But we can work all day tomorrow. Promised to take them to a show tomorrow evening, and then see the sights Sunday afternoon. But we can be in here Sunday evening."

"Sorry, boss," Nettie shrugged, "but this has been planned for a long time. They arrived this afternoon. We'll get our parts done. Arnie can update his financials on the computer pretty easily, and there won't be a lot for me to do until the subsections of the packet are ready to be put together. I'll work all night Sunday, if that's what it takes."

A bit deflated, Cliff said, "Sure. We'll get it done. Why don't you all get out of here, and let's get started around eight tomorrow morning."

As they departed, he suddenly realized, that in the excitement, he had forgotten to call Krissy the night before, as he had promised.

She was not a happy camper when she heard his voice. "I'm sorry, Krissy. I've been inundated here."

"At least, you could have taken one minute to call." There was an edge on her voice that he had not heard before.

"I know. It was damn thoughtless of me. A major...and I mean *major* opportunity has presented itself."

"What could be so important that you couldn't even take two seconds to call me, when you promised?"

"Well, it's still quite preliminary, but we've got the chance, possibly, to sell the company. We're talking big bucks...potentially, that is."

Softening, she purred, "At least you could have called me. I was worried...thought maybe something happened to you."

"No, nothing happened to me, except I'm up to my ears here at the office. To make matters worse, looks like I'm going to have to work through the weekend. Tomorrow night's probably out. Of course, you didn't say yes for sure."

"You know my answer would be yes. Can't a girl be a little coy? I was the one practically begging you to come in last Saturday night. You rejected me."

"That's not exactly the way I'd put it, Krissy. Special things are worth waiting for."

"Looks like it's going to be a long wait. Now you're telling me tomorrow night's out."

"I'm sorry. But what I'm into right now could mean a lot...maybe for the both of us someday."

"If you put it like that, Cliff, I guess I'll just have to wait."

"What about tonight? Could we at least catch a bite together?"

"I probably should play hard-to-get. I'll be ready in twenty minutes. There's a nice little bistro in Shirlington where we can have dinner."

"Make it half an hour."

"I'll be waiting downstairs in the lobby for you."

When Cliff pulled up to the front of the apartment building, Krissy waved, and scurried out to the car, jumping in before he had a chance to go around to the other side to open the door. Leaning across the seat, she kissed him on the cheek and squeezed his thigh. "Cliff,

I'm so sorry I acted like a bitch on the phone. I know what you're doing is very important...you must be under a lot of stress. Forgive me. I want to be a comfort zone for you, not another one of your problems."

"Nothing to forgive you. But thanks for saying it. I get so wrapped up in what I'm doing that I become very thoughtless when it comes to the people I really care about."

"Does that include me?"

"You little vixen...more and more every day," he took her hand off his thigh and squeezed.

They had a bottle of Chianti and spaghetti, along with mixed green salads and fresh hot-buttered Italian bread. It was nearly ten when they got back to her apartment. At the door, he took her in his arms, kissed her, and whispered in her ear, "You inviting me in, tonight?"

"If you're sure."

"I'm sure," he nodded, taking the key from her hand and opening the door.

A Barbra Streisand tape was softly playing "The Way We Were," in the background, and only a table lamp next to the couch illuminated the room. Curled up on the couch next to the lamp, reading a book, was Krissy's roommate, Mary Catherine.

"Hi," Krissy was taken aback. "I thought you were on the red-eye run tonight. What happened? Oh, excuse me, you remember Cliff?"

"How could I forget! Hi, Cliff. Got bumped. Got a puddle-jumper tomorrow morning. You two want some hot chocolate?"

"No thanks," they both replied.

"Well...ah...," Cliff stammered, "I better be going. Got a big day tomorrow."

Krissy looked at him, raising her eyebrows, and shrugging. "I'll walk you out to your car."

"Fine. Nice to see you again," he waved to Mary Catherine.

On the elevator on the way down, Krissy purred, "I'm so sorry, Cliff. I thought for sure she was gone."

"I know. These things happen. Maybe next week...no...that's no good. I've got to be at the plant with these prospects I was telling you about. I'll call you when you get back in town Thursday. We'll figure something out for the following week. Okay?"

"Promise?"

"Promise," he replied as they embraced outside the lobby, and she went back inside, standing at the window, waving at him as he drove away.

Chapter Nineteen

When Cliff arrived at the office, a few minutes before seven on Monday morning, to his surprise, Nettie was still there, standing at the Xerox, making copies of their packet for presentation to Tektron. "Almost done, Mr. C.," she took a deep breath, hunching up her shoulders and exhaling. "Took a little longer than I thought."

"You sure don't look any worse for the wear," he smiled, studying her for a long moment. She had let her long black hair out of her bun and down around her shoulders, the tips laying softly over her exposed shoulder blades above the embroidered peasant blouse that he recalled her wearing on the night they had their dinner in Chicago. Beneath her formfitting jeans, she wore her high-heeled, open-toed black shoes.

"You been here all night, working in those high heels? Don't they hurt?"

"When you're as little as I am, you need all the height you can get. But that's something you surely wouldn't know anything about. You have to duck going through doorways. I have to stand up on the bench when I go to football games to see anything."

"Well, I sure appreciate you getting our package together. Sorry about creating a problem for you and Arnie. Have a good time on your dates this weekend?"

"They weren't dates, Mr. C. We're just real good friends."

193

"Don't kid the kidder, Nettie. An attractive, young woman as you...I'll bet the guys are swarming around you like bees around honey. And don't think I haven't noticed how Arnie practically gets moonstruck each time you walk into the room."

"Come on...quit making fun of me. I admit, I like Arnie a lot. But that's all. He's not my type."

"Now let's see...you told me out in Chicago that the boys from your neighborhood...I suppose, pretty rough and tumble steelworkers...were not your type. Now, here's Arnie...smart, sophisticated, educated, serious-minded, solid as a rock...and he's not your type. Just what is your type?"

Nettie looked down at the floor, swallowed hard, and then looked up at him with tears in her eyes, "You wouldn't understand." She threw her papers on the Xerox machine and darted off into the ladies' room.

When she came out, Cliff was standing at her desk. "I'm sorry, Nettie. That whole conversation was none of my business. I sometimes forget what you went through...Viet Nam...your husband, what was his name, Nick? I'm sure he was a wonderful man. If anyone should appreciate the lingering pain that goes with losing a loved one, it's me. After Sarah...after losing a husband or a wife...life can never be the same. At least you're lucky not to have had any children to worry about."

"Is that right? Well, thank you for telling me how nice it is that I'll never have any children," Nettie seemed to rise up out of her high heels, her eyes blazing into his face. "You're the most insensitive bastard I've ever known!" With that, she turned her back on him and returned to the copier.

Cliff hung his head and mumbled as he dragged his feet back into his office, "Whew...thank you for telling me something I didn't already know."

Fortunately, the office was coming alive. Hal, Mike, and Arnie were pouring through the final package to be certain there were no mistakes. Cliff joined them in the conference room, instructing Arnie to call Nettie in. "You all have done next to the impossible...putting this classy document together on such short notice. Nettie, make sure I call the guys in Chicago to tell them, too."

"Yes, sir."

"Hal, why don't you arrange to get this to Gus and Charlie. I think it's important that you actually go through it with them, page by page. Make sure they understand it. After all, we're selling. Try to see if we have any weak spots, so we can be prepared to answer them when we meet them at the plant next weekend. You'll try to confirm next Sunday. Right?"

"Right," Hal replied. "This deal's my reason for breathing. I'd recommend that Mike go out there with us, too. In case they have field maintenance questions."

"Good idea. We ought to get out there Saturday, so we can get ourselves organized. Okay with you, Mike?"

"Sure. I've been spending a day or two at the plant every week, anyway, to stay on top of Engineering Change Orders for the field. I need to interview some applicants for our new office in Milwaukee, so I might just slip up there Monday."

"Okay, guys," Cliff shook his fist enthusiastically in the air, "let's get moving! Nettie, could I see you in my office for a minute?"

Nettie walked into Cliff's office, staring at him coldly. "What can I say, Nettie? Of course, you're right. I try to be helpful...to show how much I appreciate what you do...to let you know I *feel* for what you've gone through...and I only make it worse...all the wrong words come out," he looked at her imploringly.

"I know, boss," she shrugged. "It's just your way. Maybe it's best if we just avoid talking about these things."

"Sure, Nettie. Whatever you say."

"Don't you think you should let New York know what's cooking?"

"Let's wait and see what comes out of Hal's discussions."

Hal arranged to meet Gus and Charlie the next day, delivering the packages, and flipping through them page by page. They listened carefully, asked no questions, thanked him for responding so quickly, and said they would get back to him.

Cliff and the whole management team were on pins and needles as each day went by. By Thursday night, having heard nothing, Cliff called Krissy to let her know he may not be going to Chicago for the weekend. "I realize you may have already made other plans, but in case you haven't, I wanted to let you know I might be around."

"Gee, I have made other plans, Cliff. If you would have let me known earlier...I'm sorry."

"What about Friday night, if I don't have to go out of town?"

"I'm really tied up the whole weekend. Then I'm back to work early Monday morning. Why don't you call me Thursday evening when I get back? Okay?"

"Sure. Have a nice weekend." He was angry with himself for feeling so deflated. It was his fault that he hadn't called her earlier...couldn't call her earlier...and wasn't even sure if he'd be in town over the weekend. Yet, she obviously was seeing other men, and it bothered him, even though he realized he had no special claim on her.

Friday morning, Gus Sarius called Hal, "Sorry it took so long to get back to you. Had to run this up the flagpole to Gil. You and Cliff still available to meet us at the plant Sunday morning?"

"Sure. Thought we'd bring along Mike Gattuso, who's running field maintenance. You remember Mike?"

"Wild man Mike? How could anybody forget him? Sure. We've got the company plane. Why don't you guys meet us at Signature Aviation at National, say at eight on Sunday, and we'll fly out together. Maybe you could have a car or a couple of cars meet us."

"We're flying out Saturday, but we can fly back with you Sunday, if that's okay."

"Sure. You pick us up Sunday at Meigs around nine, Chicago time."

When Hal reported his conversation, Cliff again shook his fist in the air, and gritted, "Just maybe...this is the big one...just maybe...we're on our way. Nettie, get me Oscar McMillan on the phone."

When Oscar heard the news he seemed surprised. "You mean Tektron is serious?"

"They sure are wasting their time if they aren't. What's happening at your end? Any word on a line of credit or private investor?"

"We're working on it, Cliff. We're working on it. But that certainly is good news about Tektron. Can we help?"

"If it goes well this weekend, the next step will be for you and me to sit down with Gil Fenno, the new CEO, to start serious negotiations about price. I suppose you'd want Win there. Probably good if we kept Sidney out of it for a while."

"We'll see, boy. We'll see. Just go to it and keep me informed."

"Yes, sir."

Friday night, Cliff took Sally and Tyke to McDonald's for cheeseburgers and French fries, and then to a movie. He let them stay up until eleven, and then, before tucking them in, they held hands and went through their ritual of closing their eyes, saying their prayers, and seeing their mother.

Before crawling into bed himself, Cliff stood for a long moment staring at Sarah's picture on the dresser, and the cracked mirror he had never replaced. "I still love you, honey," he whispered, "but I suppose I've got to get on with my life. I hope you understand."

He then bent down, pulled open his bottom dresser drawer, and sorted through his old sweats until he felt his bear-toothed die. Jiggling it in his hand, he studied the bear paw side, gently set it on the nightstand beside his bed, and spoke aloud, "Guess I could use you, after all, old bear paw. If I ever needed your power and guidance, it's surely in the days ahead."

* * *

Early Saturday morning he, Hal, and Mike caught a United flight to Chicago, where they were met by Red, Smokey, and Sam. After spending the day rehearsing their presentations and attempting to anticipate the questions that might be asked, Red took them to what he claimed to be the best restaurant in Chicago, The Cape Cod Room at the Drake Hotel, where everyone was too keyed up to enjoy their exquisitely prepared Dover sole. Sam dropped them off at the O'Hare Marriott, where Cliff insisted that they get a good night's sleep for the big day ahead.

Gus, Charlie, and Lester Berry from Tektron's Engineering Department arrived on time at the little Meigs Field along Lake Michigan, where Cliff and Hal met them. At the plant they were joined by Mike and the trio Hal called the three musketeers. They spent the morning moving quite slowly through the plant with Sam explaining the operations, the assembly line flow for both the printers and the ink-jet cartridges, and Lester asking most of the questions. After sandwiches and Cokes in the conference room, Smokey briefed them on his software team and the packages they were developing. Cliff had saved what he considered the best for last—Red's engineering design activity. Lester practically crawled inside the ink-jet printer mechanism, and then spent half an hour studying and grilling Red on a prototype printer that Red had running at eight pages per minute. He queried Red on a rather vague reference in the Jet Speed packet about increasing the resolution of the dpi, the dots per inch, but Red simply shrugged, said, "Maybe," and looked at Cliff.

Cliff interjected, "If it looks like we're going to get together, before the closing, we'll show you what Red's got in the back room, but...well, I assume you understand, it really is something we don't want to talk about in detail at this time."

"You been hanging around with Hal too long, Tonto," Gus smiled and squinted at his friend. "Talking like a salesman, dangling a goodie out in front of us."

"It's a goodie, Gus. But it's still in development. Give me another six months."

"Fair enough. Today has certainly increased our interest. Get us back to the airport, let us talk to Gil, and we'll be in touch."

"Fine," Cliff replied. "Hal will fly back with you, if that's okay, but I'm going to stay over to tend to some other matters. Mike's going up to Milwaukee to interview some applicants."

"As the Tektron company plane lifted off toward Washington, and Mike caught a cab to O'Hare for his hop up to Milwaukee, Cliff turned to his three musketeers, "Well, what's the verdict?"

"I think they're hooked, if you and New York can negotiate a decent price," Red replied.

"I'm glad you decided to stay over," Sam frowned. "As I told you in the men's room, we might have a problem with EDA. Our loan is based on our being a small business. If Tektron acquires us, we may have to repay it. We're talking close to five million. I suppose that could be part of the deal...but coming up with the cash is a lot different from carrying it as a long-term liability on the books."

"You said Congressman Romanowski is in his Chicago office on Mondays. You call them first thing tomorrow morning to see if I can get fifteen minutes of his time. This issue's got to get nailed down before we start negotiating dollars. Maybe he can help with EDA." Cliff checked back into the Marriott, went down to the health club to run off some adrenaline still coursing through his body from the excitement of the day, and then ordered a steak and salad from room service. As he cleaned his plate, even sopping up the last of the steak sauce with his second roll, he recalled his first night at the hotel, when he had just taken over the company, and the terrible panic attack that had engulfed him. Grinning, he began humming the tune, "What a Difference a Day Makes." He then called home to make sure the kids were all right, carefully set his bear tooth on the nightstand, crawled under the covers, turned off the light, and fell into a deep, untroubled sleep.

He got up early the next morning, ordered scrambled eggs, toast, orange juice, and coffee from room service, pulled Hal's latest sales projections out of his briefcase to study, and waited for Sam's call concerning his appointment with the Congressman. Around ten, the phone rang, and Sam reported, "Good news...I think.

The Congressman must be pleased with us. He wanted to know if
you could have dinner with him tonight. What should I say?"

"When and where? Make sure you're included."

"I'll confirm it. You want to come in here today?"

"No. I can just as easily work here in my room. Let me know
what time you'll pick me up."

"Sure. You might want to keep your room for tonight. I understand he's a late eater and likes to sit around and have a few drinks
after dinner. We shouldn't be in any rush."

"I'd like to catch a flight back tonight." But then, Cliff thought,
Krissy's usually overnight in Chicago on Mondays. "Well, Oscar says
we should cultivate the Congressman. You're right. I think I'll stay."

Cliff worked in his room all day, going down to the health club
late in the afternoon to work out. Sam picked him up for a seven
o'clock dinner at Morton's Steak House.

After a Manhattan, two glasses of Jordon Merlot, and halfway
through a huge charbroiled porterhouse steak, Cliff decided that Congressman Romanowski wasn't such a bad egg, after all. He was pleasantly garrulous, had an unending store of jokes, and was *very* pleased
at the number of jobs Jet Speed had created in his district.

"What can I do to help, boys?" he asked, lighting up a cigar and
ordering a round of Port for everyone except his aide, who apparently was his driver.

Cliff outlined the possibility that Jet Speed might be acquired by
Tektron, emphasizing that the increased capital investment would create well over one hundred new jobs. "But, our EDA loan was based on
our being a small business. If the agency requires us to repay the loan
immediately, that's another five million in cash that we've got to come
up with, making the deal that much less attractive. We thought we
should talk to you before we make Tektron aware of the problem. We'd
have an obligation to tell them, if we can't get assurances from EDA
that the original terms of the loan will be honored. If it's appropriate,
we hoped you might consider interceding."

"How many more jobs?"

"Short term...this year...at least a hundred. Long term...sky's the limit. Potential of several hundred."

"Plus the stability of being part of a financially secure larger organization," Sam added.

Studying his glass of Port as he pursed his lips, the Congressman finally said, "Obviously, I want the jobs. You boys have been straight with me...so far." He narrowed his eyes, staring, unblinking, at Cliff for what seemed like several seconds. "Could the deal be done in such a way that they acquired you as a wholly owned subsidiary? That way, the business entity would still be a small business. I think I could get EDA to look the other way on that."

"We can certainly press them to do the deal that way...if we get that far," Cliff replied.

"Fine. You boys go ahead and negotiate your deal, and if you remain as a wholly owned sub...I'll see to it that your low-interest loan with EDA stays in place."

"Yes, sir. Thank you, sir," Cliff vigorously shook the Congressman's hand, he and Sam said their goodbyes and quickly left. On their way out, the Congressman's aide caught up with them.

"You know, the Congressman's holding his big fundraiser in Washington next month. We'd like you to be on his Finance Committee, Mr. Cross...help us turn it into a great success."

"Be happy to. Here's my card. Call me at the office and tell me what to do."

As Sam was driving Cliff to the Marriott, he looked over and shook his head, "Boy, they didn't miss a beat, did they?"

"I'm learning, Sam. Fact is, he's helping us stay alive. Nothing wrong with our helping him. That's the way the world works."

* * *

Cliff walked into the lobby, hesitated, and then turned to enter the lounge. He quickly spotted Mary Catherine, Jeannie, and several of their friends—apparently other flight attendants and pilots—sitting at three pushed-together tables, but no Krissy.

"Hey, Cliff...come on, join us," Mary Catherine motioned.

Smiling and waving at them, he made his way through the lounge to a few feet from their tables, "See Krissy around?"

"She went out for dinner with someone a few hours ago," Mary Catherine replied.

"But I think I saw her coming back through the lobby a little while ago," Jeannie added. "She's probably up in her room. She's in 212, next to me. Give her a call."

"Thanks. I will. I'm in 218, right down the hall from you." When Cliff got on an empty elevator, a waiter, pushing a room service cart, asked, "Mind if I ride up with you?"

"Come on in. Plenty of room." Cliff noticed that the hotel slip on the cart indicated room 212. As they both got off on the second floor, Cliff said, "I see you're taking that to 212. Friend of mine's in that room. Here's five bucks. Let me deliver it. You stay behind me, okay?"

"Sure. Thanks."

Cliff knocked on the door, and in his best, bass, stage voice announced, "Roooom service."

"Just a minute, please," came Krissy's voice from behind the door. In a few moments, the door opened slightly, and she called again, "Okay, bring it in."

Cliff pushed the door open with the front of the cart, and there was Krissy standing in her bathrobe and bare feet. Behind her, in the center of the room, in his boxer shorts, stood Mike Gattuso.

"Cliff!" she shrieked. "How did you...where...oh my God."

Dumbfounded, Cliff froze momentarily, bent over the cart, holding on to its corners. Then, with his eyes wide and his mouth hanging open, he slowly looked past Krissy to Mike. "Mike...," he smiled incredulously.

"Cliff...," Mike threw his hands up in the air, "what the hell are you doing here?"

Krissy had stepped aside, holding her hand to her mouth, in disbelief, at what she was witnessing.

Cliff straightened up, shaking his head, with the same strained smile on his face. "I guess I could ask you the same thing. But...hey," he straightened, holding his hands out, palms up, "you two love-birds have a nice evening." As he backed out of the room, still holding his hands up and with the same strange smile on his face, he hesitated, shaking a finger at Mike, "Just don't put this on your expense account, old buddy."

Twenty minutes later, as he was sitting on the edge of his bed, pouring a Cognac from the minibar into a glass, shaking his head slowly with the same strange smile on his face, the phone rang.

"Cliff...Cliff...this is Mike."

"Hi, Mike. Get all your interviews finished up in Milwaukee?"

"Come on, Cliff. I feel terrible. I didn't know you knew Krissy. Hell, I been hittin' on her since last fall when I started coming out here every week. She never said a word about you...although she did ask me a lot about the company. She's one hot number. She just told me that she's been seeing you, too. Hey...I'm sorry, Cliff, if I screwed things up for you...I never..."

"Forget about it, Mike. I've got no special claim on her. Fact is, you've done me a big favor tonight. A **really** big favor."

"Well, I still feel awful. And...ah...Cliff...you wouldn't say anything about this to Glenda, would you? Or the office? You know, things like this get around. I was just having a little extracurricular activity. Nothing serious."

"Mike, how long we been friends? Nearly ten years. I'm no tattletale. What you do is your business...as long as you don't let it interfere with business. I'd say, the best thing we can do is put this aside. Far as I'm concerned...it never happened. Let's just never speak of it again. You don't know it, but you've done me a favor. It's over and done with. Deal?"

"Thanks, Cliff. Can't tell you how much I appreciate this. You won't regret it."

"Mikey, we got bigger fish to fry. See you tomorrow."

When Cliff hung up the phone, the red light was blinking, indicating he had received a message while talking to Mike. The voice on the recording said, "You have received one message...," and then Krissy's voice came on, "Cliff, oh Cliff, please call me...we need to talk...I didn't...," he hung up the phone, and with the same strange smile back on his face, said, "*Sayonara*, baby," turned out the light, pulled up the covers, and lay there staring at the ceiling, trying to go to sleep. He felt like the little boy who had stubbed his toe...he was too big to cry, but it hurt too much to laugh. He had thought that, well, maybe, Krissy was the one. What a fool he had been. How could he have become so beguiled without looking beneath the surface. But it was some surface, he had to admit. Never again am I going to let myself get carried away like this, he resolved. I've got two little children to raise, and an extraordinary chance to make it big, maybe even into the Fortune 500 some day. "Never again!" he growled aloud, and then turned over on his side and fell into a troubled sleep.

Chapter Twenty

Cliff met Mike in the lobby to catch the early morning United flight back to Washington. Not a word was spoken of their experience the previous evening. Instead, they both worked at keeping the conversation upbeat about the prospects for the merger. As Cliff feared, Krissy was working the flight. He had considered taking a later flight, but had decided that he needed to get back to the office quickly, and it would be stupid to let any personal discomfort dictate his schedule. **Stupid**, he emphasized to himself.

She greeted both of them quite properly, and they nodded in return. After they were airborne, while another flight attendant was serving a light breakfast, she slipped Cliff a note, "Please call me."

He glanced at it, motioned for her to come back down the aisle to his seat, and when she got there, conspicuously tore the note in two and handed it to her without saying a word.

She glared at him, crumpled the torn note, and angrily threw it on his tray.

Mike watched silently, leaned over to whisper something in Cliff's ear, and then thought better of it.

When they got to the office, Nettie and Arnie had to have a blow-by-blow description of the meeting with Tektron.

"When will we know if they're going to make an offer? I can hardly wait!" Nettie pleaded.

"Keep your pants on, Nettie. These things take time," Cliff assured her.

"I always keep my pants on, Mr. C, don't I, Arnie?" she giggled. His face turned beet-red.

"Come on, let's get serious. We've got month-end closing to wrap up. Numbers ought'a be good. Right, Arnie?"

"No question, boss. Better than last month, even."

"You'll let me know the minute we get any phone calls from Tektron...they may have some more questions."

"No, Mr. C...we'll keep it a secret from you," Nettie grinned.

Even though Cliff was extremely busy, with the month-end reports, with making several important sales calls with Hal, and with his new-found responsibility of trying to figure out how to raise money for Congressman Romanowski's coming fundraiser, he still ached each time he thought about Krissy, and what a fool he had been.

On Thursday morning, Cliff received a phone call from Gus Sarius. "Cliff, Gil would like to sit down with you and your investors early next week, but he'd like to talk to you first. He's cramped for time, so he's proposing we fly up to New York together on the company plane to meet your people. You and he can talk on the way up. How's Tuesday morning?"

"Probably fine, Gus. I'll check it out and get right back to you."

Within minutes, he was able to confirm that he, Hal, Oscar McMillan, Sidney Martin, and Winslow Rooke would meet with the Tektron executives the following Tuesday. He and Hal would meet them at Signature at eight-thirty, and they should arrive at Oscar's office in Wall Street by ten.

Oscar pressed Cliff for his assessment of what they were going to offer, but Cliff assured him, "I have no idea, Oscar, and I think they see this as one more step in the negotiation dance."

"Well, Sidney's all hot and bothered about you possibly telling them too much. He wants to handle the negotiations. And, after all, most of it is his money."

"Big mistake, Oscar. I know these people. They're not going to respond kindly to Sidney's badgering. I think we should be polite, calm, listen to what they have to say, and, most importantly, have already figured out how much we want for the company. Once we see if we're in the ballpark, then we talk structure. I'm sure that's important to you in terms of the tax consequences, and it's important to my guys and me to understand where we would fit in after the acquisition."

"Let's you, Sidney, Win, and I have a conference call on Monday to talk through our strategy...come up with our asking price. Sid and I have already given this a lot of thought. And, by the way, there's no need for you to bring Greenberg into this. We can handle it."

"Oscar, I understand perfectly, you fellows have the controlling votes, but Hal's on the Board...he's my guy...and he'll be there."

"Whatever you say, boy. Let's talk around three, Monday afternoon."

"Fine, we'll call you then."

Cliff called Hal and Arnie into his office, told them of the plan, and suggested that they lock themselves in the conference room to figure out a reasonable valuation for the company, along with different possible structures. It turned into another weekender for Cliff, Hal, Arnie, and Nettie, but no one complained. They were too excited. Cliff did excuse himself for a few hours on Saturday afternoon to take the kids to the movies, and on Sunday afternoon to take them to see the cherry blossoms around the Tidal Basin in Washington. He asked Greta to go along Sunday, but she was surprisingly evasive, saying she needed to meet some people, that she hadn't had a day off for several weeks, and hoped that he could keep the children the balance of the day. When he told her he really had to get back to the office by late afternoon, she informed him that she had their neighbor's daughter on call for babysitting. She would have the teenager there by four to watch the children, and she would be back by nine that evening.

By the time Cliff arrived home late Sunday evening, the children were in bed, and Greta was in her room with the door shut. Cliff had thought about it on his way home, and decided that, once again, he had been totally insensitive to someone else's problem. Greta had been working every day, and evenings, too, without letup. Even though they had a cleaning lady come in once a week, virtually the entire burden of running the household and looking after the children had fallen on her shoulders. It was one more problem that he had better address. Maybe next weekend, he thought. I better have a talk with Greta.

Early Monday morning he, Hal, and Arnie went over their plans for their conference call that afternoon, with Nettie looking over their shoulders. Everyone was excited.

"Just might be on our way!" Cliff shook his fist in the air.

Around ten, Nettie barged into his office, throwing his American Express bill on his desk, "Would you like me to pay for those flowers on the bill out of petty cash?" she stood glaring at him with her hands on her hips.

"What flowers?"

Without speaking, she leaned over, circled the florist's charge on the statement, and then jabbed it with the eraser tip of her pencil.

"Oh, **those** flowers. No, I'll take care of the bill. Thanks, Nettie." He hurriedly stuffed the statement in his coat pocket, slid out from behind his desk, and pointed, "Got to go to the men's room." He had forgotten all about the roses he had sent Krissy. The embarrassment welled up in him again. What a fool I've been, he agonized.

* * *

When the clock struck three on Monday afternoon, Cliff was ready for the conference call to discuss the potential sale price of the company.

Sidney interrupted Cliff's opening comments, "How much of this did you tell your friends at Tektron?"

"Nothing...not a damn word," Cliff replied, angrily.

"Let the boy talk, Sidney," Oscar interjected. "Go ahead, Cliff."

"Thank you, Oscar. Well...our analysis suggests, that keeping the same debt structure in place, we could value the company anywhere from ten million on the low side, to forty million on the high side. The basis for..."

"Hold it! What do you mean, keep the debt structure in place? I want my loans repaid, first, before anything else," Sidney bellowed through the phone.

"Of course, Sidney," Cliff answered, exasperated. "The assumption is that they would pay off your loans, but infuse a like amount of debt back into the company. They may not want to do that. But for valuation purposes, you've got to start with certain assumptions."

"Let him go through his analysis, Sidney. Then we can pick it apart, if we disagree," Oscar, uncharacteristically, shouted back at Sidney.

"Thank you, Oscar. Our current P&L shows we'll do about thirty-nine million this year, with a Profit Before Taxes of a little under four million. Our Tax Loss Carry Forward is over nine million, which cushions this year's and next year's earnings, but for long-term valuation, you've got to figure a Profit After Taxes of about two million at our current levels. Ten times earnings would value the company at about twenty million. But...and this is a big but...we have a negative net worth of over nine million, and this year's financials are based on one-quarter actuals and three-quarters projections. Those factors significantly reduce potential value. Of course, that's the reason why we shouldn't be selling now...why we should be finding a line of credit to finance our expansion. Anyway, all things considered, that's how I come up with a price of ten million on the low end."

"You're saying, we get all our debt repaid, plus ten million for our stock?" Oscar asked.

"Yes, sir. That would be six million for the investors and four million for management...at the low end. A minimum, reasonable price."

Winslow coughed, "Well...ah...the stock distribution is a different subject."

"What do you mean by that?" Cliff asked, puzzled.

"Oh, nothing," Oscar interrupted. "We've just got to think about tax consequences...selling for cash, or a stock swap...that kind of detail. So, give us your high-end analysis."

"Well...with another ten million cash infusion for expansion this year from Tektron, we can reasonably project next year coming in with extraordinary growth...tripling our revenue to around one hundred twenty million...the market's there. That would put PBT at around thirty million. After taxes...fifteen million. Ten times earnings...one hundred fifty million. But, obviously, we couldn't sell that. They'd laugh us out of the room, with our negative worth, and what they would call a blue-sky projection. However, I think we can defend such a projection, and that, coupled with our having turned the corner into the black this year, lets us set a high-end price of around forty million. What do you think?"

"Damn right! We ask for forty million, and negotiate down from there," Sidney shouted into the phone.

"In cash or stock?" Winslow asked.

"That's negotiable...as long as we get our loans repaid in cash," Sidney answered in a sweet, syrupy voice.

"We'll need to understand the structure, and where our management team fits in," Cliff commented.

"Sure. Don't worry about that, Cliff. That's a detail we'll work out. No problem," Sidney replied, nonchalantly.

"It's more than a detail," Cliff snapped.

"All right, boys. Calm down. We'll see you and the Tektron people up here tomorrow morning. Right, Cliff? And you've got all the backup to support your different scenarios?"

"Yes, sir. See you then. But remember, let's let them do the talking. I'll present our projections without talking price, and then we sit back and listen. Right, Sidney?"

"Ya. Ya. You get us a good price, laddie, and I'll kiss your ass in Times Square."

* * *

The next morning, Cliff and Hal met Gil Fenno, Gus Sarius, and Charlie Lambert at Signature for their flight to New York in the Tektron company plane. Once airborne, Gil said, "So tell me, Cliff, how do you see this deal going together?"

"You've seen our financials, Gil. We've already turned the corner. Given the potential market out there, and the quality of our printer, with the necessary capital investment for expansion, sky's the limit."

"Seems to me, it turns on the degree of risk we're willing to assume and our potential Return on Investment. And that, of course, gets down to price."

"And structure, Gil. I think we should wait until we get to New York to talk dollars. We've got a presentation for you on our future projections, but I need to understand where you see us...my management team...fitting in. Might be good to get that cleared up before we get to New York."

"Why do you think I suggested we should talk first, before we meet your investors? Of course. The two good things about this deal, if we can put it together, aside from the financials, are that your company gives us entry into a new market, and, we know each other."

"Those are the intangibles that create additional value above the financial projections. You know that, Gil."

"Sure. There's no sense in me denying it, Cliff. If we can agree on price, we'd want to set you up as a separate division. You and your management team run it as one of our profit centers."

"Any objection to making it a wholly owned subsidiary? We've got a five million dollar, low-interest EDA loan that would not have to be paid off if we can remain as a small business entity."

"That would be a sweetener. Fine with me. I'd want our lawyers to look at it before I committed to it."

"Another consideration would be your willingness to invest about ten million for capital expansion. Without it, we can't tap the market potential that's out there."

"If you can justify the Return on Investment, we've got the cash. You know that."

"Right. Sounds like price is going to make or break this deal."

"You got that right, too, Cliff."

* * *

When they arrived in Oscar's conference room, after introducing everyone, Cliff took charge of the meeting. He handed out three-ring notebooks which included the details of their financials, as well as the projections for future growth and profitability, and then turned to flip charts to summarize the key points.

As he outlined the current year's expectations of thirty-nine million in Revenue and four million in Profit Before Taxes, emphasizing the nine million in Tax Loss Carry Forward, the Tektron people nodded approvingly. But when he got to the future projections of one hundred twenty million in Revenue and nearly thirty million in PBT, Gil Fenno spoke up, "Wait a minute, Cliff. That's pie in the sky. How many companies have tripled their Revenue in a twelve-month period? Damn few...if any. And what about the growing pains with that kind of explosive growth? We can't make our business decisions based on somebody's pipe dream."

"It's not a pipe dream, Gil. Look at our detailed analysis. I'm sure Gus and Charlie already have. Look at the independent projections of the size of the printer market. We're just scratching the surface. Look at the quality of our printer. I'm sure you have, and that's one of the reasons why you're here...And...and we're not asking you to buy the company based solely on that future projection. If we were, we'd be asking upwards of one hundred million dollars for it."

"Get real, Cliff. There's no reason for us to continue this discussion, if those are the kind of ridiculous numbers you're going to throw around."

"Did I say we were asking for that kind of money?"

"Now, just a minute," Sidney held up his hands. "Cliff's analysis is actually conservative. Why, with your financial resources, Mr.

Fenno, this could turn into a billion dollar company. We could end up practically giving it away to you."

"Mr. Martin," Gil lowered his head and looked up over his glasses, slightly smiling at Sidney, "Jet Speed's been in business for only a couple of years...has a negative...*negative* net worth, looks like it's going to generate about a four million dollar PBT...has a debt to equity ratio of fifteen to one...and you're talking an astronomical value for this little start-up venture? With all due respect, sir, unless we can start talking reasonable ballpark figures, there's no sense in our continuing. We'd be wasting your time."

"Gil, we understand all that," Cliff nodded, wincing. "Considering all those factors, but including the very real growth potential of this company...a potential that a conservative analysis supports...one that I think you, and Gus, and Charlie see, or you wouldn't be here...what do you think the company's worth?"

After looking up at the ceiling for a long few seconds and shrugging, Gil looked out the window and mumbled, "Let's see, we swallow the eleven million your investors have sunk in the business...pay you off...then maybe do a stock swap for, say five million. Additionally, we'd expect to pour another ten million into expansion, but that'd be none of your concern once you're out of it. We'd have the equivalent of twenty-five million in a two-year-old company with a negative net worth."

"Come on, Gil, you know it's worth a lot more than that," Cliff looked at him askance.

"What's your bottom line, fellows?" Gil, tried to suppress a smile.

"We think it's worth every penny of forty million!" Sidney smacked the table.

"Ten million, tops," Gil returned the smack to the table.

"No deal," Cliff shrugged, standing up. Come on, Gil, you gonna give Hal and me a ride back to Washington?"

Sidney glanced over to Oscar, grimacing and nodding his head for Oscar to speak up.

"Why don't we all just sleep on it," Oscar calmly suggested.

"You boys go back to Washington...sharpen your pencils...we'll do the same. Then let's talk again in a few days."

"Fine with me," Gil smiled. "Nice meeting you gentlemen. We'll stay in touch with Cliff, if there's any value in further discussions."

As they headed toward the elevator, Sidney grabbed Cliff by the arm, whispering, "Call us...call us, dammit, the minute you get back to Washington."

* * *

On the plane back to Washington, Gil patted Cliff on the knee, "Understand, Cliff, we want to do this deal...but you boys have to be reasonable. Your company's only two years old, with a negative net worth, and only one product. Good as it is, if a competitor builds a better mousetrap, you could be out of business overnight."

"Come on, Gil, your guys saw our Engineering Lab. Tell him, Gus, we're already working on a better mousetrap."

"He's right, Gil. They're not standing still."

"What's it going to take, Cliff? What's your bottom line?" Gil smiled benignly.

"Honestly, Gil, I'm not sure. I suppose we could, scientifically, split the difference. Call it twenty-five million."

"I don't see how I could sell that to my Board. Tell you what I'll do...Board meets toward the end of the month...on the twenty-eighth. Get me a dozen copies of your report, and loan me those flip charts. I'll lay it out for the Board...see what kind of a counteroffer we might put together. Okay?"

"Sure. But understand, time's important. We're looking at other possibilities."

"Stop gaming me, Cliff. We know each other too well for that." There was a hard edge to Gil Fenno's words and a sudden icy glare in his eyes. "You know damn well, these deals take time. And frankly, your pushing me makes me nervous. Are there some problems here I'm not aware of?"

"The problem, Gil, is that we need cash for expansion. Like yesterday. You see that in our projections and the growing size of the market. Anyway, your accountants will be crawling all over us doing your due diligence before any deal gets closed."

"Now you're making me more nervous with this urgency for cash. Why haven't you gone to a bank for a Line of Credit? Why haven't your Wall Street boys come up with the cash? Huh?"

"Gil, I don't know what financial limitations my investors have. In a way, I don't care. What I care about is growing this company. A deal with you guys gives me the financial strength to do that. Either we have the seeds of a deal that's good for both of us, or we don't. Dammit!"

As the plane touched down at National, the air in the small cabin was filled with tension. Cliff's nerves were rubbed raw, and Gil Fenno, the CEO of a major corporation, was not about to be pushed around by one of his former underlings. By the time they were walking through the Signature terminal, both Cliff and Gil seemed to realize that the potential deal was about to blow up, largely because two very strong-willed men were not about to let the other gain any psychological advantage in the negotiations.

"Hey, you two lighten up," Gus Sarius stepped between Cliff and Gil. "How long we been friends? You're both too damn competitive. Let's stop playing games. We both want this deal, so let's figure out a fair price. Maybe we should bring in an independent third party to put a valuation on it."

"Just a waste of time and money. No one's going to grasp half of what we already know," Gil shook his head.

"I agree," Cliff nodded. "You take it to your Board, Gil, let's see what they say."

Everyone shook hands as they went their separate ways, but the bonds of mutual trust had been damaged. Clifford Cross and Gil Fenno each knew, deep inside, that they no longer simply could be friends. Their interests clashed. Each was responsible for extracting the maximum possible benefit from the other. Perhaps after the deal was closed, they could repair their relationship, but even then, Cliff knew he would be competing for resources with the many other divisions of Tektron, and it would be Gil's job to push him toward achieving maximum profitability.

The knot in Cliff's stomach returned as he was driving home, his pulse quickened, his palms began to sweat, and suddenly, a clamminess engulfed his body. Gripping the steering wheel tightly, he muttered, "Another damn panic attack...is this really worth it?"

When he arrived home, there was a message to call Oscar in New York. Throwing his briefcase on the floor beside his desk in the den and kicking off his shoes, he placed the call.

Although Oscar answered the phone, apparently Sidney yanked the receiver out of his hand. "Cliff! I thought I told you to call us when you got in."

"I'm here, Sidney," he sighed. "What do you want?"

"We've talked it over after you left. Don't...I repeat *don't* lose this deal! You hear me?"

"I hear you, Sidney. What brought on this sudden change of heart? I thought you wanted to hold out for top dollar."

"Cliff, this is Oscar. Win's here too," his voice coming over the speaker. "What Sid means, is, is, it's in everybody's interest to put this deal together. We want it nailed down. Fast. What happened on the airplane on the way back?"

"Well, we kicked around the potential price. Actually got a little testy. He..."

"Don't you be screwing this up, boy," Sidney shouted into the speaker.

Cliff pursed his lips, clenched his jaws, and stared silently into his telephone, tapping his foot rapidly.

"Cliff, you hear me?" Sidney screamed, in a high, almost hysterical voice.

Taking his time to answer, Cliff finally replied, "I hear you, Sidney. What I started to say, when you cut me off, was that Gil has agreed to bring up the matter at his Board meeting in a few weeks, using our reports and flip charts. Then he'll get back to us with a counteroffer, or say they're not interested."

"What kind of price were you talking on the plane?" Win asked.

"Oh, I suggested in passing that maybe we split the difference...we threw out forty million...he said ten...so make it twenty-five."

"So...how'd he react to that?" Sidney pressed.

"Not well. But he did say he'd bring it up at their next Board meeting, so they're obviously interested. We'll just have to wait and see. Maybe in the interim you can come up with a Line of Credit from your banking connections. That would certainly put us in a stronger negotiating position. Then we wouldn't have to sell unless it really was a sweet deal."

"Cliff, we've got to be candid with you," Oscar said soothingly. "We're not having too much luck finding a Line of Credit. Your deal with Tektron appears to be our best chance. Maybe our only chance. So we're really counting on you to keep it alive...to put it together. That's how we all come out of this thing whole."

"I still don't understand. With our progress, we should be able to get a Line of Credit...hell, mostly secured by our Accounts Receivables and Inventory. I'm going to take a shot at some of the banks here in Washington."

"No! No...don't do that, Cliff," Sidney spoke very slowly and uncharacteristically, quite softly.

"Fellows, what the hell is going on?" Cliff demanded.

"Cliff, trust us," Oscar pleaded. "We've shown our good faith. We've put eleven million in the business already. We've sent you the five hundred thousand each month you needed it. Please...you've got to let us handle this. If you would like a formal Board vote on this matter, we can do it. But that's not needed. We've got to work together on this. We're doing the best we can up here under the circumstances. You just get this deal put together with Tektron, and we'll all benefit. Agree?"

"Don't be rocking the boat in Washington!" Sidney bellowed.

Oscar must have put his hand over the speaker, because Cliff could only hear his muted voice saying, "God dammit, Sidney, shut up!"

"You gentlemen hold the cards," Cliff replied, dejectedly. "I'll do the best I can with Tektron. But if we can't pursue other avenues, it's going to be a waiting game."

After he hung up the phone, he kept his hand on the receiver for a long moment, and then muttered, "Is this really worth it?"

Chapter Twenty-One

Just as Cliff was winding down, enjoying a delightful dinner with the children—their favorite, of macaroni, hot dogs plastered with yellow mustard, French fries dunked in catsup, Dr. Peppers, and vanilla ice cream smothered with chocolate sauce—another crisis erupted. Tyke went out on the back porch to feed Ginger, and she was gone.

"Daddy...Daddy," he cried, "the gates unlatched...somebody stole Ginger!"

Sally rushed over to her father, clinging onto his arm, "Please, Daddy, please...you've got to find Ginger."

"Now, kids, just calm down. It's still light outside. Tyke, you and I will walk along the back yards in the neighborhood, and Greta, you and Sally go out front, walk up one side of the street and come back down the other side. We'll all call out for Ginger. She's probably just running loose in the neighborhood. When she hears her name, she'll come a'running."

"No...no...the gates unlatched. Somebody took her," Tyke insisted.

Greta spoke up, "I'm afraid I might have let the gate open. I went out to the garbage cans under the porch after lunch. I'm so sorry. But we'll find her, children. Won't we, Mr. Cross?"

"Of course. Now let's get moving. We can make this fun...a search for our missing puppy. Who's going to find her first? Tyke or

Sally? Come on, let's go." As they went off in their separate directions, Tyke called over his shoulder, "Bet we beat you, Sally."

Tugging on Greta's hand, she snapped, "No you won't, you little pipsqueak."

They searched the entire neighborhood, front and back, switching places with each other, knocking on their neighbors' doors, but Ginger was nowhere to be found. Finally, as the last tip of the sun descended behind the Tyson's Corners high-rises in the distance, the four of them met at the street corner under a flickering streetlight, with Sally teary-eyed, and Tyke sobbing, "She's gone. I told you...I told you and you wouldn't listen...somebody stole her."

"She'll turn up in the morning, kids. Come on, it's dark. We've got to get you home. It's past your bedtime."

"Tyke's right, Daddy. She's gone. We looked everywhere. We called and called. We'll never see Ginger again." Then Sally joined her brother, sobbing uncontrollably, as Cliff led his two disheartened children home.

When Cliff turned on the lights in the family room, there, on the other side of the sliding glass doors facing the porch was Ginger, scratching at the screen, wanting in. Utter dejection turned to instant joy. Sliding open the door, Ginger jumped up on Tyke who fell back onto the floor with his arms wrapped around the little brown beagle. Sally piled on top of them, hugging Ginger. Over Greta's half-hearted objection, Ginger was treated to a large bowl of vanilla ice cream, and then permitted to sleep on the floor between the children's beds.

After they were in bed, Cliff poured himself a glass of Port and offered one to Greta.

"You know I don't drink, Mr. Cross, but thank you for the offer. I'll get myself a cup of tea. There is something I'd like to talk to you about, if now's a good time."

"Sure, Greta. Get your tea and let's relax here in the family room. I've had about as much excitement today as my body can take."

Weighing his last words as she returned to the family room with her tea, Greta said, "Maybe now's not the right time. Perhaps tomorrow evening we could talk if you're going to be home."

"Now's as good a time as any. Uh-oh, sounds serious. Well, lay it on me."

"Well, Mr. Cross, you know how much I've loved looking after the children. They're like family to me. But I've had another offer...the same agency that Mrs. Cross's mother, Mrs. Wilson, used to find me...they've called me. I felt it would be foolish for me at least not to listen. There's a family from Charleston, West Virginia, that's moving to Georgetown...apparently, the gentleman is getting a high-level appointment in the State Department...and they're looking for a housekeeper. I guess someone gave them my name and the agency's name to do whatever kind of screening they do. Anyway, they've offered me the job. Their children are grown...so there would be a lot less responsibility, with two days off each week. At my age...well, it's probably a good way for me to ease toward retirement. And the pay's really excellent...although that's not my main consideration. I hope you understand."

"Well, I must admit, Greta, this comes as quite a shock. You are like one of the family. I don't know what I would have done without you. I don't know what I will do without you."

"I understand the gentleman needs to be confirmed by the Senate before he can take the job, and that's supposed to happen some time in June. So, I told them I wouldn't be available until the first of July. That gives you time to find my replacement."

"Have you already accepted the job?"

"Not formally. They're supposed to send me a written job offer...just like you did...and then I sign it and send it back."

"Would you do me one big favor, Greta? Don't sign it until we have a chance to talk some more. I would like to think about this, and see if I couldn't come up with a proposal to lift some of the burdens off your shoulders here; to see if I might not be able to come up with an attractive package that could entice you to stay. You know, the children will be brokenhearted if you leave them."

"Truth is, I'll be brokenhearted leaving them. But I've got to look out for what's best for me...especially at my age."

"I understand, Greta. You should do what's best for you. Absolutely. Just let me think about it to see if I can't make it in your best interest to stay. Could you hold off until after Easter? I'm taking the kids to my parents that weekend. When I get back, I'll have a proposal for you to consider. Then you can make your choice. Okay?"

"I doubt that I'll have their offer in writing until next week. Then Easter's the following Sunday. Certainly. I can wait 'til the week after Easter. Please understand, Mr. Cross, I didn't go looking for this. I'm very happy here, although, I admit, sometimes I feel a little overwhelmed by all the responsibility. I'm not trying to force you into anything, but I certainly owe it to you, and the children, to at least give you the courtesy of hearing you out."

"Thank you, Greta. Frankly, I don't know how I'm going to restructure the household responsibilities, but I promise you, I'm really going to try. I don't want to lose you. More importantly, the children don't want to lose you."

"Thank you, Mr. Cross. I'm really touched by your concerns. And the way you put it now...about the children...I really don't want to leave them. I hope we can work something out. I really do."

* * *

The next morning, Arnie, Mike, and Nettie already were in Cliff's office when he arrived, wanting to hear about the New York meeting. Hal had refused to tell them anything, saying they should wait for Cliff.

"Get Chicago on the squawk box. I might as well tell everyone at once," Cliff instructed.

"Go ahead, boss," Nettie pushed the speaker button, "the musketeers are all ears."

"It's hurry up and wait again," Cliff reported dejectedly.

"Wait a minute," Hal interrupted. "We're still alive. Fenno's taking it to the Board on the twenty-eighth. They're serious. It's a question of price. He threw out an offer of ten million, which Cliff rejected, so I know we can do better than that."

"Hell, forty percent of ten million ain't bad," Mike exclaimed. "Everyone gets at least a couple hundred thousand. Cliff walks away with $1.6 million. Not that we're begrudging it, Tonto. You the man that brung us to the dance."

Cliff worried that he had been so open with them, yet he felt that if they really were going to be a team, everyone should know up front what each was getting. If there ever were a stock offering, it would be public information, anyway. "Listen, guys, I know we're itching to get some cash in here so we can expand, but we're just going to have to hang on. Let's keep our fingers crossed. Hopefully, within thirty days, we'll know if we have a deal. Don't waste any time fretting about what might happen. Let's just keep doing our jobs, and things will work out."

Even though they knew Cliff's approach was right, it was hard not to think about the pending deal, and what it might mean for the company's growth, and for them personally. So they tried to concentrate on their responsibilities, but not a day passed without them looking forward to the twenty-eighth of the month, when they hoped—and Nettie even prayed—that their dreams might come true.

* * *

While Cliff and his team were working and waiting nervously to learn what their future might be, Jumper and Joe Joe were basking serenely in the extraordinary success of their no-longer-little venture. They were moving about a pound of marijuana, retail, weekly, and Joe Joe was selling his twenty-five pounds, wholesale, at the car auction each Friday.

As the yellow bell-shaped forsythia flowers burst open throughout the valleys of southern West Virginia, and the dogwood blossomed along the mountain sides, Jumper helped his mother up the steps of the First Baptist Church of Beckley to attend Palm Sunday service. He had promised to take her, and he was a man of his word. Decked out in his new navy blue suit, starched and laundered white shirt with imitation tiger's-eye cuff links, flowered tie, and spiffy, black, wing-tipped shoes, he escorted her, in the new pink and white rose-print dress he had bought her, down the aisle to end seats in the second row directly in front of the preacher, where everyone could see them. As they stood to sing the first hymn, he was so proud he could burst. And, he was sure she was proud of him, too. Perhaps, for the first time since the day he got to ride, sitting up on the back seat of an open, red Pontiac convertible beside his teammate, Clifford Cross, in the parade honoring the team for winning the state basketball championship.

Finally, he was making something of himself. He wished Cliff could see him, actually going to church on Palm Sunday, dressed like a real businessman, like the man he was about to become. During the service, while everyone else was paying attention to the preacher, he slipped out his ballpoint pen, and holding the church bulletin down between his legs, carefully made his calculations. He had one hundred sixteen thousand dollars stashed away in the metal suitcase deep inside the abandoned coal mine. And, so did Joe Joe. They were ready to make their play for old-man Siefert's Ford dealership in Oak Hill. They were ready to bring Cliff into the deal. When he learned how much cash they had to invest...well, he'd be so impressed...he couldn't turn them down.

Next Saturday night at the Moonshiner, he would meet Cliff...take him in the back room...maybe even bring the metal suitcase of cash to show Cliff that they weren't blowing smoke, that they really had the dough. Yes...they'd clear everyone out of the back room, and show him the money. Boy, would his eyes pop!

When he rose to sing the next hymn, with his dear mother at his side, the sun shone through a stained-glass window, lighting upon his face. It was a good omen, he was sure, and although he wasn't a religious man, for the first time in his life, he felt God was blessing him. So, when the collection plate was passed, he dug his roll out of his pants' pocket and laid a hundred dollar bill flat across the top of the envelopes and other bills in the plate. He nudged his mother to be sure she saw, and then with head held high, smiled angelically at the preacher in the pulpit.

* * *

Although Cliff had a tightly scheduled week, he decided that solving his housekeeper problem had to be his top priority. As he went about his various management meetings, his phone calls to Chicago and New York, his high-level sales calls on government officials with Hal, the necessity of finding a way to keep Greta weighed heavily on his mind. Yet, by midweek, he was still totally stumped. Hiring a second housekeeper probably wouldn't sit well with Greta. Two was one too many. Yet, where could you find a part-time live-in?

Finally, he turned to Nettie, and asked what she would do.

"You've got two choices, Mr. C. Hire a responsible cleaning lady for two days through the week, so Greta can have some time off, and schedule yourself to be home early on those days. And I mean stick to your schedule. Probably offer Greta a nice raise. I'm sure you can afford it. Or, you've got a second choice."

"And what might that be?"

"Find a woman and get married."

"Oh, I see. Just like that. Maybe I could take out an ad in the newspaper. Or, send away for a mail-order bride to Cambodia or Sri Lanka."

"What about the girl you've been sending flowers to? She really must be special to rate red roses."

"Once, Nettie. That was only once. And it was very big mistake."

"Oh? It's none of my business, but I got the impression you were in the process of sweeping some young damsel off her feet."

"Well, you're right, it's none of your business. But if you must know, it didn't work out. In fact, it never got off the ground."

"So...so you're not seeing anyone special?"

"Afraid not, Nettie. Mark Twain had a saying: 'Once a cat jumps up on a hot stove, he won't jump on a cold stove either.' After Sarah died...I don't want to talk about it. Okay?"

"Well, if you ever need a shoulder to cry on, boss...mine's a long way down...but it's there. I guess we both have a few scars to nurse. But you...heck, you've got it all together. Peons like me...what's that song...I'm always chasing rainbows..."

"Hey, Nettie...someday, the right guy is going to be sitting right there at the end of that rainbow waiting for you. I told you before, you're the whole package. When the right guy comes along, you'll know it."

Nettie looked down at her hands which were tightly clasped and shrugged, "What if you know it, but he doesn't? What do you do then, boss?" Before Cliff could answer, she turned and hurried out of the room.

Before Cliff packed up the kids on Friday afternoon for their trip to Beckley, he called Greta into his den. "Greta, I don't want to lose you. The children don't want to lose you. We *need* you and want to find a way so you will want to stay."

"But I do *want* to stay, Mr. Cross. It's just that I can't pass up this opportunity."

"I know. But let me propose another kind of opportunity for you here. You think about it this weekend, and when we return Sunday evening, you can give me your answer...or some other suggestion. I'm certainly flexible."

"Yes, sir."

"So here is my proposal: I...you and I together...will hire a cleaning lady to come in one or two days a week...your call...I will commit to being responsible for the children on Saturdays and Sundays, giving you both days off. I...we...may hire a babysitter on the weekends if I have to be out for a short time, and you can hire a babysitter any time you want, if you need to be somewhere else. And...you get a twenty percent raise in your salary."

"Oh, Mr. Cross, that's very generous..."

"Don't say anything now. You think about it carefully over the weekend, and let's talk Sunday night when we both get back. And I'm open to any other suggestions you might have. We **want** you, Greta!"

With tears welling up in her eyes, Greta shook her head very slowly, "You're too kind, Mr. Cross. Yet, I would still be responsible for two little children. It's not the money. It's the responsibility I worry about, at my age. I promise I will think about it very carefully over the weekend. And, yes, we'll sit down Sunday night and talk it over."

"Good. Now I hope you have a wonderful weekend. I know I can, with the kids and my parents. Springtime in our West Virginia mountains is about as close to heaven as you can get on this earth. I'm going to take the kids hiking up some of the old trails we used as kids. I want Sally and Tyke to begin to understand what a different, wonderful world exists out there in our mountains and valleys, far away from the big cities. Ginger never really has been able to run free here in McLean. Wait 'til the kids experience the joy of seeing her cavorting through the woods, chasing after squirrels and rabbits."

* * *

Cliff and the children arrived a few minutes before the sun was setting behind the mountains. Before they could get out of the car to hug Ruth Ann and Clint, Ginger scampered straight for the dog pens where four beagles were jumping wildly at their fence, excited at the arrival of one of their own. Ruth Ann insisted on immediately taking the children to sit on the back porch steps to watch the sun go down, a ritual from Cliff's childhood days. In fact, it was one of the first memories he could recall.

"Clifford, you and Clint get over here, too." As the five of them squeezed together on the old wooden steps, Ruth Ann explained to the children, "Now, you've got to concentrate and watch closely. Raise your right finger up in the air like this the moment you see the bottom of the sun touch the tip of the treetops on the mountain. First one to see it gets a one-scooper ice-cream cone tomorrow down at the corner store. No cheating. Then, keeping your eyes right on the sun as it slowly sinks behind the mountain, you make a wish to yourself...it's got to be an important wish...what you want to be when you grow up, or something real good you want to accomplish...like getting As in school, or hoping your mommy hears your prayers. And then at the very instant the last tiny tip of the sun disappears behind the mountain, you raise your left finger up in the air, quick as you can, like this. First one to see it gets a one scooper, too. Now, if the winner is the first one to see both the top and the bottom of the sun, then you win a two scooper. But the important thing is, that you really have to concentrate on your wish for it to come true. Your daddy used to beat me all the time. He always got the two scoopers. But I got my wish to come true. You can only tell your wish after it comes true. Mine was that your daddy get an education and make something of himself. And see...my wish came true. Uh-oh, sun's starting to sink. Get ready."

Both Sally and Tyke screwed up their little faces and concentrated on the setting sun. As the last tip at the very top sunk behind the mountains, leaving only a soft afterglow filtering between the shadows of the trees, both Sally and Tyke had played the game to perfection.

"My goodness," Ruth Ann exclaimed. "I believe it was a tie! Sally and Tyke beat the three of us. I guess I'll just have to buy them both double scoopers tomorrow at the store."

"Looks that way, Ma. Hope you both made your secret wishes."

"I'm not telling, Daddy," Sally shook her head vigorously, and frowned at her little brother. "Don't you tell, either, Tyke!"

After the children went through their evening ritual of saying their prayers and closing their eyes tight to see their mother, both Ruth Ann and Clint insisted on helping Cliff tuck them in. The three adults then went into the kitchen to have some hot chocolate and reminisce, sitting around the kitchen table.

Cliff explained that he planned to take the kids hiking in the mountains in the morning, that he hoped to instill in them an appreciation for the kind of life he experienced growing up. "After the kids are in bed tomorrow night, I'm going to slip down to the Moonshiner to have a drink with Jumper and some of the old crowd. I guess you won't mind being stuck with the little ones. I know it'll be a terrible imposition," he grinned.

"What are grandparents for?" Ruth Ann smiled. "I just wish we had them every weekend."

"Cliff, I don't mean to be telling you your business," his father knitted his eyebrows, "but I'd watch my step with that crowd down there. I know how close you were to them years ago, but people change...sometimes not for the better."

"What are you trying to say, Pap?"

"Well, there's been talk around town...about Jumper and that crony of his, Joe Joe, being involved in some pretty heavy stuff."

"Oh, they've got some harebrained scheme about buying Mr. Siefert's Ford dealership over in Oak Hill, but nothing's going to come of it. I love those guys dearly, but I wouldn't put two cents in any venture they might cook up...I'm just going to have a couple of drinks with my old buddies. That's all."

"Well, you be careful, son," Ruth Ann wagged her finger.

* * *

The next morning, Cliff filled his backpack with the peanut butter and jelly sandwiches Ruth Ann had prepared, bundled up the children, and led them up a winding path behind the house into the mountains, with Ginger following behind. The dogwood already was in bloom, the leaves of the oaks and maples were beginning to form their verdant canopy above the forest floor, and the smell of spring was in the air. When a gray squirrel scampered along a lower branch of a red oak, Ginger charged the tree, barking ferociously, as Sally crouched down screaming, "No, Ginger. No! Come back."

To everyone's surprise, the little beagle spun around, raced back, and jumped up on Sally, licking her face as they both fell to the ground. "Look, Daddy...she loves me!" Sally exclaimed.

Cliff smiled and nodded approvingly.

As the scattered rays of the noon-day sun fell between the limbs and leaves, dappling the earth below, Cliff led his little band to a giant pine beside a babbling brook. Ginger immediately plunged into the cold, clear stream, struggling to momentarily perch atop a slab of rock worn smooth by the currents of a thousand years, then slipped back into the icy waters and scrambled onto shore. She shook herself furiously, spraying Sally and Tyke, then darted off into the woods, apparently chasing something. The children both squealed happily as they wiped the droplets from their eyes.

Cliff spread a blue-and-white checkered picnic cloth over a bed of pine needles beneath the tree, set their sandwiches, potato chips, and cans of root beer on it. As they ate their lunch, Cliff pointed to a prickly patch of bushes growing alongside the stream, and explained, "See, the little buds forming on the bushes...in a few weeks they will burst open, into tiny pink rosebuds, and eventually blossom into wild roses, four or five on a stem. My daddy and mommy used to hike up here with me on Sunday afternoons, and we had our own little picnics under this very tree. Grandpa Clint would cut several bunches of those wild roses for Grandma Ruth, and she would set them in jars of water throughout the house. They'd live for days...a lot longer than store-bought flowers...and give every room a clean, fresh smell. Even set them on a shelf in the old privy behind the chicken coop. Your grandpa said they reminded him of your grandma...hearty ...strong...pretty to look at, but sometimes a little prickly, too."

"Did you ever bring mommy up here?" Tyke asked. "Did those flowers remind you of mommy?"

Cliff leaned back on his elbow, squinting up through the pine branches for a few moments before replying, "No...not really. Mommy reminded me more of a beautiful bouquet of blossoming yellow roses...each full petal perfectly in its place. That's what they presented to her on the day she was named Homecoming Queen. That's what I always gave her on her birthdays and our anniversaries...and on the days when you two were born. Other times, too. Your mommy was my...," Cliff swallowed hard, stared down at the bed of pine needles, and hoarsely whispered, "...my Golden Girl." Shaking himself, he hurriedly stuffed the trash from their picnic into his backpack and jumped up, "Come on, let's get a move on...I want to show you an old coal mine over that next rise before we start back down."

"But, Daddy, we've got to find Ginger first," Sally pleaded.

"She's right back there behind you, dummy," Tyke pointed to a fallen log. Ginger was lying behind the log, her two front paws up over her eyes.

"Don't you call me dummy, you little squirt!" Sally's eyes flashed at her brother.

"Hey...knock it off...the both of you," Cliff scolded. "Let's go," he lightly swatted each of their behinds.

Topping the rise, Cliff stopped to catch his breath and pointed to what appeared to be a bramble-covered hole in the side of the hill, a few hundred feet below.

Reaching the mouth of the little mine, he unsheathed a machete out of his backpack and began hacking away at the brush and vines obscuring the entrance. Taking a flashlight out of his backpack, he cautioned, "Now we're only going to take a few steps inside, so you can see what an old mine looks like...see a few small outcroppings of coal still in the walls. Wouldn't be safe to go too far in. The rotting timbers holding up the walls and ceiling could give way any moment...crushing or trapping us inside. Here, let's hold one another's hands. Let's go...watch your step."

The three of them stepped carefully over some fallen rocks, going no more than a dozen feet into the mine. Shining his flashlight along the walls and up at the ceiling, Cliff said, "See that thin black seam running through the dirt wall? That's coal. Reach up and touch it."

As they both obeyed, Sally shivered, "Daddy, it's damp in here."

"I'm cold. Look how black it is up ahead," Tyke pointed.

"Okay, let's slowly turn around, get back outside, and talk about what you've seen," Cliff flashed the light toward the entrance. Ginger was standing outside, peering into the mine and barking.

"Ginger's a scaredy-cat," Tyke picked up a pebble and tossed it at the dog, who scampered back down the path.

"Come over here, kids," Cliff motioned for the children to sit beside him on a boulder near the mine mouth. "Now, who can tell me what's coal used for?"

"To heat Grandma Ruth's house," Sally waved her hand as she replied.

"I knew that," Tyke pushed her.

"Don't you touch me, you little runt," she pushed back.

"Stop! Stop," Cliff lowered his voice. "Now listen carefully. Coal...from old mines like this, and big modern mines like the one we can see from Grandma's front porch, not only heat lots of homes here in West Virginia and across America, but also is burned in big plants to generate electricity to heat and light up our homes...run factories...even power our air conditioners and refrigerators and washers and dryers. I know that's hard for you to understand. But as you get older, you will. The important thing I want you to remember is that Grandpa Clint, his daddy...my grandpap, Josey, and hundreds of men in this valley...thousands of men here in West Virginia, Pennsylvania, Ohio, and other states have spent their lives going into dark, damp, deep, cold, and dangerous mines like this one to dig the coal out of the earth so we can be warm, and have electricity, and have manufacturing plants that produce all the nice things we enjoy...our clothes, our cars, our homes, even our movies."

"How can coal make movies? I thought cameras did that," Sally asked.

"Indirectly, honey. I know it's too complicated for you to understand now. But someday you will. I just want you to remember now that the men in our family and hundreds of other families have spent their lives going down deep into the mines to dig out coal so we could have nice things. And many of them...too many of them...including one of my uncles, your great-uncle Isaac Cross, were killed in mine accidents...explosions, collapses, suffocations. Thousands of men lost their lives deep in the mines, digging coal in dangerous, unsafe conditions."

"You mean like that roof falling in on us?" Tyke asked.

"Yes, sir...and worse. Sometimes being trapped for days deep in a mine behind a cave-in. Eventually not having any more air to breathe, and slowly suffocating. You know how you have to hold your breath under water when you're swimming?"

"I can do that, Daddy," Sally answered.

"Me, too," Tyke added.

"But then, you had to come up for air. Well, the poor men trapped in coal mines need to come up for air too...except there isn't any, so they die."

"Boy, I'm never going to work in any old coal mine," Tyke shook his head emphatically.

"And you won't have to, son. I didn't mean to scare you with these stories, but I wanted you to at least begin to understand your heritage...and the hard lives your grandpap and so many others suffered through. That's why we've got to be so thankful for what we have...why it's so important that you get your education...why Grandma Ruth pushed me so hard to go to college, so I wouldn't end up down in one of the coal mines. But, enough of this stuff for today. Let's head back down the mountain. Time for you both to collect those two-scooper ice-cream cones your grandma owes you."

* * *

After supper, Ruth Ann and Clint took the children down to the corner store for their two-scooper cones, while Cliff spread some Jet Speed worksheets on the kitchen table to reaffirm his latest projections. Upon their return, the children played with Ginger in the back yard until dark, when Ruth Ann insisted everyone hold hands to say their prayers before tucking Sally and Tyke into bed. "Tomorrow's Easter," she reminded them. "I hope your daddy's brought new outfits for you to wear."

"Don't you fret none, Ma. They'll be dolled up," Cliff walked up behind his mother in the kitchen, put his arms around her waist, and squeezed her tightly. "Believe I'll mosey on down to the Moonshiner. After those chicken and biscuits, I can stand the walk. Best I walk home tonight, anyway, after an evening with the old crowd."

Ruth Ann put her hands on her hips, lowered her head, and scowled at her son, "Clifford..."

"He's growed, Ma. He ain't your boy no more," Clint grinned.

"Oh, yes he is...and always will be. And don't he look grand in that new plaid lumberjack shirt I got him? Our own Paul Bunyan!"

"Well, don't wait up for me. See you in the morning."

As Cliff walked down the porch steps, Clint opened the screen door and called, "Mind what I said, Cliff. Watch your step with them boys down there."

Chapter Twenty-Two

When Cliff stepped through the door of the Moonshiner, and stood unnoticed for a moment, surveying the room full of his boyhood friends, a dozen different memories flooded through him and he felt as though he had never been away.

Skeeter, who was tending bar, was the first to spot him. "Hey...look what the cat dragged in...Cliff! Where the hell you been, boy, since our reunion?"

"Skeeter!" May Belle whispered from her barstool. "Shush up. Don't you know about his wife?"

Skeeter winced and nodded. "Good to see you, Cliff."

Everyone gathered 'round him, patting him on the back, expressing their condolences, pulling out a barstool for him to sit on. Jumper and Joe Joe appeared from out of the back room, squeezed up to the bar on either side of Cliff, threw their arms around him, and ordered boilermakers for everyone.

"Damn, it's good to see all you guys. You too, May Belle," he pecked her on the cheek.

On their third boilermaker, Joe Joe called down the bar to one of the girls at the far end, "Linda...Linda Sue, get up here and say hello to Cliff. You remember Linda Sue, Cliff. She and my brother Spike got hitched. 'Course, he ain't doing her no good where he is."

"Spike still in, huh? Sorry about that, Joe Joe," Cliff replied.

"Brung it on himself. Come here, Linda," Joe Joe put his arm around his sister-in-law's waist.

"Hi, Cliff. Bet you don't remember me," Linda Sue batted her eyelashes at Cliff.

Cliff pursed his lips together, squinted, and slowly shook his head, "Gee...Linda...ah..."

"Oh, no reason for you to remember me...I was just a freshman when you was a senior. I was a junior high cheerleader, though," she brightened up.

"Can't say as I do," Cliff nodded. "But I surely would have if you looked like you do now," he winked.

"Ain't she something!" Joe Joe squeezed his sister-in-law. "We got our own Dolly right here in town. Check them headlights, Cliff." With that, Linda's pointy-toed shoe shot out, striking Joe Joe's shin.

"Ow! Damn you, Linda. Why'd you go and do that? I was only bragging on you."

"I don't need you bragging on me...you scuzzbucket. Cliff's got eyes, if he's got a mind to look," she twisted away from Joe Joe's arm.

"Come on, Jake, give the lady a seat," Jumper pushed the man off the barstool next to Cliff.

Linda Sue slid up onto the stool, adjusted her tight skirt, and crossed her legs. "Pay no never-mind to him, Cliff. He's just uncouth."

"So you're married to Spike. Always thought he was a good old boy. Sorry to hear about his troubles," Cliff said.

"Well, we're surely separated."

"I guess that's true enough. Can I buy you a drink?"

"Why, yes. Thank you. I'll have a Coors." Skeeter set the bottle in front of her, which she slowly tilted up to her lips, while keeping her eyes locked on Cliff.

"Come on, Cliff. We got some business to talk to you about in the back room," Joe Joe tugged at his sleeves.

"Be there in a minute, Joe Joe," Cliff jerked his arm away. "So, ah...you and Spike separated, you say?"

"Well, sort of. Yes, I guess you could say that."

"Maybe we could have another drink after I get done in the back."

"Sure, Cliff. Sounds great. We don't have to hang around here all night."

"I don't have my car here. I just walked down from my folks' house."

"I got my car."

"Fine. I really don't know my way around town too much, anymore."

"I could get us a six-pack, and we could drive up to the reservoir. You can see the slag dump all lit up from miles away."

"Sounds good to me. Don't move a muscle. I'll be back in a few minutes," he squeezed her thigh as he slid off his stool, and then hated himself as he followed Jumper and Joe Joe into the back room.

"Have a seat, Cliff," Jumper pointed to the wooden table and chairs as he slipped out the back door.

"What's going on?" Cliff looked at Joe Joe, puzzled.

"Just you wait and see," Joe Joe grinned from ear to ear, rubbed his hands together, and pulled up a chair.

In a few minutes, Jumper returned with a metal suitcase, bolted the door behind him, and set the case in the middle of the table.

"What's this all about?" Cliff frowned.

"Remember...," Jumper stood at the table over his case, "we told you, come spring, how we was going to be in a position to buy out old-man Siefert?"

"So?"

"Well, we wasn't blowing smoke, old buddy. Got the means right here." Jumper patted his case. "All we need is for you to throw in with us."

"Like we discussed at the class reunion," Joe Joe added.

"Now, hold on, boys. I just said I'd help you analyze the deal."

"Cliff, this ain't no pipe dream. Lookee here," Jumper took a key out of his pocket, unlocked the case, and proudly flipped open the lid.

Cliff's eyes went wide as he jerked his head back, stiffly, letting out a long whistle, "Where in the hell did you get **that**?"

"Nearly a quarter of a million smackers," Jumper grinned, nodded proudly, took out a packet of hundred dollar bills and riffled them. "Now, old buddy, are we serious, or are we serious? Count it."

"Jump...I don't want to count it. I don't even want to **touch** it. Answer my question. Where in the hell did you two get that kind of money?"

Jumper looked at Joe Joe, but before they could answer, they heard a commotion out in the bar. A loud voice shouted something they couldn't hear over the screams of women in the bar, followed by sounds of tables and chairs being overturned.

Joe Joe looked out over the swinging doors and exclaimed, "Shit...it's the police!"

Jumper looked wildly about, slammed his case shut, and dashed for the back door. When he unbolted the door, four state troopers with weapons drawn, barged through the door. As one trooper slammed Jumper against the wall, the case lid popped open, and the packets of cash spilled out onto the floor. Another trooper yanked Joe Joe out of his chair, shoving him against the wall beside Jumper. As Cliff half-rose out of his chair, yelling, "What the hell...," two troopers grabbed his arms, but before they could pin him, he cursed, "Get your goddamn hands off me!" knocking one of the troopers over a chair. As he spun around, the trooper struck his gun butt into the back of Cliff's skull. Cliff's legs buckled as the trooper smashed his face against the wall, while the other trooper struggled to his feet, jerked Cliff's hands behind his back, and cuffed him.

Cliff was still dazed as he vaguely heard a trooper mumble something about, "You have the right to remain silent...," and was led, stumbling through the front of the bar into the street where a crowd had gathered, and cameras and TV lights were flashing.

"Ain't that Cliff Cross?" a voice out of the crowd shouted. "Hey, Cliff...Cliff...is that you?" His head was still throbbing as he was shoved into the back seat of a state police cruiser.

Within a few minutes, the police cars, with sirens blaring and lights flashing, pulled up in front of the local jail, where Cliff, Jumper, and Joe Joe were removed from separate vehicles and led into the jail. The Chief and several officers were waiting for them.

"Put these three in separate cells, Chief," a plain-clothed state police detective instructed the Chief. "Book 'em on possession of illegal substances with intent to distribute. We'll get 'em arraigned Monday morning."

"Wait a minute," Cliff exploded. "What are you doing to me? I've done nothing wrong."

"Ya, buddy. That's what they all say," the detective sighed.

"Cliff? Clifford? What are you doing here, mixed up with these two?" the Chief looked perplexed.

Cliff looked at his distant cousin, Harley Snook, stared down at the floor dejectedly, and shook his hand, "Damn if I know, Harley. I was down at the Moonshiner, having a couple of drinks with some of the old gang, Jump takes me in the back room to talk to me about buying a car dealership, brings out a big suitcase full of money...and the next thing I know, the police are there smacking me upside the head and cuffing me."

"Come on, Chief. Let's get them in the lockup. We got a pile of paperwork to fill out and it's past midnight, the detective motioned toward the cells. This can get sorted out Monday morning with the magistrate. This big fella, who's supposed to be innocent...write down that we're also charging him with resisting arrest."

"You know who this is?" the Chief pointed to Cliff. "This here's Clifford Cross...the basketball star...president of some big computer company in Chicago, or someplace."

"Harley, I don't care if he's the king of England, put him right back in one of those cells until he gets arraigned."

"Well, he's got a right to call a lawyer. They all do. Although I'm not surprised about these two. But Cliff, here...you're making a big mistake."

"That's for the courts to decide. I just bring 'em in."

"Well, get your cuffs off them, so they can make their phone call, and we can lock 'em up 'til Monday." Turning to his officers, the Chief said, "You take those two into the bull pen so they can make their calls, if they want to. I'll take Cliff with me."

The Chief took Cliff upstairs to his office, shut the door, and shook his head disgustedly, "What the hell's wrong with you, Cliff, associating with these bums?"

"Harley, they're my teammates. You remember. I was just having a drink with them...that's all."

"Well, boy, you're in the soup, that's for sure. Better call your lawyer. Use my phone."

"I don't have one, except for my company lawyer. Sarah's dad did all our personal stuff. Oh, boy..." He took a deep breath and let it out slowly. He held his hand on the telephone receiver for several seconds, and then dialed a number.

"Walter...Walter, I'm sorry to wake you up so late...yes, this is Cliff. I'm in a mess down here in Beckley, and I need your help." Cliff explained the situation to his former father-in-law, answered a few questions, and then said, "I know, Walter. I appreciate it. Sure, bring a criminal attorney with you. Yes, dammit. They are keeping me in jail 'til Monday morning. I understand. Okay. I guess I have to wait until then. Thanks, Walter. And...please be sure to tell Odessa that I am absolutely innocent. I've done nothing wrong! Okay, see you tomorrow morning."

Keeping his hand on the phone, Cliff said, "Harley, I've got to call my mother. The kids are up there. What about all those cameras...is this going to be in the news?"

"Sure. It's big news. Be on television tomorrow. Probably won't make the papers until Monday."

"Shit! I've got to call my office, too. But that can wait until tomorrow morning. You'll let me, won't you?"

"Hell, you can sleep up here on my cot tonight, if you want."

"Would that be smart, with Jumper and Joe Joe down there in the cells?"

"Suppose not. Come on, let me put some salve on those cuts on your face, and make your call to Ruth Ann."

She was sitting up waiting for Cliff to come home. When he told her what had happened, there was a long pause, and then she replied, "Don't worry about the little ones. They're fine. Get yourself the best lawyer you can find. I wouldn't rely on anyone local. What about Walter Wilson? He can help..."

"Already called him, Ma," Cliff replied, surprised at how calmly his mother was taking it. But then, that was Ruth Ann, he thought...completely focused on doing whatever needed to be done.

"Good. You better call your people...and Greta, first thing in the morning. They don't need to learn about this from someone else. I'll watch the children. Your pap will be down in the morning. Is Harley there? Let me talk to Harley."

"I'm awful sorry, Ma. Okay. Here's Harley."

Harley took the receiver, listened for a moment, and replied, "Yes, Ruth Ann. Absolutely. You know that. What do you think kin are for? I promise you. Fine. Try to get some sleep. Goodnight, Ruth Ann." Turning to Cliff, he shook his head, laughing, "Your ma's a pistol. If they don't have you out of here on Monday, I expect her to show up with a hacksaw. Well, let's get you locked in. I'll put you in the back cell with a double mattress. You try to get some sleep, hear?"

"Not tonight, Harley. Afraid not tonight. But thanks for your help. I gotta believe I'm going to get out of this, but, boy, is it going to be a bombshell...in both Washington and New York."

* * *

Cliff did finally fall asleep a few hours before dawn, but then was awakened by the strains of "Hosanna in the Highest..." filtering through the open windows from the Easter sunrise service at the Baptist church across the street from the jail. He climbed up on his cot to peer through his barred windows at the church, which had been so much of his family's life. Gripping the bars tightly, a surge of emotion enveloped him, and he felt like crying. Unlike his parents, he had never been very religious, but the sight of the church, the sunrise behind it, and sound of the music made his predicament unbearable. He was engulfed in shame, even though, logically, he knew he had done nothing wrong. He stepped down, got on his knees, clasped his hands together on top of the cot, bowed his head, and began to pray, "Lord, please help me to get out of this mess. I know I could have been a better person. I've done so many things wrong in my life. But if you could see your way clear to lift this burden from me, as undeserving as I am, I promise I'll become a better person. I promise I'll try my best to make my life worthwhile. And...and thank you from the bottom of my heart for all my many blessings. Amen." Tears welled up in his eyes, and as he looked up through the bars to the sunlight, he remembered the words from Jeremiah his mother had drummed into him as a child, "Nothing is too hard for thee...nothing is too hard for me!" he stood erect and gestured with his clinched fist high in the air.

A few minutes later, Harley appeared, unlocked the cell door, and motioned, "Follow me." He led Cliff up the stairs into his office and pointed to a plate piled high with pancakes, doused with butter and syrup, sitting on his desk. "Maude wouldn't let me out of the house this morning without bringing you a hot breakfast. Sit down there in my chair. Take cream and sugar in your coffee?"

"Black's fine, Harley. Gee, I don't know what to say. Tell Maude I really do appreciate this. Guess I am pretty hungry."

After cleaning his plate, Cliff asked, "Mind if I make some phone calls, Harley?"

"Go right ahead."

"Thanks. And be sure to tell Maude I said thanks. And Harley, I hope you know how much I appreciate your...well, your attitude about this whole mess."

"You'll be out of here tomorrow, Cliff. I'm sure this fiasco will get straightened out."

First, Cliff called Nettie at home, catching her before she went to church. After explaining the situation and asking her to call Jet Speed, she replied, "Sure, boss. What else can I do? What about the children? You want me to go over to your house?"

"That's a great idea, if you wouldn't mind. I'm going to call Greta now, but I have no idea how she'll react. I offered her a better deal to try to persuade her to stay. We were going to discuss it tonight. Boy...now she's really going to want to fly the coop. Wouldn't blame her. Maybe you can take her temperature."

"I'm on my way. And don't worry. Everything's going to work out just fine. You're one tough guy."

"I don't feel very tough...no, dammit, you're right. Nothing is too hard for me!"

Cliff then called Greta, and to his pleasant surprise, she assured him, "Mr. Cross, I'm sure you didn't do anything wrong, and we can just put our little conversation on hold. You can count on me. I'll be here at least until you work out your problem."

After Cliff talked to both the children to tell them he would be home within a few days, he then placed the phone call he dreaded the most, catching Oscar as he was going out the door for his Sunday morning game of golf.

Oscar listened carefully, and then replied softly, "I'm sure you're totally innocent, Cliff. But you understand, the problem this creates for us."

"Oscar, it's going to be over in a week or two. They'll drop the charges once they hear the facts."

"Maybe. But this can queer the deal with Tektron. They're not about to buy a company whose CEO is under criminal indictment. Maybe you should step aside and we'll put Hal Greenburg in charge. He knows the Tektron people."

"If I become a liability, I'll step down, but we're not there yet."

"Cliff, you **are** a liability now. I've got a copy of the AP wire story that will run in the papers tomorrow. Listen to the lead:

COMPUTER EXEC ARRESTED IN DRUG RAID

Clifford Cross, former U. of W.Va. basketball star and president
of Jet Speed Printers, Inc., was arrested Saturday night in a drug
raid by the state police in the Moonshiner bar in Beckley, West
Virginia..."

"Do you need to hear more?"

"I get the picture, Oscar. All I ask for is that you give me a few
days."

"Okay, but keep me informed. And you better call your old buddies at Tektron right away."

"Yes, sir. I am truly sorry about this, Oscar, but I didn't do anything wrong." Cliff placed a call to Gil Fenno at Tektron, who listened
sympathetically. "Damn, Cliff. I guess the shit must have really hit the
fan. Best we suspend our talks until this gets sorted out."

"Of course, Gil. Hopefully, that will be within a few days. I'll
keep you apprised."

"Fine. And Cliff...we know you well enough not to believe any
of this bullshit. Keep your head up, boy. We'll stay in touch."

Cliff's father was waiting for him downstairs when Harley returned him to his cell. "I think I need a hug, Pap," he threw his arms
around his father, who assured him everything was fine at home, and
they had total confidence in him. Cliff was relieved that his father
didn't mention his earlier admonition to stay clear of his old friends.

A few minutes later, Walter Wilson arrived with his partner,
Jonathan Foster, a criminal attorney. They listened carefully to Cliff's
description of the previous night's raid, the circumstances surrounding his meeting with Jumper and Joe Joe, and compiled a list of the
people present who might serve as witnesses. They then outlined the
procedures that would be followed at the arraignment Monday morning, assuring Cliff that he would be free on bail by noon. Cliff introduced them to the Chief, explaining that he was a distant cousin,
who offered the lawyers the use of his office. They spent most of the

afternoon telephoning potential witnesses, made reservations at Motel 6, and then left to interview Linda Sue Karns.

After eating a ham and cheese on rye, with potato chips, for lunch, Cliff spent the afternoon trying to concentrate on a Zane Grey cowboy novel Harley had loaned him.

At suppertime, Harley unlocked the cell door and took Cliff back upstairs to Harley's office. Passing Jumper's cell, Jumper reached out to catch Cliff's arm, "Cliff...Cliff, I didn't know...me and Joe Joe deserve what we get, but you...well, it ain't right. I'll set things straight, I promise."

Cliff just stared at his old friend, patted his hand, and shrugged.

The next morning after breakfast, Cliff was permitted to put on his street clothes and was led by Harley, with Walter Wilson and Jonathan Foster walking behind him, to the Magistrate's Office, catty-cornered across the street. When he arrived, Jumper, Joe Joe, and their lawyers were already in their seats. To Cliff's astonishment, after the magistrate hammered his gavel down calling the session to order, the whole proceeding lasted less than fifteen minutes. The prosecutor rose, charging the three of them with "possession of an illegal substance with intent to distribute" and Cliff, with the additional charge of "resisting arrest." The magistrate set bail at ten thousand dollars each, which each of the attorneys indicated they were prepared to post. Foster indicated that he would have a motion to dismiss the charges against Cliff, and the other two attorneys announced that they would have motions to "suppress." The magistrate set a hearing on the motions for two weeks hence, urged the prosecutor and defense attorneys to attempt to arrive at plea bargains before the matter was turned over to the Court of Common Pleas, where a judge would set a trial date, and adjourned the hearing.

"That's it?" Cliff asked Walter as he walked out of the building, temporarily a free man.

"For you, right now, yes," Walter replied. "But for us, right now, our real work just begins. We've got to get these charges dropped before the prosecutor takes them to the grand jury to get you indicted."

"Should I stay? Should I take the kids back to Washington? Can I go back to work? What should I do?"

"I'd suggest you stay here for the next few days, Cliff, because we're either going to get this quashed quickly, or we're going to be in it for the long haul."

"Whatever you say, Walter. I suppose I can get some work done up there on the phone, if I can keep my mind on it. The kids will miss some school, but maybe I can have Nettie drive Greta over here and the two of them can take the kids back to Washington."

"Good idea. I'd love to see the children, but under the circumstances, best I don't. I felt I had to tell Odessa about your phone call in the middle of the night, and my reason for coming down. She wanted to come right away to take the children back to Charleston with her, but I persuaded her that now was not the time. She may show up here at any time. You know how...well, how excited she can get. Probably best for you to get the children back to Washington as fast as you can. They don't need more turmoil in their lives right now."

"Thanks, Walter. I'll try to take care of it."

"Jon and I will be working out of our motel. Hopefully, we will have assembled enough facts to be able to meet with the prosecutor by midweek. Keep your chin up, Cliff. We're going to get you out of this."

Nettie immediately agreed to call Greta and for the two of them to drive over to Beckley to pick up the children. "But first, boss, I think you should talk personally to the guys here and in Chicago," she suggested. "I've explained the situation to them, and they're all with you, but they need to hear your voice. Can I get them on a conference call?"

Cliff, of course, agreed, and after describing the circumstances in detail, they were relieved. "Don't worry, Tonto. We've got everything under control," Hal assured him. "Hell, we don't even need to see your ugly face. And by the way, I spoke to Gus over at Tektron, and he told me they're willing to sit tight, at least for a little while."

"Thanks, guys. I think this is going to get resolved quickly, and then we can get on with doing our deal. Just keep your fingers crossed."

After the conference call, Nettie picked up Greta, who had packed some sandwiches to eat on the way, and they headed for Beckley.

Four hours later, as they pulled into the driveway and got out of the car, the children and Ginger rushed to greet them. Within minutes, Ruth Ann had Nettie and Greta helping her set the table for supper, and filling the serving bowls with crisp green salads and mashed potatoes, carrots, peas, spring onions, and thick juicy slices of breaded meat loaf. By the time supper was finished, it seemed as though the three women had been friends forever. Nettie insisted on washing the dishes, while Greta dried. Ruth Ann cleaned up the kitchen, scrubbed the oil-clothed table, and put everything away in its place.

Cliff offered to get them rooms at the motel, so they could drive back in the morning, but Nettie said she had too much work to do back in the office. "Anyway the kids can curl up in the back seat and sleep, while Greta and I take turns driving. We'll be home before midnight. That way the kids can go to school and I can get to the office."

"You know best, Nettie," Cliff said, as he walked all of them down to the car. He, Ruth Ann, and Clint all hugged the kids, and Cliff promised he would be home in a few days.

As the car pulled away, Ruth Ann put her arm through Cliff's and reached out to take hold of Clint's hand as the three of them walked back into the house. "You're very fortunate, son," she smiled, "to have those two to look after the children...and to look after you. I guess that's Nettie's job...right?"

"Oh, she runs the office. Smart as a whip. Keeps things humming."

"She attached?"

"Her husband was killed in Viet Nam, Ma. Don't believe she ever got over it. But she's seeing Arnie Shearer, my controller. They make a fine couple...complement each other...you know, opposites attract. Arnie's quiet and studious...Nettie's like the Energizer bunny."

"She ain't bad to look at, son," Clint squeezed Ruth Ann's hand.

"I'd say she has personality plus...you dirty old man," Ruth Ann gave her husband a friendly poke. "You know, son, it's been over a year since Sarah's passing. Maybe it is time for you to begin thinking about your future. You're a young man. Isn't natural for you to be alone. Mind if I ask, are you seeing anyone?"

"No, Ma. And it's a blessing I'm not. I've got kids to worry about...and a business to run...and until I get out of this mess I'm in, that's one more obligation I don't need right now. Once I get this problem solved, and once I get the future of the business nailed down, then it'll be time enough for me to think about my personal life."

"Just don't get so caught up in business that you let some wonderful chance slip away from right under your nose."

"I won't. I promise you, Ma. But first things first. Right now, I'm going to get some work done in my room, and then try to get a good night's sleep. Tomorrow could be a mighty big day."

Chapter Twenty-Three

Tuesday was the longest day in Cliff's life. After shaving and bathing—in the four-legged tub that he loved to splash around in as a small boy, watching a bar of Lifebuoy bob about, but into which he now could hardly fit—he sopped clean a plate of fried potatoes, ham and scrambled eggs Ruth Ann had prepared for him.

He phoned Greta to be sure the children got off to school on time. He phoned the office to be sure there were no new crises requiring his attention. He phoned the plant to be sure...well, he didn't know why, but he called them anyway. Everything was running smoothly, or so they all said. Nobody needed him, or at least it seemed that way.

He phoned Walter at the motel, who assured him that he and Jonathan were pulling together a strong case to have the charges dropped, and would be making their presentation to the prosecutor on Wednesday morning.

He helped his father clean out the dog pens and take the beagles for a run. He helped his mother gather eggs and feed the chickens. He chopped half a cord of wood, even though none would be needed until at least next fall.

After lunch, he tried to take a nap, but couldn't sleep. So, he called the office again and had Nettie read him the previous week's sales reports, salesman by salesman, line by line.

249

Walter called, asking him to join him and Jon for dinner, but Cliff was too embarrassed to be seen in public, so he gobbled down Ruth Ann's lasagna, and met them after dark in their motel room. "I think we've got it licked, Cliff," Walter greeted him with a broad, reassuring smile. "Tell him, Jon."

"Well, Cliff, we have affidavits from Linda Sue Karns, May Belle Hanik, and her husband, one 'Skeeter' Hanik, affirming that you were simply a patron at the bar, were invited by Jason 'Jumper' Ramsey and Joseph Joshua Karns to follow them in the back room because they claimed they wanted to show you something. You were back there only a few minutes when the police entered. There is absolutely no evidence that you knew what they were involved in."

"In fact," Walter added, "your surprised and angry response, which is in the police report, gives further credence to your innocence. The Police Chief also tells us that he heard that Jumper fellow apologize to you, said something to the effect that you had nothing to do with it. So, we probably can get his corroborating testimony, but we'll have to talk to his attorney first. Bottom line, we've got all this exculpatory evidence, including your high standing in the community, and they don't have squat to tie you to the money or the drugs they found on Karns."

"Your telling me Joe Joe actually had drugs on him?"

"Two packs of blunts in his coat pocket. That's ten cigars laced with marijuana...about three grams a cigar...plus sixteen one-ounce packets of the stuff in his pants' pocket. Coupled with the quarter of a million in cash they seized in the suitcase, that's enough to charge them with 'intent to distribute.' When their lawyer tells them about that, they'll be ready to cop a plea. And part of the plea can be to exonerate you. So, things are looking up, my boy. We're having a conference with the prosecutor and the lawyers tomorrow morning, and I fully expect charges against you to be dropped on the spot."

"What about my resisting arrest?"

"Once we get the serious charges thrown out, no jury would convict you of resisting arrest. You were an innocent guy being roughed up by the law...by those snoopers who ought to go back up to Charleston where they belong. No way...not in your hometown."

Finally, Cliff had a decent night's sleep. The nightmare would be over, and although he wasn't sure he ever would be able to completely shake his irrational sense of shame, life would return to normal. But normal for him could still mean chaos. How was he going to raise two children without a mother? Could he still put together the Tektron deal? Would he really have a future with them after the deal was done? How would the employees and his friends in McLean react to him after the charges were dropped? People read the awful headlines—arrested in a drug raid. Five years later would they remember that he had been cleared, or only that he once had somehow been connected with selling drugs? Would his good name have been irrevocably damaged?

But after a forty-minute run with one of Clint's beagles up along a mountain path, and another of Ruth Ann's breakfasts, he was feeling pretty positive again. The knot in his stomach had disappeared. His phone calls home and to the office were reassuring, and a greeting card he received in the morning mail from Nettie and the gang perked up his spirits even more. On the front of the card was a vest-suited boss towering over meek, smiling employees, with his arm outstretched to the edge of the card. The caption read, "Dear, sweet boss, we miss you so." Upon opening the card, on the inside, the boss's hand appeared, cracking a whip over the cowering employees, with the caption, "But don't come back too soon."

"I miss you guys," he spoke aloud, smiling, as he leaned the card against his dresser mirror.

A few minutes before noon, he heard a car pull into the driveway, and looking through the window, saw Walter and Jonathan hurrying toward the front porch. Walking out to greet them, he sensed immediately that something was very wrong. "Fellas...what's the matter?"

"Some place we can talk privately, Cliff?" Walter's terseness unnerved Cliff, who motioned to the chairs on the porch, and called into the house, "Ma, I'm closing the front door. Need a little privacy with my lawyers." He sat down on the swing, rocking back and forth slowly, as the lawyers hunched down in their chairs, pulling them close to the swing.

"Got a problem, Cliff," Walter spoke somberly. "We had our conference this morning...laid out the facts of your innocence. Went well...until the prosecutor informed us that Karns's lawyer was set to drop a bombshell. Get this...in exchange for dropping all the charges against Karns, except possession, which is only a slap on the wrist, Karns will testify that you...**you** are the kingpin of the operation. The cash in the suitcase was brought in by them to give to you. You were being repaid for fronting the operation."

Cliff stared incredulously at his former father-in-law, then a slow malevolent smiled curled across his lips. He leaned forward, half-whispering, "Do you believe him?"

"Of course not, Cliff. He's just trying to save his..."

"Does the prosecutor believe him?"

"I don't think so, but it creates a problem for him. Now he can get direct testimony of your involvement...self-serving as it is. I understand he's up for reelection. You'd be a mighty big scalp for him to hang on his belt...sorry, Cliff. I meant a big fish. Would be quite a show trial here in town. Do I think we could win? Sure. But you never know for sure with juries. And...you're talking months of bad publicity, thousands of dollars. What about your business? What about the kids? Of course, Odessa's been itching to get her hands on them. You know that."

"Shit, Walter, what am I supposed to do?"

"I know it's easy for me to say, but stay calm...sit tight for a few more days. I'll try to smoke out the prosecutor tomorrow to see if he's serious about flipping Karns against you. I've got to learn where your pal, Jumper, stands in all of this. His testimony could help you...or kill you, if he's part of any plea agreement." Clapping his hands together and standing, Walter continued, "But we've got our work to do. Just remember two things, Cliff. You're innocent...and, Jon here is the best defense attorney in West Virginia. We'll call you as soon as we have anything...good or bad. And Cliff...I still consider you my son-in-law," Walter's eyes misted over, as he patted Cliff's knee and turned to leave.

Cliff nodded goodbye, muttering to himself, "A **criminal** attorney...I've got my own **criminal** attorney. How the hell did I get in this mess!"

* * *

While Cliff's attorneys were giving him the bad news, Jumper was meeting with Joe Joe at the old farmhouse back in the hills to hear Joe Joe's latest scheme. "Hey, Jump," Joe Joe punched his partner's arm, "wipe that hangdog look off your kisser. Me and Samuel got things figured out. No need for us to take the fall."

"You and that shyster lawyer of yours got things figured out? What the hell you talking about? Get your head out of the sand, man. They got us cold. And you, asshole...having your pockets stuffed with dope. My guy tells me we're looking at time. Says if we plead guilty, we just might get a reduced sentence."

"We can walk away with probation, and pleading guilty is part of it."

"Ya, sure. Tell me how we pull that off."

"Simple. Samuel's already negotiating with the prosecutor. We lay it on Cliff. He was the brains behind all this. He fronted the operation...put up his cash. We didn't have no money to start with. Once we started moving the stuff, the cash came rolling in. Might have to give up the names of a few of the guys at the auction, but tough shit. Them's the breaks. We was just meeting Cliff at the Moon-shiner to take him in the back room to pay him off. That there cash was his."

"I can't believe what I'm hearing. You want to lay this all on Cliff when he had nothing to do with it. When it was your harebrained idea to start selling the stuff retail...and I was dumb enough to go along with it."

"Don't get me wrong, Jump. I like Cliff. He's a good old boy. He was one of us...once. But we're between the rock and the hearth. Self-preservation is the first rule of the jungle."

"I guess I didn't know lifelong friends could turn on each other, like animals in the jungle, to save their own skins. Now, you listen to me good, Joe Joe. I'll have nothing to do with this. I'll take my medicine like a man. I let you talk me into planting the marijuana. I stood to profit. I knew the risks. But don't you be hurting Cliff!"

"Come on, Jump. Use your head. If I finger Cliff, it might work. We get off with just using. They drop the distributing charges. We walk, with a fine and probation. If you was to back me up, that would be two witnesses. Gives the prosecutor a front-page victory over a real big shot. You seen the papers already. Cliff's the story. We're nobody."

"Damn you, Joe Joe!" Jumper knocked over the kitchen table and hurled a chair at Joe Joe, missing him and putting a gash in the cardboard wall. "I'm **telling** you...don't you do nothing to hurt Cliff!"

"Don't you be threatening me, you goddamn lush! If you want to be sitting behind bars for the next five years...that's what that fella over in Fairmont got last winter for selling a lot less than we been moving...that's your business, but I'm looking out for number one. I'm telling Samuel, first thing tomorrow morning, to go ahead and try to cut me a deal," Joe Joe glared at Jumper, made an obscene gesture, and stomped out the door.

"Like hell you are, you piece of shit!" Jumper grabbed the planting bar leaning in the corner beside the door, ran out into the yard behind Joe Joe, and smashed the pointed end of the bar deep into the top of Joe Joe's skull.

Joe Joe's arms momentarily fluttered out like a chicken's wings, as he emitted a gurgling sound, sinking to his knees, wobbling, and then falling facedown in the mud.

Jumper froze, stared down at his friend, dropped the planting bar at his side, and muttered, "Shit!"

Blood oozed out of Joe Joe's head down over his ear, purpling the soggy earth beneath. His left leg stiffened, then fell limp. His eyes turned to glassy marbles, staring blinding at Jumper. This was the first dead body Jumper had seen since Viet Nam. The first one he had killed since then. For him, it had been so easy then. And much too easy now. Yet, this time he didn't feel the exhilaration, the rush he got each time his M16 had found its mark, deep in the jungles of that godforsaken land. But then he wasn't killing boyhood friends.

* * *

A high-finance world away from little Beckley, West Virginia, Sidney was on the phone again, ranting to Oscar. "Don't you see, Oscar, this is a blessing in disguise. Now that Cross got himself arrested on drug charges, we can dump him like a pot of hot piss. You pick up the phone and call Gil Fenno at Tektron. Tell him how upset we are. We had no idea what Cross was doing. We're reputable businessmen. You sit down with Fenno. Cut a deal. Obviously, we're going to have to drop our price. He'll know that. He'll see this as his chance to squeeze us down. But that's okay. We'll exercise our options...water down the stock...and get out whole. Better than whole. Now, don't dilly-dally around. Get it done!"

"Under the circumstances, I guess you've got a point. Cliff says he's innocent, but they all say that. I've got no problem calling Tektron direct, but part of what they're buying is the management team. We don't want all of them to walk. I think I'll feel out Hal Greenberg to see where he stands. Next to Cliff, they'll follow his lead."

"Just do it, Oscar. Get it done! I need that cash so I can settle my other problems."

Oscar hung up and immediately called Hal. "What do you hear from Cliff?"

"Nothing today, Mr. McMillan. But as of yesterday, things were looking up. His attorneys had taken several affidavits from witnesses at the bar who say that Cliff had nothing to do with those two scumbags selling drugs. He had just stopped in there to have a few drinks on Saturday night with his old hometown buddies. Cliff's lawyers are meeting with the prosecutor today, and they hope to have the charges dropped."

"Hal, you're in the saddle now. Let me share something with you confidentially. Our investors are getting cold feet over all this bad publicity...these criminal charges against the CEO of our company. They might pull the plug...call their loans...put the company in bankruptcy...take their tax losses and walk away."

"You mean Mr. Martin and you?"

"Ah, it's not that simple. We've got several investors tied up in other deals. Jet Speed is only part of a much bigger picture."

After a long silence, Hal asked, "So, what are you saying, Mr. McMillan? What can I do?"

"The Board thinks I should call Fenno direct. Try to cut the best deal I can. And, of course, make sure you and the management team are part of the deal."

"But cut Cliff out?"

"Not exactly. He'd still get his cash from the sale of his stock. Once he got his legal problems solved, Tektron probably will have a place for him."

"His problems might be solved in the next few days."

"And they might not. Even if they are, there's still the taint of his arrest and all the bad publicity. Hal, take my word for it. I've been around for a long time. You and the team should face the reality that Cliff's tainted. If we don't move fast, the deal could fall apart. All of you would be out on the street without anything to show for your hard work. If I call Fenno and try to strike a deal, can I count on you? The rest will follow your lead."

"I'm not so sure of that, Mr. McMillan, but I understand what you're saying. Give me a day. I'll get back to you tomorrow."

"Okay, but make it early, so I have time to contact Fenno. I'd like to meet with him before the weekend. Nail things down before the roof collapses on all of us."

* * *

Jumper looked about frantically to be sure no one was on the road or in the woods beyond. Hyperventilating, he grabbed hold of Joe Joe's ankles and dragged his body around the farmhouse into a jumble of weeds that once had been his grandma's vegetable garden. Stumbling up the back steps into the house, he bundled several dirty sheets of black plastic in his arms, pulled some binder twine out of a drawer, and bounded back out into the garden. He wrapped Joe Joe's body from head to toe, until it looked like a mummy. Still hyperventilating, he uprooted some hedgerow from around the garden to cover the body. "Got to get him buried...got to get him buried...**deep**, so he don't get rooted up." Too many times over the years, he had seen carcasses of cows and horses rooted out of shallow graves by wild animals. Their bones picked clean and left to bleach in the sun. Turning, he climbed into his pickup, wanting to race to town, but breathlessly muttering, "Slow down...slow down...Jesus, what have I done...be calm...be calm."

It was nearly suppertime when he reached his home, but he waved to his mother, motioning that he would eat in town. Pulling an old tarp out of the garage, he threw it into the back of his pickup truck with a spade shovel, rake, sack of lime, and a lantern.

He stopped at McDonald's to buy a chocolate milkshake and cheeseburger, attempting casual conversation with the cashier, so she might remember he had been there. By dusk he was back at the farm. First, he raked the ground where Joe Joe had fallen and over the path where he had dragged him into the garden. Then, the hard work began. It was past midnight when he finally had dug a six foot deep grave. By eerie lantern light, as the mist settled along the valley floor, and the fog rolled in overhead, he pulled Joe Joe's wrapped body onto the tarp, tied the grommets, pulling them tightly together. He then sprinkled a little lime into the bottom of the grave. Dragging the body alongside the grave, he muttered, "Damn you, Joe Joe...I told you...I **told** you...we wasn't hurtin' Cliff." With the heel of his muddy old combat boot, he slowly shoved the body over the edge, where it thumped into the bottom of the grave. He then emptied the sack of lime on top of the corpse.

It took another hour to fill up the hole, scatter rocks on it, and painstakingly insert weed roots into the dirt. He then walked backwards out of the garden to his truck, carrying his shovel and lantern in one hand and dragging his rake, upside-down, behind him.

Driving slowly in the dark through the dense fog, he did not turn on his headlights until he pulled onto the macadam road. His shoulders heaved to his heavy breathing, realizing that his night's work was not yet done.

Jumper turned off his headlights as he pulled into the alley behind Joe Joe's house. Digging his flashlight and work gloves out of his toolbox, he removed the key to Joe Joe's back door from beneath a loose stone on the walk and entered the kitchen. Feeling his way to Joe Joe's bedroom, he located a suitcase under the bed and a suit bag hanging in the closet. He stuffed them both full of Joe Joe's clothes, along with his bankbook and papers from the desk. He then pried loose a floorboard in the closet and lifted out Joe Joe's metal money box. It was locked. "Damn," he muttered, thinking that he probably had buried the key with Joe Joe. I can bust it open later, he thought, tucking it under his arm as he crept back through the kitchen and out to his truck, with the suitcase in one hand and the suit bag in the other.

It was nearly dawn when he drove up to the edge of the glowing slag dump, fifteen miles south of Beckley. Checking first to be sure no one was in sight, he tossed the cases down into the burning embers. Should I pitch the money box in, too? Don't be stupid, he thought. I can hide that away for a rainy day. Maybe in the dirt beneath my dirty oil barrel in the garage.

Now his work was done. He arrived home in time for breakfast, gave his mother a squeeze, crawled in bed, and slept 'til noon.

* * *

On Thursday morning, Hal called Nettie, Mike, and Arnie into his office, and got Smokey, Red, and Sam on the speaker phone. He explained their predicament, in effect, Oscar McMillan's ultimatum, and asked for their advice. In less than a millisecond, Mike practically spit out his words, "You tell that pin-striped pansy to kiss my ass!"

Simultaneously, the boys in Chicago chimed in, in slightly different words, "We're with Cliff...you tell him that!"

Arnie responded slowly, "If we stick with Cliff...we might all go down the drain...but...but, I can't turn my back on him now. I'm on Clifford's team."

Nettie leaned across her chair, threw her arm around Arnie's neck, and kissed his cheek.

"What was **that** for?" his eyes brightened.

"For you being you," she sparkled, lightly tapping his leg with the tip of her shoe.

"Where the hell's my kiss?" Mike grunted.

"I only flirt with gentlemen," she winked.

"What's going on back there?" Red's voice came through the speaker phone.

"Nothing worth your knowing about," Nettie answered. Then she added, "Don't you think we should talk to the boss about this?"

"Sure, but first I had to know where you all stood," Hal replied. "I'll call the big galoot right away. Then I owe Mr. McMillan a call, unless Cliff wants to handle it."

Cliff was taking out his frustration on another cord of firewood when Ruth Ann called him to the phone. "Tonto...you hanging in there?" Hal greeted him.

"Barely standing, kemo sabe," Cliff replied, realizing he would have to tell Hal about the latest complication. And then, Oscar, and the others, too.

"Well, let me tell you where things stand here," Hal launched into a report on Oscar's call, and the management team's determined reaction. "You brung us to the dance, so we're circling the wagons around you."

"I think you just mixed your metaphors, but right now, Hal, that's the least of my worries." Cliff then explained how Joe Joe Karns was attempting to blame him.

"You can't be serious!"

"Oh, he's serious enough. Question is, whether the prosecutor believes him, and most importantly, whether Jumper Ramsey backs him up. If they both stick to that cock-and-bull story, I'll probably have to stand trial. Could take months."

"But you haven't **done** anything!"

"You and I know that, and most of the people around here know that, but will a jury buy it? I'd say you guys better rethink your position. Makes no sense for everyone to lose what we've been working for because of me."

"Hey, Tonto, we're not budging. When will you know if the prosecutor buys their bullshit?"

"Hopefully, in a few days."

"Well, I'll just string McMillan along. In fact, I think I can get Gus to help me pull a few of those strings over at Tektron. If McMillan insists on calling them...make sure Gil doesn't return the call for at least a few days."

"You've got the ball, kemo sabe. Do what you think is best, but remember, you've got the whole team to think about."

"Ya, Tonto. And you're our captain."

* * *

When the county prosecutor strolled into his outer office from his afternoon coffee break, Jumper was sitting at attention on an upright wooden chair. "Ramsey? What are you doing here?"

"Come to see you. Got something to say."

"Where's your lawyer? You shouldn't be here without him."

"Don't need no damn lawyer. Got two things to tell you."

"You understand, anything you say can be used against you?"

"Yes, sir."

"Well...come into my office. Mary Beth...get your pad and bring the tape recorder in here."

Turning on the recorder, the prosecutor began, "Let the record show, that at...ah...three o'clock in the afternoon, on Thursday, April 23, 1987, Jason 'Jumper' Ramsey appeared in this office of his own free volition, waived his right to counsel, understands his rights as previously described to him, and insists upon making a statement. Is that correct, Mr. Ramsey?"

"Yes, sir."

"Let the record show that Mary Beth Brown is also present as a witness. You may proceed, Mr. Ramsey."

"Well, sir, I got two things to say. First off, Clifford Cross didn't have nothing to do with our drug operation. That was only me and Joe Joe Karns. Cliff came by the Moonshiner for a couple of drinks, and we wanted to talk him into joining up with us to buy the Ford dealership over in Oak Hill. We took him in the back room to show him the money we had to put up so he'd know we was serious. He had no idea where we got it. Wasn't in there five minutes when the police busted in."

"So, you're saying, he's totally innocent. You're admitting that you and Karns got the money selling marijuana?"

"Yes, sir."

"Okay. What's your second point?"

"Well...Joe Joe come to me yesterday afternoon, saying we could get out of this if we blamed Cliff. Said he was the mastermind. Said he loaned us the start-up money. Money on the table in the case was for paying him back. Said if we both stuck to that story, we could cut a deal with you. I told him, 'No way.' Me and Cliff was like brothers once. He said if I wouldn't go along with him, we'd both be facing jail time. So, I told him he better be packing his toothbrush and shaving kit, 'cause I wasn't lying...not if it meant dragging down Cliff."

"What'd he say to that?"

"Aw...something about me being a damn fool...and he'd be packing all right...but not to go to no jail. He'd be skedaddling out of the county. I expect he's already long gone."

"Okay. What else?"

"That's it. I ain't got nothing else to say."

"Where'd you get your marijuana, Mr. Ramsey?"

"I ain't got nothing else to say."

"Would you like to call your lawyer?"

"I ain't got nothing else to say. You can turn that thing off, 'cause I'm outta here." With that, Jumper stood up, tipped his greasy baseball cap at the secretary, and walked out.

* * *

Within minutes, the prosecutor called the news media to announce a press conference, and then called Walter. "Mr. Wilson, this is Calvin Byrd. Thought you'd like to know, I'll be holding a press conference tomorrow morning at ten on the courthouse steps. I'd recommend you be there with your client. I think you'll like what I have to say."

"Come on, Byrd, don't be coy. You dropping the charges against Clifford Cross?"

"Wouldn't you like me to tell you so you could blab it to the media first. You just be there." He hung up the phone.

Walter immediately called Cliff, describing the call from the prosecutor. "I believe it's over, my boy. He wants to milk it for the publicity."

* * *

The following morning at ten sharp, Calvin Byrd did, indeed, announce to the media and the crowd behind that Clifford Cross had been cleared of all charges through the diligent work of the prosecutor's office. "A confession has been obtained from Jason 'Jumper' Ramsey, and a fugitive warrant has been issued for the arrest of Joseph Karns, who apparently has fled the county."

Calvin Byrd pulled Cliff up beside him, shook his hand, and posed for a picture with the town's local hero before Cliff could extricate himself from the fawning little man.

Pushing his way through the crowd, Cliff got into the back seat of Walter's car. "Got to find Jumper. Drive down to Peach Street and turn left," he instructed Jon, who was driving.

"Isn't that Ramsey, standing in the back of the crowd?" Walter pointed.

"Yep. Pull over there. Jump...Jumper...get in," Cliff called, opening the door and reaching out to pull Jumper into the car.

"Cliff...hey...you're free and clear, old buddy," Jumper tapped Cliff's thigh with his fist.

"Where to?" Jon asked.

"Down to Peach Street...to your house...okay, Jump?"

"Sure, I ain't got nowhere to go."

"Jump...I don't know what to say...what you did for me..."

"Clifford, you was the only good thing that ever happened to me. Remember how you made me sit right up there beside you on the back of that convertible when we won the state's? I couldn't let you down."

"Jump, these two gentlemen up front are Walter Wilson, Sarah's dad, and Jon Foster, the best criminal attorney in the state. Jon, I want you to take on Jumper's defense. I'll foot the bill. Okay?"

"If Walter agrees, and your friend wants me to, you got it."

"Aw, Cliff...what's the use? I already said I done it."

"Mr. Ramsey," Walter turned sideways to look at Jumper. "A good attorney can mean the difference between a light sentence and hard time. I'm just along for the ride because of Cliff. You don't need me. But I strongly recommend you accept Cliff's offer."

"I suppose so, if you're willing to do that for me." Then thinking of Joe Joe's body, buried deep in Grandma Ramsey's old vegetable garden, a chill shot through his body, realizing that he may well need the best criminal attorney in the state to keep him off death row.

After making the arrangements for Jumper's representation and letting him out at his home, Cliff thanked his attorneys, promised to bring the children to Charleston more often, gave his parents the good news, phoned the office, and departed quickly for Washington. The nightmare was over, and now it was back to saving the company and caring for his children. He took a deep breath, rolling those two daunting tasks around in his head, as he crossed the Blue Ridge Mountains into Virginia.

Cliff arrived home in time to meet Sally and Tyke at the school bus, taking them and Greta with him into the office.

On the way in, Greta said, "Mr. Cross, this last week with the children made me realize how much I love them. If your offer still stands, I'd like to stay."

"Hooray!" he shouted. "All in favor of Greta staying, raise your right hand." Sally and Tyke poked their hands up in the air. "That settles it," he shook his fist up in the air.

As he pushed open the door for Greta and the children to enter the office, everyone inside shouted, "Surprise!" A bevy of balloons floated about the office, and Mike Gattuso popped a bottle of champagne, the foam spurting out over Nettie's desk.

His management team, as well as everyone from the Accounting and Field Maintenance Departments gathered round him, shaking his hand and patting him on the back. Nettie stood up on her tiptoes, hugging him.

Most surprising, Gus Sarius and Charlie Lambert from Tektron were also there to celebrate. "Gil wants to sit down with you as soon as possible," Gus whispered in Cliff's ear.

"Tomorrow morning too soon?" Cliff asked.

"Fine. Not too many people in on Saturday. Word's leaking out anyway. People are excited about you guys coming back. Nine o'clock, Gil's office? Better bring Arnie with the numbers."

"You got it," Cliff nodded, and then went through the office shaking hands with everyone again.

As the party wound down, he turned to Nettie, "Better get Oscar on the phone."

"Hal called him right away, when we got the news," she replied.

"Good. Best I talk to him, anyway."

Oscar clearly was relieved by the news and positively euphoric over Tektron's initiative. "Great! I'll be home all day if we need to talk. Get a Letter of Understanding and I'll convene the Board right away."

* * *

By late Saturday afternoon, Cliff and Gil had negotiated the deal. Gus wrote out a Letter of Understanding, longhand, which Cliff and Gil signed. Tektron would acquire Jet Speed as a wholly owned subsidiary, paying off Jet Speed's debt to the investors and purchasing all the outstanding stock for twenty million dollars. The memo would become the basis for Tektron's Legal Department drawing up the final papers for approval by the Tektron and Jet Speed Boards. Because Tektron had already completed their due diligence, the closing could occur within a few weeks.

On the way back to the office in the car, Arnie shook his head in disbelief, "Boss, I didn't think you could pull that off...twenty million for the stock. With us holding forty percent of the company, that means we'll split up eight million bucks among us. You'll be a millionaire. My two thousand shares at two hundred dollars a share will put four hundred thousand in my pocket...at capital gains rate, too. Hell, you're going to be worth over three million."

"Get out of the car, Arnold. We haven't seen it yet."

Hal, Mike, and Nettie were waiting in the office when Cliff and Arnie arrived. After Cliff outlined the deal to them, each one naturally calculated what it meant to them. Nettie gasped, "My two thousand shares will be worth four hundred thousand dollars!"

"Let's wait until the deal closes," Cliff couldn't hide his own excitement. "Come on, let's get some dinner. I'm famished."

Hal and Mike had to beg off because their wives had made other plans, but Arnie and Nettie were up for an evening on the town. But first, Nettie insisted on getting a change of clothes out of the car, which she had just picked up from the cleaners, and primping in the ladies' room for what seemed like forever. Finally, Cliff banged on the door, "Come on, Nettie, I'm hungry."

But when she came out, it had been worth the wait. Her jet black hair lay loosely over her shoulders, matching the black shirt and blouse. A silver-brocaded little black jacket was slung over her arm, and a hammered silver necklace matched the woven silver belt around her waist and the silver tips and heels of her high-spiked black suede shoes. The deep red lipstick on her full, soft lips had to have been applied with a fine, thin pencil brush. The top button of her blouse had come undone. Or perhaps purposely left that way, exposing the slightest glimpse of her cleavage. Arnie and Cliff stood transfixed, until she moved between them, grabbing both their arms. "Let's go, boys...time for a double celebration!"

Cliff took them in his car to his favorite restaurant, the Four Seasons, where he ordered steak Diane flambé for everyone, along with a Philippe-Lorraine Reserve Cabernet Sauvignon. As they finished their cappuccino, Nettie remarked, "You know, boss, this ain't exactly like the Southside of Chicago."

"Isn't, Nettie," Arnie gently corrected her.

She turned on him glaring, "Don't you think I know the difference? I was using 'ain't' for emphasis, Arnold!" she clipped her words. "You think I'm some dumb Pollock?"

"Of course not, Nettie, it was stupid of me. I'm sorry, I just was..."

"Hey, you two lovebirds knock it off. We're out to have a good time tonight. In fact, why don't I take you down the street to Basin Street Blues? It's a jumping jazz joint."

Nettie immediately brightened, "Sounds great. Okay with you, Arnie?"

"Sure. Let's go."

As Cliff was ordering their second drink, a lilting voice behind him purred, "Hi, Cliff." Standing with her hand on his shoulder was Krissy Conlon. "Remember me? Krissy with a K?"

"Why, of course. Hi, Krissy." After introducing everyone, and pausing for an awkward moment, he said, "Would you like to join us?"

"Thanks, but no, Cliff. I'm with some friends over there. I just had to come over to say hello. It's been a long time." Shaking his shoulder gently, she said, "Give me a call. You've got my number." Smiling and nodding at Arnie and Nettie, she turned away and swayed between the tables.

"One of your old girlfriends, boss?" Nettie glared at him.

"I'll tell you this much, Nettie. When she said I've got her number, she sure was right."

"Hmmpf...I'll bet you do...along with an address book full of numbers! Come on, Arnie, dance with me. They're playing a slow number."

"Tell you what," Cliff said, throwing the keys to his car on the table. "You two stay and have a good time. Take my car. I'll catch a cab. See you first thing Monday morning." He slid three twenties under the ashtray as he rose to leave.

"Come on, Arnie," Nettie tugged him away from the table. As they made their way to the dance floor, she nearly bumped into Krissy, who was following Cliff out the door.

Chapter Twenty-Four

When Cliff walked into the office Monday morning, Nettie looked up at him from her desk, smirking, "So, did you and Krissy with a K split the cab fare?"

"What are you talking about?"

"I suppose the two of you didn't meet outside. She ran out right behind you."

"Hey, there was a cab waiting outside...I got in it and went straight home."

"Likely story."

"Nettie, get in my office right now...and shut the door behind you!"

"Yes, sir."

"Sit down! Now...why are you always jabbing me? I don't deserve it. And I'm your boss. I'm supposed to get a little respect."

Nettie stared down at the floor for a long moment, and then wilted, "I wish I knew...I...I just feel so lonely all the time. You promised...you promised if I came with you, you'd look after me. I hardly ever see you, and when I do, you're so busy, you don't even know I'm around."

"Nettie...have you been living up on a different planet this past year? My God, look at what I've been through...Sarah...my arrest...turning the company around...trying to sell it. I haven't been popping bonbons. And I resent it when you're always needling me about my supposed girlfriends."

"I'm sorry, boss. I'm too selfish. I know what you've been through. I just...I just...oh...nothing."

"Just what?"

"Aw...you're larger than life. Your wife was an extraordinary woman. You've got beautiful babes like Krissy chasing after you. And me...I'm just some undersized Polish girl."

"Oh, my...listen to me, Nettie. You're a wonderful person. The first time I saw you in Chicago...after talking with you for half an hour at the plant, I said you were the whole package. And you're certainly not undersized in the right places, if you'll forgive me for saying it. Why, Saturday night when you came out of the ladies' room, all gussied up, both Arnie's and my eyes nearly popped out. At dinner and afterwards, you were perfectly poised. You and Arnie make a fine couple. I'd be proud to be seen with the two of you anywhere."

"So, you think Arnie and I are a good match?"

"Sure. Arnie's got his serious side, and you make up for it with your vivaciousness. You know, Nettie, you're like two different people. Around here, with your hair rolled in a bun, your attire, your whole demeanor...you're little Miss Efficiency. But when you let your hair down, both literally and figuratively, you're absolutely stunning."

"You really think so? You like me with my hair combed down?"

"Sure. Down...up...I like you every way. Just don't needle me. Let's make a deal. You stop that and I'll try to be more considerate. Okay?"

"It's a deal," she reached across the desk, and they shook hands awkwardly.

The next morning, and every morning after that, Nettie appeared at the office with her lustrous black hair falling loosely down around her shoulders.

* * *

By the middle of the week, Tektron's Legal Department sent Winslow Rooke a proposed draft of the Acquisition Agreement, and within a day he returned it with minor suggested changes which were acceptable to Tektron's lawyers. The final document was drafted, and the closing was set for the following Monday morning in New York. When it reached Gil Fenno's desk Friday morning, he was surprised to see that there were three hundred thousand shares outstanding. Perhaps he had misunderstood. He thought Cliff had told him there were only one hundred thousand shares outstanding. It made no difference to Tektron because the acquisition price was set at twenty million. Nevertheless, it bothered him, so he sent Gus Sarius over to Jet Speed with a copy for Cliff to peruse before the Monday closing.

"There must be some mistake, Gus. Maybe a typing error," Cliff commented upon reading the document. "Thanks for bringing it over. I'll call New York and have the lawyers straighten it out."

When Cliff called the suave lawyer to alert him to the mistake in the document, Winslow Rooke replied nonchalantly, "You recall, Cliff, at one of our previous Board meetings, we agreed to give Oscar and Sidney convertible debentures in exchange for them loaning several million more to the company...back when you were strapped for cash. Only way to keep the company alive."

"What are you talking about, Win? I never agreed to that. Waters down our stock from two hundred a share to less than sixty-seven dollars a share."

"It's right there in the minutes, Cliff."

"Win, I never agreed to that!"

"Son, you certainly did. Maybe you weren't paying attention when the Board voted to do it, but your vote to approve it is right there in black and white. We **had** to do it, Oscar and Sidney were taking a terrible risk...coming up with all that money to keep you alive when you were still hemorrhaging losses."

"What's the convertible rate?"

"Dollar a share. Same as your price."

"So, you're telling me, Oscar and Sidney are going to get back all the money they loaned the company, **plus**...let's see...two hundred sixty thousand shares out of a total of three hundred thousand...means they get over seventeen million on the twenty million we're being paid for our stock. I and my management team get a little over two and a half million, instead of the eight million we're entitled to as forty percent owners of the company."

"Cliff...you're not forty percent owners of the company. You and your team own a little over thirteen percent of the company. You agreed, son. I'm surprised that you're feigning ignorance."

"Dammit, Win! You're screwing us!"

In a calm, instructive voice, the lawyer replied, "I'd recommend you be up here Monday morning to close the deal and collect your checks amounting to $2,666,400, because if you aren't, we'll proceed without you and mail you your money."

"We'll see about that!" Cliff slammed the phone down.

"Nettie," he shouted, "get the boys in here and get Chicago on the speaker phone. We got a problem!"

Cliff began, "Fellows, I've got some awful news to tell you, and it's my fault...I should have caught it." He then explained how the stock had been watered down; how their stock would be worth $66.66 per share rather than the $200 they expected. "I don't know what recourse we have, other than walking away with nothing...trying to kill the deal...and then we lose everything."

"What about talking to Mr. Fenno?" Red suggested. "Maybe he can make things right."

"It's worth a try," Cliff responded, "but his hands are tied. He can't arbitrarily agree to increase the price so we get more money. Maybe we can work out something with options. I don't know. But, I'll talk to Gil. And, hey, guys, this was totally my fault for not catching what they were doing."

Smokey spoke up, "You're a manager, Cliff, not a Wall Street financier. You thought you were dealing with honorable people."

"They're a bunch of damn snakes!" Mike shouted into the speaker phone.

"What galls me," Cliff gritted his teeth, "is that they pulled it off legally, without me having a clue. I'm sorry, guys."

"You go talk to Mr. Fenno, boss. I bet you can pull something off," Nettie smiled sympathetically.

* * *

When Cliff reached Gil on Saturday morning, telling him that he had a problem, Gil invited him over to his home that afternoon. Over a couple of beers in Gil's rec room, Cliff explained his plight. After listening attentively, Gil rose, strolled over to the picture window, patting his hands behind him, and stood admiring the vibrant crimson blooms of azaleas mixed in among the yellow forsythia of his flower garden. Finally, he spoke.

"Cliff, I don't see what I can do. We've entered into an agreement. Our lawyers have negotiated the final document. We've made a deal. If I agreed to pay you something extra, I would be violating my fiduciary responsibility to Tektron. You know it's company policy to award options based on performance, so we couldn't give you and your team any options up front. Maybe six months from now I could give you some salary increases, but even that would be stretching it. If Jet Speed performs as we all expect, at the end of the year there will be some hefty bonuses as well as stock options."

"I appreciate that, Gil. But, of course, the value of any options will depend on Tektron's overall performance, not on our achievements at Jet Speed."

"Sorry, Cliff. Looks like you've been snookered. But you know, when you come back with us, you'll be treated fairly."

"I know that, Gil. I guess we'll just have to suck it up."

"So, I'll see you in New York, Monday."

"I expect so. Thanks for seeing me, Gil. The one thing my guys know is that you've always been a straight shooter."

* * *

Sunday afternoon, Red, Sam, and Smokey flew in from Chicago, and the management team met in the office Sunday evening, over pizza and beer, to map out their strategy.

Mike said, "Screw 'em. Call their bluff. Tell them we're outta here if we don't get what we were promised. We're all young enough. We can find other jobs. They know that. I'll bet anything they'll cave."

"They've certainly got a lot to lose if this deal falls through," Hal nodded.

"Even if they honor their original commitment to us, pay us forty percent of the acquisition price, they still walk away with twelve million, **plus** their loans repaid. Pretty sweet," Arnie calculated.

"But they put another five million in their pockets if they stick to the agreement with Tektron. You think they'll hand over that five million to us if they don't have to?" Cliff frowned.

"That snake Sidney Martin wouldn't give us two cents if he didn't have to," Hal stated.

"It hurts me to say it," Cliff stretched out his long frame and sighed, "but I think we're stuck. Fact is, Tektron's got a wealth of management talent. If we walk, they'll have a new team in here in a week. Gil's an honorable man...he's not going to back out of an agreement because we threaten to leave. Oscar and Sidney aren't going to fork over another five million to us if, legally, they don't have to. They don't give a damn about us. We've been had...and it's my fault. But the only prudent course for us right now is to collect our $2.6 million Monday, bite our tongues, and keep running Jet Speed as a Tektron subsidiary until something better comes up."

"My suggestion," Red spoke up, "is that you go up there Monday morning...make one last stab at trying to get what's coming to us, and if it doesn't work, go along with the deal. Get whatever money you can. We'll hang around here Monday until you get back, and we can put our heads together to figure out what alternatives we have. I just might have a trick or two up my sleeve."

While the others reluctantly nodded in agreement with Red, Cliff shrugged, "I can give it another shot. Won't hurt. But I don't think it will work. And...what other trick you talking about, Red?"

"Now's not the time, Cliff. You get us as much cash as you can. Make sure they're certified checks. I wouldn't be surprised if they tried to cheat us out of the $2.6 million. Let's see how things turn out Monday in New York, and then we all can talk when you get back."

Chapter Twenty-Five

While Cliff and Hal were walking out of the shuttle terminal at LaGuardia to catch a cab to Wall Street, Jumper Ramsey and Jonathan Foster were walking into the courthouse in Raleigh County, West Virginia, to negotiate a plea bargain with the county prosecutor.

"My client has acted in good faith, Mr. Byrd," Jumper's attorney argued. "He has admitted his guilt, cooperated in giving you the name of his accomplice, and, perhaps, most importantly, has cleared an innocent man, one of the most outstanding young men to come out of your county. He has restored Clifford Cross's good name, and in doing so, has restored the luster to one of your local claims to fame. We could fight this...take it all the way through the appeals process, if necessary, cost your taxpayers thousands of dollars. Nobody wants that. For his cooperation, and his remorse, I propose you recommend to the court that he be given a suspended sentence and a fine."

"You know I can't do that, Mr. Foster. He has **admitted** distributing...selling marijuana."

"We could challenge your admitting that evidence. After all, he had no attorney present when you.. ah...**extracted** that admission from him."

"Come on, you heard the tape. It'll stand up in any court."

275

"You have Clifford Cross's affidavit, saying he'll testify in any court as a character witness for my client. You don't think that will carry some weight with a jury in this county?"

"Okay. I'm willing to recommend a light sentence, **if** I can clear up two outstanding issues. Where'd you get the marijuana, Mr. Ramsey, and where is Joe Joe Karns?"

"How light a sentence?"

"For selling...five years, with recommendation for early parole. Could be out in...," the prosecutor thumbed through some papers, and then looked up, smiling for the first time, "...nine months and twenty-two days. Obviously, forfeiture of the money."

"Excuse us for a few minutes," Jonathan motioned for Jumper to follow him into the hall.

"It's a hell of a good deal, Jumper. Can you tell him where you got the marijuana and where Joe Joe is?"

"I suppose I could tell him about us growing the stuff ourselves," Jumper shrugged, concerned that disclosing the location would send the authorities sniffing around the farmhouse, around the old garden where Joe Joe was buried. "But I can't tell him where Joe Joe is, because I don't think he's walking around these parts anymore."

"So you don't have any idea where he is?"

"Police said they figured he was long gone out of the county. Said they went all through his house and all his clothes and stuff was missing. I already told them that I thought he was skedaddling out of here."

"Can you give them any names of your wholesale buyers who distributed the dope?"

"No. Joe Joe handled all of that up at the auto auction in Charleston."

"So, you can at least point the police in the right direction."

"Sure."

"Let's see what we can do."

Returning to the prosecutor's office, Jon said, "My client is prepared to cooperate fully in exchange for your recommended sentence and parole. He'll tell you where they got the marijuana, but he can't help you locate Karns because he doesn't know where he is. He can state that Karns told him he was fleeing the county. However, in addition, Jumper can point you in the direction of where the marijuana was marketed for resale, although he doesn't know any names because Karns handled those sales."

After tapping his pencil on the tabletop for a few moments and squinting at Jumper, the prosecutor replied, "Well, your story about him fleeing seems to check out. The police pretty much have confirmed that he's gone. He didn't leave much behind at his home. We've called off the search, put out an all-points bulletin, but we doubt that we'll ever see him again. So, okay, it's a deal. Let's get the tape recorder going."

Jumper described their marijuana-growing operation along the old logging trail behind his grandfather's farm, and Joe Joe's weekly trips to the car auction in Charleston to sell the crop, mainly to used-car dealers.

Apparently satisfied, the prosecutor said he would draw up the necessary papers to be filed with the court. Shortly, Jumper would be on his way to prison for a brief stay.

After thanking Jonathan Foster for his help, and giving his mother the bad news, which could have been much worse, Jumper phoned Cliff's office. Nettie knew exactly who he was, and after, informing him that Cliff was out of town, lit into him. "You expect to talk to Mr. Cross, after what you did to him? Almost destroyed his life. Don't you ever call here again!" She slammed the phone down.

* * *

When Cliff and Hal walked into Oscar's conference room, Oscar, Sidney, and Win were all smiles, sitting around the long oak table with Gil and his lawyers. "Papers are all in order, Cliff." Oscar enthused, "Your certified checks are in here," he held an envelope in his one hand, flapping it against the other. "Win's got the formality of our Board meeting drawn up. All we have to do is sign the minutes showing our approval of the sale. Here...," he pushed the papers over to Cliff, who still was standing.

"I'd like to speak with our directors privately," Cliff answered, "over in your office, Oscar. Excuse us for a few minutes, Gil," he smiled at his old boss as he brusquely turned and walked out of the room.

Bewildered, Oscar apologized to Gil for the delay, and, along with Sidney and Win, followed Cliff.

"What the hell's wrong with you?" Sidney bellowed. "There's $2.6 million laying in there for you and your boys. You want to blow this?"

"Should be eight million, Sidney. We both know that. We want you to honor our agreement. We want forty percent of the deal."

"Cliff, I explained to you that we had to give stock options to Oscar and Sid to get their additional loans...to keep the company alive. We went through all that...," Win explained, exasperated.

"Cut the crap," Sidney demanded, "it was all done legal, but if you want another vote by the Board to approve the deal, let's do it right now. Come on. Oscar, Win, and I vote yes. You two assholes vote no. Majority wins. Deal's approved. Again! Now, let's go back in there and get our money."

Cliff stood towering over the others, seething, glaring silently at Sidney Martin. Sidney started back into the conference room, then stopped, turning to Oscar and Win, "Well, come on. What are you waiting for?" They obediently followed.

Cliff motioned with his head to Hal, and they, too, walked back into the room.

The lawyer shuffled the papers back and forth, signing them, while Sidney drummed his fingers on the table. Gil seemed puzzled, and Cliff stared glumly at the moving papers, his jaws clamped tightly shut, his right foot tapping furiously beneath the table.

With the closing completed, Cliff picked up his envelope of certified checks, thumbed through them, rose, and shook hands with Gil. With a slight sardonic smile, he spoke hoarsely, "Call me tomorrow...boss," and then turning and glaring at Sidney and Oscar strode out of the room, with Hal close behind.

* * *

As Cliff passed out the certified checks to his management team, he couldn't decide whether he was attending a celebration or a wake. After taxes, he would clear about seven hundred thousand dollars, hardly what he had expected, or believed he deserved. The others would net from about two hundred thousand for Hal, down to about a hundred thousand for Arnie and Nettie. All told, the team had about $1.8 million after taxes, along with a promising, yet uncertain, future with Tektron.

Surrounding a plate of hors d'oeuvres behind closed doors in the conference room, they popped the cork of a bottle of champagne and toasted to better days.

"I expect Tektron will be roaring in soon," Cliff commented. "At least we know most of the players."

"Controller already called," Arnie answered. "Said they'd be in tomorrow morning to change us over to their accounting system."

"Anyone want to hear my idea?" Red Cermak asked.

"Sure," Cliff replied.

"Well, you all sit down, get a pad, and listen up."

* * *

After the sun went down behind the Guyandotte Mountains west of Beckley, Jumper dug out Joe Joe's money box from beneath the dirty oil drum in his garage. He then drove south to the slag dump, to the precise location where he had tossed Joe Joe's clothes down into the burning embers. Standing at the edge, the red hot heat rising out of the pit seared his face until the sweat trickled down his neck onto his chest. "Damn you, Joe Joe," he cursed into the abyss, "I never meant to do no harm. I only wanted to **be** somebody. You dragged me down...and Cliff, too, if I would'a let you. Damn you, Joe Joe, I don't want the money either. I'm done with you!" he hurled the money box down into the glowing slag and watched the metal curl and melt, crumble and disappear. "I ain't never doing nothing bad again!" He turned, climbed into his pickup, and drove back to town.

* * *

Red Cermak leaned forward, grinning, his eyes moving around the table, making contact with each person in the room, "I've been fooling around with laser printing in my spare time. Got a breadboard prototype rigged up in my basement at home. Figure I can beat Hewlett-Packard's LaserJet in both speed and flexibility. With the right software, we could get page formatting and full-page graphics."

"You file any patent?" Mike asked.

"Not yet. Wanted to see what happened to Jet Speed first. Figured the company could have a claim on any patents I filed while I still worked for the firm. But I got the papers all drawn up. Could file anytime."

"How reliable is this brainstorm of yours?" Sam asked.

"Sure beats ink-jet printing. Characters are formed electronically. Toner cartridge will last longer too."

"What price market could you aim at?" Arnie inquired.

"Same as HP...three to four thousand dollar range."

"I think we better take a little trip down to your basement," Cliff smiled. "Got to be on our own time, with our own money. Wouldn't want Tektron coming back at us. That's assuming what you've got's for real."

"Hey, fly out Saturday morning. See for yourselves. Pizza and beers are on me," Red proposed.

Everyone agreed, with Cliff emphasizing, "Let's be damn sure we stay on top of our responsibilities here. Tektron's coming in the morning and we need to be sharp. And let's not get our hopes up too high. Remember the wing walker's rule: 'Don't let go of what you've got hold of until you've got hold of something else.' Red, you know we all think you're the best, and you don't blow smoke about your projects, but going from a breadboard prototype to final design, production, and marketing ain't exactly easy. Let's take a hard look at what Red's got, think this through **very** carefully, and if, together, we might have the capacity and the potential to turn it into something."

* * *

When Cliff got home, the children already were asleep, and Greta was dozing on the couch in the living room with the TV on. On the hall table was a message with a phone number that Jumper Ramsey had called. Cliff went into his den, closed the door, and dialed the number. "Jump...you okay?"

"Ya, sure, Cliff. Just wanted to thank you for that letter offering to testify on my behalf. I think it helped. And getting Mr. Foster to represent me. He knows his stuff. Anyway, I wanted you to know it's over. I agreed to plead guilty in exchange for a light sentence. I'll be out in about eight months. I'm truly sorry, Cliff, I got you tangled up in this."

"Jump, let's just put it behind us. Let's just remember the good old days."

"Ya, we was really something, wasn't we?"

"You bet we were. Best you start thinking about your future when you get out. I hope you get into something a little more stable than tending bar. And, old friend, drinking away most of your paycheck."

"I'm going to straighten myself out, Clifford, honest I am. Won't be no drinking in prison, so I got eight months to shake that habit. Be like back when we was playing ball. Didn't touch a drop all season. Sure would like to get back into car repairing. 'Bout the only thing I ever was good at...except when you and me was play-ing ball."

"What about setting up your own automotive repair shop? You always could make any old clunker purr. I understand the newer ones are even easier, if you have the right equipment."

"Oh, I ain't got no money, Cliff. And you know I always was too hotheaded to be working for someone else for very long. But, I'm working on that too, Cliff. Honest I am. I think I learned my lesson with Joe Joe."

"I thought you and Joe Joe always got along?"

"Sure...usually...but we had our differences, too. One real big difference, Cliff, but that ain't nothing for us to talk about...never."

"How much would it take to get set up in your own shop?"

"Well, I got most of the tools. Wouldn't cost much to rent one of the old closed-up gas stations in town. But I'd need to buy some of the more modern equipment. Probably take forty or fifty thousand to get up and going."

"Jump...tomorrow morning, I'm wiring fifty thousand to the First National Bank in Beckley to be held in escrow, and available to you when you get out, to be expended, with the approval of the bank, for the establishment of the Jumper Ramsey Automotive Repair Center. You won't let me down, will you?"

"Aw, Cliff...," Jumper started to whimper, then tears rolled down his cheeks, and his shoulders shook as he began sobbing. Getting control of himself, his voice cracked, "Clifford...I won't let you down. Not never! I promise. Someday I'll pay you back. I will. You'll see. Someday you'll have cause to be proud of me."

* * *

Cliff and his management team hovered over Red as he sat at the prototype of the laser printer in the basement of his home. "Don't worry about all those wires hanging down from the breadboard on the wall," he explained. "They'll be replaced with a couple of chips. Important thing is clock the speed. Check that quality. No ink clogging up a nozzle."

Sam studied the schematic, and after it was turned off, Mike watched closely as Red tore down the printer, handing Mike each part for inspection.

"How many hours continuously have you run it without a malfunction?" Mike asked.

"Couple of weekends ago I ran it twelve hours on Saturday and twelve on Sunday without a problem. Forming the characters electronically cuts way back on maintenance...it's got to boost reliability over ink-jet printers."

"What about cost?" Cliff asked.

"I bought an HP LaserJet, sitting over there in the corner. Stripped it down. Parts are pretty standard. Tweaking the circuitry, adding a little RAM memory, and using a parallel interface can get us full-page graphics and flexible formatting. Once we get a production line up, I think Sam could hit a unit manufacturing cost around a thousand dollars, or maybe even a little under. It's going to take more sophisticated software, but I think we could go to the OEM market with a three thousand dollar product that had a fifty percent gross margin."

"Sam? Mike?" Cliff turned to them.

"Depends on the quantity, but I think it's doable," Sam answered.

"Sure as hell easier to maintain than an ink-jet printer. Nobody's ever completely solved the nozzle-clogging problem."

"Software, Smokey?" Cliff raised his eyebrows.

"Take us a few months, but we can tap into Microsoft. There are plenty of options out there for us to piggyback on."

"How long to get into production, **if** we can raise the seed capital? Surely going to take a lot more that we've got," Cliff asked Red.

"I could have a preproduction model in three or four months. Depending on parts suppliers...maybe six months 'til Sam could have them coming off the line."

"Hal, you haven't said anything. Would we be competitive? What are your potential markets?" Cliff asked Hal.

"This printer market is booming. We're looking at a demand for millions...I mean **millions** of printers...desktop printers, like our ink-jet **and** like reliable laser printers. The question is, can we get into the market fast enough to take advantage of it?"

Nettie, who had flown out to Chicago with them, ostensibly to visit her brother and mother, but who couldn't stand the thought of the team making some exciting decisions without her being in the room, spoke up. "I don't pretend to understand the technical aspects of Red's printer, but anyone can see that the small printer market is exploding. Isn't the real question, can we raise the money to do another start-up company? I'll kick in my hundred thousand, but I know that's peanuts compared to what we'll need."

Everyone looked at Cliff. After a long pause and a slight cringe, he chuckled, "So all we need is money. I think it would be wrong for us to plow back every penny we got out of the Tektron deal. But if we each kicked in sixty percent, that would give us a little over one million. We'd probably need to raise another four million in equity, and five million in debt. With our track record at Jet Speed, that might be doable. But this time, by God, if we do it, we retain control. No outside investors get more than forty percent. We offer a debt-equity package."

"Where would we put the plant?" Sam asked. "I don't know that Congressman Romanowski would be thrilled about helping get us some start-up money to go in competition with Jet Speed's Chicago operation."

"With our million up front, and with our record, we should be able to put together a public-private package. We'd need to put the plant somewhere in a high unemployment area where we could qualify for economic development money, like we got in Chicago's Southside," Arnie observed. "Cost of living can't eat us alive, either."

"And a place with a good work ethic," Sam added.

"Better have good access to our markets," Hal mentioned.

"I think you boys have just described the perfect place," Cliff stood up and stretched. "Beckley, West Virginia."

"Beckley, West Virginia! Where the hell is Beckley, West Virginia?" Smokey asked incredulously.

"Sits at the intersection of two interstates running north and south, east and west...only a few hours from here. It's coal country...with chronic unemployment...people who still believe in a hard day's work...low cost of living...and the mountains, the streams, the clean air...the sunsets on a summer evening are about as close to heaven as you're going to get on this earth. We could move our corporate headquarters in with the plant...save a lot of money. Just keep a sales and service office in Washington."

"Beckley, West Virginia?" Hal winced.

"Hey, guys. It would be a different world. A different life. No traffic jams. No alarm systems in your house for fear of being raped or robbed," Nettie went on. "Just think about it, all us city guys...it would be a new adventure."

"Let's not get ahead of ourselves," Cliff held up his hands, "but I bet I could sell it to the West Virginia Congressional Delegation...to one of the most powerful senators in the country. Does anybody veto my trying?"

"Sure would be different," Mike shook his head. "Hell, give it a try." Everyone nodded their agreement that Beckley should at least be explored. But the bigger question was, should they really try to put together a new start-up company? Did they have the ability? Could they succeed?

Late into the night, they huddled in Red's living room, weighing the pros and cons of trying to start a new company.

"We all would have a pretty decent future with Tektron," Cliff assured them. "If we left them now and fell flat on our face, there wouldn't be any welcome mat sitting out there for us in the future."

"We're all hired guns," Hal commented. "But you, Red...you've got your own patents...you could cut a sweet deal with any one of a dozen companies."

"Hey, I've worked for the big boys, and I've experienced the thrill of trying to build something from scratch. Nothing like it. Come as close to having your own baby as a guy could get."

"I agree with Red," Mike nodded. "It's like being half-asleep all your life, and then suddenly coming alive. I say we roll the dice."

"I know I'm supposed to be the green eyeshade guy," Arnie laughed, "but this past year, I could hardly wait to get up in the morning so I could get to the office."

"So, Tonto...what do you say?" Hal turned to Cliff, who by now, had slid down onto the floor with his back against the sofa, his long legs stretched under the coffee table, finishing the last piece of pizza.

"Whew...," he set his empty bottle of beer on the table. "The question is, are we willing to take another chance? It's even a bigger chance this time because we've all got some money to lose, and we'll be burning our bridges with Tektron. We'll really be out on the street looking for jobs. But...am I willing to take the chance?" Cliff dug into his pocket, pulled out the old bear tooth, and rolled it across the floor toward Nettie. It stopped a few feet from her knee, a blank side up.

"What in the world are you doing, boss?" she looked mystified, as the others watched quizzically.

"Roll it back over here to me," he motioned with his finger.

Nettie picked up the strange totem, studied it for a moment, and then threw it back across the floor toward Cliff. It tumbled to a stop, a blank side up again. Picking it up, Cliff persisted, "One more time." Putting a backspin on it with his thumb and forefinger, it bounded onto the floor in front of him and tilted over, the bear-paw side on top.

"That settles it, guys. Old bear paw says we go. I'm in. I'll take the chance. That's if you're willing to take it with me!"

"Tonto, how many times would you have rolled that old relic to get the right answer?" Hal asked, laughing.

"As many times as it took." Cliff shot his fist high in the air. "Are you in or what?"

A soft, warm silence seemed to permeate through the room. Slowly, one by one, they studied each other, smiling, and then one by one, each thumb went up until they got to Cliff, who, once again, shot his fist high in the air. Like youngsters on a basketball court, they jumped up, converging in the middle of the room, hugging each other, and simultaneously shouting, "Yes!"

They decided to meet the following morning at Red's to work out the details. It would take several weeks of planning.

As Hal, Arnie, Mike, and Cliff were getting into their rental car to drive to their motel, and Nettie was getting into a cab to be taken to her brother's, Cliff said, "Wait a minute, boys. You go ahead. I'll catch a ride with Nettie. I want to talk to her. I'll have the cab drop me off at the motel."

Motioning for Nettie to wait, he slid back into the back seat of the cab beside her. Surprised, Nettie asked, "What's wrong?"

"Not a thing, Annette," he replied. "Just thought I'd see you home safely. That's all."

"That's all?" she asked as the cab pulled out.

"Well, not quite. Truth is, I've got two great tickets for "A Chorus Line" at the Kennedy Center, Saturday night. Thought maybe we could have dinner at La Colline and take in the show."

"Are you hitting on me, Mr. C? Would this be a **date**? Or am I still just one of the guys?"

"Nettie, I'm afraid, somewhere along the line, you lost your distinction of being one of the guys. At least with me. It's one hundred percent...pure date. That's if you're willing to take a chance on me."

"I thought you'd never ask."